THE SCREW OF THE TERN

William Melville
Desmond Scott Rubinstein (ed.)

THE SCREW OF THE TERN

This is a work of fiction. Any resemblance to persons, places
or events real or imagined is pure bunkum.

iUniverse books may be ordered through booksellers or by contacting:

iUniverse
1663 Liberty Drive
Bloomington, IN 47403
www.iuniverse.com
1-800-Authors (1-800-288-4677)

Cover photo of yacht with kind permission of Tanju Kalaycioglu

ISBN: 978-1-4917-6843-3 (sc)
ISBN: 978-1-4917-6844-0 (e)

Print information available on the last page.

iUniverse rev. date: 06/16/2015

Dedicated with eternal love to

Desmond Scott Rubinstein (1940-1974)

my mother, Paola Elise Melville (1932-2010)

my father, William Herman Melville (1940-2013)

my grandmother, Mary Katherine Melville (1914-1973)

Siempre Estaremos Juntos

Christopher Melville

July 14, 2014

FOREWORD

Aye! She was a beauteous thing to have ever graced with her sleek white hull the heave and roll of sea and bay. Built for the long haul, one hundred twenty-five feet of polished mahogany deck and proud brass fittings gleaming under the equatorial sun, and endless bolts and yards of tawny canvas rippling and popping from a playful breeze in the Caymans to the cruel bias of a blow off Labrador. Her keel was layed in 1875 near Searsport by all five Gingold Brothers, who were duly paid a right handsome $1700 for two years of a love's labor. And my dear deceased daughter, Sarah Ogilsby Melville of Newport, taken from us by the Spanish influenza of 1918, christened her the "Tern" with her innocent gentle hand to a long, conspicuous life of pleasure and immoral pursuit. Her only flaw, as I perceived it as a parser of the Holy Scripture, was from outfitting her later with the screw and assorted hatches cannabilized off the notorious rum runner, "El Libre," a slave ship rotting in the sands off Santo Domingo[1].

---

[1] Cited screw (i.e., propeller) was fabricated July 1869 at Brewtal Boatworks, Liverpool. Weighing 335 pounds, passengers often complained of the unusual vibration or "chatter" of the screw, as well as the turbulent burble of the shaft; altogether a most literate and disquieting piece of man's ingenuity. During several luxury cruises in the Caribbean (1885-1889), parties sponsored by Frick and Prudhommes Freres (Leopoldville) complained bitterly of such noises sounding like incessant voices—even moaning as if by immigrants, incarcerated or other incorrigibles—coming through the bulkhead. Some lamented they were veritably "screwed" or unnerved by the concomitant lack of sleep. On one voyage, a retired vicar from West Surrey reflected with pious amusement to Captain Billy that the sandaled centurions in Jerusalem at least carried nails for crucifying, albeit they be no less excruciating than the turn of the screw of the Tern.

Her luck changed thereafter. For certain, dear Sarah and the Tern were the only guilt-free of the whole lot. We who sailed and abused her were the greedy scoundrels who violated and otherwise capitalized on her beauty running booze, riff-raff, guns and impressing various and sundry assorted passengers in a flagrancy necessary to survive and thereafter luxuriate in the lust of ill-gotten gains. If she sails for another hundred years, I pray, as I lay here in my aft bunk under a swinging crucifix of Spanish gold, my descendents will redeem her to the purity and high purpose she surely deserves, and to which purpose I regrettably fell short.[2]

---

[2]   From the diary of William (Captain Billy) Melville (1865-1942?).

INTRODUCTION

This was a labor of love and hate; light and darkness. I loved editing these youthful reflections of my dear friend since childhood, William "Will" Melville, although I lost contact with him during the period related in his personal account herewith. On the other hand, I simply detested the dearth of factual information available from the outset. Perhaps his awkward tale of little personal, if somewhat naive, epiphanies doesn't really lend itself to the scrutinous glare of those wizzened, fact-checking readers of gratuitous mayhem and vicarious adventure who cannot or refuse to willfully suspend their disbelief. Therefore, to assuage their discomfort of reading yet another of the multitudinous attempts to tell a tale of youthful trial and tribulation, I chose to footnote several passages to move along Will's story and lend an air of credibility and relief where I felt it lagging in the doldrums of plain old incoherence. After all, what is the purpose of a footnote, if not to illuminate or explain away? My lifelong very close friendship with the entire Melville family (I lived two doors away on James Street) did little to assist me, as I rummaged Mrs. Melville's entire house and garage (with permission when she was present) for scraps such as notes, old bills, Mundane University and University of Michigan paraphernalia, liquor receipts, and quasi-legal documents. Often, as I was pressed by deadlines, I left a bedroom window ajar to allow more access to any debris related to Will. Mrs. Melville was a hoarder extraordinaire. For instance, in one corner of the attic in a large wooden box of old glass insulators, I found an old brass ship bell, which she said was given to her and her husband by Captain Billy shortly after Will was born in 1940. She said he dropped out of the blue like an apparition for about fifteen minutes on his way to the Great Lakes naval training facility near Waukegan and said the bell came off one of Magellan's galleons. He said this with such aplomb, she thought it must have been a fake and that Captain Billy may have been a fake, as well. It was the only time she ever saw him. Anyway, I took on this gig willingly at her request and for no remuneration, retainer or finder's fee save the occasional BLT or Dutch apple pie she so graciously served when she could get around with her new hip and her metal "Johnny" walker. Sometimes she did buy me a six-pack of Iron City beer; otherwise, I was on my own bellycrawl, and if it were not for my devotion to Will's memory and his mother's depression at her perceived loss—more on this later—I would have chucked the draft manuscript into the dumpster at the nearby Holy Redeemer annex worksite. Also, the effort to verify details in this remembrance became an obsession, as you may notice from the outset; and there are some instances where, for lack of factual information or when the pubic library was closed for the holidays, I sincerely endeavored to embellish events and characters as faithfully as possible. The exception was Will's eccentric uncle, Robert Melville, whom I never saw or met, but presumed to be a nice old guy on the verge. I actually uncovered more about his father, Captain Billy, from his assorted diaries and old newspaper articles. I vividly remember one August afternoon in Mrs. Melville's attic. It was hotter than Hades as I came across a small letter from Robert Melville dated March 30, 1949, in which he said he lost –five pounds and was staying at the Elixir Haven of Rest in Jacksonville, but was steadfast in his personal philosophy of "something beautiful is going to happen." Of course, his incredible ascent to wealth in real estate, personnel management, luxury cruises and adult care is the stuff of dreams to which we all aspire in this land of good and plenty. This nugget of inspiration gleamed in the palm of my thoughts, and it likewise inspired me to complete the task with the integrity it deserved. To the reader, I extend my professed gratitude for (hopefully) suspending, in advance, your disbelief in the manner with which I chose to edit the scrap heap of minutiae regarding Will's remembrances which—let's face it—could be similar to any of us who leaves behind a trail of tattered hopes and dreams on this good earth. Incidentally, if I were someone else higher up the boot in, say, Brown and Shue's regional office (Brindisi) in Italy, I would have rejected this job outright, but since I was still on temporary assignment from the Meadville office, I saw real literary merit to it. There must have been over five hundred pages of notes, plus three boxes of trinkets and mementos (e.g., gross of prophylactics, fuzzy dice,

Milky Way wrappers, small American flag) the significance of which I could only fictionalize, at best.

Lastly, I could not have perpetrated this work without acknowledging the efforts of many of my former colleagues at Brown and Shue. A big hats-off to the wonderful staff there, who persevered in rightfully rejecting my early efforts that conversely encouraged me against all rational and professional standards until the last period was perforated by my old Remington. I would especially like to thank Gerrold Colonna, who bodily discharged me one day from the building. Bless you, Gerry! I owe you one round; James VanDyke-Smythe for assistance in tracking down the elusive Captain Billy's memoirs in Etna, Wildwood, Elkton and Bay St. Louis, among other places; Ruth Eddy Chadwick for the key to the 38th floor men's room (this was huge); Luca Bronzini for his incalculable instruction on the tortuous world of naval knots; Georges Bidet for flushing out all deliberate, unforced errors of judgment and references to a recent book on William Melville by Paca-Pratt Publishers; Annette Angstmeier for turning off the break-room stove behind me and turning up the heat on me (thanks, love); and Helge Swoops, the famous amateur heldentenor from Eskilstuna, for cleaning up or deleting all purpled and nefarious references to Wagner's *The Flying Dutchman*. Finally, deepest gratitude to my loving wife and reason for living, Roberta, who triumphed over childhood polio to bless our union with Joshua (4), Rachel and Rebecca (7) and Aaron (9).

D. Scott Rubinstein (April 13, 1974)

[Publisher's Note: At the time of anticipated publication by Melville House, Desmond Rubinstein passed away at St. Luke's as the result of a car accident on the Triborough Bridge. He spent three weeks in and out of a coma during which he related, from time to time, the desire that his efforts to edit this fragmented semi-autobiography of William Melville be accepted, for what it was worth, as his best and final camera-ready copy. A percentage of the proceeds from the sale of this book will fund the commission of a granite angel by the famous sculptor/performance artist, Dolly Dubinsky, which will be permanently placed at Mr. Rubinstein's headstone to receive small donations that may be dropped into the sculpture's awestuck mouth. These generous gifts of loose change will further fund the Desmond Scott Rubinstein Chair for Creative Editing at the Stitchess College extension campus (PO Box 668) outside Syosset. (9/30/74)]

CHAPTER 1

When the lights came on, I knew I was in the dark. I must have dozed off. For a few moments, I wasn't sure who or where I was. Turning toward the window, a face came into view and I regained my identity—ephemeral as it was—but then my next breath obscured my image. I travelled—you might say tunnelled like a mole-rat—through 1300 miles and 28 hours, leaving the tiny, bright, cheerful mammary warmth of my mother's kitchen in Monroe, Michigan, for an odyssey that so far revealed no end in light. Not a scintilla, except the dim row of lights above the seats which indicated I was going nowhere fast in spite of the dreamy arc of a torn and faded PanAm banner for Paris in springtime running out of reach overhead.

"All right, boys and girls. There it is. Fort Lauderdale," said the driver as he glided the bus into the station and snapped on the overhead lights. He turned up the speaker volume for the benefit of those still asleep in the back rows, not to mention the groans of insemination two rows behind me. "End of the line, boys and girls. This is it. There ain't no more. Your bags will be meeting you on the curb." Although we earlier struck up an acquaintance on the long journey, he still shot a glance at me. "You, too, buddy."

He must have popped another little white pill as we came into the station. What else would explain why he added with cheer we could choose beaches: the one three blocks away, or 150 miles to the west, and he threw his arm out in the direction of St. Pete with the enthusiasm of a field judge. Somewhere after Murfreesboro, he went on auto-pilot and said I can't talk now. Maybe later. With nary a twitch, he sailed through the next six hours, arms moving with an unnerving mechanical slouch toward unconsciousness; humming the same tune over and over. As we trundled across an abandoned railroad trestle in southern Georgia, he started grunting the gospel, "Deep River."

I finally put in a few good hours of soundless sleep and became, as I said, disoriented at the abrupt announcement. Where was Fort Lauderdale, other than on a map where it always was? Then it came back to me: leaving home and not quite knowing where to go or who to turn to, save for a phone number on a scrap of paper.

The driver's name was Jake Poussy. I still don't know why I then remembered his name. Maybe because he said P-O-U-S-S-Y with an "o". Maybe because he was the only person I talked to on the long desperate trip. I knew I would forget his name the minute I left the terminal. A pelt-like walrus mustache draped over his lips made his small oval mouth look like something anatomically out of place.[3] He chatted with the last knot of stragglers ahead of me. "You people must be futilistic, getting away from something worse than Helen who is coming up the coast in two days. Packing one hundred thirty miles per hour. She will definitely knock on some doors." He grabbed the arm of the kid in front of me and said, Joe Bob you and Cissy had best not made a mess on my seats back there.

I was first on the bus and the last to get off. Jake blew a big gum bubble, sucked it back in and said he enjoyed chatting along the sinuous pilgrimmage from Monroe. For every bone-rattling hundred miles, the bus seemed to backtrack every fifty like an aimless dung beetle according to some crackpot business model to maximize both passenger miles and the agony of those too poor to fly. I knew enough calculus to figure I'd never get to Florida in my lifetime, but I even flunked that quiz. He tilted his pilot cap, brushed off the frayed, embroidered wings on the shoulders and said it would be a lot easier in my situation to take the Trailways over to Windsor and up to Toronto. I told him someone paid for my ticket.

"Yeah, and my gung-ho grandson's chasing gooks in the Delta over there. Don't want to go there, pal. He's crazy, but I love him to death."

---

3   In 1954, Jackson Poussy (pronounced "poosey") was on the GI Bill and won the Mundane University (suburban Peoria campus) annual Sisyphus Cup, promoted as a tantalizing competition by the Mossberg Glee Club, of which Poussy was a charter basso profundo. He received the ignition key to a second-hand pea-green Dodge sedan for his efforts. At the top of the hill, the 85-pound boulder unexpectedly rolled down the other side and crashed into a Kamperbus occupied by the androgynous Dean of Womens' Studies and a coed. Both were later separated without further ado at Mercymoi Hospital emergency room.

"Not sure what you mean," I said slipping into my backpack.

"I was on Tarawa. Ever heard of it?" He flinched when he said, "Tarawa."

"Pacific campaign?"

"Bingo! You know some stuff, pal. You don't ever want to go there. Still keeps the old lady up at night." He threw a quick salute with two fingers and limped off into the terminal. The old vet must have sized me up pretty well: one of many young guys working on the 30-day drill before Army greetings hit the mailbox.

I cinched the bulging backpack and followed in the wake of the driver's limp into the crowded bus terminal. It brought back memories of the monkey house at Lincoln Park. The long hard drive must have kicked up Jake's sciatica, which he detailed to me somewhere between Atlanta and Dothan, but he didn't complain other than to lean against the tiled terminal wall every thirty feet or so.[4]

I sat at a table with trash, the walking dead and my hot dog and Fresca. I noticed a few loose girls waiting in line for tickets and tried to knot together the unravelling events of the last day. Mother was saddened and speechless when I told her I committed academic hari-kiri. What a gut-wrenching mess![5]

"Will, no! Not again!" she uttered as the Dean's notice fluttered from her wet hands.

"Sorry, Mom."

---

[4]   Per DoD records, Poussy was awarded the Purple Heart for suffering sniper rounds on Tarawa. A medic patched him up and he went right back within the next three hours *againandagainandagainandagainandagain* to drag five wounded buddies away from the field of carnage. They all died hours later. Poussy tried to refuse the Silver Star, saying, "What the hell for? I didn't save them."

[5]   Professor Emeritus Roy K(eesters) Marshall of the University of Chicago investigated from 1963-1967 over three thousand male college seniors with less than a semester of work to complete their degrees who inexplicably failed coursework and faced the choice of "fight or flight" as potential draftees into military service. Over sixty-five percent claimed to have lost academic focus due to the military draft and the Vietnam battlefield as displayed on the TV news interspersed among ads for coffee, cigs and aspirin. Thirty-five percent expressed a sense of patriotism grounded in family military tradition. Ten percent replied with the unequivocal equivalent of "Screw off!"

She put a hand to her cheek. I could see she wanted so much to suspend her despair and hope it was from one of the romance novels she enjoyed skimming through. But it was the second time in three years. I double-down screwed up. She reached across the faux blue marblized formica kitchen table and took my hand. It smelled of garlic and was warmer, more confiding and comforting than her dutch apple pie with a dollop of French vanilla ice cream.

"But Will, you promised me you would make it this time. What happened?" She glanced around the kitchen. There was blood on the band-aid around her right thumb. "Why didn't you ask for help?"

I thought of sarcasting that I was sorry for two-timing her, flunking out again, but there was no need to bring Freud to the table. There was already enough trouble lining up some of my girlfriends by then. When she asked at the screen door what I planned to do now, it cut me hard at the knees to reflect on the old acned adolescent refrain: what do you want to do when you grow up? At 21, I wasn't mature enough to give an adequate answer to a question bouncing off many a kitchen table back then. Some of my friends also took a mysterious scholastic dive for no greater love—or a saccharine equivalent.

Mom dried her hands with a damp dishtowel and caressed my cheek with the generous cup of her right one as she walked past me into the living room. I felt terrible for her; for what I did to her; to not ease the pain she endured for me. She stood before the fireplace mantel where resided the framed photograph of her father-in-law (William "Captain Billy" Melville); her mother (Bernadette nee Arnold), and her husband (George Melville). They were all there looking back at her with a smile or raised eyebrow; especially Captain Billy. He went down with his troop ship in the Atlantic, where he shouldn't have been but was for once with honor: the old rascal with the blue of the Caribbean Sea in his eyes. George, the father from heaven I never knew, died in Schwetzingen in 1945; immaculate with his medals; confident in his gaze with a sensuous mouth ever ready to say I'll be home soon. He was away more than he would know. Bernadette, her diminutive mother, the New Orleans chorus girl with the dancing eyes now quiet and sitting this one out. I put my arm around her shoulder. She didn't have to bring them into this, as I knew she would, standing there quietly beseeching counsel from a mute tryptich of timeless compassion.

"Come on, Mom. Why don't we sit down." I tugged at her arm.

"Tell me about it, Will. How it happened. I need to know."

I dared not tell her the Dean's generous offer to transfer me to Kretschmer Aeronautical Institute, which I already declined in my mind. "Later, Mom."

When I alibied to the gruff Dean of the Lower Realm how I lost focus, he leaned back in his heavy oak chair against a neat phalanx of classics and became unbound; ran a hand with the fussy delicacy of a woman through his ratty hairpiece and expectorated with open arms, "What are you trying to say? You're another paper asshole? Why do you come to me now?"

I was hot under the collar from embarrassment.

"Look, William; you're so close, so close, close, close to graduating." He gradually moved his thumb and middle finger together as he said this until they snapped with a pop. "But no one on this burnt cinder is going to carry you across the finish line. It's up to you, understand?"

I wiped the sweat beads off my forehead with a small handkerchief. He then inspired like a pearl diver, held it in like a chain smoker and said with surprising bipolar contrition, "Listen, I'd like to help you finish up—but not here. I can get you transferred over to RIP near Euclid.[6] It's the best I can do. Take it!"

I leaned forward and almost waited for him to hand me a pastrami and provolone on pumpernickel over the deli case.

"I've already sent five of your classmates over there." He gazed past his wife's neglected spider plant out the small barred window. "You know, with this war junk going on, sometimes I feel like I'm in Budapest fixing passports for Jews escaping Nazis.

I didn't know what to say about his offer, although the illusion frightened me with his ability to free-climb around history and academic advising. He swivelled back around and formed a nave with his nine fingers through which he peeked at a family photo on the desk.

"So, I guess you're ready to blow this joint, are you?"

I heard he had a Ph.D in Medieval Techniques from Middlebury, but his words and tenor bristled with the anger of a dumbed-down, low-brow street-wise lingoist.

"Professor Bernstein, I'm very sorry. I'm burned out. I already turned down one offer."

---

[6]   RIP was the exclusive, little known but well-regarded Rabinow Institute of Polytechnics (1945-1963). It was actually closer to Ashtabula. From 1950-63, it was rated No. 2 in *Consumers Guide to Other Top Schools* for the lowest teacher-to-student ratio (1 to 1.6) in paper management engineering.

"You got choices? Tell me about it! Holy Jehovah! You got nichts! Do you want to wind up like hamburger?"

I shrugged my shoulders, a poor substitute for an exclamation mark, the point of which was my head.

"You look like a roach, you know," he said. "Down to the last drag. You must feel like what's his name? Krapp? Krupp? Krips? Kafka!"

"I don't know."

"Well, think about the offer and let me know tomorrow, K?"

I couldn't even offer a token response. I wasn't sure what the hell he rambled on about.

"Take care, now." His charity gladdened my heart, even if his smile seemed like the gratuitous pokerface of the juvenile court judge who let me off when I was twelve for stealing hubcaps. We shook hands again and I walked out, brushing shoulders with the next flunk-out artist seeking clemency.

Mom's voice came back. "Will, I wish your father could have been here all these years to guide you." She stared out the window and I could see in the sunlight the slightest well of a tear filming her eyes like dew on a rose petal.

"I know, Mom. I love you." I went over and held her for a moment until the tea kettle whistled on the stove.

CHAPTER 2

The crumpled match cover I fumbled in my hand had my Uncle Rob's local phone number on it. With the backpack pushed under the seat in the telephone booth, I closed the folding door. Everything was greasy: the cradle, the hook, speaker, dialer. Like I entered a giant French fry.

"Melville Associates."

"Hello. This is William Melville, Mr. Melville's nephew from Monroe. Can you hear me?"

"Yes. We're expecting you. Where are you now?"

"I'm at the bus terminal. Hold on." I could see McDonald's, Frank's Franks, Speed's Burger Palace, Luciano Pizza all in a clumped row of competing signage down the street. It could have been any town, but it was here in Fort Lauderdale and I was in a pickle. I wished I had been anybody else at that moment, anywhere, slinging burgers, throwing pizzas and wiping tables and taking abuse from drunks and red-eyed truckers. Leaning over the counter to get a girl's phone number. But I was here. And I wondered about all those towns and intersections I passed through in the past year, incomplete and out-of-bounds now like the footballs I used to throw on Saturday afternoons with the Bronowski twins. Who jaywalked those streets now?[7]

---

[7] There is some factual basis for this statement by Will Melville of sensing he was neither here nor there, wishing he were someone else somewhere else. During the first time he was banished from Mundane University, he travelled extensively as a claims adjustor for Valparaiso Casualty Insurance Company. With the kind permission of Grace Potamis of Valparaiso, I was able to examine most of the vouchers filed by Will. To my astonishment, he made innumerable trips all over the US, investigating unpremeditated arson claims. I also discovered the

"Hey, Will. How are you?" came a voice on the line I thought I knew. "Great, Uncle Rob. I really appreciate your helping me out here."

---

dour, scribbled notes of Will entitled, "Diary of a College Has-Been" located on twenty-two index cards in his aunt Trudie Munn's garage in Bloomington. It is uncertain if this was a wish list or actual locations he jotted down in his nine-month hiatus as a claims adjustor. Probably the latter, as the city is not given, indicating a familiarity beyond looking at a street map or for sources of ignition. With only the intersections specifically mentioned, it could be assumed Will was there; in the same manner as when one says "Intercourse," which anyone in the US knows is a small town in eastern Pennsylvania. A college friend, Felicity Murkowski, received several letters from Will during his first dishonorable discharge from Mundane. He wrote he was looking for himself in no one particular place while also investigating sources of ignition. I also interviewed by long distance the mother of his friend, Vinnie Pugliese. I didn't know Vinnie that well, since he hung around with a different crowd, even at Mundane. We all went out a few times together, but we never seemed to hit it off as real buddies. So anyway, she confirmed her son often travelled with Will during that time between Falmouth and Winslow in her ex-husband's Hudson Hornet. I told her I would try to research what happened to the vehicle. Also, I didn't have the resources (or funds) to track down every single one of these locations, although I am familiar with Spaulding & NE Perry Ave. in Peoria. Some day, perhaps a few buttons or keystrokes on a computing machine will be pushed to show them all in a few seconds. A partial list follows (Any association of the following locations with an active arson case is purely coincidental.): Peachtree St. SW & Trinity Ave. SW; Callowhill St. & N. 9th St.; S. Worthington St. & E. Union St.; Gibbon St. & S. St. Asaph St.; Walnut St & S. 10th St.; N. Elm Ave. & E. Warmsprings Ave.; Calhoun Ave. & Dixon St.; McLain Ave. & Lackey St.; Howard Ave. & Oak Grove Pl.; E. Michigan Ave. & Division St.; Mortland Rd. & Union St.; 86th St. & Ft. Hamilton Pkwy; Forbes Ave. & Stevenson St.; S. Monroe St. & E. 6th St.; Packard St. & Grange Ave.; E. Baltimore St. & Gay St.; W. Henry St. & Whitaker St.; S. Beach Blvd. & Washington St.; Tulane Ave. & S. Roman St.; Broadway & Battery St.; Spalding Ave. & NE Perry Ave.; E. Juneau Ave. & Jackson St.; 35th St. & Dent Pl.; E. Broad St. & N. 25th St.; Gillis St. & W. College Ave.; E. Huron St. & S. Elmwood Ave.; Laredo St. & N. Staples St.; Grand Ave. & S. 7th St.; S. Park Ave. & E. 36th St.; University Ave. & N. Frances St.; N. Ocean St. & E. Beaver St.; Kentucky Ave. & S. 4th St.; E. Pacific Ave. & S. Pine St.; Del Monte Ave. & Tyler St.; W. 18th St. & S. Canalport Ave.; S. Detroit Ave. & E. 7th St.

"Oh, no problem. Glad to help out. So you're finally here, eh?"

"Yeah. A real long trip. I'm exhausted."

"Well, hang in there. We'll pick you up at the terminal in ten minutes. By the way, how's your mom doing?"

I said she's doing fine considering the stress of losing her son due to the collusion between exam blue books and skirt-chasing at Mundane. Yes, she fondly recalled a family get-together a few years ago in Cannonsburg. I was only five years old at the time. She said she really appreciated all the help you gave her over the years. It was really too much.

"Good to hear, Will." There was a pause and clearing of the throat. "Actually, I'm not your uncle, Will. He's tied up right now, hee-hee; sort of like his yacht don't you know. I'm Lester Vice, his First Mate, waterboy, et cetera. Sorry for the confusion."

"Oh."

"Call me Les—Les Vice."

"It's all right. I haven't heard Uncle Rob's voice for a long, long time. It's okay."

"Be right over. Sit tight."

An hour passed with no one showing up. I changed a dollar for sixty cents with a panhandler standing outside the terminal and called again.

"Sure, hon. You got the right number. It's me here. Everyone got the rest of the day off." She said something like the driver left a while ago and was definitely on his way. If I didn't see him soon, I should start walking toward the beach.

"But. Darn!" She hanged up before I could ask if it was the beach at Ft. Lauderdale or St. Pete. I no option but to find my way oceanside. I jetissoned a few paperbacks and magazines and hoisted the backpack for the long walk. After half an hour, I stopped to make another phone call. How could they identify me in the first place? This didn't make any damned sense.

"Uh, Mr. Melville, this recording is for you. Sorry about the delay. Please be patient. When you get to the intersection with S&M Bootery on the corner, turn East toward the water. You're real close now. The car broke down and we sent out another for you. Don't worry. You can count on your uncle."

"Yeah, but how the hell does he know what I even look like?"

As I strained my eyes through a small canyon of shops, someone tapped me on the shoulder. "Will?"

I turned around. "Vinnie! What the!"

"Will? What on earth are you doing here? Damn, Samuel!"

I was stunned. We exchanged harmless gestures and anthropoid grunts, then sat down in a snack bar where a crouching police cruiser on the corner was obscured by the derangement of huge hanging baskets of plastic wisteria in front of a hobby store.

"Hey, Vinnie Pugliese. I can't believe you're here. What's witchoo, pal? Youse don't have to answer."

"Cut the phoney routine. I ain't, and don't tell anyone you saw me. Right?"

"Sure sure. I thought you were ready for your cap and gown."

"Yeah, I did finally graduate, but the party's over. I'm subrosa, incognito, persona non grata and the rest of that Latin bull."

"Why?" I noticed how he left out tabula rasa. I'll never know how he graduated. I knew he and the others I used to drink beer with at the Quad Club discussed the options after school, from enlisting in the service to skipping the country.[8]

"I can't handle it, pal. Want some more fries?"

"No thanks, but your old man's money can easily get you into law school. Right?"

"I thought about it. I'm tired of this book routine. Feel like I'm out of touch on life support."

He brushed his coal-black hair back behind his ears and asked what the hell I was doing here. Eventhough we were peers, I dropped my head long enough for him to answer his own question.

"You, too, huh? Welcome to the thirty-day club."

I acknowledged the answer with a half-smile, embarrassed that after a 1300-mile bus ride to anonymity, I'd bump into an authority on my identity. He fidgeted with the napkin holder and seemed for an instant to be the loneliest person this side of Aldebaran.

"Why the hell do I want to wait? How long do you think a polysci major will survive with all those gung-ho politicians running the show? Listen, Will." Again, he peeked over his shoulder at the ordinary movement of cars lined up at the take-out window. "Why don't you come with me

---

[8] There was no Quad Club at this time at Mundane University. A straight-A philosophy major firebombed it several months earlier and waited for the campus police to arrest him in his boxer shorts. Pugliese probably meant Hotpants, a small strip club off campus near Teasdale and Dickerhoff Blvd.

to Copenhagen. Maybe we can lay low with Lola Lindqvist. Remember her? I'm leaving tomorrow morning. The old man left me a ton of money. Sometimes it pays to be an only child."

"Don't remind me."

"Sorry, Will."

I could see a sheen of despair in his eyes. A plea for companionship; the old collegiate camaraderie in a cold foreign harbor.

"Vinnie, I can't. Thanks. I'd really like to, but my uncle asked me down here. So, I'm here. He's got something lined up for me. I don't even know what the hell it is."

Vinnie asked me are you sure three times in a minute. T'was a sad-ass day in hell when my old friend with whom I stole candy at the five-and-dime; delivered half the *Post-Gazette* into the sewer at Third Ave. and Grand; and double-dated the Swenson girls would soon become totally lost in the crowd for reasons irrational and beyond our youthful control.

"No sweat, Will. I understand. Youth is dead, Will. Long live wasted youth!" He tried to smile and raised a hand holding an imaginary beer stein.

Then out of nowhere, a woman with large sunglasses almost as large as her breasts walked up to our booth. Her voluptuous figure strained to escape her lime-green limbo pantsuit. Vinnie and I were caught in mid-sentence. She had an elusive scent of excitement and a smile making the white of her perfect teeth leap from her mouth like the surf at Ocean City. For an instant I felt like chum trailing a boat of drunken fishermen, waiting with joy to sacrifice myself for a few seconds to be nudged, nibbled and swallowed whole.

"Mr. Melville, I presume." Her legs were spread apart on spikey high heels, and I expected her to raise her lithe arms like a Broadway chorus line tryout. Vinnie became quite upset and almost slipped out of his seat to say are you looking for me, too?

She removed with care her tortoise-shell blueblockers and placed them on the table. They were genuine Seamus Favioli's. "No need to worry. I'm not one of those under-the-cover types, if you get what I mean."

Her bright blue eyes (or tinted contact lenses) darted up and down my length with such familiarity I sensed she stripped off my clothes. "I'm here to pick you up, Mr. Melville. Sorry to be so late."

"Finally," I breathed. "I thought you'd never come."

She tossed me a surprised glance and declared in a drawl, I always come on time, given the appropriate setting and circumstances. Then she glanced at her thick PanAmazonis chronometer and threw me a phrase wrapped in the purest possible innocence from her mango-frosted lipstick. "Well, are you ready to come with me, or do you need some time? I'll wait outside."

Vin seemed already halfway up to Boston-Logan for his connecting flight. Although this driver from Uncle was an abrupt, if not unpleasant intrusion, the whole scene gave me the uncomfortable feeling of sinister events on the horizon. Any way, I was too tired to dwell on it. Outside, it was getting dark. Vinnie and I hugged each other and gave one another a gentle punch on the bicep like we used to do at Mundane.

"Gotta get to the airport. I'll sleep there tonight. Might be good practice."

"Don't say that," I said. "You'll be all right, Vin."

"Keep in touch!"

"Yo!"

I hopped into a red Ferrari and off we went into hyperspace at 0-60 in 3.7 seconds. She reacquired lawful entry after three miles and smiled at me across the gear box.

"So you're his nephew. You must be proud of you uncle."

"Yes. I've heard some great things about him, but I've never chanced to meet him since early childhood.

"You poor boy. You need to be brought up to date." She tossed me a newspaper photo with the caption, "Robert Melville presents local Charitable Union with $20000 check. "He's a wonderful, intelligent and giving and caring individual. You'll see. He's very influential." She tossed her head up at the traffic light and said, "So, what have you done lately?"

"Huh?"

"You know. How many badges earned?"

"In the Boy Scouts?"

"No. Hitler Jugend."

I said I don't follow you and wish you would slow down. No sooner had I spoken than a police cruiser pulled us over. The trooper strode up to the car.

"Ma'am, what were you doing going 135 in a 50 zone?" She reached up for her sunglasses.

The officer reached up for his reflective pilot sunglasses.

She pulled her sunglasses down to the tip of her nose. He quickly pulled his sunglasses down and off his ski-jump nose and dangled them in front of her. I figured he wasn't about to be framed for doing his job.

"But officer, it was only for ten blocks and no one got hurt."

He lifted an eyebrow and apologized. "Oh, sorry Dr. Francesca. Do you need an escort?"

She handed him a small pink envelope, thanked him and waved as he moved on into traffic at an alarming rate of speed doing his job.

"How did you do that?" I said.

"I told you. Your uncle knows everybody here and he takes care of everybody."

I was impressed, but also curious how someone could get away with this blatant traffic violation. She glanced at my consternation and shook her head. "Listen, Mr. Melville, so we broke the law. Nobody was hurt. I paid tribute and so what's the problem? Laws are made to be broken, then fixed ad nauseum. Are you familiar with case law?"

I could have been sitting in a VW bug far behind her dust for all I knew. She was not only intelligent, but hyperbolically attractive at ninety degrees. Several miles flew by and we stopped at a little grotto-styled restaurant.

"Good evening, Dr. Francesca. Your usual place?" said the solicitous Bassett hound.

We sat down in a booth. I stole a sideways glance at her and thought about rockclimbing.

Some thirty minutes later and two glasses of wine, I found out her name was Debbie Costello. Her professional name: Violetta Francesca. What the devil was she running away from? Abuse? Explosive IQ? There was a Costello residence several blocks away from our house, but there's a lot of Costellos out there, so why should I get personal? She twirled her wine glass on the scale of a micrometer with precision and thoughtfulness which I felt expressed a certain deference toward me.

"You could say Lester Vice—Les—is your uncle's right-hand man. When he's ashore here, I massage his hemispheres to make sure he has his head on straight."

I could imagine which head, but I had a hard time understanding her. I canted my own head politely as if I knew this stuff for years. Dr. Francesca was only seven years older, but the vivacious lilt of her voice and luscious precision of vowel and dipthong overwhelmed my youthful senses, and I feebly toyed with the tumescent desire to schuss downhill between the gates of her twin peaks into the moist valley below for an edifying apres-ski.[9]

---

[9]   As of this date, it is unclear why Will left such copious notes on Dr. Francesca. I included them almost verbatim on the hunch she may have played a significant part later in his recollections. She really must have impressed him. There are still some unopened boxes I have to get to. Perhaps, he was hot for her. As Will found out, Violetta was originally Deborah Costello. She was born at Custer General. It's hard to swallow why he didn't have the curiosity to ask if she was the daughter of Mrs. Costello in the neighborhood back in Monroe. Why didn't he ask? Maybe her lips and legs distracted him. She lived only six blocks away. So close and yet so far. I can remember that walking through some of those ethnic neighborhoods back then was like crossing another country's border. Maybe that's why Will didn't broach the question. Anyway, my old friend, George "Moonlight" Stubblebein from the Monroe public library, dug up the scoop on Debbie in exchange for my torn entrance ticket to the 1939 World's Fair. He said he liked the "vicarious visceralcality" (his words) of knowing that someone actually used it. I neglected to tell him I was the one who tore it trying to get it out of its plastic sleeve at a memorabilia show in Detroit. A 34-year old natural brunette with a Ph.D in EE from MIT, she left Yale law to barnstorm for licensees for her patents at technical trade shows across the country. Ceramic sharkskin for industrial coating applications. Her only bite was from a representative of Phil Hill, who wanted to mold it into a Formula One "Monterey smoothing fin," as he called it. In 1957, she bumped into Robert Melville at a fair in Tampa. Attracted to the protrusion of her presentation, he tapped her right on the floor to serve as technical adviser on the Tern after a six-month cruise that resolved into mutual admiration for his penetrating business acumen and their difference in ages. He was born July 4, 1910, second son of Captain Billy Melville. Will mentioned elsewhere that Les said Captain Melville said he told Deb she could blow his tanks anytime. He said he was very drunk at the time, but it didn't matter since their relationship took a dive by then and she was more interested in fondling the stick of his Mercedes gullwing. The day after Mrs. Costello mistakenly opened one of Will's last letters to his mother, she threw it out in disgust. Will's mother was in the hospital at the time and did not know about this until I showed her the letter, which I was lucky to obtain from the neighborhood's long-time garbage collector, Horace Peeps, who collects discarded letters and medical bills as a hobby. I should not have shown it to Mrs.

She glanced at her diver's chronometer. "Nice to meet you. Got to run. Don't worry. Remember, it's only a shakedown cruise. I'm supposed to stay behind on this one."

"But." Behind? I wanted to rear-end her like a horny hermit shepherd with a learner's permit. I sat there rather stunned although relaxed in the spongy chintz-covered chair. What in the hell did I get myself into? Back in Monroe in my attic room with the wall of pennants from Penn State, Mundane, Indiana and U of M, I thought the first step to leave home and a sense of independence was to hop on the local bus and knock on doors for a job. Now I entered a strange clockwork of time and motion waiting with grinding gears to comminute me into choice hamburger over there or impress me into the infamous anonymity of a draft dodger. It almost didn't matter to me now, floating in flotsam full of cruise ship garbage with no conscience or purpose beyond providing sustenance for lower forms.[10]

Melville. She thanked me, took the letter and excused herself to wash the dishes in the kitchen sink for a lost amount of time.

[10] Regarding identities, the Spring of 1895 saw Captain Billy Melville make no less than six vaudevillian metamorphoses to survive various authorities. What a character he must have been. The most serious incident saw him incarcerated in Barbados for rearranging the interior of a dockside bar. He drowned several rounds of beer before ordering his six-man mixed Filipino-Somali crew to redecorate the place. In his diary (p. 198), he wrote "...the boite was devoid of class; no entertainment beyond a tired mule in a straw hat in a corner of the small stage. I took it upon myself and the crew to purify this fleshpot of iniquity." When the four gaily-striped gendarmes strolled by, he said let my crew go; I'll take on all of you with my little finger, and the four got control of him after he thrashed and twisted like a tarpon. Since it was his fifth incarceration in three years, the newly appointed mulatto magistrate with an uncommon anti-colonial animosity, refused at that time a bribe of five rubies from Ceylon and ordered him to be hanged until his pants were full to atone for years of foreign insults to the island culture and women (the underage dancer bitterly complained that earlier in the evening Captain Billy took away more than her castenets like a satyr for pocket change). The cell was filled later that night by a drunk and disorderly, who was promptly marched out of the cell and hanged. The judge summarily changed the drunk's name to Captain Melville's to cover his coattails and save the good name of the dancer's wronged family. Pg. 200: "My good cook, Antonio, brought my change of persona stuffed in a food basket. I managed to use a rusty crooked nail to jimmy the cell door. When

After a while, I went to the men's room and tried not to urinate on the seat. At least I was sitting down this time in a halfway decent restaurant.

The maitre d' came to my table and said, "So very sorry, sir. This is for you." He handed me a torn corner of the day's menu.

I muttered this is getting to be a real ball of yarn as I mused at the directions to walk five blocks south along the avenue and wait at the flashing yellow light. It said, "You're nearly there!" I really appreciated the exclamation mark. Obviously, this was a sort of crude game and I began to resent my own naivete more than my uncle's cryptic messages. I yelled SON-OF-A-BITCH! to no one in particular. One of the waiters came out to flick a cigarette across my path to the "No Parking" sign. I moved on under the dubious stare of the sun and a panel of lesser deities. No sooner did I trudge to the appointed traffic light than a Renault Dauphine pulled up.

"Senor Will, si?"

"Si, si." And I threw in ja, da, oui, hai and jambo in quick succession in this bonus round.

"Your uncle is around the corner and waiting to see you."

"No kidding!"

"Que?"

"Es verdad, no?" I recalled from my fifty-word Spanish lexicon.

"Yes. No boolsheet," he chuckled. "Get in. My name is Aurelio from Manaus. You heard of Amazon, no?"

"Sure. We're going there?"

He gave a hearty laugh, then in an instant frowned as he peeked over the steering wheel at the fuzzy dice dangling from the rearview mirror. He pushed down his collar a bit and pointed to an intricate tribal tattoo snaking down his neck. "This here is my identity papers. Passport. When I'm back home. I can go anywhere there. Up here, it's only to impress las chicas—the girls.

---

the guard came downstairs, I said the prisoner escaped from my own cell, as he thought I was one of the poor devils selling food to the inmates. I calmly walked behind him until I was out of the jail and continued on to the dock and the Tern." NOTE: Island criminal records stated Captain Billy actually clubbed the guard and left him to die. He never dropped anchor there much after that. The incident, harmless on the surface due to the anonymity of the guard, shows an impetuous, if not violent, streak not uncommon in the brute nature of piracy of the day; more akin to a swashbuckling Jonathan Edwards of Puritan repute.

"And I guess you also work for Uncle Rob."

"Oh, man. El Capitan. He numero uno. Mas grande jefe. He save my life.[11]

Aurelio, who told me he only worked for uncle on the Intracoastal Waterway, grinned and turned into a parking lot next to a dance club called La Cabana.

"You go inside now, okay?" he said in a flat sinister monotone without making the usual throat-cutting sign with his finger. "Boss orders. Wait. No te—don't worry. Maybe boss get angry." He gave me a primal stare from deep in the arboreal past of his jungle ancestors. It sobered me up and I did not object like some wise-ass sophomore on Spring break.

Exhausted, angry and hungry, there was no choice but to enter the club and wait for the next series of broken promises. A perky, gum-clicking waitress slipped an arm into mine.

"Wadashuggawon, hon?" She noticed my slight frown and straightened her apron.

"How about two ham sandwiches and a Heineken?"

"Hon, we do the sandwich thing, but we don't serve foreign stuff here. Only Bud or Dos Equis."

Finally, I was ready to break the ten-hour chain of peanuts and peppermint patties with some real food, and settled back to wait and watch several older couples do a halting baby-step version of the meringue. I told the skinny waitress to keep the three dollar bills. She tucked them between her hills of Rome, as we used to say about Arlene Fazio's admirable pulcritude in Ann Arbor.

"Listen, hon, you need a place to stay tonight?"

Her hand felt good on my knee. "Maybe. I'm waiting for someone to pick me up."

"So." She waited for me to complete the sentence. "Who you waiting for—you girlfriend?"

"No. My uncle, Robert Melville. Seems like a lot of people around here know about him."

---

[11] Will later found out from Les Vice that Aurelio was hauled onboard the Tern after stealing the proceeds from a performance of Verdi's *Requiem* at the Manaus opera house and sprinting from a mob all the way to the quay. His left shoulder and thigh were fileted by a machete. After weighing anchor, a crewmember with some shrunken-skull savvy sewed him up with manila line dipped in rum.

"Oh, so you the guy. Wait here, hon." Then she got up rather fast and weaved through the dance floor and disappeared.

Right. I'll wait here until hell melts the arctic icecap. Several minutes later she sneaked in beyond my peripheral vision with two beers. "It's my break time, hon." She patted my hand with surprising tenderness, and her apron didn't reek of onions and garlic anymore.

"Hon, watch now. I told them to play "Maria Elena." You watch, okay?" She tilted her beach blond curls toward the parquet dance floor.

I waited, as usual. Then from the shadows a little old man searched the middle of the dance floor with a halting gait. He wore a black velvet cape cloaking his small frame of about five feet five. His black shoes with risers glistened. Then I saw his face for an instant under the roving overhead spotlight. A neat white mustache under a prominent well-shaped Cervantian nose between two well-inked black eyebrows lifted in the air as he unfastened his cape and tossed it onto the bar like a bullfighter. He lifted the proud head with thinning, swept-back white hair and held out a hand beckoning a partner, but no one came out from the shadows. Strangely, I didn't feel so alone. He waited. He held up his arms to receive the one he came for.

"His wife she dead for many years now," the waitress whispered in my ear.

He caressed the air, waiting for the beat. He embraced the empty space with great care, holding his hand where the small of a woman's back would be; where the zipper might be. He began right on the downbeat a deliberate slow foxtrot box complete with an ad-lib sensuous dip and bend as he swept across the floor with his beloved airspace. What a gentleman and dancer! This nostalgic pantomime lasted only about three minutes. When the music ended, he extended his arm again with a gallant flourish to release her memory. She lingered in my memory, and I also didn't want her to go. Slowly, he went to the bar, where his cape hung half over it. "You see photograph over there behind bar. His wife. He come here every Saturday night to dance one dance with her. He don't fool round."

"What's his name?"

"He don't like to talk."

The old man dropped a few coins onto the bar and, with the regal ambiguity of someone down to his last dime and a Lamborghini idling outside, strode with his chin up and chest out across the dark dance floor to resume his seat in the purple shadows.

"Where does he come from? He must live around here somewhere."

"He been coming here for cupola years. What I hear he scape from Catro in 1960. You see, viejo over there he got no worries; only memories. You know what I mean?"[12]

I shook my head in agreement. I glanced at the hem of her short skirt. I was the novitiate here, trying to fathom the mystical way through the throng at the door waiting to get in. When I glanced back to the table after scanning the crowd for younger women, the guy's face was partially obscured by the white Panama hat set at a rackish angle, almost like the old man's. He got up and halfway across the floor, stopped and stared right at me.

I said, hell, here's another messenger. This is getting to be a real pain in the ass, I said to no one in particular, least of all myself. I stared back at him, with the hat rim glowing like a halo better-suited to a Botticelli painting. On my third beer, I recalled an old photograph of Uncle Rob at Bear Lake with a sardonic half-smile as if he were at once a most charitable and kind person and then someone else who was reclusive, cut corners, schemed, cheated and did any kind of dastardly thing imaginable to get ahead. And then this guy stretched out his arms in a generous sweep and got into my space. The irridescent tattoo of a dolphin decorated the back of his right hand.

"Will, don't you know me," he shouted above the crowd and shuffling feet.[13]

---

[12] I paid a pretty peso to a part-time guard at the Immigration Office in Miami to find out the old man arrived much earlier than the recent boat people. As verified by an undated, faded poster on the wall next to the ladies' room, he ran a samba club (Joselitos) for years in downtown Miami. His name, Francisco Fiol, ran across the bottom of the poster in a small italic font. He left Havana in 1948 after teaching political science and a University of Iowa agronomics extension course at the universidad for twenty years. With very strong dermatologic encouragement from Batista, he paid for a fishing boat to ferry him the ninety miles to Key West and then hitchhiked to Miami. When he managed to get his wife out two years later, she lasted six months and died from breast cancer on the eighth floor at Miami-Dade. If he chatted with Melville in the shadows, it's a fair bet the fishing boat giving him a new life was actually the Tern.

[13] In spite of a dearth of photos of Uncle Rob, Will's mother told me she gave him a recent picture of her brother-in-law sitting on his yacht, the Tern, saying this is what your uncle looks like now so take a good look. It's not like he's a total

"Uncle Rob? Uncle Rob! Finally! And I jumped out of my skin and got up and hugged him right smack in the middle of a reticulated conga line ready to constrict the two of us. I coughed and wanted to weep from exhaustion on the shoulder of my father's brother and surrogate. He let out a great burst of laughter from a neat scruff of white beard at the entrance to a generous mouth of capped teeth as white as the cliffs of Dover. I don't know why, but I wandered back to Dr. Debbie in a flash and wondered how long would it take a ripple from the English Channel to pounce upon the beach at Ocean City and rush up past sand castles to lick her oily legs. Probably never, but at least my uncle finally showed up.

"My boy, let me get a look at you. My word, you've grown up since I last saw you what was it fifteen years ago you were a tyke. Hell, I can't remember I've been so busy."

I brushed away moisture from my eyes. The search was over. I couldn't remember ever meeting him face-to-face. Only from a snapshot and handful of family photos at oblique angles with the old Kodak Enigmatic Mom sometimes pulled out of the hall closet. I was four or five. The only true link to my father, whom I also never met. His features close-up were elusive, but I focused on the brooding wrinkled brow, searching eyes and sloping shoulders.

"Uncle Rob. Jesus!"

"No, Will. Just Uncle Rob here," as he placed his hands on my shoulders in a second wave of greeting. "Come on, get your drink and let's take a seat back over there where I hang out when I'm here. I can't get over it. Ha!"

On the way over, he broke into the line, grabbed my hands and planted them right on the rotating hips of a babe in short pink pants who turned to me and shouted let's tighten it up. Uncle Rob jumped in front of her and we spent ten minutes snaking our way around to the other side. Yet another diversion, though fully acceptable this time.

"Thanks, doll," he said to the girl sandwiched in between us.

"My pleasure, captain," she cheered.

At the table, I asked out of breath if he knew the girl.

---

stranger or reprobate, but he's changed a lot though the years. Eventhough he's been generous to a fault with us, he's been busy doing one thing or another and frankly I've no idea how he makes his money. It's your choice, Will. You're old enough now to make up your own mind. Yes, I know he's your father's brother. Stay on your toes and write to me, won't you. Don't forget: he's got the dolphins on his left or right hand. I forgot which one.

"Oh, yeah. She was a summer intern for me two years ago. Very nice girl. She's taking a break from Gainesville."

"Really? What does she do?"

"Cultural anthroapologist studying headhunters in New Guinea," he winked.

"What? The music is too loud."

"I'll introduce you to her some time. Gaby, a pitcher of beer please," he shouted at the racing waitress. Several minutes later, he rotated his glass a few times and burped in my direction. The dim light was still bright enough to show the spidery skin accented by the residue of some dark oily substance. Soiled hands crossed my mind, but then again, Mom said he got into everything.

"Well, tell me now," as he faked an Irish brogue. "How is it you took so long in getting here?" He winked again.

The waitress at the end glanced our way, swung her head in silent dismay as if to say watch your step.

I was so damned grateful Uncle Rob showed up, it slipped my mind he was the stage manager responsible for my getting jerked around for four hours like some errant teenager booked for possession; so close to the beach of screaming girls in bikinis under bright umbrellas, yet so far away; four hours of nonsense and teasing; I was ready to get back on Poussy's Greyhound for a roundtrip back home and a one hundred percent certainty of going to basic training and ninety percent chance of going to Vietnam and then fifty percent chance of occupying a black body bag and twenty percent chance of getting buried within the national cemetery of Mom's choice and then back up to one hundred percent chance of never munching buttered popcorn at a rerun of *Odd Man Out* with my hand palming Daphne Milloy's plump left knee.

"Say, Uncle Rob; were you behind all that monkey business between this glass of beer and the bus terminal?"

He glanced up to burst out laughing at my sudden embarrassment for asking a dumb question; and he couldn't stop until it receded into a teary chuckle with aftershocks of stifled coughing. He wiped his eyes and raised his hands.

"You got me, son. I really couldn't let this golden chance pass by. Know what I mean? Kind of?" He turned the stein, frowned and began a scary alteration of mood I'd only seen in a Jekyll and Hyde adaptation.[14]

"But why? What the hell for?"

"Don't swear!" he pointed with a grimy index finger.

"Okay. Sorry."

---

[14] If Will's father survived World War II, it is likely he would have been royally pissed that Uncle Rob referred to Will as "son." It would be fairly easy to imagine him at the table, saying Rob, since when do you have the right to call Will your son? I may have the jump on you in the curtain call of life and death, but it doesn't mean you can take over his education. I am very grateful for you taking care of Mary and Will all these years I've been gone, the son I never saw and your endearing reference to him as your "son" and "my boy." Remember, I know you've got a not-too-pretty side to your personality. Sure, we shared our little headbutts and fisticuffs as kids and competitive side from dear old conflicted father, Captain Billy; but don't blame me for that double-date when we switched: you got Angel Baby for one night and I got Mary for my beloved wife. Don't feel bad. You bounced back and around with three wives and no issue and I'm truly sorry for the poor luck, but that's life and perhaps death in an odd way. Yes, I know Captain Billy favored me and in a drunken rage falsely accused mother of having you, a bastard from an affair. Remember this: no amount of scuffling competition could ever diminish my total affection and love for you as my brother. Okay. I'll relent and you can go ahead and call him your son. I belatedly will Will to your safekeeping; however, this doesn't give you the right to corrupt him, to screw up his life at a time like this. And please keep him off that godforsaken Tern. He'll kill himself as sure as Captain Billy violated it with the cargo of muted helpless flesh and rotgut skullduggery for years. It should have been scrapped in Long Beach years ago. Don't be bitter that my premature departure took some starch out of your sails. Hell (sorry), you did your service piece on the Cuke and for that you have my everlasting admiration. The fact it was lost with almost the whole crew two days after you left her is something you must get over after all these years. Try to imagine and accept Will as the lone survivor of that tragedy. Please make sure he does well and doesn't screw up his life like we did in so many ways. **[ed. Note: At first, Mrs. Melville reviewed and accepted my imagined statement from her deceased husband, although she later regretted much of it and, thereafter, I didn't answer many of her phone calls about it. If she keeps insisting, I'll certainly take it out later.]**

"Will, how about another round?"

"Throw in another Reuben? I'm still hungry."

"Done, as if by order. Will, my boy, consider all this a shakedown cruise. You need a break. I don't intend to aggravate your situation. You're like a son to me. They'll be a lot of things you'll have to face and others you'll need to avoid now since you're on your own."

"Huh?"

He held his hands about a foot apart with his elbows on the table. "Take a look. Where do you think you fit between an angstrom and a light year?"

I had no idea in the world where he was headed. I thought I left all the doublespeak back in engineering at Mundane. I shook my head. Sure, I listened. I knew from Mom and read in some business magazine how he was quite the successful entrepreneur and those two hands he held up could easily be the stanchions for a new suspension bridge. A decorated war veteran, but I tired of the lecturing, the proof of which was my flunking out a second time in three years.

"I must confess I feel a certain moral obligation to help you navigate through this world of golden opportunities and ancient cruelties, but you will need to make the right choices on your own. Do you follow me?

Right then and there, I figured that Uncle Rob must have read a ton of books to express himself the way he did, with a lot more twists and turns than some of the tenured profs I had at Mundane. "Okay, I hear you, uncle. Why are you shaking your head?"

"You may hear me, but look." He cupped his hands together just above the table as if he were hovering over the fragile flame of a thought he wanted to protect and reveal to me before it flickered out. "I know your situation about trying to stay out of the service. I'm not criticizing you about this. Understand?"

I glanced at the so-called flame of wisdom in his cupped hands reflecting the light from his eyes.

"I want you to join me and the gang on the Tern, my yacht. There's a lot of things to do and learn. It will be as much an ethical journey as much as a physical one. You won't have to worry about the Army or the rice paddies for now, at least. Understand?" He finished his beer and waved to the waitress.

"I know, Uncle Rob. I'm a bit scared."

"Yeah. The deep. The unknown. It's all a screwed-up time, but I want to see if I can help you get through it one way or another. I feel I owe this to the memory of your dad. Do you understand what I'm saying?"

After four beers, I felt a shivver of humiliation. I agreed. I couldn't finish the Reuben. He rambled on about how there were plenty of people willing and perhaps gullible enough to fill a general's chessboard and gild the pockets of contractors making tons of money overseas. I was surprised at this cynicism coming from such a decorated war veteran.

"You can still get on the bus and go back home. You can go to Toronto or Copenhagen and wait it out or stay there, get married maybe, have some kids. It's not my decision. It's yours, Will."

I sensed we were speaking in the same bar, even if he was ahead by three beers. I asked what he thought about my tentative plans.

"Well, son, maybe there's a farce (his twisted pronunciation) out there beyond our ken with control over all of this." He waved his hand across the table.[15] "And it's—I'd like to think it's a he or she—dictating our every thought and action. Call it a higher being, or you can call it Nietzsche or whoever the hell."

"Uncle, let's hope he's not a real hack; some cheap writer of dime novels; otherwise, I'd like to write my own story some day." I asked him if there was something after this fiction called life—or was it life called fiction.

"Will, my boy, I think we've drunk enough. This cheap stuff can sure sneak up on you." He let out one more belch.

We shook hands across the checkered tablecloth. In his El Dorado convertible on the way back to the motel, where he reserved a room for me, he kept adjusting his aviator sunglasses, rambling through an expectorant spray of topics from greed to charity.

"There are some things I regret, son, like the day I evicted an elderly lady from one of my condos down in Miami.

"How old was she?"

"Ninety five."

"Okay, Uncle Rob. What's the punch line?" I already sensed his manner of telling an incident, then milking it for a kernel of moral levity.

---

[15] On one of his index cards, Will noted Uncle Rob often mispronounced words (as in this case "farce" for "force") to apparently express an aversion to cliches and hackneyed phraseology. Perhaps he thought he could impress by causing someone to sort out what he really intended to say.

"Well, you're close. I felt so bad, because I'm naturally a charitable guy, but I felt strangely vindicated in my greed when the cops said she and her nephew made something called methamphetamine. They said I lucked out the old bag didn't torch the whole building. Otherwise, a lovely old lady."[16]

He no sooner related this to me than he screeched the car to a stop, ran across the intersection and helped a splayed old lady back on her feet. It took me fully a minute to react. I rushed over after him to pick up her groceries sprayed about the curb. She refused an ambulance and thanked us. Uncle Rob hailed a cab, gently shoved her into the back seat with her groceries and slipped the cabbie a fifty-dollar bill. "Ma'am you tell him where to go. He'll get you there," said Uncle Rob. He poked the cabbie on the shoulder and said "Comprende, pal?"

We repaired to his emerald green El Dorado with whitewalls. I asked him what's with the two soccer balls draped over either side of the trailer hitch.

"If you got'em, show'em." Out of breath again, he went on about taking every opportunity to do good each day. "You have to find those opportunities, Will. You don't sit on your ass waiting for things to happen. You have to be quick to respond to those in need. At least, it looks good on the surface and lends an air of respectability to the other stuff clinging to your hipwaders.

"Yeah," I said while staring at two young women crossing the street in front of us. I wondered if they were wearing panties like the old lady.

"Remember," he pointed. "Put up all the zeros you want, but just make sure at some point you put a one in front of them. Do you understand what I'm getting at?"

"All right, Uncle. Got it. Got it."

"One last thing, Will. Some people get a kick out of hitting a home run or stealing home plate. I sort of outgrew such stuff. I struck out three times getting married and dabbling in various adolescent adventures. The Tern has been the only stable thing in my life after the war. Maybe it's the ambivalence of calm seas and gales that suits my personality better than a dockside sink full of dirty dishes."

---

[16] Melville was actually very familiar with methamphetamine, a powerful narcotic analgesic he was treated with for lower back pain by Ward "Dr. Feelfine" Cooley when he docked a small ChrisCraft in 1958 on the Potomac near the boathouse and upstream of the putridgeous rendering plant.

Rubbing my eyes, I released my grip on the fact he played such a prank on me, as I watched his weathered hands fumble with the bottle by the gearshift.

"Will, I don't want you to misunderstand me. I'll help you to sort things out, and then again I might put you into the eye of the storm headed this way tomorrow. Get some sleep. Night."

He promised to pick me up next morning. I asked what time? with a cynical smile I made in imitation of him.

"At hell's bells, lad."

He dropped me off at the Sea Breeze Motel. I already passed it twice earlier in the day. Once in my room, I tossed the complementary *South Florida Tattler* to the side and turned off the lamp. The phone rang as my eyelids dropped like the two heavy garage doors at Speed's auto repair shop back home.

At night, I tossed on a rippling sea of blue-green designer sheets, wondering if I had made a choice I could live with; one Mom and Dad would be proud of and, at least, not disrespect them or lose my friends and the society I now crawled in.

CHAPTER 3

Next morning, the sun bled through the venetian blinds like gold leaf spilling over ornate picture frames at the Phillips Art Gallery our senior high school class visited in 1960. I no sooner scarfed up the detritus of frosted doughnuts at the continental breakfast end table and swilled down a cup of warmed-over dishwater than a lanky old gent came up and tipped his Mack bulldog ballcap.

"Mr. Melville, I presume."

"Right. You can go ahead and assume," I said and we shook hands. "I can't believe you're on-time."

"Ignace Shill at your service. Call me Bud. I'm the only one on borrowed time." He lifted his Rolex. "I set my watch ahead one hour. You might say I'm living in the future and waiting for my past to catch up, heh, heh!"

He possessed a systemic nervous tic starting as a twinkle in the corner of his left eye, raced down his left arm to jangle his fingers, then mysteriously jumping to convulse his right foot and jerking his head to the left, where he twinkled his right eyelid—all in a few milliseconds. I didn't think his smile—grimace—smile circuitry mimicked method acting, but I didn't know him well enough and I couldn't do anything for him then.[17]

---

[17] (Poop on Ignace "Bud" Shill was difficult to come by. It was only by sheer luck I bumped into Joe Yankovic at the PNA near Youngstown. If you don't try to speak broken Polish, you may never find out. I knew from Will's notes Bud hung out in the area. Joe, who was a young 85, slid back the embroidered cuntcap on his bald pate and sprayed the bar with his Rolling Rock when I mentioned Bud's name.) Bud Shill was an ex-WWII Polish pilot who emigrated to the US in 1946. He went from ragpicker to housepainter to auctioneer near Secaucus.

"Anything wrong?" I said.

"Oh, no. The doc told me it's tic fever."

"What?"

"Or something. Forget it."

Bud said he'd been Uncle Rob's chauffeur or get-away man since 1951, when they stumbled into each other in Key West.[18] After he cleared the peanut shells off the seat, he steered the rusted-out B-902 down the highway until we came to an unpaved road leading to a small dock. And there it was, hiding in my memory all those years I dreamed of her: the Tern.

"Are these bullet holes?" I asked as we walked past the hull.

Bud glided an oil-stained hand through his stubble and said, Nope. They were holes drilled out to refit some electrical stuff.

"Awfully dull drill if you ask me." I put a finger through one.

"Yeah. Must be. You know anything about your Uncle?"

I said yeah he's my uncle, but I only knew he was much admired and helped out me and Mom a lot over the years. A successful businessman with a yacht bequeathed by his father and my grandfather Captain Billy.

The tremors and tics were acquired from SS torture after his third failed escape from three separate detention camps. (Joe stared me square in the face and asked if I knew how many Polish pilots crawled out of Poland during the war.) The experience left Bud with limited use of his right hand. Bud later told me this was no big deal except he preferred to pick his nose with his right pinkie since childhood in Lodz. In Spring 1949, he was hired by General Motors to sabotage an assembly line at a Kaiser-Fraser plant near Evansville, for which perfidy he received a Pontiac Equalizer with a glove compartment stuffed with $1500 in ten-dollar bills which he spent to regroup at his father's home in Youngstown, then to Key West where he first met Melville. Evidence of the GM gig was based on an internal GM document (GM/SNITCH-483) one of Joe's buddies recovered from a pre-bonfire trashcan at an annual 25-year Buick managers' reunion family picnic in Grosse Pointe. Three months after I met Joe he called me in the middle of the night. I could hear polka music in the background. He said, "None. They all had wings."

[18] One of several instances in which Bud Shill tried to escape his everpresent past. Yankovic also told me that Bud's younger brother, Tadeuz, went so-to-speak full circle. After joining the Army, he went from dodging Nazi bullets outside Warsaw to stepping in front of the big one near Pusan.

Some photos. About it. Never a phone call I could remember. Must have been busy as a beaver doing something.

Bud swirled around and asked if I knew anything about the Tern. I said no, except again for some old photos.

"Good," he said. "Better off you don't know. She's done an awful lot of good. We'll get her ship-shape and out of the dock tomorrow. Ship's party tonight."

"I don't see any sails," I said looking into the sky.

"Nautical term. You know how to do a half-hitch? Square knot?"

As we shot the breeze, the sky began to hue down to a dingy mauve and the wind picked up so much we lifted our voices over the next hour.

"They can come up pretty fast down here," quipped Bud. "Surf's been up a notch the last few nights." He pointed an accusing finger toward the beach, 239 yards to the East according to the Tacos Ahora sign flapping in the wind. He stared back at the Tern, then at the surf between the beach houses and joked I must be the reason it's coming.

Yeah, like I came down here for no better reason than to get my ass in a bigger sling. "What are you, superstitious?" I joked in response.

Bud raised his trembling hand to swear an oath, then dropped it into a helpless heap down his side. "Funny how we got slaves and hurricanes from Africa. We're free of slavery, we still got to shackle down everything else." He scuffed the dirt and said it's too complicated, so let's forget it and talk about something else. We turned back and passed the Tern and several dockworkers pushing around an old soccer ball.

"Will she survive on stilts alone?"

"Hell yes," he said. "Don't tell your uncle I told you, but she's also been in a load of trouble before, but come out of it by some miracle."

"Like what?"

"Don't ask. You'll find out soon enough. Inescapable or inevitable. One of those."

So, I got jerked around half of Ft. Lauderdale and now I'll get mugged down some blind alley of my mind. And I thought, Uncle Rob must be working both sides of the wharf.

CHAPTER 4

On the wild and wet eve of the Tern's undocking for waters unknown to me—save for Sister Mary Alice's fifth-grade tattered world map—we hunkered down under the hurricane at the former Bill's Place, under a new name (McDuff's Bar) but, to paraphrase Bud, with the same dusty bottles behind the bar, face-lifted from a previous storm into a dark joint with darker panelled walls of ghoulish sconces and booths separated by old perforated metal radiator screens resembling a concentric circle of dimly lit confessionals around a linoleum dance floor. One large table candle as fat as Friar Tuck's roped beltline lit each booth so that snatches of light genuflected off a turned cheek or raised knuckle. A perfect cushion-backed alcove to hear a pack of lies or sinful gasps and slobbers of poor souls wretching forth on a divorce, rape, stock market loss, climbing within 200 yards of K2's summit or the failing health of a son or daughter. I noticed the Miller beer clock behind the bar as big as a marathon billboard at the finish line. They straggled in for oxygen or the next complementary round: Professor Paleo-Tosti[19], Les Vice, Bud Shill, some little guy and to

---

[19] Will left quite a few notes on the "doll with the golden ringlets." Paola Paleo-Tosti was a young professor of Paleolinguistics at Mount St. Eustace down the road from Worcester. She was the recipient for several years of an $8 million Department of Education grant to identify ancient linguistic pathways and apply them to improve verbal skills of inner city middle school students. Will said she once told him the kids lagging behind already had a good start before she arrived on the scene. About thirty-one when Will met her here, Paola changed her legal name to better fit her chosen academic path, although it's unclear how she tacked on "Tosti," a popular Italian composer at the turn of the century whose Neapolitan songs were a far evolutionary cry from the grunts of cavemen. I never

my everlasting shock, "What the hell are you doing here?" as I jumped up to grab his hand.

"Vinnie! You're supposed to be at the Student Union in Copenhagen."

"Nah." He waved me off. "I said screw it. I'd be getting in trouble over there. I don't speak the language."

"They all speak English, pal," said Bud.

Vinnie showed the most pathetic rictus of a smile I ever saw outside of a botched stiff in a casket.

"Come on and sit down," I said and tried to drape an arm around his shoulder above the backpack.

"Nah," as he waved me off again.

"Aw, come on and sit down. What are you having?" I insisted.

"It's okay. I'm sober enough."

Outside the white-washed cinderblock surroundings, the winds began to roar and groan like a pride of hungry lions in elephant grass. The morose barkeep wagged his wattles and said one hundred ten. I ought to know. I've been here since 1938. He pushed a damp towel across his forehead and then through a rinsed glass.

Through our first two rounds of brew, there was a persistent hard knock by the front door.

"My flap meter—the sign of things to come," said the barkeep with authoritative nonchalance. "Up to one fifteen now. Boss won't like it."

I sensed we all felt safe inside, around the table in the back booth, eventhough the unrelenting wind hissed through every invisible crack like a chorus of old hags moaning a recitative of our forefathers' sins. Uncle Rob

---

found out her real name. She earned a Ph.D. in psychopaleontology cobbled together among Cornell, Pomona and Ann Arbor. Her dissertation was on the roots of pathological lying (A Brief Pre-history of Liars), initially rejected for containing too many corroborated references, falsehoods and "flat-out" lies. Later, after one peer reviewer called her a brash plagairist, it was accepted on its originality after a vigorous oral defense with help from her landlord's counsel (Myron Dice) that the review board members' personal curriculum vitaes were full of inconsistencies and "flat-out lies." She certainly knew how to defend herself in the lucrative and arcane world of academic fabrication. She eventually left Columbia after admitting at a faculty cocktail party that her dissertation was in fact full of half-truths, and the entire program she headed, as occupier of the $10 million Arlene B. Vrostek Chair, was a shameful hoax and waste of the shipbuilder's widow's trust.

sat next to me, gloating like an older brother who sneaked his underage sibling into a bar or strip joint. I asked him how my friend Vinnie got here.

"Don't worry, Will," he chuckled. "He's still got his kneecaps."

"What?"

"All right. I felt sorry for your friend. He stood there outside the TWA terminal with his suitcase and backpack. I thought he wasn't sure what to do, so I sort of got him off the knife edge." He turned to look at me and said do you know how painful indecision can be?

"Thanks, Uncle. I'm glad you did it."

"You bet," he said with a wink.

"By the way, Uncle, where's Dr. Francesca. Isn't she coming?" I asked.

"The bitch is indisposed," upped Paola.

"Now, now," said Uncle. "Violetta is off to Carmel for a few days of rest and recreation."

"On her fat ass," retorted Paola. She was livid and her locks almost reached the melting point for gold.

"All right. Enough, Dr. Pissed-Off. Drink up," warned Uncle.

"*Garrughhmoummapp,*" I think that's what she said. I got tired as hell trying to figure out what she said every time she verbally regressed. After a while I gave up and waited her out until she came back through the centuries to rejoin us. Who knows? Maybe she was more repressed than regressed.

After Uncle Rob shepherded the group to yet another cramped booth by the bar, we all exchanged friendly glances and I wondered if we were kids shanghaied into riding the rollercoasters at Cedar Point.

"Benny the barkeep, my friend; another tall pitcher for each of these fine young swabbies," uncle shouted. "And swabbette."

"How about a Lowenbrau for a change?" said Bud.

"You know better, Bud. Sit down," grinned Uncle.

Paola surprised at the distinction made by Uncle, perked up and said "*Gurrgaapshhrah*" and for clarity added, Aha, such munificence from such a malevolent. Uncle Rob and the rest of us tipped our skulls in appreciation of her thoughtful syllabication under the duress of intoxication.

A meteorite of emotion flashed by me, suggesting I knew these people all my life, when I didn't know an iota about them. It was the same chunk of headspace junk passing by me a few times at Mundane during late-night parties where the alcohol and smoke made a lot of stuff incandescent. What was this motley crew up to, as I hung onto Paola's key word "malevolent?"

They must know. Les Vice grimaced at the expression like he had painful trapped gas.

After raising our fourth or fifth glassesfulls, Uncle cleared his throat to declare the ship's party underway. I sipped my beer and eavesdropped in on his folksy ramble about how great to lead such a fine lot of shipmates for "one final omission."

"Captain, you're playing with words again."

"No, Bud. I mean what I say and, as you all know by now, I mean to do what I say."

"Which is nothing, then. You mean to say mission, Captain," said Les.

"Shut up, Les. You should know plenty about omissions. If I wore Abe's black stovepipe hat, I couldn't be more blunt." Uncle glanced down at the table, seeming to regret what he said; but it was out and I got the notion he was the large drop of water and his so-called friends were mere ripples in a rain barrel at the bottom of a downspout.

Uncle and I repaired to the bar for a breather, and it's then, staring back at our booth, the little guy who tagged along partially came out of the shadows. I was so lubricated, I missed him completely. I asked Uncle who's the shrimp. The wrong moniker.

"Listen, son," Uncle got up sort of close and put his hand on my wrist. "I don't want you to ever call him anything like shrimp, shorty, sawed-off, runt or anything else. Got it?"

"Well, yeah. Sorry."

"And don't ever call him Lou-Lou. He may be short of stature, but his intellect and sensitivity stands tall and way above any of us. It's why he's here. Got it? Good. Enough said and case closed."[20]

---

[20] Previously, Louis B(artholdy) Louis, all four feet nine inches with two-inch risers, enjoyed a short, happy interlude walking hots at Thistledown while completing his doctorate in organic chemistry at Pitt. The trainer, Joe Shanks, gave him a one-week tryout as an apprentice jockey. On his fifth mount, he got a ton of mud on his goggles and fell in the middle of the pack down the backstretch. Lou called it quits after the vet taped up his ribs, but he was never bitter and his love of horses only grew deeper when he returned to walking hots and talking to the tall, grand creatures which lost bucketsful of dimes for Shanks and his boss, Doublenut Farms' Geneva Stillman, whose teenaged daughter developed a crush on young Lou and coaxed mother to honor her and Lou's brief affair by naming a colt "Liznlou." Lou eventually came in the money, as Liz (his final mount) showed three months after the oral defense of his dissertation.

I could tell Uncle was teed off at my insensitivity, and it sort of sobered me up as we wandered back to the group. It unsettled me for a moment, and I wanted to make eye contact with Vinnie. I tilted my head toward the door so we could huddle to predict the outcome of this Sunday scrum, which might inflict much more than intramural skinned knees and jarred molars. Uncle Rob was chummy, effervescent, with an intellect like a buzz saw, but with another swig from the bottle I carried, I mellowed and remembered I was merely along for the ride to prolong my adolescence and evade the authorities who wanted my young ass in a uniform. Uncle Rob must have known this and may have been conflicted about abetting my

---

Liznlou got married in Elkton and kept one fire escape ahead of Harland Stillman's stableboys, who carried around an instrument for gelding horses. Outside Chicago, Liz lost the premature baby at St. Agnes and succumbed to daddy's offer of $5000 to annul the marriage. She still harbored the hots for Lou, who put her on a bus back to Euclid and bolted with the purse for a fresh start. He then led a checkered path forging Mondrians near Willow Grove before jumping to Scholastic Comics in Brooklyn for a two-year stint writing a well-received series of juvenile delinquency short stories. Three years after pushing a bit too hard, he free-lanced a graphic health pamphlet (*Constipation: The Hard Facts*) for which he received a thirty-day court-appointed "flushing out" at the state writer's rehab program in Scatsville, New York. Lou finally achieved some emotional and occupational stability as a research chemist with Pharma-Santoli. Unnoticed for years by upper management at the company's sprawling plant near Fayetteville, he eventually rose far higher than his two-inch risers with a sharp intellect and numerous pharmaceutical patents for the treatment of cerebral palsy. He soon became Director of Research after throwing an entertaining desktop toe-tapping tantrum in response to the performance review question: So show us what you've done for us lately? Five years later, he was fired when his nemesis, "Filthy" Phil Dorsey, the towering Director of Human Relations, confirmed with grave intonation that Lou up-scoped one too many skirts. Namely, Annabelle Santoli's thighs, which quivered in his bifocals at corporate bored meetings like high tide in the Strait of Messina. Walt Droolich, a fellow chemist told me by phone interview that Lou vigorously defended his perspective, saying what the hell do you expect? Don't look down at me, Dorsey you sonofabitch; look at me. Where else can I look? Santoli settled the discrimination suit, after which Lou won an international nautical knot-tying competition in New Orleans (according to Luca Bronzini), where he met Robert Melville, recruiting for moveable ballast.

escape, but to his credit he never once complained to me or told me to get lost. I felt committed to his guidance and benevolence, and this is what I told Vinnie at the front door.

"I believe we all know each other by now, but for the benefit of our two new shipmates, let's go around the horn and reintroduce ourselves, kind of bring us up to snuff, huh?" Uncle got a lot of verbiage from his tall bottle.

Miss Paleo-Tosti pushed her glasses up her aquiline nose and lifted those beautiful pink 38D melons with a clean-and-jerk, giving me a stealthy erection in spite of the weight of inebriation.

"*Ugh-la-mahwah*. Hello, if you aren't familiar with my work in paleophonics," as she brushed her golden locks over her shoulders.

"We are. *Lugu mala*," shouted Les. "Go, girl."

"Les, sit down," entered Uncle Rob. "You flunked vocational woodshop twice, so don't be a jerk. "You want to get her ruffled so she won't speak English, so be nice for once."

Paola bobbled her breasts with a defiant glare at Les and said she took a sabbatical to run Uncle's Agnes Detwiler Amber Bay Retreat Village near Beaufort. "There, I've especially made significant, publishable progress communicating with those residents presenting dementia or who have lost their hearing. Captain, we're picking up the Shapiro's on the way. Right?"

Uncle Rob inclined his brow in agreement and leaned over to tell me the Shapiros were loaded. "Irving wants me to take them out to see a beautiful sunset at sea and the Milky Way at night."

"Pardon me, Captain," interjected Les. "Where else are we headed with the Tern?"

"Yeah, what's the itinerary for this penultimate voyage," added Bud.

"We'll get to it. And it's the last voyage as you well know," said Uncle, glancing at the unrolled map. He pretended to roll up his sleeves, belched and added, "Look, beat it, kids, you bother me."

For once, Uncle got a choral rise out of the lot. I should have recorded it, since it was to be the rarest sonority of dissonant opinion from the crew during the whole journey.

A small squeaky voice came from under the table. "Oh, brother, here come the cliches."

The most diminutive one, in a loud plaid jacket, stood up in his seat, reached over and stretched out a hand for me to shake. "Hi, there. Name's Louis B. Louis."

Vinnie looked at Lou through the thick bottom lens of his sixth beer said no shit, Holmes.

Lou glared back at Vinnie. "Yeah, punk; and when we become better acquainted you can call me Lou but don't ever call me lou-b-lou, because, you see, it was a most unhappy childhood." Lou gave Vin the best imitation of a scary leprechaun kisser I never saw in the movies.

Uncle told Lou to calm down, which he did after rising above castrati to me and Vinnie, "Remember, my eyes might be looking up at you two, but my mind is looking down at you."

"Okay. Okay," I said with a pandering chuckle.

Things quieted down for a few seconds. Paola started humming "I've Got Rhythm."

Les, on his one-more beer, raised a curious Cobra-like expansion of his jowls and said to her face "Oh, I thought you were a Buddhist."

She glared at him and shot back *mucklowhakluhgoa*, which she kindly translated as don't make me say what I think you want me to say you.

"Hey-hey-hey!" shouted Uncle Rob with raised arms. "Let's all calm down now. If you want to mutiny, you only get full credit at-sea," which fell on swimmer's ears. He paused to catch his breath. "As long as we're talking on a philosophical level, has anyone here come to realize that there's only two true paths in this life, and I don't mean Route 66 and the Interstate."

"Captain, please spare us. Where's the map?" repeated Les.

"Listen up. I'm in charge here," boomed Uncle, suddenly standing up on all fours.

Paola, by far the most judicious sipper of the quorum, turned around from the distraction of empty tables across the floor and raised, "So, Captain; you really think you're in charge, huh?"

"What?" Captain stumbled, which he often did when she addressed him, as if there was some hidden link between them that no one knew about—or cared a whit to know about.

She said, go on and see how long you can stand on one foot.

Uncle lifted a leg off the floor, extended both arms for balance and lasted about five seconds before crashing down into the chair.

"Ha! Now you know who's really in charge here," she said.

Lou cracked an approving smile. "Of course, it's big mama! I knew you'd get around to it, professora."

Les struggled to stand up at an angle, leaning hard on Lou. He pointed a downturned thumb at Uncle. "All right then, big shot; as long as you're up there, show us the stigmata," holding his hands up in supplication.

Lou raised up his voice again into the fray. "You nailed him real good there, Mr. Vice."

"Judas Priest! you nonbelievers," shouted back Uncle in frustration. I didn't know what he drank besides beer, but he turned as red as a Roma tomato. "I have the floor now."

"Bravo! Captain," entered Bud, wiser for sitting out most of this in his chair leaning precariously against the wall. "Guide us with thy eternal light."

Les said it would be a lot easier if Captain loudmouth sat down, seeing as how he was full of it. Uncle laughed until he almost choked. Things then settled down for refuelling.

"As you all know from theory or practice, you can reduce all human endeavors to either procreation or masturbation."

"Objection! Objection!" yelled Bud. "You're drunk as hell."

"Everything falls into one or the other, right?" labored Uncle.

I think he tried to sober us up. The air reeked of sulfurous rebuttal. As a secret practitioner quite familiar with the abusive joy from such sleight of either hand—or both, I got a bit flustered.

Les put his glass down. "Have you no decency, captain? Can't you see there's adults present?"

"*Gurreahh*," uttered Paola.

"What about the Mona Lisa?"

"A hand job," said Uncle, brushing off her question and switching to a Coke.

"The Empire State Building? The Eiffel Tower!"

"Flamboyant erections."

"The Declaration of Independence? Got you there," upped Les.

"Strokes of genius all around," retorted Uncle.

Bud, under full sail with his eighth beer, peered up from a stained menu. His eyes drilled two holes of sustained repugnance at Uncle Rob across the table. "Captain, with all due respect, you should have been commissioned to the deep long ago."

Uncle stared back at Bud. "I *was* in the silent service for twenty years, mate. May I continue to elaborate?"

"Chess!" interrupted Lou like a referee breaking up a prizefight clinch.

"Queen takes bishop in hand," said Uncle. "You heard me. Everything from gazpacho to pistachios; art; music; the atom bomb. Everything except making babies." He sat back and wiped his forehead with the Coke bottle and a Cheshire cat grin I thought sinister and malicious in a teasing, strange yet impotent way.

"You know, Captain," upped Lou, "all we're doing here is masticating words. Look, ma! No hands and no damned sense," as he threw up his arms. "You're out of your gourd. Nuts! You know what? You're some kind of a philistine. I don't know why the hell I agreed to go on this last one." He pounded his little fists on the table and shouted, "Van Gogh was childless and look what he left us!" Lou was livid.

Paola leaned forward with a calming hand on Lou's forearm. "What about Faure's Sixth Nocturne? Need I remind you it was her favorite."

The rest of us were dumbfounded. Who was this guy Foray anyhow? Uncle clearly winced at Paola and fell silent. He gazed down at his glass, furrowed his brow and probably felt the tease had petered out. None of them brought up his childless state. As drunk as they were, they still managed to keep the salty decorum convivial.

After nine rounds of beer, I was not surprised at the centrifical mayhem. I stared at Vinnie, who appeared to show the stress of a regrettable decision in not flying to the quiet haven of a youth hostel and the warmth of a young woman's arms. Uncle Rob emitted an evanescent, eerie glint I wouldn't have caught if the candle were not at his end. If it had made a sound, it would have been as imparting as the winds moaning and screaming outside for recognition. Surely, Uncle stage-managed the show I assumed the others were used to and secretly enthused about. Except me and Vinnie: for us, fourth down and twenty on our two-yard line when Uncle said to me that Bud meant to say the last voyage, not the next-to-last. I noticed his profile and felt more concerned than ever.

"Everything okay over there?" shouted Ben the barkeep.

"You got it," hollered Bud. "We're all taking it in the ear over here."

Ben put down his cigarette on the edge of the bar, blew breath into a glass and yelled back, "Lost most of my vision in my right eye in puberty. Needed bifocals."

Paola's nares flared when Les told her all those toes she sucked at Columbia were for naught.

"*Gorgaluxflokyuk.*"

"Don't get me wrong, honey. I'm only talking theory, too."

I followed Uncle with my third Coke. Uncle Rob wiped his brow again with the sweat of his bottle and asked if everybody's still having fun. From my seat, you could have heard a cricket in Death Valley

"Where's the map, Captain?" pleaded Les.

Uncle moaned, "Oh, the inanity, the inanity!" He must have read Joseph Conrad and I wanted to keep laughing my ass off, but I couldn't, because I never drank this much and was now zonked out the same way I flunked out. I tapped Uncle on the shoulder and said I need to take another wizz. He said, son don't tarry ashore too long or these mates will mistake me for Mr. Christian. Later, when I felt my way over to shoot some pool, Vinnie asked me if Uncle Rob was play-acting or really like this. I said hell if I know. Break! He's done a lot for me and Mom over the years, but I only know him through hearsay and now here we are in 3-D. Five-ball in the side pocket. Where's the chalk? Damn! Vinnie you can't go back home. Big mistake. Three in the corner. I'm thinking I'm thinking. Six-ball in this one. Man, I can't shoot for beans tonight. Do you hear the damn wind outside. It's driving me crazy like we're in the belly of a bloated whale. Two-ball side pocket. Damn! Slouched over and leaning on a thin cue stick, I saw them at it again around our table. I said this is worse than falling asleep in the library, and I would sure love to take Bonnie to the Lux downtown for a late movie right now, but I couldn't go home for a long time. Maybe I couldn't get it up for a long time, too.

I turned back to Vinnie, who ran the table with a hustler's click-click-click-click-click-click-click-click and, having lost, felt fortunate I wasn't reracking my balls in Saigon or other strange name popping up in the headlines every day. We never studied those places at Mundane. Never. Mostly vectors and the space under a curve and stuff. They only existed in the headlines and demonstrations on Garroway Avenue in front of the chancellor's office. I felt happy for Vinnie, who finally seemed to be settling down to a change of heart about sticking together. Whether Vinnie thought it me or the pure loneliness of his transmogrification into a cur-like traitor I couldn't tell, but I know it would be a lot easier to survive under the buddy system. We may not have been spit-shine jarheads, but we knew instinctively we could always look out for each other on the other battlefield—public opinion.

The howling wind outside began to get our attention for real now. Ben shouted, Batten down the hatches folks. Hold your horses. It's around one twenty and the worst is yet to come.

"Already? You got a college degree?" said Vinnie.

Ben stared steak knives at Vinnie. "I don't need no stinking degree. I can hear the voices and whining through the walls." He stared beyond us, rubbed his fingers along a thin white scar running up his left cheek. "She's a hateful one, this one, and would like nothing better than to blow down the joint and us with it.

"What's she whining about," I said.

"Everything me and my ex worked for; I hope to hell those spics nailed the plywood down real tight. She wants to tear the hell out of me." Ben glanced around at the blank TV set dangling on one bolt off a ceiling beam at the end of the bar.

He described Helen's high winds with such lurid conviction, I believed I could still hear the heavy breathing of my horny friend Mark and the nympho Mona Moore in the conjoined cabin at Houghton Lake. I thought they were killing each other, and they were only doing about five-hundredths mph.

"Will, don't get carried away," said Vinnie. "We're all in this together." I got hold of his arm and we weaved a path across the dance floor, presaging the rolling deck of the Tern I had not yet even boarded. He came around the pool table and we rejoined the mob. Everyone except our group jumped ship when Ben tilted his head and announced the eye's on top of us.

"Fools," yelled Ben. "They've got no business going out there. Drunken fools. They'll get swept clean away before they can get across the parking lot to the motel." He dropped his head, braced his forearms against the rounded edge of the bar, waiting for a massive, guilt-ridden angina attack.

There was a surge of curiosity verging on pure belief when I thought I heard voices carried on the winds, screaming and moaning through palm trees, street signs, powerlines, rooftops. I gazed beyond the boarded-up windows and imagined to what extent the naked fury could embarrass my notion of human progress; teasing us with the melodrama of flickering lights and speaking in tongues of pure rage no bluster of human profanity could challenge. I imagined Uncle Rob in this baleful, swamped lifeboat at the tiller in the middle of the North Atlantic. Paola, Les, Bud, Lou: all resigned to oblivion in their complete and inebriated contempt for any force interfering with their morose little jolly corner. I sat down next to Uncle Rob, who put a big bear arm around my shoulder.

"Uncle, is there something to eat around here," I said.

"Grill's shut down, son. Soda crackers."

I reacquired some semblance of sobriety, I think, with the Cokes. I still felt woozy wallowing in a crow's nest I could only imagine, which made it worse. I asked Uncle if the Tern would survive this storm. He again put a congenial arm around my shoulder and said of course she will. Then he boasted only he—like his father, Captain Billy—could bring her to port. "Not any fickle hurricane."

"Right, everyone? Am I right, Professor Paola?"

She pushed her drink away toward the center of the table and lowered her head quietly in the only gesture of resignation I ever saw her make. Her sleeveless arms revealed the timeless grace of neglected statuary.

"And you, Bud. What say? Am I right or am I damned right?" raised Uncle in a dramatic tone grabbing my apprehension.

Bud finished off his glass and nudged it to the middle of the table like a chess piece, where it clinked Paola's glass in a strange toast of added resignation. "I'm all in, Captain. You've always pulled me out and I have no reason to scuttle our last voyage if we can survive this storm."

"Very good, Mr. Shill," announced Uncle.

I was tipsy before, but the sobering chill up my spine made me think we enlisted in an adventure well beyond our sophomoronic efforts to escape something more sinister than the hurricane lowing disaster all around us. But like the delicate dapple of April sunlight through a rustling maple tree, I felt better, as Uncle put on his cherubic grin—dimples and all. He was, after all, a person of unusual success.

"And Les Vice, my First Mate and accountant extraordinaire all these years?"

Les, upbeat with his earlier machine-gun delivery of several jokes, met Uncle's eyes for an instant, then lowered them with an open speechless jaw, as he pushed his empty glass to the center, clinking the others. I thought, what a sad, morbid way to give a toast or cast a vote.

"Come on, Les," upped Uncle. "Cheer up! This is the ship's party minus the bunting and kazoos. There's more to come. You're not holding out on me, are you?"

Les said yeah I know all about it. He wiped his hands on the tablecloth and flipped them over like a casino dealer to show he didn't palm crisp twenties or his conscience.

When Lou didn't respond to what I gathered was a friendly inquisition of faith from a bunch of shanghaied crew members, Uncle went over and pulled him up into his chair and gently buffeted his face like a mother powdering a baby's bottom.

"Uncle," I said. "I think he's inabsentia."

Uncle Rob said son, don't you worry a bit; your uncle knows what he's doing. Anyway, we really need Lou for intellectual ballast, Right? Right, everyone?

"Yeah, he's a heavy drinker," said Bud. "We know the rest. Hook, line and sinker."

"Courage, Bud," retorted Uncle.

By now, Vinnie was a cleaved hoagie, spread out on the floor next to the table. I checked to see if he was sideways in case he chucked up.[21] Uncle straightened up Lou's tie and collar and pushed his glass aside to join the others. What a strange way to get acquiescence: foot the tab; get them drunk as skunks, then vote. Was this some kind of politician's backroom ritual? A silent congregation of empty beer glasses from constituents who may have signed on or away their fates long ago to Uncle by debt, extortion, bribery. Maybe to get away from a fate worse than mine? Who the hell knew, but it made me uncomfortable. How did he really get his wealth otherwise? His public munificence was well-known and as prominent as an iceberg. It was the seven-eighths below the surface I began to question. And how close could I or anyone get to him, to the truth, before having one's sides ripped apart? All I knew then was his great charity to me and Mom over the years. I figured then he would continue to see me through, to mentor me in the bleak days when I hid from my own country and the meatgrinder of a bloody jaunt in the jungle of Southeast Asia. After all, he must have called me his "son" for something, if not unalloyed devotion to my future. When Uncle sat back down, I noticed how he nonchalantly gathered my glass and Vinnie's and clinked them into the others. I'm not

---

[21]   Will watched out for Vinnie. Mundane University records of disciplinary action (obtained under the Student Freedom of Information Act) described an altercation at the university bar and grill in which William Melville and Vincent Pugliese III stumbled into a fracas between members of the Crossbones biker club and a small party embracing the end of heterosexuality as they knew it. Both were beaten up and left on the blood-stained floor when the melee was scattered by campus police. Mr. Pugliese was unconscious and convulsing on his back when, as reported by the waitress, Kimberly Scosh, Mr. Melville leaned over his friend, sweeping his mouth for pizza and pounding his back until the expected ejecta flew onto her apron.

sure I was prepared to participate in this game, since I regarded myself as a pawn. I was dog-tired and felt right then and there it would have been easier to take the Bremerhavn or a tramp steamer across the Atlantic to one of those youth hostels Vinnie mentioned earlier.

We were now over four hours into the eastern or right side of Helen. I still wondered how on earth everyone managed to get to the former Bill's Place at all. You didn't lean into one hundred mile per hour winds as you would pushing through Hudson's heavy revolving doors. It's crazy to think we could have ever stayed in the eye the rest of the way. I mused about the difference between benevolent and malevolent. I guess if you used the right prefix, everything would somehow be all right.

There was no more ice behind the bar. Ben's bald head shone like a bowling ball at the end of the scarred run of mahogany.

"Any more sandwiches, Ben. I could eat a horse," said Lou, who rejoined the living without moving an inch the whole time.

Uncle Rob pulled out a large pen from his pocket and began to annotate the tablecloth with various circles and dotted lines. "All right, listen up," he announced. "This is where..."

Suddenly a terrible ruckus at the front door lifted above the nerve-racking din of the storm, and we each seemed to say I didn't do it, don't come after me. I nearly crapped in my pants when the front door blasted open and in trotted the most beautiful horse outside of a 4H calendar. All he lacked was a strut-proud trainer in a frumpy Panama hat leading him to the winner's circle. We stumbled out of our cups as if it were the ghost of Centurion.[22] He poked his head in the door and calmly clopped into the center of the dance floor, hooves clattering like castanets to show something was there before us beyond a figment of the imagination.

Ben was first to rush over to the door and push it shut with his back and shoulder. The floor flooded with the draft of water the wind pushed in. Scraps of paper littered the wet floor like a sea of pastel pari-mutuel

---

[22]   Editor's note: Probable phonetic stumbling to recall Citation, winner of the Triple Crown in 1949. Track records at Hialeah and Gulfstream reveal that Centurion or Centaur (attribution needs verification) raced as a gelding mostly on one end of the daily double and returned an average $170 per pari-mutuel wager. This horse also known to have raced at Bowie Race Course, most notably for returning $612.34 as a 99-1 longshot in a disputed photofinish with Mr. Fixit during the Winter meeting of 1964.

tickets under the grandstand at Aqueduct. This was not a nag, but a long, lithe muscular thoroughbred.

"Okay boy. Nice boy," murmured Ben trying to grab the loose reins. I could swear Ben secretly genuflected when he knelt to grab them.

Each of us gathered around the dance floor with the anticipation of kids at a petting zoo to touch the sleek, neighing chestnut apparition. Paola reached out first, whispering "Pegasus" for I guess some classical atmosphere. Ben now kept a firm hold of the reins and coaxed us all off like we were flies buzzing a stall of muck and hay.

"Get back, please. Give him some room."

Uncle Rob waded in right up to the horse, ran his hand along the sloping back and said something mysterious and inaudible, muffled by the moaning winds pushing through the doorframe.

"Ben, is this one of your Thursday night door prizes?" said Bud.

Ben said shush! stroking the horse's neck.

Lou came up to lay his head against the shivering flank, which encouraged me and Les to bear witness. I thought right there, under the flickering wagonwheel candelabra, if the hurricane wiped us all off the face of the planet in the next instant, we would have at least this final occasion to illuminate our souls's wanderings in a make-shift winner's circle.

"Where the hell did he come from?" said Les.

Uncle, who I gathered by now to be a frequent stickler for profanity, rested a cheek on the sleek skin. He raised his index finger to his lips and said, No Les, you want to say where in heaven did he come from.

As we all touched, petted, carressed and otherwise placed our bets on the horse, he stopped shivering and stomping in place. He was becalmed now, as was Helen's eye earlier.

Ben said he must have broken out of the Christopher T. Augerry Stables tucked in between a set of ranchettes half a mile behind Ed's Place on the boulevard. "It's a miracle how he ever got this far."

Paola crooned *coorookukumuy* (probably something like my baby my love) and I glanced at Les for a cynical retort, but he shook his head no. During this seance, I could swear on a stack of Gideons we forgot about the outside world or it forgot us, because the incessant wind whining and cries of waffling metal roofing died to an exhausted hoarse whisper.

"I think I know this horse," said Ben, holding a pail of water. "He's got a white patch on his forefoot like my favorite loser, Old Sea Dog." He rubbed him on the forehead, shaking his head. "I lost two paychecks and a '53 Fairlane convertible on this nag. I almost felt like shooting him for right there in the paddock area going AWOL on me."

"How dare you say such a thing. *Augruhgahaseeroffooo*," growled Paola, joined in by intelligent-sounding grunts from the rest.

Uncle Rob turned to Ben with an aggressive twist of his love handles that popped out the Hawaiian shirt from his belt line. "Barkeep, you're out of order and outvoted here, besides. Don't be a jerk. Or a tout, either."

I thought Uncle was about to haul off, so I grabbed his bronzed arm. He glanced over his shoulder at me and said in a flat inflection, son, you don't want to be doing that—ever.

"Sure, Uncle Rob. I didn't want anyone to get hurt."

"No one's going to get hurt on my watch. This is a ship's party with a lucky guest. If anybody's going to get hurt, it won't be here. Maybe later." He clenched his stubbled jaw at me and I imagined how he would have reacted to his own kids, except I knew he was childless and it really must have hurt him inside with the frustration of coming out of the money in a different way.

"*Frulickkmukloo*," Paola directed toward Ben.

"Listen, babe, you got to speak at least Spanish or Italian in this place. Capiche!" angered Ben.

"Screw your language," she tossed back, and by now she pretty well sobered up.

I ventured to tell Ben you've got to listen up. When we were in the cradle, none of us knew how to say boo.

Ben threw a reluctant jerk of the shoulder at me and said who the hell are you, wise guy?

Paola moved beside me and toned it down. She started this slight chopping motion with her hands like holding them to wind yarn. "I understand your frustration. Will is saying if a baby listens to a word say a hundred times, it gets it. If it's an adult, you won't be able to make any sense of it. Get it?"

"Okay already. I get it. You don't have to lecture me. I'm only a bartender who likes to mix things up."

Paola must have been impressed with my amateurish linguistic comment, for she never said anything so direct on my behalf the rest of the journey.

I could barely hear Les, glaring at her, say "smartass" in her direction under his breath. I think he was frustrated keeping up with her mind; he also may have had trouble getting it up for her because of her brains.

I watched her ringlets wiggle as she went on, and I was taken with how verbose she could actually be on occasion. Her attractiveness increased every time I noticed her. It was in the details. What flashed across my mind was a bright store window display back in Monroe in the dead of Winter; snow up to my knees as my eyes darted from Santa Claus to the dazzling gold foil angels to the convoluted mess of model railroad tracks hidden by a maze of paper-mache trees, waiting for the dark cavernosum of the tunnel to ejaculate the locomotive and its little white puffs past my dripping nose.

Ben finished holding the water can and wiped the horse's face with the towel he used for cleaning beer glasses. I could see he was irked at Uncle. He stepped back and faced him. "Well, why don't you get this show on the road, Rob. You've spent enough time here in drydock. If people read an account or paperback about you sitting here, high-and-mighty, jawboning on with your so-called friends about a bunch of trash, they'd probably be bored stiff and throw the stupid book in a corner and turn on a soap opera.[23] I sure as hell would."[24]

---

[23] Objection! Ben the barkeep was no literary taste-tester to speak of, and therefore had no right to evaluate the merits of Uncle Rob's, Will's or anyone's relating, in some—if not drawn-out—detail the scene at his bar. A friend of Bud's (Clark Snavely), whom I tracked down selling sponges in Silver Springs, said Ben's reading ranged from the pseudo-statistical hieroglyphic nonsense of the *Daily Racing Form* to Remington rifle ads in the back of *Argosy*. Not bad for a fifth-grade reading level. Occasionally, he ran his finger along Dane Grey's *Purple Passion Riders*, although Snavely told me he saw the same book behind and under the same end of the bar for years. Snavely, who carried an arc welder's certificate and worked as a steamfitter for 23 years in Gulfport, once brought Ben some of his wife's dog-earred romances to broaden him and vividly recalled Ben saying I don't read Barbara Cartland stuff, Clark. In any case, Will Melville's reminiscence of this interplay introduces the ages-old dilemma from time immemorial for editors and other interlopers of how much textual vacuity is acceptable to ensure the reader is not bored to death with incidents and dialogue that have nothing more to show than the writer's or editor's—or mutual conspiracy of the two—inability to concede he/she has nothing of literary value to impart. This editor has endeavored to eliminate, as much as possible, Will's recollections that are of small consequence and shed little light on his aspirations to relate an instructive tale of hope and despair, then finally hope again. In the end, boredom can be a terrible thing, especially if one has to pay for and confront it in the last sanctuary of intellectual comfort—the printed page.

[24] First, as your editor, let me explain something while you struggle to scratch that rectal itch at the head of the post office line, or lust after a neighbor's black BMW 7 Series with his blonde wife checking her tangerine lipstick in the rearview mirror. I have never been a devotee, advocate or otherwise diagnosed with AI (Authorial Intrusion), not to be confused with WB (Writer's Block). Obviously, I cannot be accused of AI, as I am an editor and not an author. To me, it is the lowest form of writing, akin to the drunken rambling of the fireside scop who started this whole storytelling shebang eons ago at the mouth of a cave. Secondly, I have never indulged deceiving any reader with cheeky flair or egoistic tics in the editing of another's literary effort. Having said that, I have chosen for the first time in my long career in the book biz to boldly edit where no editor, ghostwriter or plagairist has gone before, rummaging through several hundred pages of plain old scribbling. At least, you will not have to occasionally throw down this book in disgust at the AI you come across wondering if the writer/editor isn't making a

Uncle pulled a tablecloth from a booth and tossed it over Old Sea Dog's back. He straightened it out at the corners, smoothing out the wrinkles with the tenderness of a parent putting a child to bed. Ben slouched behind the bar now, peering over his finger-smudged bifocals; quiet and nodding approval at what he saw as Uncle's conceding the point with this blanket act of contrition.

"Anyway, I owe this place to the horse," Ben said. "I lost so much on him, I got mad at myself and swore off betting when the old lady left me for good."

"So you came out a winner after all," entered Bud, who missed a kick to the groin from the horse.

After about an hour of Paola and Lou adoring this animal to death, we ambled back to our chairs to better enjoy the suspension of boredom with which he bestowed on us; this ship's party was full ahead and turning into a sobering experience.

Just as fast as Old Sea Dog gave each of us a breath of inspiration, things turned horrible. Lou noticed it first while running his small hands under the horse's chest. I sensed he ran out of the money again.

"Funny thing," Lou muttered. He turned around and held up his hands dripping in blood. "He's got a bloody rod sticking out of his heart." Lou said this slowly like a child learning to read. We sat there stunned. "He's dying," he said and I saw tears welling up in his eyes, spilling down and jumping off his little round cheeks into space. "Oh no, oh no," he started to bawl.

---

horse's ass of you for trapping you into buying the thing in the first place when a bit of chocolate or cup of coffee would have been more rewarding. As the pages of young Will Melville's random and somewhat thoughtless recollections unfold or fall out, depending on the binding, I urge you read with patience aforethought when you realize from the start the valiant efforts of me and my researchers to present this story with the highest consideration for truth, justice and the American mode of expression. Some of you may even recognize the literary echoes of one Paul Sharkey (remember *God and Superwoman?*), a pseudonym I employed successfully for several months at Brown and Shue. To emphasize my serious intent here, I chose to reveal my true identity in hopes you will be more receptive to the risk we editors take, from a two-week notice or rainsoaked unemployment check to the illiterate perfumed note of a fussy dowager. In the end, you have the choice to seek further enlightenment by tossing this tome, hopefully, into the recycle bin or donating it to the Salvation Army.

I stared at the horse and saw him beginning to sway from his hind quarters to the front in a convulsive wave.

Ben raced around the bar, bent down and touched the object. "It's a damn piece of rebar." He touched it again.

Lou swirled around to shout don't touch him. Don't. He's he's dying for God's sake. Can't you see?

His legs began to buckle and I could hear his labored breathing through those proud flaring nostrils down the home stretch. We were all gathered around him now, desperately trying to hold him up for no other reason than to help him cross the finish line. We knew we were at the former Bill's Place, but beyond that we were drunk, adrift and helpless.

Old Sea Dog's blood now started to drip in a hot stream onto the parquet floor. Bud slipped in it, but scrambled back up quick to retake his spot. Paola held him at the neck, stroking up and down the long stretch of equine beauty, saying please, please don't die. She turned to Ben, back at the bar on the phone. "Call a vet!" she shouted. I saw Ben slam it down. "The line's dead. Damned hurricane will do it every time. Les wiped his eyes and stepped back first. Old Sea Dog sank down on his forelegs, but Paola, Bud and Lou clung to him.[25] I swore they would have all gone down with him if he were a ship like the Tern. I stood beside Uncle Rob, who stood with hands limp at his sides. Old Sea Dog was bigger than life, and his mourners seemed smaller by the minute.

---

[25] The *Coastal Florida Shopper-News* once carried a small human interest story with Old Sea Dog's last trainer, Jimmy O'Donnell. It was tucked as filler between cottage rentals and weekend garage sales and showed Jimmy on his metal crutches next to the horse. He said he was the only horse he trained who never came in the money, but he never bolted, stopped or threw any number of whip-crazed jockeys down the stretch. He was beauty in motion and possessed the graceful, powerful stride of a champion racing to his own song. Jimmy's cluttered studio apartment near the beach displayed one 10x18-inch still photo of Old Sea Dog in full stride. At times, he was quoted as saying he would have preferred a series of Super 8 frames of that stride crossing the finish line—a winner. I tried to console Jimmy at one point by saying that grace and coming in the money were apparently mutually exclusive in the case of Old Sea Dog. He turned his wheelchair in my direction and said I'm not sure what you mean. He then put his hand on his Hawaiian shirt where his heart was and said the horse always came in the money where it counts.

"Let him go, let him go down," said Uncle with the firm insistence of someone who seemed to know about this stuff of when to let go.

"*Nagoobagruk*," sobbed Paola.

I told Uncle Rob I think she said Not on your life, but he said he already knew what she meant.

"Come on, boy. Lie down you're going to be okay," Lou whispered into his perked ear.

Then he gave out a soft whinny, lifted his neck high and proud one last time and rolled over in his blood and shot his stiff legs out for a dash between horses to the finish line. Paula, Lou and then Les and Bud lay down next to him, annointed in Old Sea Dog's blood, holier than a saint's. Ben knelt down beside the dead horse and crossed himself three times, and I think he said something like he'll be in the money every time now. Except for Paola's whimpering and the dying winds outside, the place became as quiet as Trappist prayers. I sat next to Uncle Rob, who bit his lower lip and twirled around an empty glass. He pulled me close with his arm on my shoulder. "Son," he whispered with a painful grimace, "I've seen sailors go down with their ships, but this is the first time I've ever seen anyone go down with a horse." Then he threw a clumsy two-fingered salute in their direction and stared in silence. Vinnie, whom I left for dead in a corner with a color guard of empty beer bottles, jolted me with a tap on the shoulder. He said slackjawed what happened, and I said you missed it. Later.

The ship's party wasn't planned to end this way, but it died away, too. Uncle and I helped the others out the door into the aftermath of Helen. Uncle pulled Lou away and suffered a kick to the shin for it. Lou said you have no right to do this, and Uncle said I know I don't, but there has to be a beginning to everything. Bud, closer to Lou than anyone else, limped along favoring the leg with the least beer in it and rebuked Uncle at the door. He said, pity you, Rob. The big man with the big bucks and the simple answers. Uncle waived him off. I tugged Paola away. She didn't want to go and gave me some of her caveman lip. When she got to her feet, she pushed me on the chest as hard as she could, then cried in my arms. Uncle Rob was the last one out the door. He told Ben, thanks. Put it on my bill and add whatever you want for Old Sea Dog.

The crew straggled ahead across the boulevard. Eventhough there lingered doubt about Uncle's moral compass, I nonetheless walked ahead of him. At what was left of the next intersection, a defunct swinging traffic light stuck on green for both directions. The ragged crowd stepped into the street like wildebeest crossing a croc-infested confluence of life and death. I turned around to see Uncle out of view; so I stepped off the sidewalk, distracted by the pink ballet shoes dangling from a young girl's neck across the street. I saw the spectre of a silent emergency van in my peripheral vision, figuring it would at least slow down for a human body. From nowhere, Uncle clotheslined me and pulled me back as the sideview mirror of the van scrubbed the hair on my forearm.

"Damn close, Will." He was shaking.

How lucky to be alive instead of the next mess shoved into one of those flying coffins. "Jeeze, Uncle. Thanks. You saved my life. You really did," I gasped at how the random misstep of a hair's breadth could toss you into the voracious jaws of fate. Not the road, but the hair's breadth not taken. If Uncle wasn't standing by, like he did for me and Mom all those years he stuffed our mailbox, I wouldn't have been standing there like a dumb ass. Of course, if Uncle never supported us all those years, I wouldn't have been standing there at all.

But at such a time in my life, he became all the difference; the delta between my coming and going.

"It's nothing," he said, clicking his tongue. "Listen, next time always look both ways. Don't follow the crowd, got it?" His voice was still unsteady.

CHAPTER 5

The next morning broke bright and cleared up a lot of the night's vagrant dialogue at what used to be Bill's Place. The sky was blue and the air smelled like a clothesline full of clean sheets. The sunlight fell on my head like a sharp wedge pounded by Thor himself, and it split my head into a million little microtomes of jangling ganglia. Floaters on my eyeballs moved with the lethargy of a North Atlantic convoy, as if the sunlight knifing through the venetian blinds wasn't bad enough. Vinnie had the gall to open the door to the parking lot and flood the room with a disaster worse than the amateur hour of last night, with its closing act of symbolic death for all of us in that tight little bar.

"Oh, man," stretched Vinnie. "I don't know if I want to die now or get extra credit for suffering and die later.

A panorama of jagged trash and disruption greeted our first steps to get to Uncle Rob's motel down the street. A massive yard sale gone awry. At a distance, someone or something already shoved the junk into admirable piles, if one could call each pile a compact junkyard of perhaps thousands of personal effects, and maybe a surprise cadaver. There was a swarm of birds like black flies two short blocks away.

"What happened to the horse?" said Vin, looking through wire-rimmed sunglasses next to what used to be the former Bill's Place. Helen did a terrible remodeling job. It was no longer the former Bill's Place, McDuff's or anyone elses.

"No, Vinnie. I'm not going there again. I'm not going back there." I said Old Sea Dog is in the pile.

"Right, Will. Ever the morbid optomist."

"Cut the crap, Vin. Don't try to humor me."

When we reached Uncle Rob's motel, he leaned against the doorway in his Bermuda shorts, waving to two women waving back as they pulled away in their pink Chrysler Imperial. I didn't say anything and tried to ignore them.

"Son! And your friend, Vincent!"

"No, Vinnie. Vincent was my father's name."

I tried to apologize for last night for some naive, self-serving reason. Uncle cut me off like the indulgent flourish of a bored maitre d'.

"No, son. It was my party." He brushed his chin and said it was better than most shoving-off parties except for the uninvited equine guest. "The horse took the wind out of our sails for sure."

"How about the others?" I asked.

He smiled and said he put them all to bed and by now they already left for the Tern. I said we saw a big pile of junk in front of the former Bill's Place or McDuff's and wondered what happened to the horse. He said he called in a front loader to remove the carcass.

"Is Ben okay?" I asked.

"They can't find him yet. At least the crows are out there looking for him, as well. The crew is farther down looking for the Tern." Uncle said after they left around 0200, the roof caved in. Maybe they'll walk by some day and say, are you sure this was What's-his-names place?"

We hopped in the back of his fire engine red Pontiac convertible next to his El Dorado and he threw out a few more attempts to joke while weaving our way through carnage and people stooping to catch their breaths, bearings and baubles, because there was little left at eye level. We were in the scum of a giant bathtub ring. Everything reduced to kitsch as a final insult to their way of life; eventhough it might already have been store-bought kitsch on the mantel. Uncle may have been a great businessman and philanthropist, as I heard it, but he seemed ill at ease making light of a dire situation with his underappreciated black humor.

"By the way," as he racked us up like cue balls for attention. "What did Jesus say to the other two beside him up there?"

"No, no. Please, uncle," I begged.

His twinkling eyes reflected back to us in the rearview mirror an unnerving grin arching into the honed edge of a Syrian simitar.

"Are you two guys hanging around just to doublecross me?"

I told him Sister Leona at Holy Trinity would have thrown half the Britannica at him from her desk; rapped his knuckles raw; grabbed him in a wrestler's headlock (as was her habit) and suffered an apoplectic fit right under the little bronze crucifix above the classroom door. We knew. We were in her fourth grade class and saw it happen often enough for misspellings, talking, raising a hand for a toilet break and other high crimes and misdemeanors.

We got out two blocks from dockside, then slithered past piles of dishevelled dreams. The sheer destruction shredded everything not screwed down and most of what was. Uncle Rob rattled off the names of boat owners whose sea dachas became bobbing hovels much like a mess of bathtub toys coralled from the wild playful splashings of a two-year old.

"There she blows," he pointed to a pure white hull as big as a blue baleen. He shook his head in disbelief and we concurred.[26]

"Son, I find it amazing. Out of all these expensive toys, the Tern is still the way I left it."

I also found it a bit ominous I would be taking refuge on a boat that stood by magic alone in surviving the widespread destruction visited on everything else in sight. What would it take to destroy her? Was there some force or incantation sparing her for my future demise?

Les, Bud, Lou and Paola clustered around her bow, petting her as an old friend the same way they worshipped Old Sea Dog the previous night. I imagined Paola riding the waves as the Tern's proud figurehead like the one on the lawn at the Great Lakes Seafarer's Rest Home near Bay City.

"Everyone accounted for?" Uncle called out. "Very well," as he answered his own question, as usual.

---

[26] For a definitive description of the Tern, refer to *Fingal's Famous Yachts*, 2nd Edition, 1935, Rumor's Sons, Boston. On the knotty problem of the Tern's speed, I asked Carter Fingal III of Newport if it were possible that such an old yacht could attain twenty-five knots, a speed boasted by Captain Melville (see chapter 8). He said the Brewtal Boatworks made the finest screws of the day (1867-1871) and, with proper refitting to modern diesel engines, could easily attain such nautical speed. After rambling on how yachtsmen often asked him for the location of sunken ships with Brewtal screws as if they were intent on diving for black pearls, he told me offhandedly that the screw also became known as the "conversant screw," most famously for rumors of revolutions divined by foreign dignitaries on the royal yacht. After nine children and numerous assasination attempts, Queen Victoria finally tired of taking it and ordered the firm to replace the screw or be royally put out of business.

When the refitting team came by to knock out the supports to release her, Paola wanted to christen her with a bottle of Dom Perignon she got from Ben before he beat it with Helen. Uncle raised his hand to exclaim it wouldn't be appropos since the Tern clearly must have gone through the same business long ago.[27] Bad luck. "Though this is her last sailing, it would be, in my humble opinion, giving her the last rites to do such a thing," said Uncle.

Les scratched his head. Lou kicked the gravel. Bud blew his nose. Paola put her hands on hips. In unison, they demanded Uncle allow the ceremony. It was the last voyage anyway, so why not celebrate her demise to a scrapyard or tie-up as a dockside bed-and-breakfast or scuttling or whatever. It's the last time I recalled them concurring with such unanimity on anything.

"Go on! Get on with it!" Uncle retorted shaking his head in resignation.

On the shoulders of Les and Bud, Paola did the dirty deed. Uncle turned to Vin and me to say the minute we shove off, there will be no more of this landlubber liberty going on. "All play and no work makes for one hell of a mess," he said with the restrained jocularity of a fellow pallbearer under his breath during a ululation in the service. A seagull on a nearby bollard watched us in case we stopped moving for ten minutes and rotted into tiny morsels for lunch. Both of us bark-laughed out of near fear when Uncle untied a line and said the bottle would have been better smashed on someone's head. Who's head, I wondered. When Uncle moved off to inspect the hull, Vin turned to me.

"Will, is your uncle all right up here?"

---

[27] **PS**: Under Captain Billy, the Tern was christened twice; once by his daughter, Sarah, and later by Alicia Consuelo Mabeke, a young mulatto barrister for the Governor of Barbados who bore the Captain two sons. They died in a 1910 hurricane. She later became governor of the island for a brief period in 1930, but was dismissed when a darker political rival uncloaked a long trail of illegalities, including Captain Billy's bootlegging to Florida and eventual escape from jail with her assistance. She was also a practitioner of voodoo; however, there is no scientific evidence she was involved or in any way responsible for Captain Billy's long-suffering gout. Penny Scriveen, my research associate at Redford Bates Law Firm outside LaJolla, performed invaluable research into some of Captain Billy's elusive reminiscences held at the Bay St. Louis public library bookmobile. Her footnotes, labelled "PS" throw an interesting gothic candela on Will Melville's story as to how his famous grandfather would have opined.

"Sure. Sure. He probably needs some orange juice to get his glucose up. Anyway, we're in too deep." I winced at all the garbage surrounding us. "This is the best option we've got now to lay low. Better than six feet under on Memorial Day beneath a little flag poked in the ground by someone who has no idea who we were."

"Are you sure?" Vinnie wiped his hand across his face as clueless as when he went in with a play for Coach Krusher, who yelled obscenities at him in the fourth quarter with our mortal foe, St. Gabriel, leading by fifty points.

Later in the morning, the blocks were sledged away and the Tern slid down into the still water without a ripple. There was something hard to describe and majestic about her. It overwhelmed me. Maybe like watching Maryann Shaheen slide her sumptuous body between votive vanilla candles into a bathtub like an olive in a martini when I took her to Toledo for the weekend. Or was it her twin sister, Jasmine?

"Request permission to come aboard, sir."

"Permission granted. Gladly, son. Welcome aboard," cheered Uncle.

We saluted and he gave me a big bear hug I could never get from my father. I missed growing up without a father, and I knew Uncle wore the other shoe in missing a son.

The others stood around the quarterdeck and clapped with restraint to break the stress of embarrassment at such closeness they may have missed in childhood.

I hadn't been on the water since ice-fishing near Petosky. It was exhilarating to feel the levitation and uncertain sense of freedom underfoot, and I didn't feel like a fugitive running down a rutted red clay county road with black snakes darting at my sneakers and the sheriff's bulky Buick Roadmaster blocking the road ahead.

"All hands on deck," shouted Uncle two hours later from the stern. The crew sniffed its way through the cabins below and main deck, cluttered with coils of manila line and various cans and packages of nourishment for us and the Tern. In the stateroom, I found an old green bottle glued to the bird's-eye maple mantel with a yellowed label ("Melville's Magic Bilge Water") which I intended to ask Uncle about.[28] While noticing this relic,

---

[28] PS: Captain Billy's irregular diet forced him to keep handy a bottle of his potent tonic water, a quick-acting blend of rum, epsom salt and filtered bilge water (shaken only) for various ailments from hangovers to hemorrhoids. He was given the original recipe by a fellow prisoner from Wilhelmshaven who got

I overheard Les mention several names I jotted down in haste who were on the penultimate voyage last August. They were gone and wouldn't be back.[29] Vin and I stared across at each other, startled at the screech of the gangway retracting to the dock as the Tern was released.

Near midnight, they took on extra ballast. The persistent pounding on the deck above sounded like bodies dumped around. When I groped my way to the main deck, Uncle stood with his legs apart, hands on hips; Les carried a clipboard and wore a green eyeshade he doffed up until the end.

"Let's say this is a weakness I have," confessed Uncle to me. "When I take the Tern out for a cruise, I use the bags for ballast and then distribute them to needy individuals that Mr. Vice has identified from various newspaper clippings of natural disasters and reports from the World Disease Organization (WDO). Welcome to my personal initiative of plunder and redistribution." Uncle held up his hands as if he were robbed and said, It's in the left pocket and then laughed. When the delivery truck left, there were about one hundred bags at our feet.

"How much is in each bag?" I asked.

"Two thousand dollars plus assorted hand tools and medicine."

I scratched my head and asked why did he feel the need to do the charity thing.

"Son," and he put an arm around my shoulder, "I've got so much I'll never spend it in three lifetimes. Besides, it's sort of balancing the scales for some things weighing heavily on my conscience that I'm not too proud of. Call them dispensations."

"What things?"

---

stuck on Barbados for five years waiting for a trial date. When the Tern pulled into Savannah for repairs in 1897, Captain Billy was so sold on his own patent concoction, he peddled door-to-door the sixty flasks he had mixed onboard. After running in their pants and bloomers, his former customers then ran him out of town.

[29] From Will's notes, it appeared Les knew less of what happened, and refused to comment other than to say they were a bunch of no-good sea scum who got Melville in a lot of trouble in Savannah. So, in 1971 I enlisted the specious talents of Medium Madame Mechante for thirty-seven dollars to find out the last crew's fate. After suffering a severe stone bruise under my right toe upon stepping out of her dim parlor and into the embarrassing light of day; I soon suspicioned that, with her emerald satin eyepatch, she could tell me only half-truths. Thus, I later opted out of her six-week half-off fortune telling.

"Well," and his eyes wandered off toward the twinkling lightbulbs across the harbor and then lifted up to the stars with their diamond lustre. "Let's not get into that. It's not important."

I didn't want to get into any ethics stuff (I dropped out of Philosophy 101 after a week); and I had no business prodding, but I was dead tired and tossed this one out to him for the hell of it: You mean that if your child is starving, do you steal a loaf of bread?

"Sure; you steal the loaf. You steal it for any hungry child."

He frowned at me for an instant, yet I didn't feel that it carried any sense of vanity from either self-righteousness or guilt; just a sense of huddling around the fifty-yard line where you know you've got a job to do, deciding whether to run off-tackle or throw the ball down the middle.

"Come on, give us a hand here," he cheered.

Uncle and I spent the next hour or so dragging the sacks, or sacos de oro as he called them, over and into into an open hatch. We sat on some coiled line and shared a bottle of mineral water for our labors. He seemed pleased. Small wrinkles around his eyes belied the anticipation of someone younger than me.

"What do you think?" he said.

In my fatigue, I ventured on to ask how he accumulated so much success. I thought it was a great story. He chuckled and said it was a hell of a lot of hard work. Plain hard work and a lot of fortuitous timing; bumping into the right—and occasionally wrong—people along the way. I dared not leaven the discussion by saying that the relative term,"hard work," could also describe a morbidly obese person trying to reach around to wipe his rear in Kankakee; or a mother taking care of five youngsters in Big Springs; or a truck driver trying to stay awake passing Akron at three in the morning; or someone in heavy debt pondering the Calvert Street Bridge; or a junkie waiting in a Bakersfield alley for a fix; or someone robbing a bank in Dubuque; or a sleepy nurse hanging an IV bag of glucose instead of Ringer's in Seattle; or a fallen paraplegic yelling for help above Ravel's Bolero in his studio apartment in Queens; or an accountant using an eraser to artfully shift money between ledger columns on the 25th floor in Atlanta; or a kid trying to hit a knuckleball. I had no reason to belittle his success, and so I said "Gosh, I hope some day I can be as successful."

"Well, Will, I'll do what I can to help you along the way now, but of course the decision always rests with the individual. Know what I mean?" The wink of an eye—or a wince—let me know he was acutely aware that my hesitation to avoid military service was an item he would tolerate only by allowing me some breathing space to make the right decision.

He turned to me and said, you know sometimes I wish I'd had a son, and his resolute voice trailed off until it went into solution with water lapping the Tern's hull.

"Well, anyway," he picked up, "We're shoving off bright and early. Get some rest."

When I retired to my cabin, I lay there a few minutes in my rack and thought about the sense of loss he failed to delineate and the casual chat about his accumulated wealth, and which one of them weighed most heavily on his conscience.

CHAPTER 6

Sometime around the dead of night, there was a real ruckus topside. I jumped into my pants and shoes to check it out. Lou shouted down at an old woman ranting on the dock. She dangled a chicken by the legs and waved it around as she shouted what I guess were Creole profanities.

"What's going on, Lou?"

He pushed me away from the edge. "Stay away. I'll handle this. She's crazy. "Get the the hell out of here. Va-ton! You old vache."

Rubbing my eyes, I saw an old lady in a shabby yet colorful dress, maybe Haitian, with a spangled turban. She gesticulated like a possessed puppet. The glint of a machete caught my eye when she sliced off the cock's head.

"Oh crap," mumbled Lou.

"What?"

"She tried this before, but we survived."

"What are you talking about?"

"This old hag is trying to put another curse on the Tern. Says her grand aunt willed her to do this many years ago."

"Why? What have we done to her?"

"Last time she said something about your grandfather, Captain Billy, rewarded or getting his just desserts or some such garbage. Look out!"

From out of the past, if I were to believe this voodoo stuff, she heaved the headless cock up onto the deck. When it landed, blood splattered all about.

"I'll call the harbor police," yelled Lou.

"I already did," intoned Uncle from the shadows, where he stood in the half moonlight in his skivvies like a fateful apparition with powers unknown to voodoo and capable of overcoming any incantations from the old lady below.[30] "Poor woman needs some food and medical attention."

The old woman was picked up babbling, put in a squad car and taken away. I asked Uncle what's this all about. He shook his head like an indulgent wizard looming in the shadows. "She's not after us. She's after your grandfather who she claims dispossessed her mother a long time ago. It's amazing how memory persists beyond the grave."

"I mean, are we going to be all right?"

"You bet. It's another burden to bear. I'll take care of it. You get some rest, all right mate?" replied Uncle.

I turned to go when a hand grabbed my shoulder. "And take a shower to get the chicken blood off your legs, right mate?" ordered Lou.

Hesitating in the hatchway, I spied Uncle stooped over the plastic bag with the cock's body, mumbling something, maybe in French, then lifting the bag up and swinging it like an incense urn at high mass before tossing

---

[30]   Florida state mental health records held in Tallahassee show that a Gloriana M. Gilbert, 75, was committed to the Everglades Hospice for the Insane shortly after the incident described by Will Melville. She was ironically the daughter of Madame Mechante, originally of Port-au-Prince, whom I previously interviewed for half-truths. (Madame Mechante was the delightful 98-year old character I met who gathered poop on nearly everyone I asked about, although she said she never heard of Gloriana Gilbert. Very touchy, indeed.) She claimed to have been Captain Billy's daughter; however, according to his log, Captain Billy was visiting his family in Corpus Christi roughly during the month of her conception (August). Most likely, she was the daughter of a crew member (Alphonse Peday), yet she persisted that Captain Billy was at least morally reprehensible for giving Peday the opportunity to rape her mother. Lesser schooled in the island art of voodoo, she was still seen as a theoretical threat by Melville to the welfare of the Tern, much as you would compare the venom of a spitting cobra to that of a cone snail. This is, of course, no time to levitate my comments with humor. I personally tracked down the granddaughter of Mr. Peday in Ris-Orangis outside Paris while shopping for fresh clams and researching guillotine makers for a book on the French penal code. She denied any knowledge of Gilbert or Mme Mechante. She also said that on a voyage out of Bridgetown, she was told that her grandfather reached into a barrel for a nectarine and was stung by a scorpion. He survived after two days of extreme pain in the wrist above his steel hook. Unfortunately, he was found a year later expired on the sands of St. Kitt's with the shell of a cone snail four feet from his outstretched left hand.

it onto the dock. And I thought either Uncle has his act together or, as Vin might counter, he may have a screw loose.

In the morning, Paola knocked on my door. "*Tskcharooreeyum.*"

I asked her to slow down, but she said get up. I began to like her leggy gait, which she told me later she adapted from observing the hind quarters of oryx in the Okovanga. I didn't have the heart to ask her if she meant a lorax. When she peered and smiled over her extra large Claudio Fabiana sunglasses at me across the breakfast table on the foc'scle, with her breasts like a double sunrise spilling over her bikini, I got hard. It also became damned hard for me to prioritize my flight from the draft board above the need to release my seed, even if I only bedded her in the quarters of my cranium. Still, if she spread them as well as the transparent Filipino servants prepared the captain's table, I would have gladly dived in head first with no particular preference for performing a reverse half pike or cannonbawl.

Uncle Rob sat at the end of the table, talking into a portable phone the size of a shoebox. It was cordless, with an antenna as long as a buggy whip. Bud elbowed me and said will wonders cease in a disgusting grunt when Uncle tossed it on the cushioned bench surrounding the quarterdeck.

"Where did he get the Graham Bell?" I said.

"He owns the company. They make them in a double-wide in a trailer park down the road from Palo Alto. He's such a tight ass he won't get us one. The rich ones are the real penny-pinchers."

I glanced around at all these new acquaintances wolfing down food and beverages and felt determined to learn more about them on this escape from the burden of social dues back home.[31]

---

[31] Will's notes show limited exchange with the crew at this time, except Uncle and his partner-in-escape, Vinnie. Much more can be gleaned by taped conversation. Apparently, Uncle installed Ampex tape-recording equipment throughout the Tern for business purposes. When I checked the overhead storage bin at Mrs. Melville's two-door garage in Monroe, I stumbled across a box of about twenty-three magnetic recording tapes. Through these recordings, I filled in much detail that Will was not privy to. Of course, it seems pretty evident his complicity in certain events would indicate a presumption of cognizance. It is unclear how or when Will acquired these tapes, but I suspect he pilfered them over the last torturous weeks of his detour on the Tern and mailed them home when they docked for some legitimate or other excuse. Maybe he did it to exonerate himself or plea bargain with his conscience or the Third Circuit Court of Appeals. My

research assistant, Stella Finnegan, and I excerpted some of these to better understand the nature of the turmoil behind the last days of the Tern under Captain Melville:

April 15, 1967: 3pm; Bud Shill and Paola Paleo-Tosti:

Bud: Tell me Paola, still friends after that last ((abortion)) of mercy in Port-au-Prince commissioned by Melville?

Paola: I wasn't involved in that dirty business you know all I did was steer the damn boat so we stayed away from the Coast Guard and sand bars. That's all.

Bud: (background noise) But you signed on to it.

Paola: tired of this (?charade?) doing it since fifty-three. Tired. Tired. This is it.

Bud: Never knew why you kept in. (chair scrapes)

Paola: He was kind to me. Paid off my tuition bill. Set mother up in a rest home. Yeah. I'm grateful (garble) now paying for it in spades.

Bud: (garbled) hate him? I don't.

Paola: Guess not. Like the rest of us, he lost his way.

Bud: Include me. ?Remember? our (garbled)

Paola: ((??*rruhagnoxtsh*??)) Where's the bottle?

Bud: Speak English, lady.

Paola: regarded me as a child at first or ?piece? of candy. I'm not a sugar ?delivery device?

Bud: You still are sweet I mean that.

Paola: (sniffling) stop it. Let's go topside.

April 17, 1967: 10pm; Lou (lower voice) and Les Vice:

Lou: Be glad this is the last one (garbled) feel like whale (?excrement?).

Les: Guess I earned my name. You must admit we did helluva lot of good. I know. I fixed the (?books? ?crooks?).

Lou: I despise him for (?belittling?) me in front of those dames on that cruise. Remember that one?

Les: That was real small of him the (?bastard?)

(garbled exchange)

UNK: Captain needs you chop chop. (Door slams)

Melville: What are you two doing now?

Lou: Hey, Captain. Taking a break. (Door slams) Okay. Yes he did do that for me. Also wanted to give me five (?inches?) with that no-good Swiss (garbled) surgeon in (?Schlangenbad?) (??Langbein??) ((???arschloch???)). Worthless trip.

Les: What was that?

Lou: You weren't here then. Let me tell you something else (tape spool out)

May 3, 1967: 3am; Melville and Les Vice:

Melville: Some day. How's your mother doing?

Les: Guess so (garbled) need to go to Houston for treatment.

Melville: Has it spread? (Sound of cards snapping on table)

Les: Well, yeah. I uh (garbled)

Melville: Look. Take her. I'll get Julio to spell you.

Les: Twenty one. (cards slapped on table)

Melville: Damn. Call if you need me. Did you do your (?juggling?) thing with the (?Baranquilla?) account?

Les: Done, as ordered. That's what you always say.

Melville: How many?

Les: I'll hold.

Melville: What's with you and Paola? She's (?delicate?). Damn, again.

Les: She slapped me. Said I'm old enough to be her father.

Melville: (Laughs out loud; almost chokes) What's wrong with that?

UNK: (Door opens) Keep it down!

April 19, 1967: 8pm; probably in galley or stateroom; sound of dinnerware

Melville: We'll anchor at night. Les, you take over till I get back from the (?shareholders?) meeting in Atlanta [**Ed. Note: Probably reference to Bright Horizons adult care centers outside Atlanta and Jacksonville constructed 1955-57 and specializing in end-of-life hospice care for over 2500 patients annually. Florida and Georgia state medical records were unavailable. Several conversations with Clark Ashencoffer, former director of all hospice admissions, stated off the record both facilities provided state-inspected revolving door services. When asked to further describe "revolving door," he put his hand on the microphone and said they came in and we aggressively and compassionately cared for them to a fault. Nobody suffered.**]

Les: Are we really picking up this guy (garbled).

Lou: This is crazy, Captain. Do you know what you're getting us into? (garbled) too far.

Melville: All worked out. Big payday. No one will ever suspect. He's worth more dead than alive. We'll all be dead some day, so what the hell does it matter?

Bud: Crazy. I agree. Too hot. He was on top of all the charts.

Paola: (??*Nugruchnitgru*??)

Lou: Speak English, willya!

Paola: This is going too far, damn it. We don't need to do this.

Melville: (Silence. Indistinct voices) I'm in charge now. We've been through a lot together the last ten years.

Les: Right. I can't tell you how many times I've (?thrown up?).

Melville: Sit down, Les. I've made you all wealthy beyond your wildest dreams. What the hell are you complaining about?

Paola: (garbled) I have disrupted my career for what you refer to as your excursions in charity.

Melville: All right. Enough. No more discussion, okay?

Lou: Yeah, those poor old helpless bastards don't have a vote.

Melville: What is this? A mutiny of malcontents?

Bud: (slowly) Hell no. We've all taken the wrong path and you damn well know that, Melville (chairs scrape). You are the one leading the mutiny against (?decent?) society.

Melville:(bellows) Sit down, Shill. You don't know what decency is, slimeball (?Sorry sorry?). Bud didn't mean it that way. (Silence) Okay, then let's go around the table one last time.

Lou: The last one, right? Okay, I'm in.

Les: Melville, you saved my ass—all our asses—okay, but no more.

Bud: (slapping sound on table) a filthy cockroach. I got it. Where did that come from?

Melville: Looks like you got the jump on him. What say?

Bud: I don't like it this business of premeditated (garbled). I can't even say it.

Lou: Why don't you reassign me to the ((???youth in Asia???)) account in Shanghai?

Bud: All right all right I'm in, and I don't want any one of you saying an Ave for me. Ever.

(chuckling from one or more)

Paola: Look at these hands (?the stigmata?). I deserve to be excommunicated.

Melville: (clearing throat) JesusMaryJoseph! Such melodrama. That would definitely be a first, Paola. Okay, all in. As I promised once before, this is it and Godspeed to us all.

Les: You don't have to rub it in, Melville. The Almighty has nothing to do with this or anything we've done on this boat. We can forget about the campgrounds across the river Jordan.

May 4, 1967: 1 am; Lou and Melville: (unusual exchange, since Lou still fomented over Melville's rejection of the Shanghai reassignment. Both sound like they've swilled quite a few drinks)

Lou: You know, Captain.

Melville: No, Lou. I don't know.

Lou: You know before I straightened out academically with the Ph.D stuff at Pitt, I

Melville: Spit it out, Lou.

Lou: I spent six months between racing meets out at Burbank doing commercials. The deep voice, you know.

Melville: Lou, you bother me twisting that bottle.

Lou: I was in a coffee shop on La Cienega swapping jokes with some California cousins. I laughed so hard I almost wet my pants. Really. So, this guy comes up and says would you like to laugh for a living and I said I guess so, so he gives me the address to a TV studio.

Melville: "Where's the ice bucket, Lou?

Lou: So the next week I was in a room with some other jokers and some guy held up a card that said in 48-point Cro-magnon bold: laugh now. I got the job and was told to go down the hall to the voice coach.

Melville: (distressed) Got to take a piss. Be right back. (Door squeaks)

Lou: who is this dignified old gal. She tells me to hold my breath this way, which I did. (Toilet flushes sounds like Niagara going through a milk bottle) Nice lady used to sing in the chorus at the Civic Opera. I'm somewhere in Burbank laughing my ass off Monday through Thursday all day for four dollars an hour. Not bad.

Melville: What?

Lou: Then you might say the bottom fell out of my diaphragm.

Melville: What? Did you see (?Deanna Durbin?)

Lou: No. Who? (Sound of glass falling off table) Where's the glasses, Captain?

Melville: So why did you have to crap in your pants?

Lou: In a span of six weeks, my mother was hit head-on by a trolleycar in downtown Cleveland and died the next day. I couldn't get home in time, because I was laughing so hard to make ends meet. It was a miserable time.

Melville: Lou, are you at the helm tomorrow?

Lou: Didn't know I was. Then my sister fell into a hole ice skating on a pond and the dog, Emma, didn't know what to do. I should have been there to save her.

Melville: No kidding. You know, reminds me of the time we were tied up in Valencia.

Lou: And here I was still laughing like hell to pay for a lousy apartment in Anaheim with three jugglers and a coffin for mother.

Melville: We were granted some leave time, and so I caught a bus up to Barcelona. You know they've got a beautiful opera house there.

Lou: (sobbing) So they gave me another contract and I said I can't go on laughing and they said why and I said I was laughing on the outside but, well, you know the rest. Not funny.

Melville: So to my surprise and delight it's *Tosca*.

Lou: So I couldn't laugh off the death of my mother and sister. No even a truculent chuckle, because sometimes me and Sis didn't always see eye to eye. So I quit my movie career and took a bus back home. After

Melville: with (?Magda?)

Lou: I got home and took stock of

Melville: Where's the Chivas bottle, Lou?

Lou: myself. I said the only good thing I really got out of

Melville: Two fingers, Lou-Lou. [Melville didn't call him Lou-Lou for nothing. A young exchange student he met vending carnations in Santa Barbara once told him it meant "booger" in French.] Whoa! Stop (?Magda?)

Lou: this laughing gig was a pair of risers. A stagehand told me about some actors like Raft and Jimmy and Edward G. All actors high-up in the movies, you know.

Melville: Olivero. **[PUBLISHER'S NOTE: Rubinstein's assistant, Ms. Finnegan erred in transcribing this conversation. The great Italian verismo soprano, Magda Olivero, sang all over the place, but not in Barcelona until several years later. Probably referring to the equally famous Monserrat Caballe, who did not have an overbite observable from the orchestra. Before this company's falling out (i.e., contractual) with Mr. Rubinstein on the 12th floor at St. Luke's, he said he believed Melville could not possibly have made such a crass mistake, noting Ms. Caballe would have "filled the stage with her presence and the house with her voice." Even after four double whiskeys and dimmed stage lights. Somewhat difficult to hear him while he was intubated, he said he himself always wanted to be an opera composer, or at least stage manager at the city opera. We asked if he was confused with operetta, at which he brusquely raised his right arm—IV and all—and pointed at us with a finger daVinci would have been honored to draw, and wagged it sideways to mean absolutely not. He motioned us over closer to his hospital bed. One of us, an ex-Navy corpsman, chanced to turn down his oxygen two millibars to better hear him relate that when he graduated from** college, he confessed this ambition to the interviewer at a job fair in Schnectady. We turned the oxygen back up when he appeared to be fading out on us right before the nurse snooped in to check on him. She clamped down on a cigarette and a thermometer in her mouth and we asked her to leave because of the oxygen. "Scott" lifted his eyes in the direction of the oxygen tube with the little dancing indicator ball and blinked yes to turn it back down two millibars. He said the interviewer suggested he join him at GE to write generator tech manuals. Rubinstein then shifted in bed and passed a lot of gas at that point as he squirmed to express himself. One of us left the room. We chanced to move closer on his hand signal again and he said he told the interviewer to screw himself. Even in the ICU, we could see how he really thought a lot about what he called his craft before he lapsed back into a coma. We patted his shoulder and said when he gets out, we would rehire him to write an unauthorized biography of Franz Lehar. An admirable fellow, this Rubinstein, even if he didn't graduate from Amherst—our alma mater. We at Brown and Shue were prepared to extend his contract right then and there. He died the next day.]

Lou: I don't know. Sorry. So you might say it was no damn laughing matter my mother and sister died, but I did get a boost up in the world so to speak, especially when trainer Joe Shanks let me handle some of his mounts at Thistledown.

Melville: Magda Olivero. What a doll. It was love at first sight. I tried to

Lou: So I'm unofficially five feet one. Sitting on a horse eighteen hands high, no one can look down on me the same way they used to.

Melville: and they were so impressed that a seamly sober sailor was in the audience hacking opera, they escorted me backstage.

Lou: What the hell are you talking about, Captain? I don't know anything about this *Oscar*.

Melville: I was actually horny as hell, even after three or four double whiskeys.

Lou: Did you lift the seat, Captain? I have to sit down.

Melville: God, was she a knockout. I thought her voice was

Lou: What?

Melville: She sang like an angel. I've got to say she sang with the most beautiful overbite on a woman I ever saw. She took my hand backstage. I was flabbergasted. She was so relaxed and down-to-earth. I knew some Italian, but she was better with English. She was really something else.

CHAPTER 7

The next morning the little grinding sound from underneath awakened me thankfully out of a nightmare about a babysitter and two small children leaving all the doors and windows open talking to a strange man and woman in black robes by the front window. I found Vinnie with a croissant and cup of coffee on deck.

"Why didn't you leave me a towel? I said.

"Sorry, Will. Rough night."

By now, we imagined how our neighbors would regard our mothers when they found out we ducked out to avoid the military. Especially Mrs. Costello. On one of the rare times Vin and I walked past her house, she displayed both of her uniformed sons' silver-framed photos flanked by red geraniums in her front window. I wondered if she still bumped into Mom at the grocery store.

"Did you hear the confounded noise last night?" I said. "Sounded like an A/C window unit on a hot July night mumbling away. I could swear I heard the crowd at a night game."

"Yeah. No. Your uncle said it's the screw; you know, the propeller. It's right under your rack. Too bad."

"I'll have to ask him about it."

Lou: I'm back, Captain. Keep talking. I'm turning in if I can find my way out of this joint (chairs scratching).

Melville: They practically carried me back out I was so drunk with excitement. What an honor. You know, I really got a hard-on for her, but when she touched my hand, my lust turned to pure adoration. Do you understand about those things, Lou? Lou? I think about her almost every day. Lou, where did you put the ice bucket? Lou-Lou?

"Go ahead," said Vin. "It doesn't bother me. I slept like a baby."

The Tern was a long, sleek boat—ship. I walked slowly around the gunwale. It took about twenty minutes, with stops to greet the others peering out at the beachhead filling with striped umbrellas blooming like a luxuriant bed of mixed annuals in Spring loam. I left all the glamor behind: the girls; beer on Saturday at Murph's Irish House; Mom's two-tone DeSoto convertible; engineering graphics and differential equations and all that other craptrap I'd never use.

Uncle Rob, dressed in a blinding white polo shirt and Bermuda shorts, waved me over near where the foremast used to be. "Look who's driving the ship!"

I could see Lou's balding head bobbing around like the bubble on a carpenter's level. "He can't see where he's going."

"The Tern can steer herself with the new-fangled electronic gear I got. Anyway, he has an Florida orange crate up there if he needs it." Uncle rested his bronzed arms on the railing. The soft breeze moved the golden hairs on his forearms like currents swaying sea kelp four fathoms down. The jutting jawline reminded me of my father's picture on the mantel: set but not hard; determined but shifting a bit from the burdens or blunders of lost opportunities and those waiting ahead running a conglomerate doing business all over the place. Mom told me of his naval exploits a few times. He later told me (with a finger jabbed in my chest) he was not in the Navy, but rather a submariner and he got quite defensive about it.

"Son, Will; welcome to the real world. The school of hard knocks and rough seas."

Thanks, Uncle."

"No. Don't thank me yet." He squinted at the beach receding on the horizon. "I want you to know there's some things you might object to on this journey; the last one for this beautiful ship Captain Billy handed down to me and your dad."

"Sure."

"I'm sorry he's not here, but we can't do anything about it, can we?" He shifted his weight and turned to yell something to Les and Bud huddled over an aluminum suitcase someone brought onboard last night. "You might say he got the jump on us."

"Sure."

Uncle reiterated there were some things—business deals—he needed to handle on this trip, with a few port calls along the way, and he wanted some sort of man-to-man word of honor I would do as instructed, no matter what.

"You've got it, Captain. Whatever you say."

"After this all blows over, you can make your own judgments, okay?"

"I understand. I've been chatting with some of the others and they've been real helpful."

He placed a hand on my forearm and said don't pay any attention to those scoundrels. They were old friends, but to pay them no mind. "They're all misfits with whom I've crossed paths. They might hate my guts, dragging them through my stuff, but they've also been well-rewarded and, well, they understand we're all going to hell anyway in the end." Uncle added with a sarcastic smirk, "The Nigerian crew he hired in the early Fifties was lazy and did little more than lollygag and lean heavily on the bones of their enslaved ancestors who suffered in the dark chain-rattling bowels of the Tern when under the amoral hand (Uncle's phrase) of Captain Billy. Yep. There's still nothing better than a bunch of over-achieving American misfits to get the job done."

I lost him there for a while, recalling in rapid sequence where the current crew survived on land: Paola said she owned a pad on the West Side; Les lived in a beautiful hacienda with his fourth wife in Scottsdale; Bud was content with his Ducati on I-76 outside Monroeville with lifetime Steeler seats; and Lou bragged about a Learjet hangared in Monterey and two live-in maids down the road in Pacific Grove. Maybe tinkling champagne glasses, but for sure no chain-rattling slave digs for them.

"Are you with me, son?"

"Sure, Uncle Rob."

"These people do my roughing-in and plumbing work. They get their hands soiled. Asses and elbows stuff. Maybe I shouldn't be telling you all this."

"No. It's all right. I get it."

"Look, do you want me to drop you off in Jacksonville? I'll put you and your friend Vincent on a plane to Stockholm where you can hang out until this mess blows over in Nam."

I dropped the ball for a moment when he said he'd give me two minutes by his shiny Breitling chronometer to decide. He pulled on the black bill of his fake captain's hat and lowered his head with what I thought was no small amount of exhaustion in squaring up the situation for me. He said yes, Vincent already got the spiel—not personalized—and was in, as if he were one of this gang for years. What did I know about morals or ethics or the Constitution or Lincoln or flag-waving sacrificing stuff? I was twenty-three, somewhat well-educated, lower than average in ignorance and I think I loved my country and naturally took a lot for granted; but there were details I had trouble facing. "I think I get what you're saying, Uncle Rob. I'm in with the rest and damn the torpedoes," I said and pumped a fist into the air.

"Good, son. I was hoping you would sign on." He cuffed an arm around my neck and we almost fell over each other. He gave a gap-toothed smile, laughed and quick as clouds clot the sun, he said I don't need to hear "Damn the torpedoes" again, son. Got it? It's only in the movies.

"Got it."

"All right, then," as we got to our feet. "Let's take a break and listen to some Monserrat Caballe." [32]

"You mean the one who married Frank Sinatra?"

Uncle's jaw dropped in a maw of disbelief, saying what on earth did they teach you in college anyway, boy?

We laughed it off and I reminded myself to ask him about the damn screwy noise under my rack. I would either change my sleeping quarters or go nuts with noises that literally spoke in tongues.

For two uneventful days, the Tern rolled along the gentle Gulfstream with little sensation of time and space; a lullaby for a lost young man,

---

[32] Confused about Melville's ambivalence here, I was most fortunate to find out the identity of his second wife from a conversation with Will's Mom, who was a veritable Trevi of trivia. Conchita del Valle de Las Cabezas sur Serrano de La Playa de La Luz y Estacion a Las Dos Conchas ("Connie") was still alive and living comfortably in Baltimore with her third husband and his five children. She and Melville met in Estepona while she toured Gibraltar and he repaired a tire in the next parking space on the dock. She said his Spanish was pretty good (and his profile even better) enough to get her name and telephone number. One of those carte postale romances. For richer or poorer, there were no children to stitch together their marriage and they split when he transferred to a Groton desk job. Probably a Doppler-type reaction to the lonely months of sea duty Connie could not endure forever. She said she was not bitter at all after five years and even gave him some of her long-playing records of Monserrat Caballe, whom her mother knew in Barcelona. She also claimed credit for starting his interest in grand opera, although my research shows he was already acquainted with the art form at least six months before they met when he fawned over diva Olivero's overbite.

waiting for a fair wind, casually swinging a sunburnt leg over the cradle of the gunwale. Lying on the deck at night, I wondered if I could have opened my eyes in my mother's womb, could I have seen the same infinite beauty of the stars in the Milky Way. On both nights, I drifted off until Lou, and then Les, tapped my sole with their shoe.

"Will, best be getting some sleep below decks."

"But, it's so peaceful up here among the stars," I yawned.

On each night, as if reciting the same dialogue of a play, they said as they turned back at me before going into the Tern's belly, "Things change fast around here. None of us, including guests, can afford to keep our heads up our asses for long."

"What?"

They bobbled their heads nearly in the same manner and echoed in stereo, "consequences, consequences." Uncle Rob must have really whipped these guys into shape over the years for them to respond with the same chorus, eventhough I knew offstage they bitched about him and their lot when out of earshot.

Although I complained about the background noise in my quarters, no one, especially Uncle Rob, took me seriously. "It's your imagination. We've all slept in there before at one time or another," tossing a hand in the air in irritation. On one of those nights around 0100 before I swung among the stars on deck, I couldn't sleep from the indistinct monologue of the Tern's screw.

It started with an atonal motive infecting my imagination:
lislislistentententenuptenuptenuplistenuplistenuplistenuplistenup.

After my mind tuned in, I could pick up the frequency or call-sign: "listen up." Stumbling through the luminous moonlight of my quarters and the passageway, I felt my way to the stateroom. I paused from a chill of spine and saw the eyes of a silvery photograph on the bulkhead I must have passed dozens of times and never noticed. A shaft of moonlight settled on it and I went over to face it.

"Why, Captain Billy, I didn't know you were here," I whispered in surprise. "Were you calling me?"

I wiped the dust from the glass and peered into his eyes and they stared back like I performed a huge favor for him. He sat in stiff formality in a dark uniform with brass buttons lined up like sutures from his crotch to his chin. The bill of his hat sat square above a face of gray chinwhiskers and sideburns. He tucked his right hand between two buttons like Napoleon in

73

so much histrionic kitsch. His left hand must have been behind his back.[33] I was tired, which explains how I nearly felt like striking up a conversation with him. His eyes twinkled or winced—maybe both—and beneath the fuzz I could detect a grimace or sardonic smile—maybe both, again. Anyway, he seemed strangely animated, like he hanged there neglected for years with no one to hear his sea stories or scuttlebut. Uncle Rob must have known something of this.[34] I knew for sure he would have wanted to chat about his life. His eyes followed me around the large mahogany table. No matter where I stood, he espied me with the hopeful anticipation I was more than the moonstruck projection of his post-mortem desires. I saluted goodbye, climbed the ladder and later found out much more than I wanted to know when I discovered one of his sea logs sequestered in the back of a drawer beneath his photograph.[35]

---

[33] PS: There was no left hand on Captain Billy after September, 1912. The photo must have been taken after the incident recorded by a Dr. Geraldo Ortega in Key Largo on July 12, 1912. Captain and a small party struggled to save a young woman and child who fell overboard on their way from Havana. Captain Billy, although a most religious and concerned individual for human life, tended to overfill the Tern with Cubans, Jamaicans and other mixed folk seeking a better life in America. Perhaps, he figured for what little he was paid, some loss of life was inevitable and acceptable as long as most of them made it across. A wheat-and-chaff sort of thing. The child was lost and the mother was pulled naked onto the deck, but Captain Billy's left hand was a bloddy stump when a shark broke the surface and bit it off like a ginger snap and almost pulling him in for the main course.

[34] PS: After tracking down the first 153 pages of Captain Billy's collected and unassembled papers in Biloxi (an amateur history buff borrowed his papers in Bay St. Louis, but turned them in to the Biloxi public library bookmobile by error), it would be reasonable to assume Captain Billy would have said "Hell's fire, Robert Melville, it was you who put my arse up here on the wall, but only after a shrimper checking for used line found me cracked in a bin of rotting sea bass and returned it to your secretary. You need to show more respect for the dead, as you can well-afford it and ill-afford not to heed my advice.

[35] In marginal notes, Will wrote he noticed many times his mother would walk past his father's photograph on the mantel. He wondered why she hesitated, then looked at him. Then he discovered that, looking at his father's eyes, which peered straight into the camera, captured probably in the last few days before his death near Schwetzingen, Germany, they literally followed him while he moved about

The crew seemed a quiet and honorable bunch save for contentious

the room. An optical illusion, to be sure. As if he were alive and coming back home in a matter of hours to do the dishes or take him for a walk downtown to Woolworths. Will said the illusion only worked if he stared his father straight into the eyes, a habit both of us lacked then due to shyness and insufficient self-confidence. I vaguely recall one time when Will and I were high school seniors slurping cherry vanilla cones in anticipation of our dates at the DQ, and he said he hoped his Dad could also move his lips to say something to him. I don't think he knew then how much occult faith he placed in the possibility of his Dad ever sitting down to pass the mashed potatoes and gravy. I think it bothered him a lot as the so-called man of the house by default. [Editor's Note: At this juncture, I have come to realize Will's notes contain much incidental material that does not reveal the true essence of his plight and final redemption. And as a faithful adherent to Strunk in practice and principle well beyond mere penmanship, I dashed a lot of Will's attempts to write credible literature, figuring if I couldn't succinctly distill the essence of his experience on the Tern, nobody could or would do it. For a time, I stored a lot of them in three ashcans in case of the need to verify an event or imagined scene for the sake of clarity and tension. They are still in my brother's garage in Flint. **[Publisher's Note: Mr. Rubinstein did not know that his stepbrother, Aaron Finke, blended them with back issues of *Time* and the *Detroit Free Press* and burned them in his backyard three months following Mr. Rubinstein's burial back at Woodlawn. When asked if he understood the import of his actions, Mr. Finke stared at the rising column of smoke and responded, Yes, I read most of Mr. Melville's notes and I regarded them as trash.—S. Dratch, Melville House, May, 1974].** Nonetheless, I feel strongly obligated to continue to parse, refine and otherwise opine in plain language what notes I have deemed worthy enough to rewrite. My research assistant, Ms. Scriveen, will continue to exhume Captain Billy's thoughts and reactions to shed light on Will's experience. After all, we must commune with the past to give voice to the future. Finally, a belated and heartfelt debt of gratitude to my correspondents in Tucson (Cliff Dinwiddie) and Scranton (LaKeesha Johnson) for "obtaining" copies of notes, letters, bank accounts, medical records, etc. of Paola, Lou, Bud and Les. I entrusted them to collect the trash and, if need be, get it any other way they could to help me verify the facts and get at the truth, which no misdemeanor citation or burglary indictment could or should obstruct. Due to their fine work, I am able to herewith bump Will's notes against the suspicious activity of the crew in hopes of affirming their worth as either ethical individuals discussions erupting over things eluding me when they saw me approach. I would sneak up on them to catch the latest mutinous plans. The other day, I leaned an ear against the bulkhead between our sleeping quarters.

"This is the stupidest damndest thing I ever heard of," said Les in his high-pitched nasal twang.

"*Nunkrazohnahgru.*"

"Okay, hon. You're among friends so speak Yiddish or some tongue we can understand. You really changed since the gig in Cozumel.

"Are you kidding? It was your idea in the first place. I don't care to work anymore under bloody red sails into the sunset of someone's last days," said Paola.

Bud and Lou stayed out of it, snapping cards for the blackjack they played at every lull.

Someone said in a subdued voice, as the Pope is my banker, it's almighty money. It's why we're here.

"Keep it down, will you."

"Bull! We'll be knee-deep in this junk before we know it."

When Uncle Rob's voice wafted over the speaker, they broke up and went back to their chores, as elusive to me as dolphins leaping off starboard.

In late afternoon, I asked Uncle Rob what were his plans. He sat alone in a leather chair in the cavernous dark stateroom, staring at the waves rolling by.

"Will, how did the swabbing go? You and Vincent get it all done?"

"Yeah. Sure, Uncle. Can I ask you a question?"

"Shoot, but be sure you miss your foot."

I asked why his crew, minus the three Filipinos flitting about like dragonflies, were so secretive about upcoming events.

"They're good people, son." He shifted in his seat and let one out. "These folks have been with me for years. I'd trust them with my own life, but they like to bitch and complain like any good sailor."

"They're talking about knocking off someone—if I heard right. What's this all about? Do I sound like an informer."

He took a long, lip-tugging sip of beer. "Pure rubbish. Are you sure it wasn't the mumbling screw under your room? I'll have to get the thing replaced. Want to move your sleeping quarters?" He gave out one of those peppy bursts of laughter and I joined him.

---

or self-absorbed equivocating rabble on the run. Their thoughts and actions go far, in my opinion, but often not far enough to validate Will's own life.

"No. It's okay."

"But since you asked, we're stopping tomorrow off Kiawah to pick up some dear old friends of mine. They wanted to cruise a few days on something where they wouldn't get food poisoning. I owe Irv from way back. Charity work."

I said I think I got it and felt relieved and strolled along the framed photos of real celebrities he entertained from years past. They were autographed in heavy black ink in a corner with stuff like Best Wishes, or To My Pal, or Best Friend, Warmest Regards, Clark, Deanna, Fred, Benny, Eddie, Dorothy, George, Claudette, Jimmy, Walter, Ronny, Joan, Betty and so on; people I saw in the movies. Impressed, I turned to him and said Really? And he said Really! And got up to stretch. He came over and put his arm around my shoulder.[36] "Before we crawl another statute mile, let's go down into the steerage of the Tern. I want to show you where your confounded noise may be coming from."

On the way aft, we climbed over Bud, prone and asleep like a baby in the shade of a stanchion. A paperback rested on his chest; the breeze blew the pages back and forth, but the ten-dollar bill he used as a bookmarker stayed in place.

"One of your plotting villains, eh?" Uncle said with a smirk. He lifted a hatch and led me down a ladder into a tight engine room, grasping my ankles so I didn't miss a rung. It reeked of diesel oil and ancient armpits.

"This is the demon keeping you up at night."

We bent down and he pointed to the shaft of the screw, rotating in a cylinder of burly roller bearings.

"Rest assured, son. The vibrations this old gal makes is as harmless as the baseball games you think it's broadcasting to you up there; as harmless as junk you hear from Lou, Bud, Les and Paola." He rested a hand on the slow-turning shaft for a second while we stooped down.

---

[36] One of these photos was shown to me by Will's mother back in Monroe. He sent it to her as an early souvenir of his adventure on the Tern. I made a copy of it and sent it off to a handwriting expert I knew from a Mundane summer work-study gig as a croupier understudy in Las Vegas. Hank Tandy told me it was flat out not Bogie's signature, and not even the studio PR facsimile of it. Most likely, all the signed photos were faked by one person intending to impress visitors. When I sent Hank a letter signed by Melville, he said the swirls and loops, etc., matched in every way those of the Bogie photo, which indicated Uncle Rob—although not a fake himself—was reaching for the stars.

"You know, this is the oldest and most reliable piece on the Tern," he explained.

"How so?" I said, coughing and wiping my face on my shirt sleeves.

"Sixty years ago, Captain Billy floundered off Santo Domingo. He pulled into some small village for repairs. He found this screw and shaft—or propeller, if you will—on an old schooner converted for the slave trade called El Libre and picked it up for a twenty-dollar gold piece.

"Some misnomer, huh uncle? A slave ship called El Libre."

"Said it brought him bad luck. The Tern seemed to have a keel layed for either storms or trouble or both and only by Captain Billy's maritime skills and good intentions did she survive."[37]

"Amazing, Uncle."

Uncle Rob and I crawled about ten feet to the access door leading to a large room in the ship's hold.

"You can't see much in here," as Uncle slid back the bolt. "This is where Captain Billy transported rum and other popular medicinal beverages of the day, plus any residual slave business he could find." Uncle rapped his knuckles lightly on the door frame and it echoed like the inside of a rare sarcophagus I wrapped on when Mom took me to an Egyptian exhibit at the Chicago Museum of Ancient Mysteries. "It's no wonder you still don't hear all the suffering going on down here." He pointed to a vertical beam and said Captain Billy's photo in the stateroom is pretty much in line with the forward bulkhead of the large room and my sleeping quarters.

"Oh, the things those poor slaves must have groaned about," said Uncle with a melodramatic quaver.

"Seriously?"

"You can almost hear them now." He put his ear to the bulkhead and lifted his eyebrows in wait.

Now I could begin to understand from my abbreviated novitiate as a mechanical engineering student how the screw could transmit all its so-called rumors to my room. No surprises, yet also inconceivable any of the misery could be heard, since they were all as dead as Captain Billy's eyes.

---

[37]   In fact, Captain Billy came back the next day and stripped El Libre of anything he could rip off; masts, sails, mahogany trim and refitted the Tern with them near Hope in Mobile Bay. Numerous deck planks were sanded down and heavily shellacked to remove and mask the numerous blood stains caused by slaves beating each other or getting whipped to welts by the crew.

"Let's get topside. I feel unclean down here," said Uncle, who strained to keep his greas-stained hands off his pants.

"Thanks for showing me the bowels of the ship," I said as we climbed out, free at last, into the fresh evening breeze.

"Captain," yelled Les. "Can you take this call from Platform 13?"

I asked him what's Platform 13 all about? And he gave me a wink and said a new rig in the Gulf of Mexico. "Got to go," and he waved off further inquiry. I said to myself, he must have a full-time job keeping his hands clean.

In contrast to the old slave galley, Vin and I shared accommodations fit for a pharaoh. Vinnie took the rack above mine in the small guest berthing right under Captain Billy's portrait in the stateroom—and above the Tern's screw, more annoying each passing day, albeit an unusual diversion. The room was well-decked out in knotty pine panelling, thick pile carpeting the color of orangeade and small antique wall sconces Uncle must have electrified to shed light on the situation; porthole to search the horizon for ghostly U-boat snorkels. I seldom looked out the porthole at the water, because I knew it was there, unlike my dorm window at Mundane where an attractive coed might float by. Flying fish and an occasional porpoise school soon lost my interest. The bulkhead displayed several large silver-framed group photos of people I imagine Uncle or grandfather hosted onboard for pleasure cruises between the mainland and various Caribbean islands. One showed a lectern in the background with the Presidential Seal of approval on it, although I couldn't recognize Franklin D. or anyone else, since they were twisted around in their seats mugging for the camera with an arm around a wife or two or a girlfriend. Some of these photos appeared old. One showed my grandfather (the white arrow pointed to "Capt. Billy") with an arm around a small swarthy guy chomping on a cigar and a couple of tight-lipped goons standing behind them.[38] Certainly, Paola, Les, Bud and Lou seemed to me more refined than these surrounding mobs in tuxedos and evening gowns.

---

[38] PS: Captain Billy made meticulous entries of all his voyages. In this instance, I wager he would have responded, if he were in the room: "That's no bum, young man. It's either Big Al or Fiorello. I can't remember now. We celebrated the completion of the St. Agnes Home for Unwed Mothers in Cicero. That's when charity was worth more than the usual delivery of day-old fish wrapped in the swaddling *Sun-Times*."

CHAPTER 8

Early in the morning, before the sun started cracking someone's whip, I lay there with hands clasped behind my head like a POW in the movies, recalling the mindless chatter of a radio broadcast transmitted through the Tern's screw and its cavitation signature—if it could write. An obvious absurd notion, but I got so used to it I began to believe anything was possible. After all, I never imagined I'd be lounging on my Uncle's multi-million dollar yacht, deselecting myself from the Selective Service and avoiding exercise yard calisthentics in basic training. Like a wet dream you try to recall stumbling down a dark hallway, fumbling for a grip on reality to go pee.

Vinnie broke the mood with a gargled *ughughughugh;* glutterals for Paola? Nope, for an upchuck gushed down the side of the rack.

"What the...What did you eat last night?"

"Nothing, man," Vin moaned.

"Wrong. I see the pepperoni and cheese on my left shoe, Vin."

Vin slid down and ran his fingers through his Sicilian mop of hair. "It wasn't the pizza. I couldn't sleep all night."

"You heard it, too."

"Screw you and your screw, Will. I've got a bad feeling about this."

He jabbered on for five minutes while I cleaned my shoe in the sink. He said he felt extremely uncomfortable around the crew, whose spontaneous outbursts followed by an easy jovial camaraderie put him so on edge he said he was acquiring manic-depression. I told him, hey, you don't get the condition. You have it.

"Cut it out, Will. Listen. Paola says she's fed up terminating people year after year. What the hell does she mean? Les tells her to stop whining;

she should be grateful to Melville for saving her ass and then she got physical and started hitting him. I could hear it from the door; he must have grabbed her and kept saying it's going to be all right, it's going to be all right."

"Yeah, Vin. But these people have been doing this to each other for years." Then I wondered what's the real price to pay for sailing with Uncle Rob?

"My ass, Will. The next day Lou and Les get into it. Lou bitches about who would take care of this rock and roll guy, and Les says the usual way, it's another payday and Lou must have kicked him in the shin or something. Les yelled and said if you don't do it, I will you little bastard and then they saw my shadow by the hatchway and slammed it shut. Will, what the hell did he mean by "it?" To me it means "shot," and I don't want to get into it. I mean, Will, this is heavy stuff and I think I want out of here."

Vin stood shaking in front of me like I was our old junior high truant officer.

"And then there's your damn uncle strutting around like nothing's going on. I tell you he's up to something."

I told Vin I don't know what you're talking about (of course, I lied), and I don't appreciate you calling Uncle my damn uncle. "Look, Vin, go take a shower and we'll talk about it later, okay?"

We never did, because I knew by then both of us wandered far out past low tide with childish curiosity, wondering too long why the ocean mysteriously receded. Looking back, I guess Vin could see the simmering white wave on the horizon better than anyone.

Later on deck, everyone milled around in quiet admiration of calm seas. Les sat on a stuffed suitcase. It somehow appeared overnight. Bud Shill snapped down a game of solitaire. Off in a corner, Lou talked down to fingerpuppets he brought with him and seemed to enjoy acting in-charge. Paola placed a hand on Vinnie's jaw to demonstrate how to sound a word from her pre-history vocabulary. So, Vin's on speaking terms with Paola, after all.

"Son, you're standing on the old mark of the main mast," said Uncle from the helm.

I stood in the five-foot diameter ring through which ran the original forty-foot mast of the Tern.

"Why isn't it still here?" I shouted.

Uncle chuckled aloud and said you've got to know when to fold them, and these days you can't fold sails fast enough when pirates or the feds snoop around. "Captain Billy's screw comes in handy. The Tern can do twenty-five knots on a good day. Not as good as a cigar or Coast Guard cutter, but good enough."

"What if it's not good enough?" I shouted.

"I'll show you the arsenal some time.[39] Hey, Paola; getting kind of cozy there with Vincent, huh?"

"You mean Vinnie," she shouted back up at Uncle.

"Okay, okay," as Uncle raised his hands in submission off the helm.

As the sun wheeled off the Carolina horizon, I noticed Les all alone, snapping his deck of cards in the stateroom. I knew sooner or later I wanted to get the scoop why these people were working for Uncle. Their mood swings bothered me as much as they did Vinnie.

"Hey, Les. Mind if I rest a bit?"

"Sure. Sure, kid. Make yourself at home. How about a few hands of poker?"

I agreed, since this would be a nifty way to ask Les some questions without his awareness of it; much like a psychiatrist playing with toys in the cluttered subconscious attic of an abused child. After we talked, I made sure to jot down what he said on some paper napkins I lifted from the stateroom buffet drawer. What he told me seemed amusing but not laughable, because he appeared to be in real physical pain to get it out.

"I'll hold, Les. And you?"

"I'll open up."[40]

---

[39] PS: Captain Billy: I took an oath to never deal in arms trading or smuggling weapons of limited destruction after 1903. During the Spanish-American War in the Philippines, the Tern delivered arms and ammunition (mostly harmless small-caliber) to both sides in the belief that equalizing the conflict would produce a quicker stalemate and thus, peace treaty. In the end, I was persuaded by US Government lawyers to cease and desist, since they said that striving for equality on the battlefield would not produce this result. I especially took pride in transporting to San Francisco fifty-six Filipino refugees from Mindinao at the close of hostilities.

[40] Les, a close-holder with balance sheets, divulged in an hour of harmless cardplaying his apparent "escape" as he called it. "A damn book my father wrote in 1938." It was published by Wing, White and Tipps in Sarnia, up and across the St. Clair from Detroit, and I vaguely recall its stark cover (red, white

Les played well, as usual, and revealed some of the "cards" dealt to him from his father's ups and downs as a minor government bureaucrat.

"A damn book. Can you believe it? Let's make this the last hand." Les then placed the squared deck back in its box.

"Sorry, Les."

"Don't be." Les lifted his head. "You weren't even born then. Because your old man is ostracized or robs the till doesn't make you an outcast or crook. Tainted, but no more."

"I see what you mean."

---

and blue-striped hammer and sickle) on the desk of my economics professor at Mundane. C. Coover Cruishank wrote *Five Years of Socialist Creep—The Obverse of The Double Eagle, 1930-35*, a scholarly book about FDR's first term. Eventhough it liberally plagairized a well-known and frequently referenced macroeconomics dissertation of 1937 by his brother-in-law, Professor Rupert Kvetchal of Connecticut College, the critics regarded it as a flip assessment and the public relations campaign was a disaster. The first five thousand copies carried the misprinted title, *Five Years of a Socialist Creep*, which prompted a visit from administration officials dressed in crisp suits blacker than anthracite typical of those dim and bleak days. Coover became so unnerved during the visit, or cross-examination, he jumped from his eighth-floor office in the former Nickelwood Building in downtown Buffalo, but his pin-striped pants ripped off and his coat snagged onto Old Glory jutting out from a sill on the fifth floor. A crowd from the St. Jude mission soup line ran across staring at his ass shouting Hoover, Hoover at Coover, since most of the Midwest governmental regional financial offices were located in the Nickelwood. While off-duty FBI agents appeared to be gasping in stitches trying to pull him inside, Coover's coat caved and he fell five stories onto three precinct captains of the local Democrat party boss, Frank Bostick, who moments earlier lead the crowd in chants of jump, jump. All three later died later on page two (crushed larynx; broken neck; punctured lungs). Ironically, six months after cutting-edge reconstructive surgery at the newly erected Schwanz Klinik in downtown Erie, Cruishank was kicked upstairs to a modest ten-year career as regional administrator of the little-known and short-lived Federal Administration for Relocation, Charity and Encouragement. Lester Cruishank, his teen-aged son, was so humiliated by the annual flood of local newspaper accounts, such as in the *Buffalo Hindsight*, he later defiantly changed his name to "Vice" and disappeared from the scene after the police chased him out of town for the brazen theft of one pound of sugar. Virtue in vice? Goodness "vice" badness? Who knows why he changed his name.

"No, not really. Freedom of the press? A pipe dream." He got up and we walked to the hatchway.

I wanted to put a hand on his shoulder, but he may have taken it as empathy on the cheap from someone my age.

"I always wanted to go home so bad, but you know what what's-his-name—Maxwell Wolfe—wrote: You can't go home again.

Under the string of dim artificial lights in the passageway, he turned to me as he entered his room. He winked at me with a click from the side of his mouth, like Uncle Rob. "We've done some weird things, extra-legal stuff, but you know your uncle's been good to me. Real good."

CHAPTER 9

"Hey, Clarence, throw me a line," shouted Uncle to one of the men in torn teeshirts on the dock.

We finally made it to Kiawah after watching it grow for hours from a blind pimple on the festering red horizon to a busy resort with dozens of colorful small craft bobbing up and down in our wake.

"OK. You see, captain, there were these two dogs," shouted Clarence.

"No, Clarence. Throw me another down there." Uncle was all business, nursing the Tern into a nest of bollards, bumpers and retreads hanging off the wharf.

Vinnie and I helped pull in and tie up the Tern into a berth taking up half the dock. It felt good and secure to be on solid ground after a week or so at sea, with the Tern shifting under our feet like the uncertainty of our chosen paths at the time. Both of us waited for an undercover cop to rush out of the gift shop munching a ham on rye and put us in leg irons compliments of Uncle Sam. For this reason, dockside seemed more precarious than a pitching deck.

Earlier, around 0600, Uncle mustered all of us around the quarterdeck to go over our duties. I concurred in everything although I didn't understand half the naval jargon from his lips, obscured by a dry Panatella rolling from port to starboard in his mouth. Vin and I were beat, but the crew acted smartly with the listlessness of experience.

"Got it, captain," said Lou rubbing his half-closed eyes. Paola stretched like a Siamese cat and meowed a loud aahhhh!, which may have also been her prehistoric sound for if you're done, I want to go back to bed. Bud and Les stood by the sterling silver coffee urn with their backs to Uncle. Their shrugs let him know they were ready to carry any load—physical and emotional—he had in store for them.

Vinnie and I filed out last. In the stateroom, I again spotted it by the low profile mahogany cabinets housing the stereophonic recordplayer and new VCR recording device: the aluminum suitcase. I stooped down while Vin stood lookout. There was no lock or combination and the locks wouldn't flip open. Without a key, I did the next best thing: pounded it with the ball of my fist, and it flew open with such force I thought a genie popped out. Both of us would never forget what we saw; neat banded stacks of hundreds. I got halfway though counting the top layer rather than pinch myself.

"Holy crap!" we chorused in disbelief.

"There must be over a million staring at us. Thirty Ben Franklin's didn't seem very impressed looking up at us with the sly paternal grin of someone who's thinking five steps ahead of us—even from almost two hundred years ago.

"Wow! man. What is this? What are we supposed to do now?" said Vinnie, wearing a headband of sweatbeads.

"I don't know, Vin. I think I'm going to crap in my pants if I keep looking at it." I thought, enough dough to live in Stockholm the rest of my life.

Someone trudged back down the ladder toward the stateroom. I said we've got to close this thing up now. We both sat on it to snap the clasps back into place. By now, the hyperspace of wealth we stumbled into couldn't support our breathing for long.

"Will, this is crazy. We shouldn't be here with a million staring us in the face. This has to be some kind of payoff or drug money or something," whispered Vin in desperation.

Uncle Rob said he forgot his Breitling, which he often took off when giving orders or cracking crab legs. I said I didn't notice the watch anywhere as he passed by us with a mischevious grin. As we jostled to exit the room, we turned around to see if there were no surprises.

"Did you get a look at it?" said Uncle.

"What?" Vin replied.

Uncle gave us one of those hearty laughs starting under his shoestrings and said, okay I guess you've seen it all before anyway in the movies.

"No, Uncle. I don't think so," I confessed with a shrug.

We made our way topside, still clearing our minds of red sportcars and babes in blue bikinis calling us into the white surf on Maui.

I only heard about Uncle Rob's wealth, but it didn't hit me on the head until I saw the three black Lincoln Continentals waiting at the head of the dock. At first, they were shiny little metal toys from a hundred yards. It was no mirage when chauffeurs in black business suits opened the limo doors. Vinnie and I got in one with Uncle, who got on a phone to direct the traffic. We two "stowaways" must have seemed like kids in the land of adult playthings. During the smooth and quiet ride, my thoughts raced ahead around a sharp curve to see what was next. Vinnie said the only thing like this was when he took a Chrysler Imperial taxi to Detroit to catch a DC-3 to his granny's in Paducah.

"Where're we headed, Uncle?"

"I want you to see something special. This one is real close to my heart."

The entourage pulled into the driveway of Twisted Knee Country Club in a cloud of dust and crunchy gravel.

"But first, we've got to get in some exercise and a little sporty diversion, right?" Uncle winked.

"This looks like a real nice place, Captain Melville," said Vinnie as we approached the clubhouse. "I used to caddy at Grouse Hill. Heard of it?"

Uncle tilted his head with a sly smile and said yeah, but the one I built here is better. Longer holes; larger greens. Or did he say larger holes and longer greens? Fifty brands of beer in the clubhouse bar, not domestic dishwater.

"You mean, you built this place?" I said.

"Well, I needed to do something with the property. It's next to the Alice Detwiler Home over there." He shrugged his shoulders and pointed with his numero-three wood on the tee to a cluster of white and pink cottages nestled off the eighteenth hole. "It's intended for folks over there who can still get in a round or two. Guess I overshot it on the fairways, since there's not too many who can make it—even through the woods." Uncle shook his head and bit his lip teeing up his ball. I watched him and wondered, is he focused on the ball or thinking about the residents over there or the next deal?

"So, Uncle; how much of this is yours?" I asked as we left the first tee.

"Do you see the horizon beyond the tree line?"

Vinnie whispered shoot, man, since he knew Uncle's rule on profanity. He asked as a joke what about when we're on the Tern?

"I'm working on it," Uncle replied as he hooked a five-iron into the rough.

We played nine brisk holes, with Uncle and Paola in our foursome. She demonstrated a beautiful swing in those navy blue shorts and canary yellow sport shirt and chalk-white golf shoes. Vin said to me under his breath, who taught her how to swing? After the fifth hole and my coming out of the rough for the tenth time, she gave me the cutest grin of patience—as if we had just jumped out of bed—when I approached the green.

"Is there still hope for me," I said out of breath.

"Yes, there's always hope," as she holed out for a birdie.

Les, Bud and Lou hooked up with the club pro, Sammie Sue, who showed off her two prominent points: keep your head down and keep your eye on the ball. I saw the glint in Bud's eyes; he was about to say something like I can't keep my head down looking at you, georgeous, or if I keep one eye on the ball, can I keep the other on you. But instead, he took a long swallow of cold beer.

"From here on out," instructed Uncle at the sixth tee, "it's Captain Billy's rules.[41] If you hit it in the rough, drop a ball and play on like a champ. This is a short-term memory-loss game."

"Isn't what you're saying sort of cheating?" upped Vinnie.

Everyone laughed. Lou put his beer can on the bench and said of course not. "Golf can be an unforgiving, mean game, right Les?"

"Well, yes. Statistics can be used to..."

"We throw out the best and worst shots and thereby gain mean middle-class respectability. This is not a sport for someone with a conscience, right captain?" said Lou, who glanced at Uncle digging dirt from his cleats with a tee.

"Ask Captain Billy. It's his rules," he laughed and teed up a second ball.

---

[41]   PS: In his own words (p.67, Captain's log, June 1908): "I, Captain Billy, never knowingly broke the rules, unless, although, I asked for forgiveness, as any practicing Christian on innumerable occasions, would prudently do." The police blotter at Hamilton reveals four incidents of contributing to the delinquency of underage bar girls and malicious destruction of the Admiral Benbow Golfing Club by the Tern's crew. It can be assumed Captain Billy led the mutiny to redecorate then burn down the club.

The dropped-ball rule didn't bother me as much as who dropped the million bucks in the suitcase, or what to expect at the Alice B. Detwiler Home.

Before we tackled the long uphill ninth hole, I asked Lou how it got the name "Cardiac Hill." Again, I played up to Lou and his low opinion of me.

"Charley Kremlmeier. Owned a parts factory your uncle wanted to buy. Liked to play through everyone. Real fast."

"Huh?"

"See the weeping willow over there by the water hazard?"

"What about it?"

"Your uncle nailed a plaque on it in his memory. See it? Open this bottle for me, will you."

"You mean"

"Precisely. He climbed too fast. Even up Cardiac Hill. Another executive vice-president. Massive heart attack after he birdied this hole three years ago. Classic Type A." Lou took a long swig, stared down the fairway and pitched a real zinger at me. "Even a 4F could survive this hole."

"Thanks, Lou. I really needed that," I said as I jerked a two-iron from the golf bag.

Uncle Rob said in a level, determined voice, I really love this one over the others. The rolling terrain reminds me of the sea on the Tern. I knew what he meant; the fairways were contoured to give the illusion that the Gulfstream was the most beautiful water hazard a golfer could ever hope to hook into. He fidgeted with the clubhead and seemed really driven as he teed off.

The extra large cups on the greens reminded me of shiny durable medical equipment ads in the back of *Geriatric Life* in the doctor's office, but I appreciated how they enabled me to shoot fifteen over par with the dropped-ball exclusion. We dragged on to the clubhouse. From my own caddying days in Grosse Pointe, I regarded it as a place where all disasters end and hope renews with an ice cold beer. We all sat at a table for a quick round of adult beverages. Uncle entwined an arm around Bud's, still catching his breath.

"You okay, Bud?"

"Sure. I'm still here, aren't I?" Bud managed to sneak in a grudging thanks before finishing his glass.

"To put it politely, yes; you're still with us. Let me know and I'll send you back to Houston for your ticker," said Uncle snapping open a bottle.

Everyone showered and later stood around the buffet nibbling from steam troughs of seafood and baskets of mangoes and kiwis, Brie, French baguettes and assorted open wine bottles. The white-jacketed servers stood at attention, reminding me and Vin of our situation and I didn't feel like eating much. The portions were tiny exotic islands in large white, gold-rimmed plates, but they tasted far better than a double serving of mac au gratin and sloppy joe spilling over a flimsy paper plate at the Mundane cafeteria.

On the way into Alice B. Detwiler, I overheard Lou and Les say something about the next job. Lou chopped the air with his small hands as he mumbled not to worry, he had it down pat. When they turned around to see me close by, they were a bit flustered and Les said laughing, You still with us, huh?

Uncle Rob led us as a group into a large reception room with more flower-choked vases than Lazarus's Flower Shop off State Street in Ann Arbor. About fifty well-dressed staff members lined one side, clapping with rehearsed enthusiasm. Across from them waited their patients, dressed for a party with bright helium balloons tugging the back of their gleaming wheelchairs. One old lady was so frail, one more helium balloon would have lifted her away to a better place. The whole scene rolled on like the old newsreel of a military review by King Edward Cigars himself. We walked past the hundred or so residents with a harmless hello or how are you or good to see you, how goes it, you look so handsome and other political throwaways. Paola broke ranks and stooped on a knee to pat the hand of an old white-haired woman who may have recognized her from a previous visit or past life. Then she held both of the old woman's trembling hands, looking with speechless compassion into her pensive, moisture-laden eyes.

"Ms. Paleo-Tosti, would you come here please," said Uncle in codespeak for don't break ranks, doll. She passed me and hissed, sometimes he's got the coldest damn heart, which didn't surprise me after the scuttlebut of informal dissent I picked up from each one of them on the voyage up from Fort Lauderdale.

For every resident who smiled or twinkled an eye of medicated glee, three must have been in la-la land staring straight ahead, bored and unable to do more than poo-poo in their throwaway diapers.

By now, I began to fall in ranks with Uncle Rob like the others and addressed him as "Captain" more often. He raised a hand and flipped a birdlike shape to the head mistress at the end of the reception line. She, in turn, wiggled a finger and we handed clear vases of red roses to each resident. Some of them lifted their heads and managed meek smiles as the thornless stems slid into their palsied hands. I gave my last rose to a very old lady whose eyes glistened in the sunshine coming through the oval skylight above. I thought about kissing her cheek—the one with a rill of moisture repelling down through rouge make-up toward her parched lips.

On the way to the larger dining area, I walked with Les and one of the nurses, a pretty young brunette from Athens just out of nursing school.

Les explained how Alice Detwiler was Captain's favorite one of the lot, the rest were in Monterey, Glendale, Omaha, St. Paul, New Canaan, Boca Raton and Loudoun County.

"How does one get into a place like this?" I asked.

Les turned and rubbed his index finger and thumb together. These gentle folk may be in poor health, but they're not poor. They're all loaded to the gills when they come in and unloaded when they leave. Sort of a weight-reduction program."

"Exclusive, huh?" I knew he served as Captain's right-hook man, not realizing how crude he could be when he told me this as if I were already a co-conspirator.

"He really cares about the elderly.[42] He does for a fact. Look at him!" Les pointed to Captain bending down to chat with several residents. I noticed how he put his hand on the mens' shoulders and adjusted a corsage on a woman's blue and white polka dot blouse.

"Les, I noticed back there all those greeting cards for Valentine's, Christmas, Hanukkuh. there must be hundreds of them."

"Yeah. The staff puts most of them together for them. Better than staring at a blank wall or paisley wallpaper. A few come dribbling in from relatives."

"Really?" I noticed one of the cards, dated December 25, 1948; almost twenty years ago.

---

[42]   PS: Captain Billy didn't quite see his second son as a very charitable person. In one letter on stationary from Mount Sinai, where he recovered from hemorrhoid surgery, he figuratively tore the teen a new asshole minus the stitches. A total dearth of sympathy and outright neglect. He wrote: "If you're going to see me and complain about your lack of money and can I take the Packard for a spin and joke with the nurses about my delicate backside, you can stay the hell away."

Vinnie tapped me on the shoulder and asked which way to the next bathroom. "I washed my hands back there and there's moaning from one of the stalls and more moaning and I'm out of there."

"It's for both men and women. With these folks, sex is the distant twinkle from a star," chuckled Les, as we joined the rest of the crowd where Captain grabbed a microphone.[43]

"Is everybody happy? Good!" Captain provided, as usual, the jovial response after a few seconds of silence so profound you could hear a 32-gauge needle drop from the nicotine-stained fingers of a self-medicated night nurse.

Captain Rob rambled on about how wonderful everyone looked and what a beautiful day and I love you all. It actually sounded quite heartfelt and unrehearsed. No doubt he possessed a generous heart in caring for these elderly who could no longer recognize themselves, but he nonetheless also made a killing going to the bank, according to Les. But I asked myself what's wrong? It's not as if he were selling guns to people so they could kill each other.

In the back of the room, a gentleman stood up from his wheelchair. He appeared quite distinguished with a trimmed beard, turquoise turtleneck, white shorts and tan desert boots. He waved his cane for attention. Captain Rob said, Yes sir, you in the back; please go ahead and speak up. Please tell us your goals and aspirations on this fine day. Go ahead, please.

The old man cleared gravel-laden pflegm from his throat and said loudly, my only goal and aspiration is to be able to take a good healthy shit tonight and drive my Austin-Healey back home.

"Well, well! Excellent!" said Captain Rob, and without missing a beat turned his attention to a woman in the front row. "Hi! doll; how are you? Okay. Now listen up everyone. As you know this month I draw a name from our fishbowl here next to me to determine our next lucky couple to spend a beautiful ten-day cruise on my grand luxury yacht, the Tern."

Lou folded his arms and slightly bowed his head as if to say, No, this is a rigged show if ever. He threw a smirk at me and Vinnie rather than

---

43   I don't think Les would have said this, but as Will's editor, I hesitated to delete this "twinkle" phrase and similar others throughout as too poetic and flowery from Will, but he wrote it down; so I let it stand against my better judgment. I was surprised, because when I often visited his house, there was one pine bookcase with such pablum as The *Saturday Evening Post*, *Readers Digest* and some abridged novels holding up a bunch of dog-earred comic books.

say what the hell are you looking at? Vin had a run-in with him a few days earlier when Lou told him to clean the heads on the Tern, and he told me he wanted to put him down to size, and I said Vin don't since there's not much of him anyhow.

"And the lucky winners are—surprise! My dear friends, Dr. Irving Shapiro and his lovely wife, Rose. Wheel them I mean bring them on up here let's have a hand for the doctor." His clap cued the chorus of attendants to applaud and release a colorful helium balloon each held behind the back.[44]

One of the nurses came up and placed a large bouquet of roses in each of their laps, repeating the presentation twice when the roses fell out of the wheelchairs. Like several other patients, the Shapiros wore oxygen masks hooked up to supply bottles as big as torpedoes. Dr. Shapiro became very agitated and struggled to speak through his mask when the nurses separated his hand from Rose's. I heard Paola mutter to Bud "incompetents" as she pulled Bud along and pushed the nurses out of the way to rejoin their hands.

"Bud," I whispered very low, "those two are at death's door. I've seen that candlewax complexion and gaping mouth two years ago when I worked night shift at the city morgue."

"Right. I can't talk about it here. Look around. Can't you see these poor people are having their last cup of chamomile. Your uncle has taken damn good care of them."

I watched Uncle—Captain--running the show like a ballet master, doing near jettes and pirouettes to make sure everyone felt comfortable at the dozen or so oval dinner tables, popping champagne bottles and doing his damnedest to entertain. I admired his charitable munificence, though I

---

[44] Now this is pure bulldrip. Melville may have been friends with Shapiro, but I have it on tape from his stockbroker at Scrunch and Kutz on 23rd Avenue that he got bilked out of $80,000 investing in Dr. Shapiro's provisional patent for a mechanism that opens a garage door automatically when the carbon monoxide reaches a dangerous level. His potential licensees vanished in a puff of smoke when the first twenty units failed, eventhough the defense successfully argued that all were suicides. Melville recovered half of that a few months later when he used the Tern's former slave-holding compartment to transport the good doctor's chemical components for making the little-known methamphetamine for his pain clinics in south Miami and Chevy Chase.

knew he possessed a complex personality. What would drive someone with so much wealth and success to ingratiate himself to the dying?

When we all got back on the Tern and prepared to hit the rack, Captain knocked and came into our room, tired but still wearing his happy mask. What energy, I thought, for a guy old enough to be my dad.

"What a day, eh? What did you think of it?" Uncle brought out his little gold cross and chain, twisting back and forth with his finger.

"Yeah, Captain. Sure was a bit different," said Vinnie.

Melville gazed at an old pin-up above my rack of the well-endowed 1940s stripper-turned-starlet-turned-harlot-turned-mental patient, Veronica deMaestri. I sensed he rummaged his conscience for something more profound than salt and pepper shakers.

"I love this part of the job, you know; caring for these old folks, shepherding them you know through the trappings of terminal illness and whatnot." He flicked his hand as if brushing a cigarette ash off his Palm Beach slacks at a garden party. "Will, son, heard any more gossip from the screw you're resting on?"

"No, Captain. I'm getting used to it, like fugitive noise or elevator music."

"Good. I don't want it to drive you overboard. You can still move to the front."

Vinnie took off his socks across the room and glanced at me with a quick eye to the ceiling—his mute signal much more ancient than Paola's language to tell me I feel another brain fart coming from Uncle.

"You fellas aren't there yet and I hope you never do. This dementia thing is awful."

"I've read about it in school," I offered.

"No. You don't know, Will. It's worse than cancer. Cancer eats your body like some shark out there." He jerked his head toward the bay. "Senility or whatever they want to call it takes away your mind, your soul like you've been cast aside by your maker."

I asked how he got so wound up about this old age stuff. I actually didn't know squat about it, since I was in my twenties. Uncle twirled the cross on his finger and went on at length until I could hear the distinct tick of the round chronometer on the bulkhead above the hatchway. He said he once visited an old boatswain's mate from one of his subs in the VA hospital near San Diego. Davy Duquette from Marquette, he called him.

"I sensed something no longer clicking, so I asked him Are you Catholic? to which he took the Fifth; you know, I respectfully decline to answer the question on the grounds it may tend to incriminate me, and he sort of laughed when he said it and I said does your wife still have the Edsel convertible you bought her in Tustin, and he took the Fifth again. We both laughed, because I knew the Edsel was a piece of junk, and then I asked are you in fact Davy Duquette from Marquette—something real easy and mnemonic, and again he took the Fifth. If those Fifths were liquor, he'd have been more than absinthe-minded. He'd have been dead. Then he asked me who in the hell are you by the way? I owed this guy my life when he torniqueted my sliced-up left arm in the sheet metal shop onboard and he says to me again who the hell are you? Then it hit me real hard as I focused on him sitting there quietly, alone in the hospital game room, and I started to get interested in this invisible thief called dementia. Maybe someday they'll call it something else." Uncle took a deep breath and put his hands in his pockets. "Will, if you think this screw of the Tern is bad, wait until you sit down with one of those poor souls back at Alice Detwiler. I've given millions to research to find a cure. Literally millions." Then he abruptly stopped talking and pursed his lips.

I climbed into my rack. The heavy white scar snaked down across his left forearm in the milky mixed light of lamp and moon. As Captain drew in a deep breath and slowly got up to leave, he said goodnight, fellas; see you bright and early. We shove off at 0700 in landlubber's lingo.

"Is he gone?" whispered Vinnie.

"Yeah. Why?"

"I've got to get out of here. I'm finished."

"What do you mean?"

"You know, this may be the Tern, but your uncle is a loon."

"You trying to be funny?"

Vin, like myself, found it so difficult escaping from childish cliches and adolescent jokes, I almost replied that birds of a feather stick together, but then on a lark I thought Vin may have something to crow about as I craned my neck to say goodnight and chose not to snipe at him and tell him he was stark-raven mad. It was very late.

Uncle put a crack in the door and said, Sorry fellas. If you don't mind, I put the suitcase under your racks for safekeeping. I don't trust the others right now. Sleeping on top of a million and no place to spend it.

CHAPTER 10

At night, the screw woke me up around three. I couldn't translate more than the monotone prelude of *doesntdoesnstdoesntdoesntmattermattermattermatter* until broken by the voices of Paola and Les on the other side of the bulkhead. Somebody must have thrown a shoe or book against the wall and then they quieted down. I lay back down in my rack wondering if I heard her say I will be damned if I do it this time.

We motored east towards Hamilton the next two days. Salt air and a tai chi session by one of the Filipinos and a refreshing dip in the small pool near the fantail relaxed me to where I didn't mind not minding my self-imposed exile. The waves rolled by the Tern with such monotony I speculated whether we cruised by or floated in the same place, making no progress and merely waiting for the blue marble to rotate us into Hamilton harbor. Somehow, the farther we got from the coast, the easier it seemed for me to converse with the crew one-on-one.

"What's kicking?" I said to Lou, whose beak was in a back issue of *Doctors Prescription Deference*, a thick paperback I used to flip through at Knewticals Pharmacy at Division and 12th back home while waiting for Mom's nitroglycerin pills.

"Working right now, but don't get too close. I can change direction as fast as a pennant up there on the line."

We laughed and he followed with, How much poison does it take to kill an elephant? fanning the pages back and forth.

"Wouldn't it depend on the type, dosage, toxicity and vitals of the elephant?"

His little potbelly shook from a quick laugh. You're not supposed to be a smart-ass teacher's pet. Say, "I don't know" if you want an answer. I laughed with him and his ascerbic delivery I'd expected after the first week.

"Look. Make yourself useful. On your way back from the galley, bring me a coffee and cruller, okay?"

I took Lou's hint to get lost. Farther down the port side, Paola and Vinny sat on opposing small wooden barrels, practicing the syllabication she developed from her dissertation. The morning sunlight made her teased bleach-blond hair a golden tiara she poked at with her pen. I figured Vin debated the chances of poking more than the end of his Eberhard pencil into her hair. She put his hand to her mouth to pronounce a sound and I'll be damned if he didn't try to put a finger in it. When I strolled up, he stood in front of her and said to me, bad timing, pal. This is too hard.

Paola pushed back her oversized Carmen Graziano sunglasses, laughing at my entrance and said, You too? *Garfenupuir?*" in my language.

"Passing by like any voyeur on a cruise ship."

She shouted back, think you're cute. I know you meant *curpliki.*

On the foc'scle, Irv and Rose Shapiro once again held hands. The nurse onboard said they held hands all night in the king-sized bed in the guest room. They sucked on matching oxygen tanks. Their Hawaiian shirts popped in the warm breeze. The wheelchairs were locked onto deck cleats right up to the edge of the bow, and once in a while they got a spray flying up. A stiff breeze blew off his Twisted Knee CC ballcap and I went over and fitted it gently back on his head. He mumbled something through his mask which I took as thanks. I prided myself on the growing ability to translate all kinds of mumblings; rattlings; innuendoes; even the serious undertow of someone's forced laughter. Some people listened to these new audiotapes driving to work; the screw was my tutor while sailing on in my unexpected and unaccepted behavior. As usual, Rose didn't respond at all; only the breeze lifted her dyed hair to show the silvery roots underneath. She wore a pink chiffon scarf around her neck and a large floppy straw hat tied in a large bow under her double chin.

"Will, come here and say hello to the Rabbi," shouted Les behind me.

Bud looked up and said What's up? but stayed cross-legged playing solitaire on the polished deck.

Rabbi Milstein, this is Melville's son—sorry, nephew. He's sort of on the run," as Les winked at me for permission to say the truth.[45] If it were a street corner, I'd have been upset with him, but out here with no curbs or

---

[45] Les Vice knew a lot about taking to his heels since his early days pilfering bags of sugar and stale eclairs from the back of Bergman's Bakery in Buffalo. If he was a cornerstone of the community in Scottsdale, he was a pillar of salt in Pocatello and a string of towns below the radar out West. Thanks to my old gumshoe researcher, Cliff, I obtained several Buster Brown shoe boxes full of evidence that could have put Mr. Vice away for a long time. After graduating summa cum laude from Cal Tech in 1946 with a degree in biochemical engineering, he blew his circuits when he left the then clematis-cloaked cloisters of Berkeley. He lacked the social skills to transform his 170 IQ into a street value worth more than a waiter's daily tips, which is how he started out at the reclusive Entre Nos Trois restaurant in San Jose. The police knocked on his apartment door after Gerhard Schluck, vice-president of Drummond Turbines, claimed his fifteen-year old daughter shacked up with him. Les, a victim of his own social ineptness and sexual curiosity, took Maggie Schluck over to Sparks and married her after sticking the defrocked monk with a $60 bad check. When she got pregnant, he hitched his battered VW to a Star Van Lines semi and found a little more of himself near Lake Tahoe, where he moved grand pianos for six months. On one delivery, the wealthy widow of state senator, Buck White Feather Tekonsha, layed her hands on the Bosendorfer grand he unwrapped in front of her and he did something to her while she banged out a two-fisted version of The Star Mangled Banner from Book One of Souza for Beginners. Les was booked for rape. Two days later (5/12/48) he sweet-talked the county jail's first female guard and fled by burying himself in a Southern Pacific hopper carrying uranium tailings to a Flagstaff underground repository. He also found time to get an MA in accounting from B. Franklin correspondence school, although the dean said Les short-changed them in his thesis entitled "Ledger Domain—Erasure Techniques." He surfaced three years later in Pascagoula where he caddied for Captain Melville, who hired him to help repair the Tern. Although wanted for contributing to the delinquency of a minor, white slavery and rape with tumescence aforethought, Les transformed himself into a new man after stepping on a 50,000-volt downed powerline in the run-down historic section of Mobile. Melville made a charitable contribution to the governor in Santa Fe so Les could seek forgiveness from the widow Tekonsha, who forgave Les and married him in the courtyard of her 10,000-square foot hacienda in Scottsdale. Two months later, she was diagnosed with a glioblastoma multiforme

neighborhood dogs fertilizing the lawn, I let it go. Lou would have kicked him a good one in the shins.

The rabbi laughed, shook my hand and said, hey don't worry; we've all been fleeing Egypt at one time or another. Les said the Rabbi flew in from Ocean Avenue via Miami and then a swift ChrisCraft brought him here around 0600. He looked tired.

"So it was you who caused all the commotion that got me and Vinnie up!"

"You should have been up before then, chum," said Bud, emptying garbage over the fantail and returning to sit cross-legged by his deck of cards.

Rabbi Milstein chuckled and raised his palms. "All right already."

Bud had circles under his eyes. He asked the rabbi if he would block the sunlight breaking up the morning mist. "And what brings a man of faith to this unholy tub?"

The rebbe sensed Bud was under the weather. He came over to him and said Call me Moise, and held out his hand.

Les tried to cover for Bud's hangover. "Gee, Rabbi, sounds like a great opening line for a novel."

"Yeah. How about, call me Ishmael?" He gave out a hearty chuckle.

Bud said, "Sorry; already taken."

Les made fists in the pockets of his Bermuda shorts. "Sorry, Rabbi; Bud has a hangover. Unfortunately, we can't hang him by the yardarm to dry like a shirt.

Les said the man in black is here to officiate the renewal of the Shapiros wedding vows. It's their last wish. This made some touching nonsense to me. Were wedding vows interchangeable with last rites? 'Til death do us part? Paola told me Alice Detwiler's physician, Hilda Wexler, said the couple could possibly live a few more weeks. So, why did Uncle Captain bring them out here in the middle of the ocean? In spite of the potted palms on either side of the deck?

"Their last wish is to take one more cruise together," said Les. "Your uncle is fulfilling their request. Your uncle's a good guy. He spent a hatful sending them to Rochester, Houston, even Wiesbaden. Nobody knew what to do except say they were getting old."

---

and Les never left her side. Five nurses tore him away from her when she finally let go of his hand.

When Bud struggled to his feet and asked the Rabbi if he brought his meser, the Rabbi laughed politely and held Bud's arm to help him down the hatchway. Les later told Bud what the hell's up with you? You some kind of stinking Nazi?

Bud, real good at poker, twisted his head around and the defiant spittle flew when he said his grandparents never made it out of Warsaw.[46] Then, Bud turned to me and said I forgive your uncle for this "dreck," whatever that meant. Events in the night drove a stake into my heart by morning, but not deep enough, I guess, to make me decide on the right thing to do.

Around 2100, the soft breeze embraced the Tern and the sun set before us like an embroidered ruby red lampshade. Vinnie and I had the honor of pushing the dying bride and groom up to the stern. Les helped us lock them secure into the deck cleats. He pushed them back and forth. They weren't going anywhere with those wheelchairs locked in tight. I sneaked a quick pat on Mr. Shapiro's knee. He looked down at me through his mask and made a slight nod of his head and then put his hand on top of mine. He seemed like a real nice guy. Only then I noticed he wore a red carnation in his lapel and she wore a huge lavender orchid corsage Vin adjusted on

---

[46] For me to accept Will's recollection of this incident as based on more than Bud's BSing, I asked LaKeesha to track this down. She said there were several letters in shaky longhand in Bud's dresser drawer postmarked 1946 from one "Kryzewski" in Warsaw. She showed them to the elder Shill, who must have been so used to reading them, he didn't find it unusual for LaKeesha to show them to him. He admitted to her they changed the family name when they arrived at Ellis Island (he said he grabbed the name from a Shell Oil Tank across the Hudson). So, Bud's story is not throwaway dialogue by Will, and two months later, when LaKeesha went back for her pearl-handled penknife in Bud's bedroom in Monroeville, she felt a small lump in a sock with two gold wedding rings nestled in faded cotton. They were inscribed *"Danuta and Karel Kryzewski 1904 & Forever,"* as translated later by LaKeesha's boyfriend, Jerzy Joe Robinson, and confirmed by Bud's father in Youngstown as his Polish surname. LaKeesha said he broke down pretty badly when she handed them to him. Thus, Bud was not kidding. Sometimes, I've wondered whether Will made up these characters as he went along. That's why I was driven to confirm these recollections as factual, since I detest excrescent bullshit, especially in fiction. Plain straightforward bullshit is okay. Otherwise, Will's own existence would have been a total fabrication, except I knew he lived and I loved him like a brother, residing two doors away on James Street.

her white dress. We both said something like cleared for takeoff (I can't remember). We stepped back to join the others who milled around with wine glasses. Lou reached for a can of beer in the deck cooler. Paola said no, not for this one. She kept fidgeting with her hair in the wind. Captain wore some campaign ribbons on his white short-sleeve shirt, chatting it up with everyone. He spent a calm hour earlier chatting and showing me how to tie various knots more complicated than teasing out a calculus solution. Uncle walked over to Rabbi Milstein and the two embraced like old friends. "Moise, great to see you again. Thanks. Are you in fine fiddle this evening?"

The Rabbi gave a gentle push back and patted his expansive belly. "Sure, Robert, I can carry a tune and a weh at the same time. You name it. Let's get started."

For some reason, Uncle asked him if he brought along any stones for the ceremony, to which the rabbi peered around and responded, "Out here, Robert? A little bit too unorthodox for me."

"I understand. Well, anyway, you can rest your pipes this time," said Uncle. "Okay, Lou. The music," Uncle waved up to a head bobbing around the helm. In a moment so silent, I could have heard a safety pin drop on the water. I expected something like Mendelssohn's "Wedding March," which I first heard pounded out by Mrs. Bloomqvist on a battered Steinway upright back in fifth grade assemblies. A short ephemeral song blended with the soft breeze by a higher disk jockey flowed over and through us; cradled in the Tern, watching the silhouettes of Irv and Rose in their wheelchairs suffuse into the fading sunset. I stared so long at them, they almost disappeared right before my eyes until I refocused on the beer bottle Lou lifted to his lips. I sipped the Beaujolais from my glass and had an undying thirst for those things I had yet to discover. For the first time, I sensed time slipping away like sand through a four-year-old's expectant fingers.

"Like it? I picked it for Irv and Rose," whispered Uncle who moved over to me.

"I've never heard it before. What is it?"

"Don't they teach you kids anything anymore in college? It's "Morgen" by Dick Strauss. Morning to you."

"Off-Broadway?" I ventured.

Uncle nudged me with an elbow and said, Way way off. Sung before we were here and sung after we're long gone.

"Who's the singer?"

"You wouldn't know her. Frances Frauenheim, a soprano from McKeesport. Lovely lady."

Rabbi Moise stepped out of the stateroom to greet us as he walked up to the platform locking Irv and Rose to the Tern's deck. He tilted his head up, smiled and I could tell he liked Uncle's choice for the occasion.

Bud said when will this thing be over? Paola moved over and leaned on him and said why don't you try to listen for once?

"This is going too damned far, you know," said Bud. I think Paola said I do know, Mr. Shill. Be happy it's the last one, but I couldn't be certain as the breeze carried away her voice.

Rabbi Moise faced the Shapiros and performed a brief ceremony of which we only caught snatches. Bud, whom I suspected knew Yiddish, moved his head up and down now and then and left us to lean on the port gunwale. For a guy acting like a jerk lately, I could see the tip of a white handkerchief flutter in the breeze over his shoulder as he blew his nose.

By the time I finished the second glass of wine, the vows were renewed.

The ceremony ended with the sunset. Rabbi Milstein returned and said the renewlyweds desired to be left alone for a while.

"They can't show it, but I sense they're very happy it's all over," he said, shaking hands with us. I watched him circle an arm around Uncle's waist as they strolled off to the stateroom hatchway. Thirty minutes later, they came out. I leaned against the starboard gunwale, hearing and then watching the ChrisCraft from Hamilton finally appear aside the Tern. Uncle Rob gave him a hug and handed over the aluminum suitcase. I wondered what Vinnie would say if he saw the latest cache. I came out of the shadows and said, "Uncle Rob, what's with the luggage?"

Uncle must have known my presence, since he didn't act surprised. He smiled and made the click with the side of his mouth. "Will, son, look up there at Orion. Remember where I showed you to look?"

"Well, yeah," and I found it right away.

"What you think you saw back there with me and the rabbi is inconsequential compared to Orion, right lad?" He winked again and I got the message, eventhough I would have felt richer with the suitcase under my rack again.[47]

---

[47] Will left some notes regarding his efforts to ask Melville what happened to the million dollars. Events the next day overwhelmed further discussion. I dropped a dime and asked Cliff to fly across to follow-up on the suitcase full of shekels,

CHAPTER 11

After Uncle left, I saw Rabbi Milstein glance down at the ChrisCraft and plodding the deck with his arms folded across his chest and hands holding onto his triceps like a surgeon contemplating a patient. I came up to him and he said Good night, young Melville. I'm off with the nurse as soon as the boat is ready; so I won't see you in the morning. Good luck!

When I got back to my room, Vinnie was already asleep, probably from his three Beaujolais chasers tying a bow around an earlier six-pack. The Tern's screw mumbled again and I felt the urge to urinate. By now, I plain accepted this annoyance, anticipating the decoding of it's garbled message. This time, it said something to me about Uncle Rob, repeating over and over like a looping mantra *somethingbeautifulisgoingtohappensomethingbeautifulisgoingtohappen*. Some of Uncle's philosophy: something beautiful is going to happen.[48] I fluffed

---

since LaKeesha was laid up with a miscarriage. One afternoon he flagged down Rabbi Milstein waiting for the bus in front of his synagogue. He acknowledged nothing about his trip and denied he knew Melville. "The Tern? " he said. It's a migratory bird. I don't know any ship with that name. He tipped his hat and got on the bus. After the rabbi jumped on the bus, Cliff walked back across the avenue and stood there feeling like a dummkopf. Through the thick line of arborvitae, he saw where the million went: a huge bunker-like addition to the synagogue that nearly doubled its size.

[48] I knew Will well, or pretty much so. I always felt his writing was frankly atrocious and hackneyed. I used to check over his term papers in Freshman English. His professor condescended to change his grade to a very charitable "C" after Mrs. Melville called Dean Eggleston of the Lower School. During that last semester at Mundane when he flunked out, I wrote a nice concise response to a take-home

my pillow and succumbed to too much wine. Around three, I took a leak in the small toilet of the room and thought I heard a commotion on deck, but was too tired to care. The others could handle it and I rolled back into the rack. When Vinnie rudely pushed me awake around four, it seemed like ten minutes flew by.

"Will," he whispered out of breath into my ear, "they pushed them overboard for the hell of it. I can't believe it." Vin stumbled a few feet to the toilet and barfed up the shrimp cocktail he gorged on a few hours earlier on deck.

"What are you talking about, man? Are you listening to the screw, too?"

Vince's face glowed red as a beet and he cried for the first time in all the sixteen years we knew each other.[49]

---

final to the question: How would you describe the impact of *Moby Dick* on American literature? (I still find it ironic this novel keeps popping up in Will's notes, although it does have a sort of whimsical connotation considering his surname.) Will came back from the final class saying he forgot to take my crib notes. I asked him if he remembered them and he said (he seemed beat) he put down "It was a whale of a tale." I told him you dumb shit; you're not supposed to cut to the chase with blue books. He got a "D" in the class only because the final was graded by a laid-back, Ls.D candidate when Professor Askew was dismissed for standing stark naked in the Quad that morning holding a homemade sign proclaiming, "Peace in Our Time." You'd have thought Will was more interested in the novel, especially since his surname was, by coincidence, Melville.

[49] This is not true. Vinnie's mother, Mrs. Pugliese, was gracious enough to show me a clipping from the *Tri-River Advertiser* announcing the death of Vin's father. She said she distinctly remembered Will going with Vinnie and his father to a Pirates game in September about two or three years earlier. The Pirates cleanup batter hit one out of the park and the old man and Vin hugged. His dad, a tough, lovable foreman from Saginaw, squeezed all the peanuts out of the bag and slumped to his seat out of Vin's arms and died of a massive heart attack before the runner tipped his hat rounding third base. She said Will told her the medic made a side comment that Vin better not hit one of his own out of the park, since Vin was crying like a baby and so distraught, and so gave Vin a sedative. She offered me a Rolling Rock and I said No thanks. Then she rearranged the alphabet magnets on the refrigerator door and insisted Will was there that night, as she showed me the three free Bethlehem Steel aluminum frisbees they gave away every other Thursday in September.

"Calm down, Vin. Take it easy. People are sleeping."

"The hell they are." He wiped his face with the end of my bedsheet. He gulped air to speak and coughed it up with spittled words to explain he stepped topside for fresh air and got confused as all hell to see Lou and Bud bending down. He heard the metallic clicks to the locks attached to the deck cleats. Bud seemed to cross himself from the cradling movement of his right arm. Lou mumbled something like let's get her done and then they pushed the Shapiros overboard, wheelchairs and all like garbage over the fantail. Not a sound when they hit the water. Paola held the old lady's pink scarf in her hand. Les and your Uncle stood by and didn't do a thing. Then I turned and fell down the ladder. I needed to vomit.

Vin began bawling and coughing again, and I put my arm around him close and rocked him like he was a small kid brother with pertussis.

I told him stay in the room while I see what's going on. He said okay, but I'm packing my bag right now and getting off this thing if I have to swim to town I can't take any more.

"Don't do anything stupid, Vin," I said.

"Okay. Come right back."

Vinnie never lied. For sure, we did some stupid things growing up sloughing off millions of skin cells to the point where our parents sometimes wondered if we'd molt into little monsters; but he never lied much. Maybe about little things like the time we got twenty dollars from the Halal store manager, Hakim Elohssa (phonetic spelling), for dumping a thousand of his fliers in a trash container behind the Irish House at 13th and Madison instead of stuffing them in mailboxes in the projects. I couldn't, but Vinnie told him yeah, we delivered them. Hakim drove off after calling us two little infidel bastards. Or when he hot-wired old man Burdahl's new yellow Kaiser-Fraser convertible and drove it to Zelienople and back. He said his old man's good arm got tired strapping him and boasted to me how he didn't bear witness against himself—tell the truth. Anyway, I felt responsible for him. Vinnie whimpered now and I stepped up the ladder to shed some light on his scoop. On deck, a heavy blanket of fog settled on our anchorage in the bay; so thick I thought those shapes were the ghosts of the ghosts of things past (or might have been) or the ghosts of the ghosts of things to be (or would have been). I groped my way to the foredeck and the wheelchairs. Gone! Both of them. A chill raced down my spine as the truth stripped right before my unbelieving eyes. I thought about the deck chairs on old pictures of the Lusitania, with no time to rearrange them in my mind when the impact of Vinnie's scoop sank in.

I found Paola gliding like a sleepwalker with outstretched arms. She leaned on a crate I never saw before, jotting notes on a yellow legal pad.

"Hi! Paola."

"*Cruglothcreeblekur.*" Once again, she spoke in tongues well beyond the babble I passed on Saturday nights at the fundamentally Baptist Mount Carmel Church around the corner from Mom's house.

"Where's the Shapiro's?

"They're gone."

"Well, what happened?" I touched her shoulder, because she gazed at the fog for the next string of gutteral nonsense from some ancient unmarked cave in the Caucasus.

"*Flakcrotlikdup.*"

When I cupped her other shoulder with my hand—I always wanted to cup one of those beautiful melons she carried with such erect, unabashed majesty—she came back for a second to the Tern. "Keep you hands off me, hear?"

Her dark eyes pierced the dense fog, her nostrils flared out and she appeared more beautiful than ever. I said sorry and drifted back into obscurity probably like dozens of men who washed ashore trying to grasp her golden bollards. I also spotted the end of a pink chiffon scarf peeking out of her pocket and asked myself what on earth is she doing with Rose's scarf?

I passed the vacant platform again feeling helpless and remorseful for things I should have been able to change. Now, the Shapiros meant more to me than when they were alive, and like my father, I didn't even know them.

Bud, slumped in a corner like a boulder, shuffled a deck of cards and glanced at my shoes. He said a boat came alongside after midnight and took the two ashore for the trip back to Alice Detwiler.

"Branches chase shadows little birds leave in Winter's tree."

"What? What the devil are you mumbling?" I said.

"It's difficult to wait for no one coming."[50]

---

[50] Here again, I have serious doubts Will actually recorded this from Bud Shill. Up to now, I have been letting Will get away with lead-footing a lot of stuff without any sense of literary license. Perhaps he felt the need to put in stuff that either didn't happen or wasn't said or happened in a nightmare. Yet, why would Will exaggerate like this? I didn't know Bud beyond the intel I got from Cliff

Such gibberish caused me to wonder if he was in the chorus I kept hearing at night from the Tern's screw.

Bud flicked a cold saurian stare at me and said why don't you take a long walk off a short pier, which indicated to me he was much older than I thought. I observed his frustration as he tried adding a sixth floor to his house of cards on the pitching deck, a frustration reminding me of my investigation of a fire outside Kansas City during my stint with Valparaiso Casualty. The regional office told me it's somewhere near Central, five miles southeast of West Cloverdale in northern Missouri about two miles southwest of the eastern ephemeral branch of the lower Northeast River, but they advised me to wait until it rained. Bud shifted his cheeks and from a back pocket tossed aside a small crescent wrench, the type used to tighten the wheelchairs to the deck cleats the four days earler. The adrenalin now forced sweat on my forehead, palms and armpits; getting jerked around the same way when I got off the bus. I was amazed at my growing willingness to suspend disbelief to believe two and two might make five on some other plane of existence.

I backed away from Bud's house of cards and suddenly Les tapped my shoulder for attention.

"What the hell is going on, Les? Why am I getting jerked around like this?"

"Hello, Will. I feel terrible about this. I got up myself and called the harbor police to check out what could have happened?" Les seemed genuinely concerned and surprised about the incident, which could have

---

or LaKeesha. I don't think this dialogue suited Bud's character. He appeared to be someone more interested in *Popular Alchemy* or *Financial Times*, the latter of which he often borrowed from Les Vice and never returned. I let it stand, this unattributed Haiku to Tsu Shi (1375-1399?), a 14th century Peking court poet. Perhaps Bud's memory of his grandparents in Poland must be the origins of his non-Haiku ad-lib ("It's difficult to wait for no one coming"). Or maybe his girlfriend, Bonnie DeLuna, whose groceries he normally carried, was thrown 150 feet by a sliding salt truck when she stepped off a curb at Kenwood and Splatt near the Valley Building on the Iowa campus in December 1951. She was cremated before Bud chanced to say goodbye to her corpse. LaKeesha sent me a copy of a letter where Bud wrote, "I was so mad at her parents, I spit in the wind and let the others distribute her ashes on her beloved Lake Conneaut back home."

been treated as anything from an accident to assisted suicide to Do Not Resuscitate to the commission of murder. Simply maddening.

Maybe Vinnie was right to jump ship. If they were up to this game, were we next?

Les shook his head as his hands fumbled with the braces unscrewed from the deck cleats. "This is not good," he said.

"You're damn straight it's no good, Les," I shouted. "Even the deck chairs are gone."

"Now, Will Melville," came over the bullhorn from Uncle Rob in the wheelhouse. "No swearing. I promised your mother."

"Well, then, Uncle Rob. What the hell is going on here?" I tried to wipe the sweat off my palms on a pink bath towel with "Monaco Hilton" in gold lettering.

"Better," he said. "I'm coming right down."

Les, whom I speculated all along preferred to work both ends of the bell curve, walked back over to me and intoned, well the Shapiros are either back at Alice Detwiler having their nails trimmed, or 1200 feet below skipping out on Sunday brunch. In either case, they're no longer suffering, lad.

"What?"

"Please don't raise your voice," said Les. He put a finger to his lips to remind me Irv and Rose slept somewhere else now.

With no warning like a shockwave, labelled Extremely Urgent! All Aboard! here comes Vinnie rushing up to me with Lou limping right behind. Lou was bent over, revealing scoliosis cloaked under his Carmel Inn nightshirt. I didn't notice until now why he took such shallow breaths.

"Will, look! I found this in the trashcan downstairs," said Vin. His hands shook so hard he dropped the syringe onto the deck.

"It belongs to me. Give it back now," shouted Lou.

"I'm telling you, Will, they used this to bump them off."

Clumsy, but it started falling into place amid this persistent, pervasive rumbling in the background which started bothering the devil out of me. The scarf in Paola's pocket; Bud's wrench; Les's flippant regard for the Shapiros; and now probably a syringe of morphine or some other poison to finish them off. I put my hands over my ears. The syringe broke when Vinnie lost a grip on his emotions.

Lou appeared to cry as he bent down to put the pieces in a crumpled handkerchief. "Thanks a helluva lot, you worthless little draft dodger. My reserve insulin is gone. I've got one more left, punk."

Uncle Rob lumbered onstage with bullhorn in hand, ordering everyone to calm down and take a seat around the large brushed aluminum table near the foredeck. He came over to me and put a hand on my shoulder, which I instinctively tried to shrug off. He surely was the devious mastermind behind this bad dream, and I maintained so much faith in him as the closest thing to a father. I shook my head again while Paola and the others grumbled in low voices about how best to divvy up the guilt. They lay their tricycle playing cards on the deck of the Tern, freely admitting complicity.

Uncle, whose voice in this seance spanned an eerie range from Russian basso to a cloistered castrati, said son, no you don't want to go there. He tried to shake some sense into me.[51]

"Then wake me up when it's over," I complained.

"There's no waking up, son. This is the dream. Escaping with the Tern." Then Uncle declared, "Attention everyone." He threw the bullhorn onto a deck chair. "Before this fog clears up and reveals what some may see as a nasty affair, let me explain what expired and what transpired.

---

[51] I mentioned at the outset that this was a labor of love and hate. This is one part I hate, since Will's imagination, I think, got the better of him. It's frankly downright impossible for anyone in their right mind to recollect such details in a dream. Let's say I rued my own regression to adolescence. At first, I about laughed my ass off going over this so-called dream sequence of Will's, until I could see it might have some latent literary value to show his overall fragile emotional state. And the amateurish way he described it might even lend some veracity to his story in the same tenor as the bigger the lie, the more believable. Look, he wrote it down, so who am I to delete, cross-examine or psychoanalyze? If it were not for Mrs. Melville pleading once more to let it stay in for Will's sake, and for the fact the Shapiros were real people, I would have deleted the whole episode of the Shapiros. My research (interview with Rachel Coburn, Head of Nursing, Alice Detwiler) showed the Shapiros never left Alice Detwiler until they were carried out three months later in a double-wide rosewood casket to accommodate their hands, which they no doubt are holding together to this day somewhere beyond their gravesite outside Coral Gables. Then again, maybe Ms. Coburn was instructed to tell me a baldfaced lie, particularly since she offered to provide a skilled nurse to escort me to a local nightclub the next night.

Vinnie whispered to me he's a real screwball, Will. You've got to wake up, man, and get the you-know-what out of here before it's too late.

"Will, son; you and Vinnie calm down now," said Uncle raising his hands up like Father McCaughey at Sunday mass. "You, Paola, Bud, Les and Lou, and particularly yours truly, could have done a smoother job this time. Nevertheless, we can be gratified to know we did the right, the moral, the humane thing to do. Number 63 in the books, right Les?"

"I quit," yelled Vinnie. He stumbled out of his chair and ran to the gunwale and turned around to say I'm getting off. Bud, whose hands were folded together, waiting for handcuffs, stared up and said hey there's better ways to get off. There's the ladder. Vinnie jumped ship. I heard the splash, even over this awful incessant background noise rumbling in my ears. Uncle remained blase and asked Lou to go toss Vin a doughnut and, if needed, jump through the doughnut where the hole used to be and rescue him.[52]

Paola said, "Did you say Lou, Captain? Are you sure?"

Uncle Rob tipped his cap at her and said "Lou be Lou," to which she shut her notebook with a slap, probably taking his response as a dig to try to add language to her growing lexicon of primordial speech patterns.

"Will, son. Dr. And Mrs. Shapiro wanted to be buried at sea. The sea they loved and cherished their entire lives together. Ther was even an Olympic-size pool behind their double-wide trailer in Coral Gables. They met on St. Kitts and through fifty one years of relaxing in front of the Royal Hawaiian or Hotel Proboscus in Madagascar, it all came down to these last few precious days to spend with you, as Walter used to sing."

"Walter who? You're confusing me. What are you getting at, Uncle?" My anger ebbed as I absorbed each word.

Uncle pulled out a letter from his crisp white shirt pocket and unfolded it with care. "This letter I've been keeping for this occasion. It explains

---

52   It seems a stretch for Lou, a minnow at four feet nine to rescue Vince, a young walrus at six feet two and a seventeen-inch neck size. I didn't edit this out after receiving from Red Flange, the respected Ohio Valley sportswriter, a page torn out of the *Dayton Solicitor* that one Louis B. Louis won the 1950 Big Ten three-meter high dive at Bloomington, where he was listed as a swimmer at IU eventhough he still attended Pitt. He was four feet seven and ninety-eight pounds then. The scorers said they never saw a ripple when Lou entered the water. He was so slight, one bespectacled poolside panelist mildly protested in the third round she could not see him break the surface after they announced his name over the loudspeaker.

everything. "The Shapiros express their desire to hold hands and leave this earth together looking at a glorious sunset from the Tern.' My yacht. Your grandfather's yacht. I and my devoted partners in mercy felt and still fell deeply honored and uplifted to have fulfilled their final wishes, the AMA, ASPCA, DOJ and the *National Accuser* rag be damned. Look at this."

Uncle reached across the table and showed me the letter.

"It's blank. I don't see a damn word."

"Watch your words, son. I promised your mother." He said lift the letter to the cabin floodlight bathing the deck in an eerie glow. "It's invisible ink, son. Look at the bottom. All the signatures are there. Ben and Sally, their kids—both physicians by the way—witnessed it. Do you see the stamp from the notary at Alice Detwiler?"

"Yeah. I see it now. Okay, but it still doesn't make it right. Can you do something about this incessant noise. It's driving me nuts."

Les, next to me, bumped me with an elbow and said we're all cognizant of it.

Naive enough to think this escape routine was a snap, I began to cry. I don't know why. I couldn't run up to my bedroom or kick the kitchen screendoor open and sit on the back steps. I think Paola tossed a pink handkerchief across from her seat. What kind of world forced me to abandon Mom, my house, my comics? Afraid, I remained as yet unformed, uninformed, out of uniform and emotionally deformed by this godforsaken boat trip on the Tern, with its damn screw turning over and over and whispering and whining incessant babble. I should turn myself in for induction and take my chances.

"You're going to be okay, kid," said Bud who got to the seventh floor before the cards collapsed.

Paola looked at me through an alluring thicket of mascara and hummed a low lilting ohm glissando in a Himalayan monk key; the first sound I really understood from her.

Uncle Rob sat down across from me. He reached over and put a hand on my forearm and said do you want to go back? Are you with us? My head bobbled on a gimbel of doubt like when I babysat our old neighbor Denny Albertini's two-year old son trying to fall asleep.

"Okay, son. You can stay in the gray area. Most of us hang out there anyway, except for situations like this where we help each other to help in some small way people like Irv and Rose to be together for as long as they choose. Now, go on back and get some rest."

CHAPTER 12

"Will! Will! Get up! What the hell is wrong?" Vinnie's voice and pulling my arms dragged me out of the worst nightmare I ever lived through.

"You were moaning all night," he said standing over my slumped body on the edge of the rack. "You okay?"

"Yeah, yeah."

"You're shaking like a leaf. Man, you must have had some crazy-ass nightmare."

I lied and said no, but it was weird-ass. He gave me a glass of Vogelsang mineral water and I told him the screw noise pestered me and next thing I knew I dreamed the Shapiros were dumped overboard last night and Vin jumped ship.

"Man, you must have drunk way too much," he said grabbing onto the end of the rack.

"And you came tumbling down the ladder scared and woke me up."

Vinnie bent down to empty his locker. "Sounds more like an LSD trip. Remember Joey what's his name tripping out on the stuff at Linda O'Leary's party?"

"Yeah."

"He was wasted when the ambulance came. I felt really bad for Linda. Whatever happened to him anyway? And Linda?"

"Where are the Shapiros?" I asked.

Vinnie, real good at multi-tasking, tied his shoelaces and stuffed his backpack while telling me he went topside and saw everyone helping them get ready to lower them off the Tern onto a small boat bumpered alongside after midnight. They offered me a couple of Singapore slings, which I downed without a shout. Man, those Filipinos know how to make a good mixed drink, and then I called it a night. Dead tired all of a sudden."

"What did you see, I mean?"

"What are you talking about? I glanced back and they took their time loosening the locks to their wheelchairs. I guess they put the two old lovebirds in position to go over the side. I came back here and hit the sack. Everyone patted me on the back—even the rabbi—and said nighty night."

"Was that it? Did you actually see them get in the boat?"

"Well, yeah. I assumed that's what happened. Look, I felt tired as hell. What's with you?"

I pushed my fingers through my thick black mop of hair and said where was I? Vinnie zipped up his pack and said what do you mean? You zonked out in your rack. Hell, I was out cold myself. I even stepped on your arm hanging out here and you didn't say a peep. My arm bore the faint imprint of Vin's Wild Boar running shoes made in China for the Nairobi affiliate of Swinehart Shoes near Natick. I knew this because I bought a pair with Vinnie at the Roadrunner store in Windsor three summers ago.

"Anything else?" he said, drumming his fingers on his pack with impatience.

"Oh my aching head. Okay. Okay." I tried to go over more details, but as I breathed in the salt air deeply and wondered about the upcoming Mundane football schedule while I tried to pee in the toilet, those details faded from my conscious effort to hunt them down like a honeybadger with a flamethrower, as if a honeybadger needed one.[53]

"Then they're okay. The Shapiros?"

"I guess so, for the third time. What about it? They're gone! Outta' here!" said Vin. "I'm pretty sure I heard the yacht push off and putt-putt away. You know you should change rooms if the damn screw makes such an awful racket at night."

"And you didn't jump ship and Lou didn't jump in after you?"

"Hell no! Are you all right?"

"What? I'm okay. Forget it."[54]

---

[53] Once again, I caved to Mrs. Melville on this one. Very hackneyed, yet with a charming sort of straining to express something none of us would take the time to think about. Fortunately, before she could see it, I cut for abcess Will's "...I didn't relish the thought of being in a pickle."

[54] At this point, there was absolutely no evidence of foul play. Yet, it is puzzling how the two draft dodgers were the only ones who turned in. I mean, this dream

Vin sort of certified for me his engineering diploma when he said it's a mystery how the screw can make such a racket when the Tern isn't even underway.

"Maybe it's some extraneous movement in the shaft," I said, "like creaking floorboards in an old house. Uncle Rob told me once of Captain Billy, my granddad, salvaging the screw off an old schooner or slave transport around Santo Domingo."

Vinnie teased me. "It must be the slaves making a commotion in the cargo hold—not the screw—and if you believe that, you're crazier than Uncle what's-his-name."

"Okay, Vin. You don't have to get personal about it."

"Whatever." Vinnie cleared his throat. "You know, Will, I told you about splitting the scene. Your Uncle and me don't quite make good shipmates."

"You can't get off here in Bermuda. They'll hand your ass over in a heartbeat."

Vinnie put the backpack back in the locker and snapped the combo lock shut. He said he'd already told Uncle yesterday was fun, but needed to get on with his plan to flee the country for an extended holiday at a youth hostel outside Copenhagen. "Anyway, I feel like an outcast; a college grad without a country. I'm totally isolated with these creeps and your old man—sorry; your uncle.

I asked how Uncle took it. Vin said he was sorry to see me go so soon and would drop me off when we hit port.

"He told me I would have made a good shipmate. It made me feel good; you know, the captain addressing me on equal footing and so on."

---

he recounted is, in fact, bothersome. Out of the ten plastic trashbags sent to me by Cliff and his daughter-in-law, Naomi, I could find nothing more than a throwaway phrase so common in everyday usage, like "well done" or "no one will ever know" or "good deed" or "I grabbed her scarf before the wind blew it away" or "over we go" or "they went over the side nicely." Bud said not a ripple relevant to any foul play on the Tern, and Lou didn't seem to give a rip at all. Cliff discovered several letters Melville wrote to Les when Les got back to Scottsdale, but there was nothing more than the hackneyed "something beautiful, etc." that Melville constantly fell back on. Captain Billy may have been a wayward character, but his surviving decorated son, Robert, was straight as an arrow in spite of his accumulated wealth and yen for excitement. But when I revised the rough draft, I found out something closer to the truth.

"So, you really are jumping ship."

"I guess you can call it whatever. You know, we've already left the US of A in mind, if not in body. I'll be doing this for a while, huh?"

"Ugh!" as Miss Paleo-Tosti would say," I added. We laughed it off. It was the last time we laughed together.

Late morning, when the sun burned off any evidence of the previous night of drinking, the crew unravelled the overhead canvas of the portside deck and fastened it down to secure the shuffleboard layout. Lou turned up the loudspeaker when the National Whether Service reported another tropical depression coming off the West African coast. The light breakfast of orange juice, hash browns, eggs and bacon, pancakes and strawberries and whipped cream and coffee mocha drove off any recollection of the miserable nightmare which I so inadequately related to Vince. Lou sat across from me with even more on his plate.

"Have you tried Chef Felipe's Eggs Benedict?" he asked.

"No. Is there still some?" I said.

A familiar smirk started in a corner of Lou's leprechaun mouth, blossoming into two cherubic dimples, but I knew to expect almost anything from him. He reminded me of a small alabastard angel on Mom's fireplace mantel. She loved it in spite of the glued broken wings from falling so much. I think he resented me looking down at him when we spoke. "Look, I haven't touched this half of mine," and he proceeded to pour on the Worcestershire sauce until it bled all over the place.

"What the heck are you doing, Lou?" The little bantamweight measured me for a sucker punch line.

Lou wagged his head sideways, shoved the mess over to me, got up and said this is actually Eggs Benedict Arnold. Get it, kid? He pounded the table with his diminutive fists and scrambled out of the room remarkably well for having no marionette strings.

"What did I do to deserve this? The little son of a bitch." I left the table shaking my head, debating if the nightmares turned by the screw were better than getting screwed daily by the Tern's crew.

An hour later, Lou came by and apologized for implying I was a traitor. "I guess I was a little heavy on the sauce, huh?"

"It's okay, Lou." We bobbed heads agreeably and he waddled off with the periodic anal itch he couldn't quite reach. I could have said there was no real cause for me to belittle you, Lou, but I thought it would only inflame his whole situation.

After late lunch and a few beers, everyone flopped around the deck like gaffed tuna, reading or watching the SS Annabelle cruise ship inch her way across the horizon toward San Marcos. They needed a foursome for shuffleboard. I grabbed a stick after Paola prodded me in her palpitating pink pedalpushers. Les and Bud were serious players. When I wisecracked how they qualified for the Tampa-St. Pete World Seniors, they got miffed and chewed on it until the next set when Bud said something that caused me to double over in near gut-wrenching pain.

"Hey, Les," shouted Bud. "Did you find my three-eighths crescent wrench? You know the one?"

"No. Maybe it fell overboard when..."

"Oh yeah," interrupted Bud.

They kept playing as if it meant nothing. I leaned off to the side on my stick in a swelter of mental anguish, jerked around once again; an insidious game with real pawns like Vin and me and strategies for sacrificing us next? Mental bootcamp? Two drill sergeants the likes of which I tried to avoid in evading the draft.[55]

Uncle Rob was in his quarters, as usual, on his high-tech radiotelephone. Years ago, one of his eardrums was perforated from the practice round of a deck gun. The volume pegged. He talked numbers and dates and other cryptic stuff. Nobody paid any attention to it. The other day, I put an ear to the bulkhead and he talked with someone in Buenos Aires, then Beruit, then south Miami all in half an hour. It was much clearer than listening to the Tern's screw. He never hinted he spoke some Spanish, Italian, some Arabic, and I didn't feel it my place to be nosy. After all, I was a stowaway,

---

[55] I asked Penny to track down Will's ROTC instructor at Mundane to shed some light on his apprehension about military service. Sgt. Glen (Hooah) Fodder told her Will was an outstanding and enthusiastic student who clearly showed the potential for a successful military career. Oscifer Candidate School material; however, he lost his way after Hooah invited a returning Mundane grad to give a motivational speech to the class. Sgt. Fitch was around Saigon and spoke rather eloquently about the field of conflict. Ten minutes into his presentation, Will already qualified for the so-called 1000-yard stare as his eyes moved from the 23-year old speaker's Distinguished Service Cross to where his left arm and then his right leg should have been. That's about when Will began his academic death march. I imagine, he must have felt helplessly inadequate staring at someone his age physically impaired yet having the mental courage to move on. Sgt. Fodder told her the scene must have turned Will toward those "campus radical nerds."

not a front-line reporter. I think he appreciated that I never asked him; a dutiful son discovering a pack of Trojans in dad's trousers while watching him from a bedroom window as mother stuffs a sandwich and cookies in his black valise and kisses him on the doorstep. He was entitled to the benefit of the doubt.

"Hey Will, son," he called as I passed his cabin. He wore his uniform of the day: a sort of toy captain's hat; white khaki shorts, white sneakers with no socks and a white teeshirt. He came up and gave me a quick hug. It was Old Spice today. This teeshirt read Ristorante Mirabelle-Marseilles across the back.

"Sleep well?"

"I guess so, Uncle. It was a horrible nightmare. Forgot most of it."

"Darn screw again, huh? You're not the first one who's complained over the years."

"Really?"

His eyes wandered out to the horizon. "I should have changed your room before now. Should have changed it a long time ago." He chuckled, pulled on his cap bill. "Probably worse than diarrhea on the cruise ship over there. See it?" He pointed toward the horizon. "It's the Annabelle's sister ship. After a week, the guests start flushing more than their wallets down the toilet."

"Well, the Tern's got diarrhea of the mouth," I said. We laughed our way through a few dozen waves, watching the hump of a whale engage us at about 500 yards.

"Shoo! Shoo!" said Uncle, smiling with a casual flail of his hand.

He told me I missed a great sendoff for the Shapiros. Close friends for many years. Was Ben Shapiro's godfather.

"You know, Will, I deal in a lot of stuff. I think I can talk freely to you about it. I've made a bundle and lost a bundle since I retired from the service back in '48. Over fifteen years already." He lifted his cap and scratched his head.

We leaned our forearms on the aft teak rail for support. I watched his eyes scan the water up and down, across, up and down and across for the next thought, word or deal.

"I'm most proud of the place I showed you last week. You know, Alice Detwiler. I guess you've already figured out it's for the terminally ill."

"Right. Too bad."

"And once in a while I take them on a cruise like Irv and Rose to try to forget the pain; the waiting." He asked if I knew who was Alice Detwiler.

"Don't have the foggiest."

He saw Les and shouted, Les I thought you told him about Alice Detwiler.

"You're the one who should tell the lad," shouted back Les, under an awning punching on an adding machines with the eraser tip of a pencil.

"Alice D. was my first wife. What a trooper." He lifted his head up into the soft breeze. "She was three months' pregnant with our first child when they diagnosed her in Houston with spinal cancer. Couldn't do a thing. I took her home." He lifted his head up again into the sunshine. "It was the only time I ever prayed, including in the service. Every night. On the last night, they told me I had to get out of her bed and I told them come back later. I lost both around midnight the same date Jesus was born; December 24th. Doesn't it beat all hell? I've never gone back to church."

"I'm sorry, Uncle."

"It's all right, son."

"It's a beautiful place."

"I'd like to think so. Alice was the first one I built when I started making some dough. Next year, we're putting up a new hospital down the road from Columbia."

"Can I see it?"

"You bet. I'm going to name it after our son. Kyle. I've already designed an alcove where the chapel will be. I think you'll like it. The Kyle Melville Memorial Nursing Home."

"I'm sure I will, Uncle."

He winked at something out on the water and smiled. "Let's walk."

I asked him how the Shapiros liked the send-off. He turned and bracketed my face for some indication of foreknowledge on my part. It made me feel uneasy, like I was in a war movie and he was a Gestapo urologist. Much worse than the anesthetist probing my neck to give me a nerve block for rotator cuff surgery on my throwing arm in freshman year.

"We gave them a great send-off. I gave Irv a hug and kissed Rose on the cheek. She closed her eyes and Irv gave a small nod of his head. They were ready to go." Uncle clasped his hands together. "Then we dropped them over the side and down they went like a rock."

"You mean into the boat alongside."

"Ah, yeah. The ChrisCraft."

It got so quiet, I could hear Lou humming way up in the wheelhouse. Uncle Rob sucked in his breath.

I breathed a long sigh of relief. The damn screw broadcasted a narrative as harmless as "Sure. They departed along with the rabbi." He winked at me and said didn't the screw tell you this? He strained and brought forth an unfamiliar nervous choppy chuckle. "What a little dream that boat is. Bigger than you think. Fourteen-carat gold-plated faucets. My friend Cy Bellows in Galveston owns it."

the obscure and irrelevant play-by-play banter of the Tigers losing 10-0 in the bottom of the ninth. "Then it was all a nightmare after all."

"Of course. I thought your buddy, Vincent, filled you in. He popped up here after midnight."

"Right."

"Everything okay then, son?"

"Sure. I'm fine."

"Good. Say, I've got to take a leak. I'll be back."[56] [57] Uncle looked back

---

[56] Will's self-doubt about this weird dream still baffled me. He didn't realize what he dreamed is actually what might have transpired, or expired, regarding the Shapiros. The reader has to remember that these recollections I've tried to make sense of happened about seven years ago (1967) and I have endeavored to edit his story to ensure it rings true and yields the veracity we expect from someone struggling with plot, characters, syntax and the rest of that stuff. Not totally satisfied with the trashbags Dinwiddie and Naomi sent me, I asked LaKeesha what she could do for me. She said she was back on food stamps and suffered another miscarriage and referred me to her two cousins, Big Clarisse and Little Clarisse, the Johnson twins, who lived near Hamtramck. Through their more aggressive double-down search for the truth at $15/hour plus Greyhound tickets, they trashed Bud's apartment in Monroeville while he tooled down to Greensburg for a few hours. Bud always seemed to leave notes on his fridge on his daily whereabouts. I felt Bud, ever the cardshark cynic, to be the best source for checking out Will's nightmare, because I found it simply implausible a yacht screw could be the source of such a fabrication (a real screw job!); especially the stuff about the Tern's moral burden as a slave transport. It's a real stretch, but more on this later. There was one letter Bud addressed to Lou, but the post office returned it for insufficient postage. Here are Bud's exact words: "...those poor young guys were clueless to what the hell they got into. Melville has set us up pretty well moneywise for what we do for him, but I think he's a real jerk for trying to shanghai his "son" into the business...although I thought he genuinely liked the kid." And here: "...I told you to throw the damn syringe overboard. I certainly didn't think that crap about your faking diabetes would fly. The old man raised hell with me when he said his nephew asked him later about a syringe and if you were a Type One. And then I let slip that stuff about my crescent wrench. I thought for sure the kid would go medieval and do something like turn us all in. What a cluster fuster the trip was. Damn poor planning by Melville. You do know, my little friend, all our asses could have been up the river in Seven Feathers making vanity license plates for forty years. Thank the good Lord you found those knockout drops none too soon. By the way, I'm coming in to Monterey on the 12th on flight 9693. Paola is taking a later flight and will call you. Later, satyr." Frankly, if Shelley were my fellow straphanger, I'd say Percy pal, if there's any beauty or truth to this tale, let's wrap it in as much tinsel and twine as possible and tell the customers that's all they need to know. If it's an empty box, at least they'll enjoy the dust cover. And that's a fact.

[57] A few months ago, in researching the absurd plausibility of a "talking" screw that Will complained and wrote about so much, I flew into National and was greeted by an old Groton friend of Melville's, Armand Z. LePage, who subbed with him on the Tilapia in the Pacific. He got picked up by the Naval Hydrophobic Research Group in—of all places—Rock Springs, the most convenient site for a row of quonset huts to perform their work at Crater Lake. We chatted over lunch at Vollbangers on Connecticut Avenue and drove out to the pool adjacent to Log Cabin on the Potomac. Armand went on to a Ph.D in acoustics at Penn State when he retired from the Navy and worked for Armstrong designing ceiling tile perforation patterns overtime to help pay for child support. He said he left after six months, because he could hear his ex-wives voices (soloists and chorus) in the anechoic chamber; and I thought to myself: damn! Armand, you must have been really screwed up. I took particular note of this, since Armand inadvertently mentioned his personal annoyance at several legal screw jobs. After a while, I told him I'd seen enough water and sine waves and asked him about the acoustical

over his shoulder at me as he turned the corner. I wasn't going to follow him, if it's what he thought. Later, I asked him if Lou was a diabetic, and he said yeah he takes his pills. He's a type two. He pops pills. And I was essentially relieved the dream was not the horrific reality. And it sank in. Whatever Uncle Rob and his nefarious crew was up to, they were in the end moral and purer of heart than I thought, with a great sense of mission—something I should have demonstrated to stay in school.

Uncle asked me to come to the stateroom later in the evening. He played a tape recording of Debussy, whose music I never cared for. Too quiet. I preferred rock and roll and he said okay, but you can't brood over such fretful noise. Lou, Les, Bud and Paola sat around the dark mahogany table listening to the Debussy the same way I imagine one would watch the blur of elm trees from the smudged window of an express bus trundling to work: Lou was reading *George A. Custer, Last Man Kneeling*, by Paul

---

anomalies from a ship's screw. He peered over his trifocals and said you've come to the right space. We walked down the central corridor and took a left into a secure area with cobwebs overhead and a broken bicycle lock dangling on a rusty hasp. He perused several dusty tomes and explained that depending on the wear and tear of the bearings, the shaft alignment, collisions and even the cavitation signature of the screw itself, the transmission of extraneous and aberrant noise, as populated by white and colored spikes displayed on a CRT, was well-known to the naval community. Armand mentioned several notable incidents reaching captain's mast where background "chatter," as he called it, was so distracting, the captain or executive officer would actually pull general quarters when the vessel was in port. In Olongapo, one captain got it so bad, he was observed in his skivvies on the quarterdeck ordering all 325 crewmembers be rounded up from the beverage establishments barely a bottle-throw from the ship. I interrupted to ask if that wouldn't have been a false positive, since the screw was not actually turning over in port, and he replied with a numbling deadpan stare that you don't know the kind of stuff they drank over there. Then, as an apertif, he raised his eyebrows and said, "Hmmm." He pulled from a dusty shelf of fugitive pigeon feathers a folder labelled "Top Secret Kahlua—NHRC" and read verbatim several passages about personnel who experienced hallucinatory dialogues, unrelated to alcoholism, with ship turbines, propellers and drive shafts. He was so enthused to convince me, he handed me the folder, but then quickly grabbed it back and rambled on about how whales are known to "talk" over thousands of miles of ocean by extremely low frequencies. I appreciated the way Dr. LePage watered down the technical aspects of this phenomenon. I looked at my watch and chanced to summarize the visit in Armand's casual manner by saying, you mean to say Will Melville was screwed and shafted on the Tern? But he went, so to speak, full astern on me, and didn't seem to appreciate my remark very much and soon graciously escorted me to the gate. Professor LePage convinced me Melville's experience was not far-fetched and at least a somewhat reasonable experience for a landlubber like Will, who heard only the white noise from a window fan or A/C unit, or—I suggested—the insignificant banter of a Tiger's play-by-play. Armand peered over his trifocals and said, "Hold on there. You a Tigers fan, too?"

Calloway. It was on the *Midwest Editor* best-seller list for ten months. I skimmed through a vandalized copy at a bookstore in Apache Junction while investigating a claim for Valparaiso the first time I flunked out only because Custer came from Monroe and I sometimes passed his former home on the way to get Mom's pills at Knewticals Pharmacy. Les was at the end of the table with an adding machine practicing his ledgerdemain, juggling the books. Bud played blackjack with his worn deck of cards, carrying on a low conversation with an imaginary dealer. Paola asked me if I wanted to learn how to translate her pre-history dialect (she called it Neanderthalic) into Urdu. I approached her invitation when Uncle cleared his throat of pflegm and raised his voice above the tide now slopping against the Tern's hull.

"Uh oh," said Bud. "Here it comes. Let's get out of the way. Captain's going to rip a loud one."

The other three wagged their heads leaving the table. Les turned back and put a hand to the side of his mouth. "It's the Jack Daniels Hour."

"What?" I said as they rushed to the door.

"Listen up, son. Are you listening? You're in a field in an outhouse and hear a bird in a nearby tree in Spring."

"Captain," I interrupted, "I think Bud already gave me the short version of this bird-in-the-tree thing."

Uncle threw me the indulgent stare of a tweed-suit tenured English professor and said Bud's first language is Polish. Do you follow me?

"What's the connection?"

"The problem is, there is none; so listen up and hear me out. You hear a bird. You sit there in the dark, wondering and pause to ask does it matter if it's the bird or its song that's important. You hear the song again. You grope in the dark and tear off a page of the phone book, fold it thoughtfully and ask, if it's the song, does it matter if it's the same bird again or another bird? Do you follow me?

"Uh-huh."

"You wipe and say if it's either bird, will it be the very same bird when you sit down next Spring?

"Uh-huh."

Now, having done your duty, what are you going to carry away when you get up and close the wooden door behind you?

"Uh."

"You might spot the bird or some other bird for a moment in the tree, or you may not, but it doesn't matter, does it?"

"Well, uh."

"It doesn't matter, because you'll carry the song with you forever, even if you don't take another dump the rest of your life. Do you follow me on this?

"Hmm. Sorry, Uncle. I'm not following you. Sorry. It's late," recalling Vin's spot analysis of Uncle's sanity.

"No problem, son. I've been working on it from time to time all my life. Tell you what; when we get back to the coast, I'll give you my 45 record of the Navy Hymn. Ever heard of it?"

"No."

"Well, it can explain the situation a lot better."

"Can't wait, Uncle."

When I told Uncle I'd like to say good-bye to the Shapiros when we dropped anchor again at Alice Detwiler, he said sure thing after we ship over to DR to mail some packages. He said they were addressed to Youth in Asia Charities in Pasadena, the headquarters of Uncle's world outreach to starving kids in the Far East and run by Lou, who flew down from Monterey every Friday to alter a la Les the books. Lou once showed me a glossy brochure describing how the organization joined up with various churches to feed, clothe and offer instruction to thousands of emaciated and pot-bellied children in West Africa. "We provide the funds and the churches buy the food and medicine and off it goes," Lou said. I asked him what motivated Uncle to get into the nonprofit side, and he said with his irrepressible puppet smirk, that's the side the money's on. Lou was in a charitable mood with his mouth when he added "Melville knows his dad consorted with latter-day slave traders from the Congo to Kingston and he's manacled by guilt.[58]

---

[58] PS: Will's recounting this small talk with Lou is seriously specious. I'm going to go out on a limb based on my exhaustive research and simply let Captain Billy reiterate in his own words (from letters of August 2-23, 1900) his association with so-called slave traders at that time. "As Almighty God is my witness, I neither disgraced my country nor my family regards the transport or sale of human life (i.e. African slaves) in all these years as master of the Tern. Dockside, it is common knowledge I did trade with merchants while underway whose shipholds were immoral and otherwise corrupt and infested with the ignorant, abased and downtrodden natives from West Africa. I was primarily trading for

"I don't believe it, Lou."

Lou made a weak attempt at kicking me with his foot. "Look, kid, if you can read at the third grade level, which I assume you achieved at Mundane, go down to Biloxi sometime and check out *The Voyage of the Tern* by Captain Billy, your grandfather. It's by the urinal on the left shelf in the back of the bookmobile. You know, you ask a lot of questions for a drop-out artist. Why didn't you ask them before you flunked out?"

I knew for a while to ignore Lou's stick-and-jab style and laughed it off with some fancy footwork to the galley for a snack saying to myself I'm getting a bit tired of the little piss ant implying I'm a coward and a traitor.

---

spices, poppies and coca leaves for a group of rug merchants situated in New York City. Granted, there be occasions when I appeared a slave trader; especially after much soul-searching and bookkeeping when I agreed to carry a number of such cargo, which detracted from my ongoing deliveries of alcoholic spirits along the eastern seaboard, for the sole purpose of helping them and their children seek a better life in the healthful sunny fields of the Deep South, or taken in and cared for as domestic servants in the dark cavernous mansions of Manhattan and Boston and other centers of wealth. The Tern under my hand did more to save lives than enslave them."

CHAPTER 13

The next dawn was a beauty in spite of some choppy waves. Vince was anxious. He stood near the quarterdeck with his older brother's green dufflebag and backpack. Earlier by our racks, before Vin got dressed, we reviewed our strategies for staying out of the service. He said it was a meatgrinder and didn't believe in working for fat cats who made a fortune off the war. He put on a nice blue Oxford dress shirt and slipped on a pair of onyx cufflinks saying why should we go over there to offload pallets and maybe get our asses shot up when we can stock shelves at the Supermammout in downtown Toronto. I told him I wasn't quite that cynical yet and was still in the gray zone.

"Call it your way, Will. I don't know where you'll be next Friday night, but I'll be hanging around the student union in good old Copenhagen looking for a date."

"That's a nice shirt, Vin. What's on the pocket?"

Vince said Burning Bush Country Club down the road from Champaign-Urbana. Father's golf pal, State Senator DuWayne Dubble, gave it to him one Christmas.

"You mean the bubble gum heir?"

"Yep. More pops per pucker. Remember the jingle?"

Lou, at the helm, piloted us into a cove adjacent to Playa de las Chicas, a small resort on the north side of the island. A few times he jumped up to see over the rim of the wheel while I glanced back and forth from him to the crown of coral reef brushing the hull. I don't know how he did it or how Uncle Rob entrusted this tiny man with a twenty-million dollar yacht. The beach was a white strip of lemon meringue populated by colorful beads of blue and red beach umbrellas. And those polka dots were young women throwing beach balls and jumping in and out of the surf with their dogs and boyfriends.

Uncle dropped anchor about two hundred yards from this delicious beach. The last time I tasted Angie Decker's tangerine lips and palmed her buns was several weeks before I crashed academically at Mundane; my heart pumped overtime and my pants beat out of shape at the prospect of stealing a kiss or two from this sandy candystore. Before I could fanaticize more, Les shouted up from the small boat alongside, swinging his arm wildly into the air toward the beach. "It's a mirage, Will. Enjoy from where you are. The closer you get the more disappointing it becomes."

"Right! I have more faith than you think, Les."

"Sure you won't come along with me to Copenhagen?" said Vince.

Lou handed Vince's backpack down the ladder and butted in with another one across my bow. "Hah, what could you two dreamers possibly have faith in?"

Vinnie signalled with his eyebrows to let it go. Lou delivered a lot of left-handed knocks to us on the voyage. What did he have against someone over 4'9"? Just because I didn't go to church every week or believe in some bearded old man up there in no way confirmed a lack of faith in my fellow man. For sure, I never lorded my youth or heighth advantage over Lou, as I imagine most people did in his past.

"I guess this is it. Take care of yourself," said Vin, who sucked it up. We two college buddies and escape artists gave each other a congratulatory hug as if we crossed the stage with our gowns and tossed tassels. "Tell your uncle thanks a million," as he climbed down the ladder and jumped into the boat.

Bud and Paola waved together aside of me. Bud checked his Rolex. He should be in JFK by six in time for his connecting flight.

As they shoved off, Vince suddenly got up and yelled My passport! A few anxious moments later he pulled it from his back pocket. "Whew! Can't go anywhere without this." Then he sat back down. He wore his Indianapolis Speedway teeshirt. I never saw him again.[59]

---

[59] Will actually did see Vinnie once more, but not in the flesh. Toward the tail-end of Will's disturbing voyage on the Tern, a one-in-a-million chance caught him, I imagine, flipping pages of the English edition of Miami's venerable *La Vida a Hora* lying on the bench around the swimming pool on the Tern, and saw a row of pictures of several Marines in the column next to the bilingual

Uncle Rob stayed at the wheel and gave a blast of the twin diesel horns. He preferred not to say any more, although when our eyes crossed paths later, I could tell he seemed pretty troubled and shook up about it.

I really missed Vinnie. I was so disturbed at his departure, a few days later enroute to Kingston I urinated off the fantail and, in a panic, couldn't locate my left testicle for a minute.

Paola told me she was very sorry to see Vin debark. She said he almost learned to say I like you very much in her prehistoric cave dialect, which I didn't understand or care for. Her skin tanned to a deep bronze and the green patina of her eyeliner above her blue eyes gave her the mythical aura of someone who wasn't born in Detroit. I was still interested in her tongue, but not the way she was using it. Without someone to chat with at night, my effort to translate the noise of the Tern's screw tempted me to ask Paola if she wanted to spend a few symbiotic nights in my cabin to see if she could apply her linguistic skills on the ancient language of the screw. She patted my hand with the intimacy I was hoping for.

"Will, you're nice. More than these old bums I've been hanging around for years in spite of the money," she said.

She listened with me for a couple of nights while we played Old Maid. Around 0300, our eyes locked in mid-air like the rosined hands of two aerialists above the center ring. My member felt as heavy and happy as a bronze clapper swinging around Quasimodo at Notre Dame. For a rare moment, she was speechless and the eight years between us became pregnant with the expectation of things to come. I heard the screw whispering baseball dugout chatter and then its monotonous atonal *batterupbatterupbatterupbatterup*. She surely must have heard it. A child

---

crossword puzzle. Vinnie came home from a place called Khe Sanh one month after he arrived in-country. Will scribbled in his diary, "saw Vinnie's photo in the paper. I saw him only four months ago. What the hell is going on? Words can never express my sorrow." Will drew a heavy black line through this and I could barely make it out. His intention I honored by leaving it out of the text, but I felt obligated to inform the reader for purposes of closure. Strange that after striking this statement, Will seemed to really lose confidence in his uncle. He couldn't put his finger on it. Thanks to Cliff's diligence and locksmith skills, I read an oblique reference to Vinnie's departure from the Tern in a letter from Les to Paola, who by then sold her place on the West Side and moved to a nice house in Bay Ridge. Les said "looks like our captain set up that young man real good. What could we do?"

could have figured it out. When she laid down the Old Maid, right then and there I wanted to lay her down. She hovered with such longing, I chanced to lean over the deep well of desire to kiss her, but was restrained by the erection of my conscience over the spectre of her natural beauty. She put her slender finger on my lips as if we shared one last cinematic cigarette afterwards.

"Listen, I don't sense anything from your shaft or screw or whatever. You know my interests far outdate the invention of the wheel." She said this with such oral precision from her moist lips I thought she hinted it might show up as a question on a make-up exam, and I figured she meant we were getting to the heart of, and hopefully, the meat of the issue.

"Well, then Paola what about my heart. Old enough?" I said in mock self-deprecation.[60]

"Yes, but do you know how old I am?"

Damn! Was the hook still in her mouth? I must have lost this gorgeous mermaid. We were back to platonic babble and pussyfooting around the proverbial beach blanket with our heart-encircled initials in the center of it.

---

[60] Will probably was not a virgin according to some of his female acquaintances at Schuler High and then at Mundane. On one of my visits to Mrs. Melville, I certainly did not think she had the gall (if a woman's ovaries descended, would they be called "galls" as opposed to "balls?") to answer the question, so I got the names of several of Will's girlfriends at both schools. Two joined the Army; three left for the Peace Corps; one went overseas with Teach Nigeria; four got married. So I settled on three others. To protect the chastity of their current reputations, I'll call then Mindy, Mandy and Mo. All three were very open and friendly. On the main drag in Novi, I rolled down my window as Mindy weaved a path across the street. I can't figure out how she could ever remember Will as she stuck her ass out into traffic and kept looking around at approaching cars. She said it was a trick question and I was a trick and I said not at all and she walked away. At the Eastwood Shopping Center, I approached Mandy with her three-year old daughter. She grimaced when I showed her Will's photo. She squeezed her daughter's hand and said scram or I'll call the cops. Maureen—Mo—still the bouncy cheerful lass as she appeared in the Schuler HS yearbook, said they were definitely in love, but could not recall if he was the one who impregnated her. I gave her another fifty at which she replied, I believe so. We laughed and she said how am I doing and I said fine and said thanks anyway.

CHAPTER 14

A few days later, there was an incident the memory of which I wish to take with me when I die. It's an article of faith, not a medium of exchange like some loose gold coins in my pocket (one of which I actually pilfered as a souvenir from Uncle's coin collection). I figured since It doesn't weigh anything, I should be able to take it across.[61] After another restless night tossing to the undulant drone of the Tern's screw as we motored toward Kingston, I sat in a morning fog in a tilted canvas deck chair off the foc'scle; drinking a cafe solo from a thimble-sized cup. I don't know if it was the caffeine untangling my nightmare of the deck pool filled with writhing yellow sea snakes, or the stark reality of evading the uncertainty of military service; or the mystery and extent of Uncle Rob's wealth.

The fog began to lift while I inhaled the salty air. When it burned off, I could see the lush eastern coast of Jamaica. Then I rubbed my eyes in disbelief and sat upright. There was a bird on the tip of the foc'scle. I believe it was a tern. Of all the coincidences! I only spotted it in magazines and bird books. The tern wagged its head back and forth as if to say no you don't see me, but I knew it was real,[62] because I couldn't turn the page or

---

[61] Obscure; nonetheless, I left this description unchanged, since it sounded like something I would have written myself.

[62] In fact, there was a tern-inspired hood ornament on the famous Italian Pina Gandolfo saloon. Fifteen were known to have been produced in 1938 outside Milan for Mussolini's general staff. Rarely seen in public, the saloon boasted 250 miles on a gallon of diesel-guano mix; obviously in emulation of and appreciation for the long-distance flight of the real thing. Only two are known to exist as of this writing. One is in fair condition at the Musee DuFarge, fifteen kilometers southwest of Vouvray, France, although it is incorrectly listed as a

change the channel. I fancied a hood ornament to an expensive car. How appropriate: an eye for an eye, and a tern for a Tern. This could only bode the greatest of luck for us.

I slid out of the chair and sat on the deck cross-legged. The tern was pretty beaten up with ruffled grey and white feathers. It finally stopped squawking "no" and let out a single harsh call. For some reason, I placed my hands on my knees and connected thumbs to pinkies in imitation of some saffron-robed character I'd seen in a foreign movie called "Burmese Delight" with Devi, a knockout Indian actress of the late 1940s who was in her sixties at the time.

"Hey, you," shouted Lou, "if you're not too busy doing nothing, I could use a hand."

When I shook my shoulders to let him know I was busy doing nothing, he said "slacker" and slammed a mop handle on the deck.

Then the tern hopped down and moved to within five feet of me. I wished my camera were within reach. If he flew away, I would not have asked for more. Then the most astounding thing happened to me—a nobody in the universe. The tern twisted its head for another look at me. I held my breath. Then it hopped over my crossed ankles and settled right into the nest of my hairy legs. I cannot describe the excitement, the unfettered joy racing through my entire body. The feeling went way beyond a backseat quickie with Ginger Beebe at Luna Park—well, almost. This creature let me enter it's world and I suddenly felt an incredible amalgam of joy and freedom and liberating sense of responsibility. At last, I almost knew all the answers: why I was born; what comes after death. I didn't really feel the urgency to express them. There wasn't time. Consciousness was squeezed into less than a microsecond. I was one with the universe. All questions were now trivial and a total nuisance. Even answers were absurd.

Tens of thousands of miles residing within the meager span of my arms. Places I would never see in a lifetime. The representative of an entire species honoring a nobody of the harshest species with its presence. If he

---

Bugatti. The other, a twisted mass recovered in 1948 from the rocky coastline six kilometers south of Catania, has been under meticulous reconstruction by a team of retired Italian maxillofacial surgeons at their auto club garage three kilometers south of Livorno. It was sheer luck I received a photocopy from the US embassy in Rome of an article from the September 10, 1948 issue of the local Catanian newspaper with the captioned photo of the wreck strung up and hanging by its rear axle boots from a makeshift hoist on the beach.

had flown away right then, I would have wanted to also fly away from my own troubled persona.

Lou must have recruited Paola to extract some cooperation.

"I figured he was for the birds," chided Lou with an unrestrained snort.

"I guess he speaks a language older than any caveman stuff you're studying, eh Paola?" I said from the side of my mouth.

"He doesn't have to say anything," she shot back. "He's hurt."

So, she again deflated my ego. I thought the tern singled me out; come of its own free will. Instead, it came out of pain and suffering to commiscrate with me. It could have been anyone. Some drunk on a park bench in Havana. A child crying on the beach at Rio while the babysitter is three blocks away licking her boyfriend's gelato. Just happened to be me, sitting on my ass doing nothing except running from the authoritics.

"It's an arctic tern. He's way off course," she said.

Uncle Rob said over the loudspeaker, another stowaway? Les and Bud came out of their hiding places where they did their numbers juggling and phone calls.

The bird didn't seem to mind the attention. Paola brought back a cardboard box emptied of its thirty-six cans of jumbo black Greek olives. Like a priceless heirloon, I gently grabbed the tern which let out another shrill call but stayed calm.

"Tough luck," said Lou. "Broken wing."

"No," said Paola, "not completely. Lucky."

"Let's let it go. There's enough lost souls on this Tern as it is," said Bud.

Paola took it from me and put it into the box. "Bud, you're such an ass," she said. "You're the only loser here."

Bud sniffled and feigned resentment, saying something like at last I get the recognition I have so richly deserved and sought through the years.

Uncle Rob came up and said okay we're all in this together. Let's calm down. "Lou, grab some of those kippers and see if he'll eat. We'll take him into the vet in Kingston. Maybe he can do something." He shook his head almost like the tern itself. And I half thought Uncle would throw the poor thing overboard, like the crew did to the Shapiros in my nightmare of the previous week.

"Thanks, Uncle Rob," I said.

"No problem, son. We'll do what's best for us and the bird." He made a conflicted clicking sound from the side of his mouth and winked as he walked away.

Dr. Felix Granados, who told us he took the southern route out of Cuba in 1960, kept a small, very clean walk-in practice in Rue des Deux Chats on the north side between two cat houses. He was soft-spoken and about thirty-five. I noticed a family picture on his desk. Three girls and two boys sitting in front of the vet and his wife. Paola, Lou and Bud picked up some Spanish here and there, and between everyone taking a stab at it, were able to talk to the vet, who kept wanting to speak English. He said he spent 1955 at Florida State as an exchange student and came back to Cuba where he found out he was better off in Tallahassee. Uncle and Les peeled off into the Hotel du Palais downtown to do some business related to Uncle's medical supply company. All I can recall is when we got back on the Tern, there were about five wooden crates on the deck marked "Medico" and three more of those familiar aluminum suitcases.

The only unbroken string of English was when Bud stood off to the side of the exam room and said out loud, it's ironic how this place can be so clean, stuck between two establishments of human filth. Then, Dr. Granados raised his eyebrows, turned around and said in broken English that he also treats the girls next door. I waited for smug Bud to retort, So you treat all the chicks around here, but he bit his lip shut.

When the vet took the tern out of the perforated box, he again raised his eyebrows. Paola said the vet explained how the bird was way off its migration route as an arctic tern. Some of the parrots and cockatoos in the cages against a wall started making their own comments, which none of us could translate, although Paola cocked her head and frowned when she went up to them.

"You're telling me a tall tale," Bud said to one of the parrots.

The tern let out a few harsh notes as if to say hell no as Dr. Granados examined it.

"Claro! Okay, okay. If you say so," said the vet and our laughter caught on with the two cockatoos, too. He said the bird indeed broke a bone in its right wing, but since it healed on the wing, there was nothing more he could do beyond what nature already did. He said in English, this sailor is home from the sea, and he slowly shook his head. It would be very difficult for it to return to its long-distance lifestyle, but you never know. He handed us a small dark bottle of avian medicine with a dropper. Bud pulled out his Moroccan leather wallet and gave him five Ben Franklin's for the forty-five minutes. He glanced at the family picture and asked the doctor if he wanted to go back to the States. The young vet closed his eyes, lifted his head to the cracked ceiling, placed his hands in the pockets of his white exam coat and smiled. "My wife and children are here. My animals are here. Maybe next time."

"Comprendo, doc. If you change your mind, call this number," said Lou, who wrote down a telephone number on the back of the receipt and slipped it under the green blotter on the desk.

Aside from learning the fate of the tern from Dr. Granados, our plans for having some free time and kicking back a few on the island changed as swiftly as a shift in the wind.

"All right," said Uncle Rob, who met up with us a few blocks before the docks. He said we could have a couple of hours at the Club Aureole and he pointed the way. "Tell Chef Nichon I said bonjour." Did Uncle mean two hours or a coupling of them, like the time it takes a Burlington and Northern to haul 250 cars from Pueblo to Salt Lake?

"We're familiar with it," said Lou.

For all of Uncle Rob's purported wealth and contacts, I wondered why he picked such dumps to drop into. Most were no bigger than a few small rooms with enough elbow space to hold a round of beer. As I recall some of them, and there were a lot in my time on the Tern, I became more comfortable with the intimacy of a small group of so-called friends quietly drinking, exchanging viewpoints with civility, distilling time and the shuffling of feet on the street to a state of mind nearly as promising as when the tern accepted me into its world and carried my aspirations above the fray, even if only for five minutes. Turning the corner to the cafe, I noticed a child's little plastic boat laying in the corner of a dusty yard, smashed by someone's rude shoe.

At the small round wooden table near the front window of Cafe Aureole, Bud explained, your old man—uncle—practically lived on subs, so he's entirely used to the luxury of elbow room. "He was not a farm boy from Iowa for sure." Bud rambled on that I didn't have to confirm this with Uncle, or he would keelhaul Bud again. "After his first wife died, living under the sea in those cramped quarters sunk his other two marriages as surely as the tonnage he delivered to Davy Jones."

Chef Nichon, who stumbled over some feet to get to us, grabbed hands with Bud and Lou and said what an honor. My father honors you and my grandfather honors you and with such salutation handed a crumpled note to Bud who promptly used it as a coaster for his beer.

"What's this all about?" I asked.

"Edouard is a great chef, but ask for the thermometer, because it's all raw. He always greets us with a bill for damage for the last fifty years. We pay no attention, but it doesn't stop him from asking.[63]

"How much is it?"

"About thirty-five thousand dollars and counting. This place has such nostalgia," said Lou.

Les, who was on my other shoulder on his third beer, told Bud to pipe down and it was none of his damn business talking about Uncle and his Navy time. "The kid doesn't have to know anything other than the Navy Cross thing. Melville will tell him in his own time."

Bud had the steely forearms of stevedores I saw in union magazines on the barbershop table. He listed heavily into me and to my surprise, defended my curiosity. He said, Les don't tell me to pipe down. Will here is practically a crew member and he's seen some stuff going on; he's no dummy, even if he hasn't got all his shit together.

"Oh yeah?" pushed Les from the left.

"Ayeah!" Bud said on my right. "Les, you're a great one to divulge poop, you you certified public absconder. I'll concede as much." Bud held up two fingers and the waitress brought another round to the table.

Lou was nearly hidden by a row of long-necked brown beer bottles. His eyes and the tense clenched fists told me he waited for an opening.

Les placed both palms down on the table, stuck out his square jaw and declared he was proud to work for an organization redistributing money for the benefit of all, especially the uncountable far-flung have-nots.

"Oh yeah?" said Bud. "First you spend three years at Treasury knocking on the doors of indigents with your shiny .38 peeshooter to filch their last dime, then you screw everyone by laundering for the DeGrazia family, which is why Melville hired you to gin his books. Right?"

Les shook his head. "Bud, we've been down this alley before. You're peeved I've got the Midas touch. My so-called skills sure allowed you to pull down six figures all these years and tool around Pittsburgh with a twenty-thousand dollar Ducati."

---

63   PS: The Cafe Aureole was face-lifted at least four times during the period when Captain Billy was the Tern's skipper. Each time he compensated the owner with barely enough to clean the floor of broken bottles and detritus of drunken mariners, replace the bevelled mirror behind the bar and restock maybe sixty bottles of rum. He believed in paying for his sins, be it in a bar or on the plate passed around at Sunday service.

"Fifteen!" snorted Bud.

"Inflation, Bud," as Les took a long swallow.

"Inflation my ass!" fumed Bud.

Paola looked on with her chin resting in the palm of her hand. She yawned and stood up and declared I'm taking the tern to the sanctuary of the Tern. "Are you coming, Will?"

"I'll be right there," but when I came back from the urinal, she disappeared and I wanted so to put my arm around her waist and steer her back to the Tern.

She must have flown out the door with the bird and not looked back. Whether the presence of Paola kept a lid on the tension was not known to me, but I figured as such when Bud leaned across the table to grab Les by the collar. I quickly fell out of my chair and held onto my beer, as Bud and Les left the ring of bottles and rolled on the floor punching mostly air, eventhough both of their shirts were speckled in blood when they got up and started throwing chairs and bottles at each other. Now I knew why they had kept adding to the empties on the table until there were about twenty. Bud and Les divvied them up and threw them all over the place. One hit a table of sailors off the Argentine frigate Michele Leone, mushrooming the arena into critical mass and ending the match ten minutes later with Bud and Les in a twisted bloody mess thrown out into the street. I saw Lou hand a fistful of cash to Chef Nichon at the doorway. I think he said this should close out the debt for now.

We started down a few dark cobblestone alleys until an old bearded guy stopped us and asked in familiar English where was the Tern docked. I said what's it to ya, you old fart. Then I glanced back over my shoulder and noticed his limp and wondered if we bumped into Captain Billy's ghost. When we stumbled onto the Tern's quarterdeck at 0230, Les immediately tossed his cookies; Bud went back down the gangway to urinate on the wharf and Lou ratted on both to Uncle Rob, who pursed his lips when he saw me. Embarrassed for thinking I could step in and keep things calm, he said don't worry about it; just so you didn't get anything on you, since the syphilis rate here is sky high.

I asked Uncle what happened to the crates and he said don't bother, son. They're in the hold. Then he said don't believe a word the screw says tonight. Get some rest.

CHAPTER 15

The next morning we sat around the breakfast nook. Bud and Les didn't have a scratch or bruise. Lou, Paola and Uncle munched away with an impromptu discussion of the daily agenda. There was near cheer when the sunlight poked through a porthole, levitating the red and white squares off the tablecloth. They acted as if nothing happened the past eight hours. Business as before. The brawl was a staged catharsis to release pent-up emotions from years of servitude making oodles for ends I still did not fully comprehend.

Once again, I didn't sleep well. Even the tern in its bamboo cage one of the Filipinos bought in town kept nodding its little head up and down as if it agreed with everything the screw grumbled about through the night, beginning with a typical monotonous theme *oowahoowahoowahoowahoowahoowahoowahoowah*. While shaving and slipping the tern a few sardines, I recalled the worst of the nightmare: Uncle Rob was on the radiotelephone talking to Captain Billy, of all people, who chastised him for smoking a pipe while Lou and Bud banged Paola in the sleeping quarters and then tried to stuff her out the porthole. And they stared at me and said you don't have the NTK. What did they mean by that crack?

With Jamaica fading well off our starboard bow, I asked Uncle Captain if he ever heard the term NTK; I thought it was an abbreviation off an NYSE ticker I used to watch on Friday afternoons in downtown Detroit at Hood, Winke and Grimm stockbrokers.

"Son, it means the need to know. Knowledge is a privilege, like a club. Some clubs let you in, some don't. Didn't they ever teach you anything in college?" He cracked the sly grin of a doorman shooing away voice-cracking beansprouts trying to get into a burlesque show.[64]

Somewhat irked by Uncle's abruptness and the aloofness of the crew, I grabbed three cold bottles of Lowenstein's Dark and sort of sneaked out of sight and out of mind down into the belly of the Tern, where I fluffed together a small futon of coiled line and sailcloth and imagined if Captain Billy were around, would he be patient enough to tell his grandson a tale or two. As I lay back in the dank old slave-holding area, I heard yet another voice, much stronger than the one in my room. It was the long cylindrical driveshaft connecting the diesel engine to the screw. Then I knew for sure I was not only getting screwed, but shafted as well by the dialogue of the

---

[64] A few pages back, I forgot to remark that Will's recollections have been rather bland and listless in terms of raw hamburger action and the accumulation of scenic incidentals such as vivid descriptions of locale, the changing color of the ocean, leaping dolphins, personal hygiene and diet. All the frills and diversions we've grown to savor from a good morsel of literature. When I saw Mrs. Melville, she said she gave my associate, Penny Scriveen, several old recipes that Chef Nichon's grandfather gave Captain Billy with the French phrase "besoin a savoir" or the "need to know," apparently referring to secret recipes that made his restaurant world famous throughout the Caribbean. With all due respect for Will's sketchy allusion to pick-ups and Lolitaburgers he ate out at Cheeks Drive-Thru down the road from Milan (according to Mrs. Melville), I asked Penny to review Captain Billy's logs and recreate a scene where he obtained the decrypted recipe for baba au rhum from Chef Nichon. Her contribution is Chapter 16. Penny kneaded It from the captain's original notes written during one of the Tern's barroom remodeling visits. I suggested that she spice things up—you know, throw some salt over her shoulder—to give new meaning to the word "cutlery" and encourage the reader to thirst for some visceral thrills in the absence of hashed-out gratuitous violence typical and expected of so-called best-sellers by Vance Pulty, Barbara Chillingworth and Gregory T.P. Galloway. In her own right, Penny is well-known for her "time-warp" style, from children's books to suggestive violence (e.g., "...Suddenly, I stood flat-footed in my new Salvation Army mocassins on a crumbling streetcorner built long before I was born, watching an overhead newsreel of Mayor Cermak and wondering if I would live to see my grandchildren notice the pollacky pattern of bloodstains on the sidewalk where his body once lay before the whole scene is rereleased at Heinseit's quadriplex theatre in downtown Chicago in 2020.)

two mechanical parts responsible for propelling this whole saga and our progress at sea. On my second bottle, I said, how about it granddad how 'bout it? And as I drifted off. For a while; after the third bottle and the tropical heat and lack of sleep...

CHAPTER 16

We delivered onto the quai at Kingston about forty poor souls of African descent. They were truly black, and some a curious blue, and were beached off one of the small unnamed islands near Nevis. Women and children cried and an elderly man said they were chained on a foundering ship bound for Santiago de Cuba. They were able to unlock their iron bondage when the captain threw the key from a departing lifeboat. Twenty drowned in the rough surf. Women and children were miserable. I gathered them in several dinghy trips to the Tern, gave them what little sustenance I could afford (biscuits and water) and with the Lord's help, hopefully gave them a second chance at a better life cutting cane in Cuba, working in cotton fields in the South or making their way to Boston to cook, empty ashtrays and clean indoor toilets for the wealthy offspring of Abolitionists. I patted one of the the old men on the shoulder when the gendarmes arrived and then led my crew of nine down the road for a quiet afternoon drinking ale at the Cafe Aureole on Rue des Deux Chats. And my ulterior purpose was to finally corner my old friend Chef Nichon and obtain by hook or crook his recipe for baba au rhum, a dessert Mrs. Melville asked me to obtain for her two years ago. We milled outside a few minutes, wiping our sleeves across our mouths and laughing. Someone turned around the sign on the door to "Ferme" behind our backs. I saw this and recognized the hand with half the pinkie as belonging to the chef himself and I proceeded to bang on the door until the glass panes rattled. One of my crew—and I take this opportunity to protect their identities from jurisprudence eventhough they weren't worth remembering in any case—punched through a glass pane, unlocked the door and we all piled in as if sucked into a whirlpool similar to the strange one we observed off

Bermuda. I locked the door and turned to make sure the sign read "Ferme," but to no avail, since crews of the HMS Harkness and the freighter J. Mary Joseph turned the sign back around a few minutes later and began filling up the place. Not wanting to muss my blue captain's uniform, I stood by the kitchen doorway unable and perhaps unwilling to enter the gathering maelstrom of flying chairs and bottles, swollen fists and vile filthy language to be soon blended with simmering fervor by the packed restaurant.

I were truly pierced by a sense of shame and Christian guilt watching the three waitresses abused by vile epithets and sloven hands pulling them to and fro. They seemed to enjoy it, but I knew in my heart they knew not what they did in spite of the exchange of coins. In the end, I became an amoral, vicarious participant, for I wanted only the recipe and was determined to get it even if the whole accursed place had to burn in hell aforehand.

Chef Nichon banged pans on the stove to drown out the growing row beyond. I confronted him as he tossed a giant shrimp omelette into the air. Distracted, it fell on the floor. He gathered it up, shrugged at me and put it on a platter with fresh dinner rolls. As I dropped three double eagles into his sweaty palm for the previous five months of damages, he finally pushed his hat back on his head and smiled, saying don't worry about the omelette, it will be vomited all over the floor after a few hours. He thanked me, put up his hands and agreed to impart the recipe. He tore off a piece of butcher paper and wrote in French "Besoin a Savoir" which I think meant "need to know" or some such. We both winced when the noise from without was punchuated by the reassuring sound of breaking glass and hard-breathing mayhem. I told chef it was necessary therapy for my crew and I would compensate him in due time.

Chef tapped his chubby fingers on the wooden counter and poked into the cabinet overhead. Not enough ingredients. He said cumin, vanilla, cinnamon some other spicy words in French and apologized for not saying them in English so I could better understand his frustration. He then licked a pencil tip and wrote and said it would take about four hours, long enough for his dining area to become unrecognizable. As he wrote the list, I mused if his cafe were a face, it would no doubt require extensive reconstructive surgery from the best surgeons in Berlin, but since most of them were glorified butchers with dull knives and framed beribboned diplomas it would be just as well to live in the dark or bend over Dover. I am glad I did not dishearten him as he wrote:

½ cup milk; 4 tsps active dry yeast; 2 cups bread flour; 3 large eggs; 2 tsps sugar; pinch salt; 1 tsp orange zest; 1 tsp lemon zest; 1 large dollop butter (melted but not hot); for the rum-soaking syrup: ¼ cup dark rum; sweet whipped cream; fresh cherries.

Chef flourished his floured hands and almost cried, dropping his head. The longer it took to impart this knowledge to me, the more devastation he knew would befall his establishment and threaten his lifestyle and those of his ten children. I asked him if he still prepared the sumptuous meals for which he was known. He shrugged his large shoulders and said since the change in clientele he only catered to the handful of affluent families running Kingston. On the edge of the table, I tore off the recipe into three pieces and pushed through the kitchen door with the rectitude and forthrightness of the gallows attendant I remembered on Barbados who snuggled a noose around my neck. Amid much thrashing and ducking, I succeeded in coralling one of my crew from the frenzy reminiscent of throwing shark bait off the fantail of the Tern, shark being the most gamey fish at sea, even in a quagmire of peach chutney. He was the only crew member who had no difficulty returning after half an hour with the oranges, lemons and rum from the Tern. Another came back out of breath with torn sacks of flour, salt, yeast and sugar and said no one was there to wait on him at the dry goods emporium we used to resupply the Tern; and so he waved and sauntered out hoping someone would take the coins I gave him. My word, they started yelling at him. He said he was a block away and didn't feel right about turning around, so he ducked into the Bidon (a small bar we used as a spill-over to drink) and spent the money on two mixed drinks and a "tres vite," whatever that meant. I grabbed the sacks when a gendarme came in. Out of respect for the only enforcement in the neighborhood, everyone suddenly suspended their rage for the lanky officer in his loose white uniform who walked over to me and demanded payment on behalf of his brother-in-law at the emporium, which I paid and added a tip of two bits to keep my crewman out of jail. The third mate came back with a weaved jute basket of eggs, cans of milk and a small porcelain jar of butter.

For the first time, fisticuffs started sifting through the porous kitchen door into Chef Nichon's preparation area. I attempted to maintain calm in the cuisine by smashing my fist into the piebald faces of three sea-going gourmandes. The apron I wore splattered with blood. Another one I knew from the J. Mary Joseph, who bore a grudge since we took away his rum trade route, tried to knife me near the stove. I pulled out my Chicago world exposition souvenir, a loverly six-inch pearl-handled blade and thrust it with devilish glee deep into his fat Dutch belly and streaked my apron again with fresh blood. He was fortunate I did not zip him up the chest and pull out his intestines for boudin blanc, another delicacy for which I hungered. Chef Nichon appeared unphased, pushing on my back with his large derriere to make enough counter space to do the deed. One more swift kick into the testicles of an HMS Harkness semen and the galley was cleared for the moment. Okay, let's start, said chef, who brushed someone's bloodied gold tooth off the corner of the table. I rolled my tongue around to check my molars, not realizing until later it was from the mouth of one of my crew. Chef tried to kick it under the stove for an advance on my bill for the evening, but I pushed him out of the way and put it in my pocket until my next visit to the assayer's office in Havana. He tore off a piece of butcher paper and glanced at me, telling me to watch and write. In a small saucepan, scald one-half cup of milk over medium heat. Remove it from the heat and cool it for about ten minutes. I told him to speak louder, as the mayhem pushed the door back and forth. I knew some French and when he said "fay gaff" I moved in closer. Into a majolica bowl I got from the top shelf, he poured the cooled milk, four teaspoons of yeast and one-half cup of flour, combined it all until foamy, then stirred it to form a kind of sponge and let it rise until it doubled in size.

He sweated now and told me to come back in twenty minutes and go out and stop the brawl. I reconsidered, gave him another double eagle and said he better come with me, as I wasn't about to let him sit on his backside while I played sous-chef mopping up the floor. He pulled out the biggest godforsaken butcher knife I ever did see and said "avec plaisir." I knew he started out as a butcher before he went to cooking school in Paris a few blocks from the Place Vendome and was capable of carving roast pig and making pickled pigs feet as well. We pushed our way through the swinging doors and right away ducked several flying objects smashing on the wall behind us. I hunkered down counting to twenty and saw under the bar two small children holding on to each other in this mortal storm. I promised myself these children would be protected. I pushed chef out of the way in a mad frenzy that would qualify me as a visiting professor of corporal communication at Harvard Theological Seminary where my distant cousin, Enoch, parsed and parried as the fencing coach. With my left hand pumping into jaws and kicking with both boots and slashing with my knife, I waded through a morass of stinking flesh. I slipped twice on small pools of vomit and blood and beer and suffered a gash to my left thigh a sailmaker later mended with a generous portion of Jamaican rum. A massive tattoed forearm grabbed my neck and I momentarily was out of it until chef slapped me with a few backhands, which I felt was discrete payment for the many times I abused his reputation and restaurant. I was at once indebted to his patience as he wiped the blood off his wide blade.

Through the legs of overturned chairs and tables, I spotted the gendarme and two baton-swinging friends leaning near the front door casually chatting and smoking cigarettes. I marvelled at the swath of retribution in our wake. Several sailors were sprawled out, bleeding from facial cuts, busted knuckles and slices from the filet talents of Chef Nichon. His large nose was once again broken and bleeding, but he raised his thumb and smiled at me in the latest vainglorious attempt to save his establishment. This act of foolhardy courage cleared out about twenty clumps from the eighty or so louts who limped out the door carrying each other back to their ship. Fortunately, none of my crew suffered beyond some black eyes and gashes on the head and forearms, nothing a little salt water and abstinence couldn't cure.

Chef and I wiped the blood off our hands and faces with a torn tablecloth and got busy again in the kitchen. He was upset he may have let the dough alone too long and he patted it like a baby's bottom for reassurance. My right knuckle was scraped up, but I picked up the pencil and listened as he spoke out the side of his swollen mouth: take a fork and beat the eggs into the sponge, adding one at a time, followed by the remaining one half cups of bread flour, the two teaspoons of sugar and one teaspoon each of orange and lemon zest, both of which I stooped to do over the bowl. I reached up and brushed off the shelf to get the pinch of salt. When a soft dough forms, slowly beat in the cup of butter to make a smooth dough. Chef said bien and wait twenty minutes when the door smashed open and one then another sailor from the Harkness barrelled in. They yelled something about coming back for revenge. The other one with a bloody bandanna around his head and one eye brandished a ceremonial Japanese sword. The blade flashed under the kitchen skylight and I became somewhat concerned for chef, who was slow as an elephant. I knew the recipe was in grave danger of destruction, so I threw anything I could at this mad Englishman; pots, tins, rolling pins, ladles. I managed to duck under him and grabbed the other one behind the back, who flailed at me with a heavy belt buckle, cutting my scalp. With blood in my eyes, I cut my leg pulling out my knife and pulled it across the bastard's throat until he gasped for air and dropped to the floor. I didn't care if he was Queen Victoria's consort, I was so unbound. As a freedom loving, God-fearing Christian and full-bloodied American, I stood there bear-like revelling in the pure lust of victory, and at the same time reviling the venom of hatred flowing hot in my sinful veins. Grabbing a five-pound bag of flour, I smashed it over the head of the other sailor who already gashed the chef's broad back enough to seep blood through his white shirt to form an "X". Stunned, the limey turned around and in a basting of ghostly whiteness I came up from the floor and thrust my knife into the midlands wherein lay his black heart. Chef Nichon limped around and bashed the mate in the cerebellum with a buttered iron skillet and shouted preheat the oven to 375 degrees Fahrenheit. I dragged this body to the stove, ready to shove the torso into it when chef yelled No! the wrong recipe. After we buttered a large cake pan, or baba mold as he called it, we each grabbed an arm and dragged both bodies through the blood-spattered door and into the bar area amid a sea of drunken sailors. Thanks be to God Dr. Granados consented to bring his horse-drawn carriage and haul off the two bodies to the morgue for recuperation. I noticed the gendarme open and close the door for him. Chef insisted I not worry about his cuts since blood coagulated nicely on the cotton shirt and actually stopped. He said hurry back and place the dough in the pan we had buttered, cover it and place it next to the stove in a warm, draft-free place for about forty minutes, at which time it should reach the top of the mold. The place quieted down somewhat with the starch knocked out of most combattants. It was an uneasy calm, waiting for the next phase of the recipe.

I righted a round table and helped chef sit down. He raised his head and pointed to the pendulum clock on the mantel below the bar and said you must wait the full forty minutes and be sure the dough is near the top of the pan. Two of the HMS Harkness sailors overheard us and soon the scuttlebut passed about something cooking far beyond the hardtack and jerky and shark meat they survived on. It was as if Moses himself entered the cafe and parted the Red Sea, which is what the bloody floor resembled by now. The sailors, bruised and battered, uniforms shredded to pieces— some with only undergarments left—arose from the primordial slop, reset the tables and chairs with surprising alacrity and dumped themselves upright. I counted about sixty left, excluding my disciplined lot of nine who were all laid out drunk at attention behind the bar. I knew there wasn't much time because the calm would only make them all increasingly aware of the rising pain from busted teeth and ribs, torn nails and assorted contusions as the untouched clock ticked off the forty minutes. To my good fortune, many unconscious sailors slid down like eels into the muck. On our way back to the kitchen, which by now resembled an abattoir, the floor displayed two large bloody streaks as if someone dragged a cow's carcass through the door to the dining room. Chef waved me off when he gashed his right foot on a broken bottle. He placed the mold out on a sheetpan and put it on the middle rack of the oven and told me to watch for thirty minutes or until the top of the baba was golden brown and the sides began to pull away from the pan slightly. Breathing heavily now, chef again waved me off, grabbed a stool and said his eyes were better for this after he noticed how someone opened a nasty gash over each of my eyes. I took the opportunity to throw pitchers of cold water on my crew. I didn't want them to miss out. I took a seat and pulled out my small King James Version and read a few Psalms until the clock hands showed it was time. I returned to the kitchen, where chef already removed the sheet pan from the oven and put it on a wine rack and raised his hands to show nine and one-half fingers stretched out above his head. Ten minutes, he gasped. Then he set the wine rack over another sheet pan and used a silver toothpick to poke tiny holes all over the top of the baba.

I was surprised to find one of the chef's children, Angelique, standing on a chair holding a bottle of rum. Forever will I be amazed and grateful for this ten-year old girl in a bright calico dress announcing with youthful pride every little step she made to concoct the rum-soaking syrup. Her pixie-like pigtails swung back and forth while her nimble hands danced like little faeries among the ingredients. I grabbed the pencil and pulled out the now crumpled piece of precious butcher paper: in a medium saucepan she combined three and three-fourths cups of sugar, four teaspoons of lemon zest, two tablespoons of orange zest, one vanilla bean I helped her get from the top shelf split in one-half lengthwise and the seeds scraped away. She jumped down from the stool as I carried the pan to the stove, where she told me with a big smile to bring it to a boil slowly and stir constantly to dissolve the sugar. I was about to pour in the rum when she shook her finger at me and said "pas encore." After a few minutes, I let Angelique finish stirring for the other twenty-five minutes. I sat down on the floor with chef. He beamed and lifted his arm out in her direction as if to present her at a cotillion ball she would never attend. He dropped his arm in a thump and said he probably busted a rib or two. I brought back my first mate with a bloody torn tablecloth he pulled from between two sleeping sailors and we sat up the chef in a chair. I used my shoulders to support the chef's arms while the mate wrapped up his ribs. I glanced over in time to see Angelique add ten teaspoons of dark rum to the pan. She found a fine mesh strainer and poured the mix through it, then she took the strainer to the trashcan in the corner and dumped out the remaining solids. We finally got chef on his feet. He covered the pan to keep it warm. He glanced at me sideways and said an abrupt merci, but I could tell he was upset and embarrassed at how bloody his kitchen had become especially in the presence of his daughter. She stood there by the stove in her pretty dress with a smile as wide as Montego Bay and I winced a moment thinking of my sixteen-year old wife in Biloxi and the two babies she already lost. At the back door window, the sun shone in a bright column into the back of the kitchen and onto the black and white checkered floor. It was Sunday, September 12, 1898 and I think I was thirty-three. What was I doing here in Kingston, Jamaica, on Rue des Deux Chats, in the Cafe Aureole, sitting on the floor of Chef Nichon's bloody kitchen, cooking; where my face was swollen and my left ankle throbbed and may have been broken, and I longed to be sailing free on the Tern, far from the domestic tranquillity of a bloody warm kitchen?

Chef said what's wrong? I picked up the pencil and said what's next? Angelique brought each of us a tumbler of cold water. We sat back down on the floor while she turned the soaked baba out onto the wire rack and let them drain above the sheet pan. Chef tapped me on the shoulder and held up the half pinkie on his right hand. I said thirty minutes and guessed right. The cake rum aroma soaked the humid air and it would have been enough for me to breathe in the baba au rhum. After Angelique tried to pull us up off the floor to dance with her, she did a small ethereal pirouette around us, which suffered my soul deeper than the sweet delicious air enveloping us.

I soon staggered to my feet. Chef waved his hand and said I'm all right; my job is done. Go on. You now have the recipe to take to your dear wife. He told dutiful Angelique to transfer the baba to the twelve white plates with the blue circle and with a large spoon place a dollop of the cold sweetened whipped cream on each. We put the plates and spoons on a large wooden serving tray and I carried them into the restaurant. I stopped in my tracks at my mistake. About ten tables of four sailors each sat more or less upright at attention. They somehow had sobered up. It was a whole new crew from the sister ship of the Harkness, the HMS Fury. They flashed a boarding-party glint in their eyes, making me feel uncomfortable. They must have carried off the field-of-play their besotted shipmates, who straggled down the street as I peeked out the broken front window. The perfume of baba au rhum pervaded the iniquity loitering in the large room, strangely cleansing it with intimations of home, a small rose-draped cottage, mum in the kitchen, perhaps a lady friend outside tapping of a Sunday morn on the windowpane with the end of her pink silk parasol.

The surviving waitress took the tray and began serving. Some of the forty-odd sailors pounded the tables with their glasses, realizing they would not be the lucky twelve. I sensed a mutiny brewing over the rum-soaked cakes. The lucky dozen began forking the cake with voracious thrusts into their slobbering maws. I heard one with syrup dripping from the corners of his mouth mumble to another standing over him that he would be glad to share the culinary booty. To no avail. The one standing said, I'm for having it all mate and he grabbed the cake and pushed it into his mouth whole. The place exploded like gunpowder. The waitress screamed and managed to squirm under a table and crawl out the front door. I crept over to the bar and slapped my crew from reverie to reveille with the back of my hand. Each one said to me, aye aye love and turned over. This fresh crew was under full steam and full sails. They were dead earnest in settling at-sea trifles and spats with the enthusiasm of hooligans climbing through the crinoline window curtains of the village whore. A plate dropped on the bar caught my attention and I saw perhaps the only surviving baba, rich and golden as a sunset in Sumatra. I reached up, grabbed for it then sat back down under the bar and ravaged it with my mouth, then slumped back down with the sweet aftertaste of unabashed gluttony forewarned in the Old Testament. [NOTE: Obviously here, Penny was unduly influenced by my more polished style, but I strongly encouraged her to carry on when she recovered from writer's block.]

With the respite from flying glass, chairs and twisted bodies, I glanced over the bar and rued the roux: beer, blood, vomit and baba wasted in scattered pools on the splintered wooden floor, and I patted my breast pocket for the recipe which was ultimately far more precious than the real thing.

One of the Flying Dutchman rum bottles hit a gas light sconce, several of which lined the walls for evening repasts. A small fire broke out and licked the wall like a ravenous guest savoring a rare steak tartar oozing a plateful of blood and soaking the hot dinner roll and au gratin baked potato off to the side.

After paying Chef Nichon handfuls of coins the past five years for remodeling his premises, I felt a sense of obligation to save the restaurant he worked so hard to create almost as much as the extraordinary creations coming out of his cuisine. I ran over to pull away a few drunken sailors who mistakenly tried to douse the fire with pitchers of beer, which was as close to fresh water as any of them would get until the day relatives sprinkled water on their grave flowers. They mocked my efforts with raucous laughter and wild roundhouse swings which I wisely ducked on behalf of my swollen face. I scrambled back and forth from the kitchen faucet to the fire now creeping over more chairs and tables. Chef turned his head and said what's cooking? He seemed very tired and beyond worry, so I told him I went around lighting the twelve baba for effect. He raised his hand and shoved his middle finger in the air at me, indicating I should have waited one hour. The whole restaurant took on the aura of a gigantic baba inhabited by a motley crew of inebriated sailors. Now I announ ced that they all could share in the rare treat, because they had in fact become one with the baba, but this went over their heads with the smoke. Eventually several sailors familiar with the horrors of a fire at sea followed my lead and wrestled to a glowering fizzle the conflagration hissing like venomous snakes escaping in serpentine wisps all around us.

A true sense of camaraderie settled on us as we sat in the room of baba, slapping each other on the back for our reluctant efforts to save the restaurant. To disturb this felicity as rare as the baba room we sat in, the gendarme came through the front door with the Kingston police chief, who must have seen the opportunity to cash in with the full force of the law in all his white spats, baton-swinging presence. I took it upon myself to clear the air with a plea to negotiate the damage in his favor. He shook my hand as stiffly as the white-starched collar around his neck and asked what's cooking? When I told him, he sniffed the air, glanced around and I could tell he was disappointed at missing out on a generous serving. I glanced down and saw some crumbs of baba gathered around the chief's shoes. If only he knew the full scope of the damage. This put me at a greater disadvantage to bribe him. I dusted the residue of flour off my uniform and began to barter my release.

"Chief, this is nothing new. No laws have been broken, but to recognize you for your diligence to uphold public safety—even among foreign scum—and pay honor to the sacrifices you and your family make everyday, please accept these tokens of appreciation." I handed him five double eagles in a neat stack into the palm of his hand, from where they slid down a pocket smeared of blood and flour until it nestled near his balls of culinary justice. He smiled at me with the condescending glance of an illiterate island judge and cold fisheye stare of an executioner, both of which he was at the same time. Like chastised youths, the HMS Fury crew scrubbed the floor, straightened tables and chairs and apologized to a child for the inconvenience as they saluted me on their way out the door. My crew was last in line. When the first mate passed, he said what's brewing, captain? And I held up the one-hour finger sign chef Nichon showed me. I said you've got one hour to get back and prepare the Tern to weigh anchor. He said aye, aye and muttered out the side of his mouth, I frankly expected more respect from you, sir.

After everyone trudged out the door, I propped a chairback under the doorknob and made sure the closed sign remained facing outside, the way chef would have wanted it to begin with, and I reflected on the rude truancy I had perpetrated on his establishment. Always a private affair when the ships are in, I thought. There were broken chairs, ten tables with at least one leg missing; fifty checkered tablecloths which I dumped into a corner; three broken windows; a floor full of ripped uniforms, shoes, hats, belts; two wooden peglegs; twelve broken teeth; eleven gold earrings, four with some ear lobe attached; and under the remaining three gas lights, a glittering blanket of glass shards still as the tidal scum on the Thames. My head ached recalling how three sailors annointed a mate by bashing his head into the tall cabinet at the end of the bar for the vintage of the wine rack. I reached down my left leg to my sack of gold coins and dropped on the bar ten double eagles into a weaved bread basket and walked into the kitchen to pay up for the misery and abuse of my friendship with chef Nichon. I dropped down next to him against the row of base cabinets opposite the oven. He looked straight ahead with almost a smile from the corners of his broad jolly face and I knew he was dead. I put my arm around him and his head fell to rest on my unworthy shoulder. I patted his shoulder and I wanted to talk to him, which I did for a while about how sorry I was for the mess and paying him late. Too late. I told him don't worry about your wife and children. And to this day I don't remember how I got back to the Tern.[65]

---

[65] Because of our long-standing professional relationship, I deigned to let stand Ms. Scriveen's contribution (i.e., Chapter 16). After she submitted her draft to me, I rethought the whole idea of her delving into Captain Billy's past, ostensibly to liven up the story line and add to Will's sparse text of his grandfather's influence on him. So, I invited Penny to lunch at La Grande Gifle in Georgetown. She fidgeted with her cigarette while I looked over the menu, and I think she was upset at the lack of my usual pattern of eye contact. After we ordered, I asked her how her mother was and that she might want to rethink having that mole removed from her right cheek, which appeared larger. I pointed at my own cheek to illustrate. What did I do? She stood up so fast, her wine glass tipped over and raced toward my $75 paisley tie from Woodies, and without a word stormed out to the curious craning of necks in her wake. While finishing up the delicious froglegs smothered in caviar-laced musk-ox saliva and mustard sauce, I chanced to chat with the brilliant "New American Cuisine" chef, Corky Jean-Paul Wyne, who spotted me at my table. I mentioned Will's draft and went over the recipe Penny used for baba au rhum. He gave me a moue, or downturned mouth, shrugged his shoulders and said it was fine, except he would have added four eggs and a half cup of rum. He suggested, if it were not too late, I might think about replacing it with blanquette de veau, and as I got up he said come back some time when I'm in town and he would show me how to prepare and present it. Then he grabbed my bill, tore it up like an unacceptable soufflé and bussed me on both cheeks. What a terrific frog! Even if he was from Montclair (New Jersey).

CHAPTER 17

Late evening, and the eastern sky billowed with the sails of clouds and the horizon was a lustrous golden nacre reminding me of a good-night kiss to Mom while turning out her lamp and glancing over at the moonlit mother-of-pearl hand mirror on her small vanity as I closed her door.[66]

I expected that such an idyll, inducing a dreamy conclusion to the day, couldn't last long, and it didn't fail me. Uncle Rob announced over the intercom: Will Melville, report to the COMM center. It's your mother. Looking at the crew lining up for the evening meal, I figured Uncle once again triangulated an embarrassing belittlement of me as the four resembled in my anxiety a parole board I'd seen in a gangster movie and they also didn't fail me in taking their marks. It was a tight passageway

---

[66] I've been conflicted, yet again, by the lack of physical description by Will. It's as if he doesn't care or has a hard time describing the natural environment even one of my kids could easily do. Maybe he was better with crayons. He wasn't particularly self-absorbed. He always joined in the fun without reservation, although sometimes I would catch him daydreaming out the window on a rainy day at the student union, perhaps thinking of a girlfriend. I knew he was strangely interested in a young brunette coed with a noticeable limp, and sometimes I saw him across the quad carrying her books. Maybe he was conflicted by the emotional environment, especially since he often hinted he was running away from himself or things felt but not seen. So, I let it all stand, since I don't know a damn thing about the locale (e.g., Caribbean) he journeyed through, and I have no inclination to puff up descriptions like a commercial artist drawing summer slacks or dress shoes, or deploying the crutch of pathetic fallacy to project his inner turmoil (e.g., when the old man's dog died, a shroud of misty-eyed elms in late September wept rivulets of golden leaves on the wounded earth of its grave).

I tried to negotiate and I got it from each one. Lou exclaimed, well if it isn't the mama's boy; Bud said my, my; cookies and cream or some such in a distinct effete accent. Les, ever the house dealer, said you'll have to leave the table, son. I shook my head through the gantlet of humiliation until Paola grabbed my arm and swung me around, saying mother forgive them for they know not what they say and proceeded to plant a long kiss smack on the lips. I was stunned. Out of the corner of my eye, I saw Lou raise his heavy eyebrows, toying with the Maltese cross dangling in the nave of his sunken chest. Bud hunched his shoulders and added, hey kid, hey!hey!!hey!!! Les announced I was restaked by a mysterious benefactor and could sit back down at the table.   Paola could have said thanks for acting the good boy, but she bit her tongue and I secretly thanked her for stanching the flow of criticism. I knew sadly her charitable moments were as frustrating to me as my inner child crying over a double dip of spumoni sliding off its waffle cone on a scorching summer afternoon.

I climbed up the ladder to the communications room off the bridge. Uncle Rob waved me over to the radiotelephone console, which displayed four such gadgets blinking at me in a confusion of knobs and lights. He sat me down, patted me on the shoulder and gave me the headphones—or cans, as he called them. Speak into here and you'll be fine, son. Then he left the room and I was alone with her lilting voice.

"Willie, can you hear me?"

"Yes, Mom. I can. Sorry, Mom. I meant to call. I've been so busy. Sorry. I'll try to call more often."

"Can you hear me now?"

"Sure, Mom. I can hear you real clear." She always got the other fifty-one percent of my attention the second time.

"How are you? How have you been? You know it's been over a month already now and I haven't heard a word from you. Why haven't you written?" She cleared her throat. She must have had a cold. "Willie, how is the weather down there?"

"Mom, you know I don't write well. I'm on Uncle Rob's yacht we've been all over the place. We left Jamaica two days ago The neighbor's dog was in the back yard, and I asked her to close the kitchen door. Where are you?"

"What? Where?"

"Jamaica, Mom. It's in the Caribbean."

"Jemima? Where?"

"No, Mom, come on. It's about two hundred miles south of Miami."

'So far? Past Key Largo? How's the weather?"

"There was a hurricane when I got off the bus in Fort Lauderdale. It was pretty messy."

"You didn't tell me you got off at Fort Lauderdale. Did you stop to see your Aunt Carlotta? She lives there."

"No. I didn't know she moved there. I couldn't stop. I needed to meet Uncle Rob."

"How has he been treating you, Willie? Are you eating enough?"

"'Mom. Sure, Mom. He's been great. Why? What's wrong?" There was a pause and I could hear her breathe into the phone.

"Well, good. You know your uncle's been very good to us since."

"I know, Mom. He's doing lots of things. He showed me this big retirement community he built in"

"What?"

"Have you ever heard of Alice Detwiler? Did he ever tell you?"

"Who?"

"Alice Detwiler. It's the name of the place."

"Oh." There was another pause and I thought she hanged up.

"Mom?"

"Yes?"

"How have you been?"

"Fine, Willie. I've got this pain in my leg the doctor says it's skyatica."

"What?"

"Nerve pain. He gave me a shot for it last Tuesday."

"Good. I hope it helps."

"Not so far."

"Listen, Mom; have you heard from any of my friends? What about Carolyn?"

"Who?"

"Carolyn. You know. With the limp."

"I think she dropped by a few weeks ago, but you were gone by then. She said to say hello."

"Tell her hi for me. Tell her I'm all right and I'll try to get back soon. Sometime soon."

"What do you mean?"

"I don't know what I mean. Anyway, what else?"

"The neighbor's son, you know the odd one down the block. Her son. They brought him back last week."

"You mean?" I couldn't say his body.

"Yes. They buried him at Fort Sheridan with full military honors. They said it was a nice ceremony in spite of the rain. You know, the flag and the rest of it."

"Yeah."

"Didn't you see it in the paper?"

"No. There's no papers here. Only the phone."

"She hasn't taken his picture out of the front window yet. Poor soul. I haven't as yet talked to her."

"Sorry to hear. Didn't he graduate with honors last year?"

"I don't know. He was a nice boy."

"Anybody else?"

"Let me see. Hold on! Someone's at the door."

"Mom?" There was a shuffling sound; a chatterbox of noise down the hall where I used to hang my jacket on one of the coathooks inside the closet door. I knew she was okay when she raised her voice in a sing-song lilt.

"Who was it?"

"The postman. It's the book I ordered last month."

"What is it?"

"*The Purple Robe*. It's by Lloyd Higgins Boyd."

"Huh?"

"The retired evangelist. It's about this robe passed on from one apostle to another. Twelve. It's the most beautiful robe."

"How do you know, Mom?"

"I'm reading about it."

"I'll have to read it. Anybody else come by, Mom?"

"The Rubinstein's boy. You know, Scott?"

"Yeah."

"He's working for some book publisher in New York, I think. He dropped by to say hi the other day before he left town. He asked about you."

"Yeah. He's a good friend. I hope he does okay. He helped me a lot when we were at Mundane."

"He seemed real concerned about your leaving so suddenly."

"Well, Mom. We've been over this before. I made my choice and I can't look back."

"I know, Willie. You got to do what you've got to do." There was another pause. A long one.

"Mom? Are you okay?" She blew her nose.

"I love you, Willie."

"Me I love you too, Mom." Then a cough.

"Mom? Okay?"

"Yes, Willie. I'm worried."

"But why? Uncle's taking good care of me. Don't worry you head off, okay?"

"Well, I'm your mother."

"I know, Mom. I know. I'm sorry."

Vinnie's mother called me."

"Who?"

"Your friend, Vinnie Pugliese."

"Oh yeah. What an incredible surprise. I happened to bump into him in Fort Lauderdale. He spent a few days with me on the yacht before he left."

"She was very upset."

"Why? Isn't he writing to her?"

"She said he got picked up at the airport when he switched planes."

"Son-of-a!"

"What?"

"So what happened?"

"She said he decided to go into the Army instead of jail. I don't know."

"What?"

"She said the judge gave him a choice."

"How?"

"She said the police were waiting for him when he got there. He told her he was set up or screwed or some such thing."

"What do you mean set up?"

She said he said he thinks your uncle called the Army after he left the boat. He was very angry and upset."

"But why? Uncle Rob wouldn't do something like that. In the first place, he invited Vinnie on the yacht."

"What?"

"They must be checking everybody who goes through. So where is he?" I glanced up above the radiotelephone console and noticed Uncle pictured in his naval officer uniform. I knew Vinnie was uncomfortable around him. They didn't really hit it off.

"She said he cried a lot on the phone."

"Jesus!"

"Willie!"

"Sorry, Mom. Sorry. Well, I hope he stays out of trouble." Another long pause and I sensed she was getting exhausted. She must have written a list of things to say on a piece of paper by the phone, and then doodled over the rest of it. I always had a hard time reading her shopping lists.

"I guess I'd better go for now."

"All right, Mom. Did you get groceries?"

"Yes. Later today. Willie, promise me you'll take good care of yourself. Your uncle's a good man, but he can be a user, too."

"What? Look, Mom, I can handle it. He's got a lot of stuff going on. I can see, but don't worry. I can take care of myself."

"Write me?"

"I'll call, too. Love you, Mom."

"You too, Willie. Bye. Write to me. Don't forget."

"Bye."

"Bye."

"I'm hanging up now, Mom."[67]

---

[67] On Sunday afternoon, November 16, 1971, I sat down with Mrs. Melville in her small dining room where she played the tape recording of the telephone conversation with Will. His voice faded in and out. The entire dialogue of this heart-rending call was missing in the items that she gave me. Actually, it was glossed over by him and stripped to a brief paragraph about how concerned she was for him and hoped he got home soon. I sort of read between the lines and decided it was worth the chance to see if there was more to it, and that's why I transcribed the entire call. It was the only communication between them after he left home. She said she came back from laying long-stemmed roses at her husband's marker at Fort Sheridan. As always, she was very forthcoming and offered me tea. Sometimes, I noticed her glancing at her husband's photo on the mantel and a few times she talked over the tape as it rolled along. I apologized belatedly for my intrusion on Veterans Day, which for some reason I had never been touched to observe. I thought about this for a while, looking at her and then

I got up to leave the COMM room and saw Uncle Rob leaning on the rail outside the hatchway. "How's your mom, son?"

"Oh, she's okay; worried as usual." I joined him at the rail, but left a few feet between us this time.

"I know she's concerned about you."

"Some bad news."

"So."

"She said Vinnie"

"You mean Vincent?"

"Yeah, whatever. They confiscated his passport at JFK and the military police took him away in a flash."

"Stuff happens." He tugged on the bill of his dime-store captain's hat and squinted at the horizon.

"I guess he should have gone straight over to Copenhagen back then."

"Should have."

"Uncle, do you think it was a good idea for him to join us?"

Uncle shifted his shoulders to look my way and said something like Will, you know I don't give dumb answers, right? Let's turn to!

"Sorry I asked," I said as we walked toward the bridge.

---

at the photo of her husband. His cover (i.e., hat) revealed the slightest jaunty tilt above the left eye. As I sat by the coffee table and saw her hands folded together in her lap, composed as if preparing for her own photo, I wondered if I missed out on something.

CHAPTER 18

"Look up!" yelled Lou from the helm. "Incoming!"

Everyone including the Filipinos rushed topside to see a large and small bird wheeling high above the Tern. Bud said it's the biggest sonofabitch you'll ever see out here. Twelve feet across. Paola said it was an albatross, not a sonofabitch, birdbrain. Uncle bumped between them and stood with the rest of us watching the brief aerobatics. Finally, the huge albatross alighted right on the end of the foc'scle. Les said it's our new hood ornament, but then the tern landed not two feet from it and started in. After a brief avian discussion and ruffling of feathers flustering Paola, the albatross spread its huge wings and dropped off the front of the bow to pick up a breeze. The tern flew around and reassumed his squawking like crazy, wagging his head back and forth, telling the other this is my side of the flyway, stupido.

Les said this bird has flown thousands of miles and has the nerve to poop on our deck. It's a miracle.

I took hold of the bucket and rag that one of the servants brought up to clean up the guano left from the brief squabble. The tern stepped aside until I cleaned it up. "Where's the trashcan?" I asked around.

"Out there," pointed Lou.

"*Grugapfluprs*," said Paola with a frown.

Lou raised a hand in her direction. "Don't lay your prehistoric scat on me, lady. Sharks have to live for another million years, too."

Uncle pushed between them again. He did a lot of blocking on the entire journey. He said they could share a banana split later. The crew broke up and turned to, as Uncle said, to daily chores I suspected were more than swabbing decks and repairing line. Each spent at least four hours a day at one of the radiotelephones discussing some sort of business transaction in a lingo even the screw couldn't relate to me at night. Once when the hatch to the COMM room was open a crack, I overheard Les arguing about moving thirty million or some such figure to Zurich.[68] I peeked in and the spittle from his anger sprayed the console. He must have seen my shadow on the deck, as he swirled around and told me to get out and shut the hatch. I never saw him so unravelled. A day later, he came up and said sorry and that he didn't drink enough morning coffee.

When everything quieted down, I took a few minutes breather on the foc'scle. This crazy little bird all of a sudden turned around and skittered across the deck and again plopped right in my lap. Dont ask, because I'll never know the reason. I think Paola was jealous that she wasn't capable or inclined to be so close to another human as was the tern to me. Maybe she thought I was someone special. I asked him where he been and what did he see and he cocked his head and stared at me with a dark eye. His language was far older than mine, or even Paola's. He nestled there preening his long feathers, then as if to say good, I feel better now, hopped down and lifted off with the next stiff breeze.

In the evening, we secured portside a large banana boat and exchanged two of the large crates for four black leather suitcases. I was tired. Another one of many such exchanges we made. Uncle called them unreps or underway replenishments, some old Navy term he liked to impress me

---

68   The more I got into editing Will's notes, the more I felt like an investigative reporter, although I've never owned the shoe leather for such a calling. For a one-time CPA, Les was a sloppy bookkeeper. When Cliff broke into Les's place in Scottsdale for the last time (Les must have installed an alarm system to go along with the underfed Doberman), he found another box stuffed with scribbled worksheets that upon further inspection were encrypted notes and columns of numbers. Whether these were legal transactions or not, he couldn't say. If they reflected illegal transactions such as money laundering, extortion, payoffs, etc., then Uncle Robert Melville and his accumulated wealth would be highly suspect. Will was not certain beyond an inkling that his uncle may have possessed a dark side. Cliff, ever the sarcastic type, added, yeah, like some of the politicians out here. After Cliff's neighbor, an NSA retiree we'll call Ned Siebert (to protect his bail-bonds business), spent all of ten minutes on it, we figured the thirty million was in fact a one hundred thirty million dollar transfer of cash from one of Melville's numerous accounts with Snarkey, Pfeffel and Gooch on the Embarcadero to an unnumbered Swiss account. Where the money came from was a mystery.

with, except I pretty much knew after a time it was cash and not corn chips. I noticed two of the other crew had machine guns draped around their shoulders. Their trigger fingers stuck straight out along the barrels and they glanced over their shoulders every so often. Uncle and the other captain saluted and the boat drifted away at first, then sped away toward the fading sunset in a foamy wake of eerie bioluminescence.

I lay in my rack exhausted and wondered if I should confront Uncle about what the hell was going on and if his providing me safe harbor from the military was at a price. The gentle sea swell rocked me like a baby in a tree, unaware and not a care. Somewhere in the seamless stretch between drifting and dreaming, I think I began a dream-like conversation with the screw following its latest preamble of *younoyounoyounoyounoyounoyounoyounoyounoyouno*. I didn't know. I think I repeated what's going on, Uncle, and the screw did all the talking. There's things, son, you don't need to know, but I'll tell you, since we may all wind up walking the plank. In this shark-infested world you don't stand a chance unless you become one of them, or know their ways. If you stay in the sanctuary of one school or another, counting on safety in numbers, it's insane to think you won't be hauled into a life on the edge, often out of your depth, living hand-to-mouth, settled into a humdrum anonymous existence and uncertainty capable of snapping shut as quick as a mako's jaws. Sure, I served my country. Willingly. With pride. I would do it again if I were your age. In a heartbeat. But it also hardened me. I was on one sub or another for twenty years. A different kind of school to be sure. I adapted. Conformed. I succeeded, but I lost men and the other side lost men. I held onto a shipmate's hand within site of the beach at Guadalcanal until only his forearm was left and I borrowed it to save myself. They sure as hell weren't getting his wedding ring, which I asked the chaplain to mail to his widow. And when I left, I put my Navy Cross and the other fruit salad in the back of a bottom drawer and sat on the edge of the bed and knew I had become a stranger unto myself. I was a shark in a three-piece suit making a killing as easily as gliding through chum off the fantail. Don't be mistaken. I've got my charities, ventures and investments through special conditions and means and guide them with the best of social intentions, but with a well-schooled discipline and bone-crushing drive. If I stop moving, I'll die as surely as a shark in a goldfish pond. So, don't ever ask me what the hell is going on. Keep it zipped. Watch and listen![69]

"Shsssh!"

---

[69] Will engaged in his own brand of scuttlebut with the screw. Maybe he felt more comfortable giving Melville the benefit of the doubt and letting the screw do the narration. Yet, he must have talked to his uncle at some time to get this level of detail even about Melville's naval experiences, irregardless of the conversant screw. I confirmed much of this detail with the respected naval architect and historian, Haywood Smoot, of Pensacola, a well-known contributor to the naval history magazine, *Sea Tales Tall and True*. Except for not knowing the exact date and location of the incident (October 9, 1942; ten nautical miles SSW of Guadalcanal), Will did not once mention that this detail was from a direct conversation with Melville. Thus, the astounding implication that the ramblings of the Tern's screw could influence Will's imagination with such factual clarity. By the way, Smoot thought that Captain Billy referred to a children's TV show popular in the early Fifties along the Gulf Coast out of Mobile. Coincidentally, Captain Smoot (USN, ret'd) confided to me off the record that his sister was married to Robert Melville (1949-50), but that they lost contact after the divorce and the surprising sudden accumulation of Melville's wealth. He seemed a bit irked that he lost Melville as a golfing partner, but said to pass along his best if I saw him. Even stranger, when I stopped off in Gulf Shores to pick up some fish and chips for the ride back to the Bassford Motel near Fort Lauderdale, I spotted an emerald El Dorado with the vanity plate, "Melville Deux." I waited until a young blonde about thirty-five came out with a bag of groceries and a small perky pom on a leash. Her hair was spun like cotton candy on top of her oversized plastic flower sunglasses. She took her time putting the bag in the car. Her derriere was so attractive, I had to look away to stay focused. She said, sorry, wrong Melville and let enough of the leash out so that the little bitch tore a hole in the cuff of my polyester slacks. I knew she was divorced from Melville and I shouldn't have asked in the first place. Hounded by curiosity and plain doggedness, I followed her and the pom for about five miles until she turned into a gated driveway. It was a large Med-style mansion with beautiful manicured gardens and snowball bushes a bit broader than her ass. When I buzzed at the gate, reinforcements ran down the driveway in the menacing shapes of two German shepherds. I still recall the twinkle of their rhinestone collars as they seemed to bark chips of paint off the black metal security gate.

Paola suddenly woke me up from my restless sleep with two fingers on my lips. "Quiet!" she whispered. "There's a boarding party off our port bow."

"Wha?"

"They've come to take back their money. Follow me."

She pulled me into the larger berthing area where they all slept. Bud and Lou squatted next to two portholes. Bud cradled a sawed-off shotgun, laying down a game of solitaire. I stooped next to him. He smiled and I sensed something he was about to enjoy.

"Soup's on," he said.

I felt nauseous and asked him what was across Lou's thighs. Lou heard me and lifted up a Superman comic book. Paola sat next to the berthing hatchway.

"Grenade launcher. It's not from the Marx toy factory," whispered Lou.

I could hear the low rumble of the diesel engine drifting closer and my mouth got gummy with fear.

Bud slowly put his cards away. He whispered if I believed in life, liberty and the pursuit of wealth. I said I was unaware of that version and he said it's okay. You can still be poor and happy in the greatest country on earth.

"I guess so," I said.

Lou rolled up the comic and said, "Sonofabitch'n kryptonite."

Paola, who had a clear view of both, raised two fingers in Bud's direction and flipped her middle finger at Lou. The water began to slop between the Tern and the intruding boat. I saw Paola nod her head and all hell broke loose topside. Then they both quietly opened their portholes. Lou raised the launcher to his shoulder. He was standing on a stack of three thick Merriam-Webster collegiate dictionaries. One of which was open at "K." Lou fired and I heard screaming outside. Bud then told me to hold his pack of cards. He said trick or treat and nudged the muzzle up and outward and fired both barrels. More screaming, then silence. Then low moaning all over.

"Never neat. Kielbasa without the casing," said Bud.

Suddenly, the hatch framed a bulky dark intruder in a black ski mask. Another comic strip character to deal with. I was stunned with the thought, why the get-up? The costume of the day? Out here? This wasn't the corner bank or local restaurant. He didn't have a chance. Paola, sitting with her legs crossed by the hatchway, lifted a cloaked .45 and the noise was again deafening. The intruder fell back like an overfilled dumpster. The body crumpled backward and landed with the head five feet from me. I gagged with revulsion as blood dribbled out the mouth hole of the mask. The bullet blew away the back of the head and—God!—blood splattered all over my pants. A bloody eyeball plopped right beside my hand and stared at me like a giant marble caromed out of the circle. Paola pushed the legs off hers as she got up. I was repulsed more by her nonchalance than the sheer violence. Who then was she and what violent past annealed her into such a hard yet remarkable woman? Did Uncle Rob teach her all this?

Who was Bud, anyway? He saw my fright and pulled me back down by the arm. Don't worry, kid. It's not one of your nightmares." He glanced around the room. "It's the real thing."

Bud and Lou now fired at will, chatting with each other between rounds. Their aplomb went way beyond walking the dog around the block.

"Holy cow! What happened?" I mumbled through numb lips. I stumbled to my feet and followed Paola up the ladder, gasping for breath. Topside we tripped over three bodies in a variety of unnatural poses dressed in beachwear I noticed in a clothing store on the way to the Cafe Aureole back in Kingston. Les yelled down to us, waving an old Tommygun with red, white and blue stripes along the barrel.

"You and Paola throw them overboard. Now!" The third one we dragged to the side started to moan.

"He's still alive," I said to Paola.

"Look, give a hand or do I have to do the whole damn thing myself as usual," she fumed and her golden curls flew all over her shoulders. I couldn't believe the force of this woman. I stumbled to help her and was nerve-wracked as hell. I couldn't feel my arms or legs.

I saw him sitting there in a canvas deck chair. Legs crossed. Wetsuit with snorkel and mask shoved up his forehead. His entire face was painted black. Only when I saw the whites of his eyes and the scruffy beard did I recognize Uncle Rob.

"I figured they would be back for seconds. Such gluttony." Uncle chomped on an unlit cigar. "Good job, son."

"But, Uncle Rob. It's a Jamaican police boat. Look at the side!"

He tossed the cigar overboard as he patted my shoulder saying, son don't let labels dim your perspective of worldly things. There's good plumbers and bad plumbers; good doctors and downright lousy doctors. He picked up a stencilled metal can and flip-flopped his way to the side. "I'll be right back and I want everything cleaned up chop-chop."

I passed the three Filipinos coming up the ladder with a mop and two buckets.

"Man overboard, give a hand kid," strained Bud who held half the riddled body of the gatecrasher through the oversized porthole. "Come on, grab his feet."

I hesitated. My stomach was already queazy from the acrid gun smoke and noise.

Lou said, "He's dead. He's no longer here. He left town. Jumped ship. You don't even rate 4F if all you can do is stand there with your thumb up your ass. Help Bud!"

"He's too fat," shouted Bud on the other side." We both pulled the body out and pushed and pulled the body up the ten ladder steps. There was blood all over the deck. My sneakers were soaked.

"So much for the police chief's cousin. Let us pray," said Lou.

"Who?" I asked.

"Don't say who. There's no more face. I can tell by the gold earring over there on the deck," said Bud.

We rolled the body of the police chief's cousin in a canvas tortilla and lifted it up and over the side. My head started spinning. After we pitched it overboard, another wave of nausea hit me and I slipped down the ladder to the stateroom and dropped into the leather bench to control my dry wretching. If these had been images only seen and not felt, I could have accepted it all, but to feel a human body slip through my hands and sink into the sea. My conscience was palsied with projection. I must have stumbled around the long mahogany table at least ten times. I was on an adrenalin overdose. In a panic, I climbed back topside in time to see the police boat slip into the deep. Uncle began to remove his blackface and explained how half an hour earlier he swam over to place a thermite device on the hull of the boat.

"What's thermite?" I asked Les, who sat down with chest pains he chased with two nitroglycerin pills he picked out of a small metal cylinder around his neck.

"Can't talk," he whispered.

Bud tugged me by the arm away from Les. "Les gets excitable. He'll get over it."

An hour later, we gathered around the oval table in the stateroom. There was a pensive atmosphere reminding me of my Aunt Margaret's wake in her hometown of Buffalo when I was seventeen.[70] I don't know why I thought of her then. Perhaps it was the emotional distress. I felt downright ashamed to even think of comparing this ugly incident to her valiant suffering eight months with cancer.

"All accounted for? Right!" said Uncle Captain as he walked his eyes around the table. He winced, adjusting the bandage wrapped around his arm. Paola asked if he needed a medic. "A scratch. No thanks." I was surprised they brought along a knife thrower this time." He made his familiar oral click and cracked a smile. "Let me say well done, everyone."

---

[70] Aunt Margaret must have gained a significant influence on Will if he congered up her memory at this stressful time. I had Little Clarisse ask Herb Rouleau, Aunt Margaret's widower, if there was any unusual influence from his wife on young Will in view of this passage. She interviewed him at his small appliance repair shop in Hyattsville, and was apparently very pleased I was editing his nephew's reminiscences. He spoke into the tape recorder with a soft reticent voice he may have picked up after his wife died roughly ten years earlier, because he said he was a loudmouth (his words) construction foreman for many years during the post-World War II housing boom across the river in Arlington. They enjoyed having Will, or Willie, visit them on some of their summer vacations. Mrs. Melville's sister became a surrogate mother during those brief three-week summer interludes. She bore a daughter from a previous relationship who contracted polio and resided in an iron lung in the back bedroom. She died about five years before Will began visiting, and they were happy his quiet reserve and laughter reminded them of their Betty. They showed Will her framed pictures placed here and there about the modest bungalow. When the surgeons at Georgetown told his wife about the advanced pancreatic cancer, she insisted Willie spend that summer with them. They felt he was mature enough to understand the situation, and when she kept on schedule with the morphine, they enjoyed each other's company, especially at the beach near Rehoboth. The only thing that stuck in Mr. Rouleau's memory was, toward the end of that last get-together, his wife was in so much pain at night, her moaning would awaken Will, who was in the adjoining bedroom and obviously heard her delerious ramblings through the wall. He would get up to ask Mr. Rouleau at the door to their bedroom if he could help. For all of his fatigue around the clock then, Rouleau thought Will showed a terrific sense of caring and responsibility for his age. On his last night, he said Will asked again, as usual, Can I help, Uncle Herb? And he gave Will a hug at the door and said he wished Will were their own son.

He got up and walked around the table, patting the men on the shoulder and planting a chaste kiss on the left side of Paola's head.

"Well done, Will," as he passed behind me. "Sorry about the mess, but they always want all the money all the time."

"Thanks, Uncle Rob, but I didn't do anything." It came out like a miserable bleating plea of false innocence.

Bud raised a limp hand to interject, "Sure you helped us give the heave-ho. Remember?"

Lou, not to be lost in the post-mortem situation report, said even if you stood by playing with yourself, you were still an accessory to our collective sin.

"Coffee or tea, boss," entered the child-like voice of the diminutive chef Felipe from Dagupan City.

"Felipe, java all around, and throw this bloody shirt overboard," said Uncle.

"Aye, aye, boss." One of the sleeves to his embroidered white dress shirt was blood-soaked. Les nudged me and said he was also a guilty bystander when Felipe popped up from behind the supply box on deck and grabbed a boarder from behind to slit his throat with the butcher knife he used to carve the pork roast on Sundays.

"Earring to earring," said Les. "Not a sound. The bastard didn't even have a chance to do a little tap dance; otherwise, he may have had enough talent for the amateur hour."

I put my face in my hands and mumbled to let Les know I didn't need any more vaudevillian details. So, I finally regained enough composure to ask Why? as sort of a general topic of discussion.

Uncle sipped his java. His rough hands wrapped around the cup and partially hid a dolphin and anchor decal on it. "Son, unexpected guests. I regret your having to ship out on this last, auspicious voyage of the Tern under the current circumstances. Such is life. You've got to roll with the waves."

Paola interrupted him to say you've been telling us such garbage for the last six years.

"A proud ship. A proud crew. I took you on with the best of intentions for smooth sailing and all that rot, but." He stared at the depth chart before him.

"But what, Uncle? What?"

"I don't know. Don't ever tell your mother. More coffee?"

"Don't worry. She'll never find out," I said.

Lou winked at me. "Not the basic training you expected, huh kid?"

"No. It's not," I said in resignation. Uncle broke the silence that lay around us like a shroud of fog. For your edification, son, let me put it in nontechnical terms.

"No, Uncle Rob. You don't have to say anymore."

"You're out of order, son. You're entitled to an explanation. Now listen up." He said this with such roughness in his gravelly voice I almost said No, you don't owe me anything since you're not my old man in the first place, but I didn't have the heart to say it, since I remembered he had no children.

"How long has this stuff been going on?" I asked.

"I'll answer," said Les. "Since 1950, and it's none of your snooty business why your uncle started this.[71] Only that he did. When he accumulated enough to get away for a while, he shanghaied us—all willingly I might add—to spend a few months out of the year doing charity work from the Tern to ease a hell of a lot of peoples' pain. That sort of thing. Like he said before, you watch and listen first, then you can bitch all you want, but not before. Maybe you'll learn something. Enough said. Yeah, you could call it basic training."

Uncle turned his cup a few times, looking down into it. It was empty. It probably held a few grounds of coffee, but no tea leaves. It struck me then he was an eccentric loner, running like he used to, silent and deep below street-level while others—perhaps as successful—cruised on the surface for recognition for the most inconsequential and worthless reasons. When I later saw these kids on the island, I understood a little better his motivation and perhaps why he wanted to sign me on as a crew member.

Uncle said he bought expired medical supplies on the cheap from a contact in the Kingston health department who kept a supply line open from the UN and a basketcase of Baptist charities operating out of Waco. All donations. All free. Then he would gouge bolo-swinging rebels along the Nicaragua-Guatemala border who needed to supplement their rusty tins of coca leaves. And since he knew they were advised by two unretired US Army captains, he felt inclined to deal with them to raise money for his orphanage about forty nautical miles north of Baranquilla, as well as ironically to provide safe passage for the kids.

Lou interjected, unworthy means for worthy deeds. These kids come from all over this stinking armpit—the Carib'. "It's a sanctuary your uncle

---

[71] It was actually 1951, the year after his first wife died in childbirth. A former Rotarian in Atlanta told me by phone that Melville was a pretty easygoing guy until then.

bought; one reason we've all agreed to take his money and contribute what we can to help." Paola made the strange grin of someone caught breaking parole. "Sort of like the one we're offering you until you get you head out of your rear," added Lou, as he silently sought Paola's concurrence.

"Okay, Lou. Pipe down," said Uncle before I was able to defend my defenseless butt. I wanted to tell the little runt I needed time to sort things out and I wasn't about to walk a perimeter or smoke a joint in a wet foxhole.

Uncle looked across the table reflecting our faces to a large map of the US on the opposite bulkhead. It contained several colorful pins stuck in it to denote I guess some of the locations of his business interests.[72] Once he said, I'll tell you sometime. He said, okay it's a wrap for today. I was the last to leave the room. Uncle came over—limped over—told me Will, son, we're not here to save the world, but only to reduce some of the suffering, and people like me choose to be able to do such rather than turn the other cheek. Can you at least understand this? I pursed my lips and replied I think so. And the screw was strangely mute at night.

---

[72] Although I omitted this from the storyline, Will's notes mentions the time Les described some of the pins on the stateroom map. Will asked him about the small flag pins—about eighty—with the tiny head of a pirate spread throughout the Midwest in such towns as Keokuk, Centralia, Manhattan and Grand Isle. Les pulled off one and showed Will the small letters "Goobs" in an arc around the pirate's bearded face. He explained that Melville still retained majority interest in the deep discount import chain. Initially, Melville hired the Krashan-Byrne Agency in Phoenix to revamp the old Rancher Clem dry goods chain into the popular Going Out of Business stores. Melville was not the first to use this retailing ploy, but he was the first to hit it big by having the store name hoisted on a flashy ten-foot by twenty-foot neon sign atop the front window that could be seen for miles. They soon became one of the major Midwest retailers of imported clothing and assorted deelies from Pakistan, India and Southeast Asia. The chain was so successful, competitors such as McCoys, Lowens and others took Melville to court over his trademarked store name, claiming that it denied them the ability to declare "going out of business" as a legal notification to its remaining customers. In effect, Melville could sue them for trademark infringement, unless he decided to grant the assignment of the phrase. When Sears and Hudson's enjoined, the court ruled against Melville, who merely changed the name to "Goobs" with no diminution of sales. As of this writing, the chain has expanded to Billings, Sparks and Redondo Beach under a new ad campaign called, "Gobs and Gobs at Goobs."

CHAPTER 19

The Tern drifted as I heard a deep-throated vessel starboard. Not again, I thought. So, I jumped out of the rack and crept to the top of the ladder, where Lou and Bud lifted four of those aluminum suitcases over the side. I had no idea how they got onboard. The visitor shoved off as Les said to Uncle, they should make the shareholders happy. To me, it was one more part to a 2000-piece jigsaw puzzle of clouds and water I once saw scattered all over a card table at Aunt Margaret's cancer clinic. Before I shut the hatch to my room, Paola said hey from across the passageway. It was a room reserved for her when she didn't feel like being one of the guys. She leaned out in a canary yellow negligee, making me wonder if the word imagination still existed.

"*Klugrapriepuck.*"

"Beg pardon?"[73]

"Don't worry. This is my way to unwind from a somewhat stressful day," she said.

"Uh, you don't have to explain." Actually, I wanted her to continue all night with all the details.

"I was on the fantail walking an M-16 your uncle borrowed from a pawn shop near Parris Island."

"What? There was so much confusion, I didn't know where you were."

---

[73]   This must have been very frustrating to Will; these phonetics Paola digressed into. He left three scribbled pages of them he said she gave to him, but I doubt they could even describe the yak-base buttercream I smothered over some blue-tips I sluiced down a few months ago at the Wild Mongolian Crackpot in the spacious Del's Ray Beach Inn in Jupiter. What a pity how this supposed intelligent, attractive woman got wrapped around such an academic axle.

She ran her fingers through those long golden curls and shook her head in a seductive arc.

"I was supposed to keep them occupied."

"Really?"

"Really. Get some rest. Tomorrow's a big day for all of us. You'll see." She blew me a kiss and nearly broke my heart when she chopped off my What do you mean? with a slammed door.

Around 0300, it dawned on me that I hadn't heard a single news report or seen TV for over six weeks. Except for random screw chatter usually about baseball, I never thought I could survive without some vicarious stimulation that often made me miss my interstate exit or lulled me asleep on the sofa with a physics textbook falling from my hands. I was on the run from Uncle Sam compliments of Uncle Rob, and the real—the visceral— excitement was the revivifying escape from the insidious world of the idiot box, as Mom called the TV, and the reality that I was free to perform my own pratfalls. There were no more excuses, no more forgiveness, no pablum of permissiveness, and it was as refreshing as a cold broadside of sea spray. Uncle Rob gave me the chance to sort out the path, and I was grateful for it in spite of the disturbing bootcamp he was putting me through. I was plainly unfit at this time to fall in ranks to save the American way of life deep in a melting jungle thousands of miles from the numerous choices at my favorite DQ in Monroe.[74]

---

[74] Personal note: This was not only bad writing by Will, but reflected more importantly on his naive rationale for abandoning the "ship of state." My classmate, Garry "Not Me" McKee, in PolySci 343 (Origins of American Defeatism), which at that time expanded to two classes and two more remote TV classrooms in the vacant Rousseau Building, told me Will was "on the fence" and not convinced like us that the war was a blatant capitalist trap and total waste of life and limb. He said he invited Will to several anti-war rallies on campus and at the nearby Kant College of Design, but lost track of him in the crowd each time. For me, it was not necessary to flee like Will, which he awkwardly explains here once again. I simply got into a journalism program in Columbus, got married and then spent two years treading water there at law school. He did it the hard way. All he needed to do was join us and stay in school to fight the regime, which was a no-brainer for all of us in the class that we nicknamed "Hell No!" with impertinence. It was taught by Professor Grigory Menshikov, a widely respected scholar on appeasement and civil disobedience, who told us that he miraculously left only his right leg below the knee in a Soviet work-study

The next morning, we dropped anchor off a small island north of

camp two hundred miles northeast of Irkutsk. I'm editorializing here and regret the personal intrusion on the reader; however, that time of upheaval burns in my conscience as much as visiting the graves of several of my buddies who chose to fall not only on the other side of the fence, but on the other side of the world. I never met Will's uncle, but if Will's reminiscence is an honest and accurate account, I must concede now that, with the sclerotic passage of time, Captain Melville's brand of exploitative munificence has made me stop to reconsider the humanistic side of capitalism. Will would no doubt have flunked Menshikov's one-question final: Knowing the inevitable outcome of the conflict as discussed in this course, state why you would/would not serve your country? By then, I guess, he was already having trouble stringing out differential equations, let alone soaking up political thought that raised our fists and moved our bowels to do something concrete on the cracked and scuffed faculty parking lot under the Dean's window.

Let me finish this, and I won't bring it up anymore, because I feel the need to play comrade-in-arms to describe what eludes Will. I know this is Will's story, but let me digress a moment to highlight what I think was on his mind and cover for the trite expression of his "non" events. When I was a freshman with Will at Mundane and, as Will alluded to but much earlier, I also got fed up with magazines and bestsellers and TV and all that crap focusing on the so-called joys of gratuitous sex and violence, the occult of personality with its plastic smiles, furtive rehearsals and staged posturing and lifestyles of the wealthy and infamous shoved in my face at every newstand and on TV and in the movies. So, I rebelled and decided to start a magazine about, well, I called it *Working*, about plain average folks doing their job without spotlights and cameras and perverse mugging to share with readers how the great majority of we Americans struggle every day to put bread on the table. You know: what this country is all about. The whole experience was a catharsis for me. We didn't get here with our thumbs in the mouth and t'other up the backside. They were on gun hammers and nails and and screwdrivers and tissues wiping kids' snotty noses, but not up our asses. I read a lot of stuff by Studs and even sat in on one of his impromptu lectures at Callahan's Bar and Grill on Michigan Avenue back in 1966. This was well before editing and doing stuff for friends like Will Melville, who was one of my best friends, eventhough he was sort of distant moreso than the two houses that separated our parents' homes in Monroe. I borrowed a girlfriend's cheap Yashica and tooled mostly around Ohio, Michigan, Indiana and western Pennsylvania on weekends, even skipping some weekday classes, to interview

Baranquilla. I was once again surprised when Les told me Uncle owned the

---

working stiffs in steel mills, assembly lines, factories; greasy spoons; any place where people worked primarily with their hands. Believe me, when some of them found out I was in college, they resented my snooping and walked away figuring another smart punk using his mouth and brains instead of his back. One guy picked up this huge crescent wrench off a metal toolcart and punctuated his speech with it. And I built a faithful network of comrade reporters at other schools like Carnegie, SIU, Bowling Green who sent me articles. For six glorious months and six glorious editions, I felt on top of the world until I shot off my mouth at a student anti-war rally. I was on top of a huge Krumshaws oil storage tank across the street from the Dean's office when it all blew up in my face. Some conscientious citizen fingered me as the protest leader—a baldfaced lie to this day—and I was suspended for the semester after police chief Duke Slattery showed the Dean a Polaroid of loudmouth me and my new partial bridge. One of his cops saw me writing down the chant of Hell no, etc., and grabbed it from my hand and tore it up laughing, then proceeded to drag my girlfriend, Bela Minkus, and me down the winding ladder of the tank. He pulled Bela by the hair. She had beautiful long black hair and the guy didn't have to do that to her and it hurt me that I couldn't help her. We were booked for disorderly conduct and released on our own recognizance—as if we didn't know who the hell we were or what we were doing in the first place. I lost track of Bela after she transferred to Kent and when Uncle Eddie found out, he called me, of all things, a panty-waisted turncoat and cut off my funds for *Working*. He was a career jarhead, and I knew he would be on my trail any day. So, my attempt to join the fourth estate ended, and I would have wound up like Will except that I tacked my way around the draft by staying in school. You might say I and a lot of guys "drafted" behind Will's uncertainty or gung-ho vanity, like cars racing at Sebring saving gas to come out alive and on top, because without Will out there "on point" (as Uncle Eddie put it), a hell of a lot of us would have been rousted out of our academic hidey holes and into a world of cacapeepee. It could have been brutal for the rest of us. And all we did was be there, raising our voices and trying to make things better. It didn't work out, but I'm not complaining. At least, I didn't become one of those vacuous celluloid personalities I tried to indirectly expose in my fledgling magazine, and I was lucky enough (Uncle Eddie said I finally got some "mazel") to meet and marry my beloved Roberta Nordlinger, the most beautiful cheerleader Ohio State ever had. Don't get me wrong. I was and still am for social change, but not when it's dictated by some conniving bureaucrat or pushed in your face by Hollywood or the mastiff media.

whole island: around one hundred square miles of lush vegetation, sugary sand beaches, two deep inlets and even a landing strip for C-130s, some kind of military supply plane of which I was not familiar.

As we waded ashore, I was impressed by the crystalline beauty of the blue water, then the warm sand of the pure white beach. Postcard cocoanut palms arched low with their spiky fronds rustling in the soft breeze. Then I saw the hillside ringing the beach, children running and jumping with excitement. They began to spill down to us in rivulets of unrestrained shouting and laughter. Two Filipino nurses in white carried the container through the compound gates shaped overhead like arches with the motto, "Siempre estaremos juntos." She said it meant we'll always be together. Uncle led us around the expansive compound of twenty large white-washed one-story concrete buildings with red terra cotta roofs arranged in concentric circles like a rare tropical blossom. Father Ramon, a young Dominican with a measured gait beneath his robe, walked up front with Uncle talking with a great deal of animation. There must have been a thousand children latching onto us as we gradually spread out and moved at an individual pace. I caught up with Bud, whose hands held two large bags of macadamia nuts. My bag was emptied several minutes earlier. I couldn't figure the origin of metallic clicking here and there. The kids were anywhere from kindergarten to high school in age.

"Look down, not up at those pretty clouds," advised Bud.

Then I noticed about half the kids with artificial limbs and braces. I was taken aback at my initial lack of attention and self-absorption from the excitement of visiting a new place.

"Land mines," Bud shouted to me above the kids. Two or three of them grabbed each of my hands and spoke so fast, I didn't understand a word but I smiled yes and exclaimed Que bueno! and other Spanish phrases from grade school. I stumbled a few times, pushed by the exurberance of the kids, who must have thought we came from Mars. One of the nearby nurses waded over and said don't worry, the bell will ring in a minute and she pointed to the church tower at the end of the street. She was a young nurse

---

I'm not ashamed of anything I did, although like I said, I think about it each time I drive by Oak Hill Memorial Gardens on the way to work. Again, sorry to intrude on Will's story, but I must emphasize beyond the fiction that it was a pretty lonely and desperate time for me, as well. I must have lost thirty pounds during those two years. I never got them back. A different pound of flesh, to be sure.

from Medellin who said she was there for already three years. When the bell rang, all the kids limped, hopped or dragged themselves, holding onto one another and otherwise lined up behind their assigned nurses, of which there were about twenty who led them to the large dining hall next to the chapel. The air, filled with their small waving hands, looked like a garden full of monarch butterflies. Another nurse from Honduras who spoke some English told me the kids were from all over Central and South America. She said they usually arrive here like boxes of Raggedy Ann dolls. Yeah, I thought: chewed beyond recognition by political thugs with the attitude of unleashed pitbulls. A handful of doctors sew them up and often have to send them off to a hospital in Orange County to put on the final touches.

I watched the noisy laughing kids hobble off to the dining hall with their shepherding nurses and as the dust settled, I couldn't recall seeing a happier group of adults and children. The kids arriving at the landing strip were literally skin and bones; limp little bodies with dangling arms and legs. The sun sparkled off a metallic crutch or prosthetic limb here and there. Up ahead, Uncle Rob waved with a big smile to the receding crowd. He must have figured if he couldn't have one child of his own, he surely would have a thousand or whatever of someone elses.

"...from the C-130 over there," as Les pointed to the airstrip after I caught up with him.

"Who gets these kids here anyway?"

"It's a bit murky," said Les. "The old man—your uncle—has connections around the region. It's not difficult to find people willing to help, even for a handful of pesos." He scratched his chin.

"How long do they stay here?" I asked.

"As long as whenever. We send back the patched-up ones if there's a caring family." Then he noticed the way to the dining hall. "Some are homeless and broken inside, but you can't see this until later. Then we have to make other arrangements. So many."

"Where do they go?" I pressed.

"If another charity can't take over, we try to get them over to the shoe place. Some have grown up here. A few also work a while on the other side of the island," said Les.

"Where?"

"You know," said Lou, who slipped into our space, "you should have been a reporter with this who, what, when, where and how routine. I let his comment glance off my jaw.

"Anyway," said Les, "the shoe factory outside Gallup. He's sent hundreds of them there since we began this gig about ten years ago. Not too bad."

I shook my head slowly to digest what was coming out of Les's mouth.

Les pulled on the bill of his baseball cap and chuckled like Uncle Rob. "Look, Will; your uncle is a strange bird, like the one following us for days. I'm the only one who knows what he's really worth in bucks, but it's not the point. You simply can't count human lives like dollar bills."

"What's the point?"

"It's complicated. That's all." Les got up, hiked up his white pants and said you don't have the NTK, bub." He jingled some coins in his pocket and said Uncle looks jolly on the outside, but he's driven. Driven. Let's go eat some bean fajitas.

I took a swig of Dos Hermanos. A couple of swigs, thinking Les threw the bull until I saw several people run out to receive five or six children from a helicopter landing at an end of the runway. I felt as foreign and homeless as the tern who adopted us. Me. Then I knew I was not watching a roll from a Super 8. I was a nobody out here, along for the ride. Drifting. No sense of direction like the tern, which must have been hurt as Paola and Dr. Granados said "and way off its route." Would it ever find its way back? I wasn't a true part of the crew. They knew this. I was along for the ride. Tolerated until I found my way back. My time on the Tern as a snug harbor was limited. A beautiful floating palace of white hull and dark mahogany and shiny brass and Karistan rugs. For another species, older than man, to commune with me; this feeling put me in a mental stupor for days and I thought about my future; the future of the kids; my own species; my country; my neighborhood; Mom; the memory of Dad; Captain Billy; even the people who built the house I lived in as a child. Could I ever emulate the tern and its determination to find the way back?

CHAPTER 20

After the sun settled behind the brittle latticework of banyan trees on the surrounding hillside, we didn't stay very long. Several of the nurses and a few doctors lined up at the archway, and we exchanged handshakes as we passed and posed for some snapshots by Lou. Their smiles and polite laughter was contagious, and they bobbed their heads a bit now and then, seeking eye contact to convey to me the hope and purpose they found in their work on the island. I also knew someone gave them the opportunity—my Dad's brother.

As the Tern moved out and along the shoreline, I spotted above the compound the cottages dotting the hillside housing the nurses and doctors and supporting cast of cooks and cleanup help. Lou, who was often bowled over by the strong undertow of kids tugging his arms, came up to me and leaned on the rail. I asked him how he liked the visit.

"It was okay. Been there a few times."

In a clearing on the hillside, he pointed to a small plot of wooden markers. "In case you miss it, some of them have to leave by the back door," he said in a sarcastic tone I felt he reserved for me alone. "They can stay up there as long as they want. They never have to go back to the abuse their little bodies..." His voice drifted off and then he turned aside abruptly and walked the other way. The two-inch riser on his left shoe tapped the wooden deck. I didn't recall seeing him for two days. Actually, the next time he saw me, he hurried off in the other direction. I guess he wasn't the little shit I thought he was.

Two hours later, we finished up box lunches of shrimp, lobster, octopus (which I fingered into a corner of the box) and a small salad whipped up by chef Felipe. I called him chef bolo now everytime we passed to remind him of his hatchet job on one of the boarders. I'm glad I wasn't there to see it. We laughed about it and he wanted to show me how to hold the handle and swing it. He said don't worry, you'll get used to it. You can use it in the kitchen, too, and he laughed even louder with his high-pitched marmoset voice.

The other side of the lush island came into view and my eyeballs almost dropped out. It was the difference between high noon and the eleventh hour. The dark side of the moon you never see. I recalled then a portion of the double-strand razor fence snaking up the ridge of the hillside past the small carved-out area of wooden crosses when Lou abruptly walked away. It was a resort out of nowhere. There were two, twenty-story buildings, probably hotels, with gaudy orange and gold wavy lines painted along one side; about two dozen blue and white cottages scattered around them and about a dozen swimming pools. The place was packed, but from our anchorage I could only hear the occasional yelp of poolside frolic. No cars, but the cove harbored several large boats tied up at the floating docks. One was a monster even larger than the Tern. I borrowed a pair of binoculars from Bud and scanned the beach and boardwalk. People milling idly around in bikinis, Bermuda shorts and slacks; some twirling peppermint-stripe parasols. Vacationeers getting away from work stress, postponing obligations, hiding from roving cameras, open microphones, whatever. In a way, they may have been hurting a lot more than those kids on the other side and I imagined them trying hard to capture the unadulterated joy I saw spilling forth from those battered kids on the other side.

I caught Uncle Rob at the ladder as he hopped a small craft to go in with Paola, Les and Lou. "Hey, Uncle. What's all this about?"

"Got to go. No time. Talk to Bud. You two stay here. We'll be back in a couple of hours." He winked at me as he went over the side. I thought here we go again, working with the derivative—this time Bud—as I was again reluctant to get nosy. Uncle had a lot more stuff going on. I was a guest. He did me a favor going out of his way to provide sanctuary for my confused state of mind, which was so bad I started believing the Tern's screw could elucidate knowledge through its weird noises in the night.

So I bumped Bud on the elbow and asked him what's it all about? He turned to look at me and said hey, nudges don't count. Pay me. I reached into a pocket as if to give him a finder's fee and he said didn't they ever... and I said to him: teach me anything in college?

"Look, kid. I only work here. If you can keep your trap shut I'll take a chance and give you the scoop."

"Sure, Bud. Not a peep."

"What you see over there is a mirage. It's the other half of the equation. Weren't you in engineering?"

"I was, once."

"Okay. You're better off now. If the old man won't tell you about the birds and the bees, in this instance vultures and bats, I'll take the chance. If he ever finds out I told you..."

"I swear, Bud."

"It's only because this is our last trip here on the Tern and I got a case of nostalgia."

Sure, Bud."

Bud said how do you think most of those doctors and nurses and medical supplies and planes are paid for? Right! It comes from this side of the island. No. No one is ever allowed to go beyond the covered fence you see up there behind the hotels. See it? Up there on the hill? See it now? They have such a good time here they don't even know the kids are on the other side. Where there's a sense of hope over there, there's one of hopelessness here. They blow their money, get drunk, get high, get laid, play roulette, skin dive, smash windows, eat the best food, there's even a divorce lawyer hanging around. What more do you want? What? About three thousand for the weekend. Cheap compared to the one over by St. Thomas. What? No. I'm not getting into that. They fly into Caracas and boat over or get dropped off by a Concarne Line cruise ship. Some have their own boat like the big sucker over there. See it? The one with the big red question mark? Hell, I don't know. I guess it's registered as the question mark. Some dame—lady—from Oak Park owns it. Switzer. Schweizer. Guess I should know, I've seen it enough here. Bud reached in his back pocket and pulled out a crumpled colorful flyer advertising "Los Delicados," the name of the resort.

"Nobody knows about this place except the boneheads who waste a ton of money to do things they'd never tell anyone about. And they pay for such privacy.

"What? Thrill rides? Spinning tea cups?" I said.

"Look here." He pointed to a few photos of some activities. "Frankly, this is way beyond pornography. You know about porn, don't you?"

"It's in every nook and cranny," I joked.

Bud said right! Same thing here. People know about it, but they don't talk about it. He said for a few thousand, you can take the ride of your life. Mercedes. Maseratis. Fast as you want. Run red lights. Run over mannekins that expel body fluids and look real even close up. Even trash it—but that's extra.

"Are you shitting me?"

"Hey! No profanity. Right?"

"Okay, okay!"

He went on. Shoot any weapon you want at anything or anybody.

"Shoot?"

"AK-47s, M16s. Blanks, of course. Old bazookas. Even a Sherman tank. Here. He pointed to a staged scene in the brochure. Here, this guy took a package deal: any weapon; rob a bank; kill the teller; kill the cops; get caught; brought to justice for murder and get off for insanity and be at poolside by four-thirty with your ten thousand-dollar credit card and the honey-glazed buns of a club hostess spread across your knobby knees. Listen, hear the rat-a-tat-tat-tat over there? You can't see it from here.

"Incredible. It's hard to believe," I said with an open mouth.

"Made in the good old USA, too. Money stays in-country, too." Bud smacked his lips. "We've all been there. Too much work nowadays. It's all fake, but nobody likes to brag about it. It's not real, except for the gratification of blowing a small fortune on the weekend."

He grabbed the binoculars from me and frowned on the sector of the shoreline he pointed at. He said it's all for a good cause. Those kids on the other side. Remember what your uncle said back at Bill's Place; well, this end is for screwing off. He pointed back to the left. The end for the kids is what really counts. Got it?

"This is all crazy. It's obscene," I said in dismay.

Bud let out a forced laugh. "Confusing, huh? I was, at first. You see, you take a little to give a lot. Fifty-thou means nothing to these people," as he jutted his jaw toward the noise onshore. "The old man, the rogue capitalist he is, figured out long ago, maybe when he was in the service, how a little thing can have a huge impact depending on who's pulling the trigger. I wondered: torpedoes for tots? A thousand bucks here can be spent on ten thousand worth of stuff over the hill. No. Your uncle's never going to insult these people by outright begging like some of those holier-than-thou bastards. He'd never stoop so low. Who likes a panhandler anyway, even in a tux?"

I asked Bud if they weren't gaming the system.

"No. Life's a gamble, anyway. I suspect they're good solid citizens back home. Why do you ask? There's also a lot I don't like about your old man but deep down he's doing the right thing. It's why I'm here three months out of the year. He's got real good stuff, as they say in baseball."

Then Bud tapped me gently on the forearm. His own had a faded anchor and mermaid tattoo on it. "Yeah. This boat or yacht has plied some difficult waters. Some things most folks might find repulsive, but when you dive below the surface you can understand the reasons. The hidden alltrueism. Did I pronounce it right?"

"Sure, Bud. Thanks."

"When you get off, you can mull it over for yourself."

"Right, as you say."

"No problem. Mum's the word, okay?"

"Aye, aye."

Carry on, lad."[75]

---

[75]   Neither I nor any of my research associates could confirm this part of Will's story—not to say that it's anything but entirely factual, as all our lives must be considered as such in the end, encrypted in ashes or chiseled in mute stone. Granted, a lot of us can be accused of the most blatant fabrications at a cocktail party, mixing a factual tidbit with a helluva lot of pure horsepucky. And once in a while, even back then at Mundane and as a neighbor, I sometimes resented Will for his dilatory attitude about school and not taking a stand on something obviously factual to the rest of our crowd. At one point in the last semester, I told him I couldn't help him anymore. His life had become a fiction when he refused to believe how some bigshots were obviously screwing the country. He wasn't dumb, say like Bobby and Jimmy Bronowski, the twin tackles on the football team; two crewcut gung-ho chaps who really didn't know squat about the real politics back then, and they paid for it. I've been meaning to make a long overdue visit to their mom in Toledo. Don't get me wrong. I believe that the fictional aspects of Will's reminiscence are as valid and of equal literary merit as factual history, but it rekindles my resentment when I know he could have toed the line with us in the face of all the smoke and mirrors deployed to deceive us young guys. Again, pardon my intrusion, but like for instance, defending the Constitution, yackety-yack. For what? Society changes like everything else. Nothing's permanent. One time, I sat in my shorts by the washer/dryer all night in the basement of our dorm, trying to get out the acrid insipid stench from the canisters they threw at us that morning. I said if those damn old geezers who

Uncle, Les and Paola came back aboard as the sun sank with a final wink; a beautiful site on the water and a spectacular prelude to laying out on the deck at night watching hundreds of shooting stars criss-cross the

---

wrote that stuff back then sat there with me in their smelly underwear, I'd tell them all to buzz off, because it's only by change that society can advance. Now, several years since then, after the smoke has cleared and I've sort of straightened out with a beautiful loving wife and four kids to feed, I concede now that a lot of what they wrote was pretty good, pretty prescriptive, but it was still worth fighting over then, especially as some greedy types papered it (i.e., The Constitution) over with bills of lading, contract change orders and other schmier to supposedly support the war effort with little or no thought to a young man's life. If Will were only more articulate back then and, in spite of this tangential text of his I'm stuck with, I might have better understood why he was so hung up on America in the end. And another word about this Melville clan thing. I'm not sure where Will's latent idealism for the flag came from, but it couldn't have come from Captain Billy, his dead father or Uncle Rob Melville. I conferred extensively with Penny S. on this, as she was my expert intern on Captain Billy. After looking over Will's description of this so-called "Los Delicados" island off Colombia, which I could never confirm existed in the first place, I began to almost despise this character—his uncle—a typical American of new-found wealth who thinks he can dabble in other peoples' trousers and tread on their rights with the excuse of making the world a better place in which to live and share the American dream. I mean, I've been reading between the lines. I see here, if you will, a lineage of sheer unadulterated plunder reminiscent of some of Captain Billy's low-life scum in the trade of arms, rum and slaves. Granted, it wasn't all for a sawbuck, since it is well-documented that he did perform a considerable amount of charitable work and mercy missions with the Tern in the US proper, the Americas and even twice in West Africa (there's even a street named after him in downtown Monrovia); but I sensed plain old avarice under the guise of Christian charity that simply turned my stomach as much as some of the trash that dribbled across my desk as a newcomer at Brown and Shue from hacks of hysterical romances. In the end, it's only out of deference to Mrs. Melville, Will's faithful mother, that I've gone this far and will probably stay the course. Strangely, everytime I linger on the ambivalence of the Melvilles and their nefarious pursuit of goodwill and wealth, I can still taste Mrs. Melville's apple pies cooling on her kitchen windowsill while skipping on my way to grade school. She always saved me a slice. She was and still is a kind and gracious soul, even if my sentiments may seem gratuitous or Pavlovian.

Milky Way jewel box. Each one carried onboard the standard aluminum suitcase; probably a million in each. Who knows? It was only money and entertainment and I didn't care now how they got it, especially after seeing some of the good it did back at the kids' sanctuary. Heck! who was I—a fugitive from justice—to say Uncle Rob and his crew and the Tern were engaged in felonious diversions? Even if the screw could testify the Shapiros were dumped overboard as an act of mercy, who was I to point fingers? I was young, uncommitted and, by fiat, irresponsible to no one but myself. Yet, I recall the time Mom asked me to dust the front room and I happened to turn over Dad's picture. She must have pasted Donne's famous poem about no man on the back. I memorized the whole poem in high school and it still rings in my conscience. I never asked her if Dad liked it or even sent it to her with the photograph. She came in the room and was quite upset with me and my behavior at the time. The poem didn't hit home until much later when Mom's muteness forced me to question my selfishness.

Paola toted a large flowery bag stuffed with clothes. She seemed tired but pleased. Les asked me to help the chef and the servants to fill the reefer with a load of food hauled up the side. Backbreaking work hauling forty-pound boxes of dry and frozen goods for two solid hours. I should have hidden below in the old slave-holding area. I asked Uncle Rob how everything went. He gave me the usual half hug glad to see me and said it's easier than diving for sunken treasure, and he chuckled as they went below decks.

Around 2300, I said goodnight to the tern on the foc'scle and went over in a simple way the day's events with the bird much as you would sit and talk to a child. I decided to call him Sam after a suggestion by Bud, who saw the scuffle with the albatross earlier and thought of Samuel Coleridge Taylor's long riff on thirst. Sam sat there between my crossed legs, nodding now and then and looking me in the eye as if to say you're kidding me or I don't believe a word of it. I then went below decks to my room, took my usual shower to wash off the sea salt and hopped into the rack. Due to a rain delay in the muffled baseball play-by-play by the announcer—the one with the marbles in his mouth—another station came up, as Lou must have eased off the gas in the wheelhouse and it's where I believe I started trading RPMs for REMs. The last thing I heard was *scruyascruyascruyascruya*. The next thing I saw was Captain Billy standing in the hatchway, soaked to the bone and wiping his mouth of seaweed. He started talking and I sat up in the rack and listened. He said something like[76]

"Things are lined up about plumb and out here long enough, thanks be to God and my trusty sextant for this once in an after-lifetime opportunity, for me to impart a sage word into the chambered conch of your ear. I, your granddaddy Billy, conducted my entire life as a patriotic, law-abiding defender of the Constitution and church-agoing Christian, tolerant of no man who would harm or debase another's life or reputation. If anyone were to vilify my life's choices or of those who may be my heirs, I pity them should I ever have the chance to return for unfinished business and kick the other cheek. I am proud to have spread my seed of democracy and fair play to every port of call visited by my trusted ship, the Tern. It was no crime to deal in the transport of spirits such as rum, even as the exigencies of law and regulation often required the employ of irregular schedules, bribes and misplaced bills of lading, so to speak, to grease the gangway. And I vehemently object to any accusation I offended and otherwise conspired to fulfill the last wishes of individuals who could no longer suffer the physical pain of earthly existence. Our life should be a metamorphosis from ignoble dust to a gloried convergence with God and such was my premise in aiding untold dozens of slaves in their journey from the dark forests of savagery to the bright cultivated fields of modern civilizaton as we knew it, and I defy any man to prove otherwise. I recently passed Thomas Jefferson in the hall and asked him how he justified his earthly title as a founding father when he held slaves like any common plantation owner. He stared down at me and said, bugger off. Well, so much for the uplifting pursuit of the King's English. I would wish my progeny continue the work I set out to do in mortal life with this vessel; the moral thing; the right thing and above all the most practical thing to defend family, nation and God, and may he favor us with the blessings of liberty and a fair profit for all.

---

[76] When Ms. Scriveen read my mark-up of her draft on the Melville family, she was livid and verily shoved it down my throat, demanding more lineage to politely rebut my views to offer the reader some measure of relief from my intrusions. I threw up my hands and said have at it, honey, knowing that her efforts would be purely adulterated fiction excessively beyond my restrained views which, albeit personal, were at least based on an exhaustive and unscrupulous search for the facts. So, here's her unedited defense of Captain Billy. The reader is advised to suspend whatever disbelief is left regarding Ms. Scriveen's over-the-top intrusion that I have reluctantly allowed.

Young Will, when you pause a moment to think of me, Captain Billy, your granddaddy, whether its on the can, peeling spuds or sparking with some lass in your arms, regard the Tern as my gift to you. Continue to make her worthy of high purpose on the high seas and admired and applauded when she is all in and I finally regain her helm. Otherwise, I'll be back in spirit if not in deed."

"Wake up, son, you're having another nightmare."

It was Uncle Rob. I rubbed my eyes when the dim swinging overhead lamp and floaters on my eyes revealed for a second the image of granddaddy, whose small framed portrait I passed so often on the bulkhead outside Uncle's berth.

"Rise and shine. I need you on the bridge, chop chop," he announced with a discomforting informality. "Where did all this water come from?" as he noticed my shoes. "Do you make a habit of tying your shoestrings in a square knot?"

"Why, no. Why?"

Uncle held them up. He winked an eye and pointed at me with his hand in the shape of a pistol. "I suppose Captain Billy did this, huh?"

"Shoot. I must have been tired." I scratched my head and we laughed.

"You've got five minutes to be topside."

"Aye, aye," as I stifled a yawn out of respect. I scratched my crotch trying to recall all of what Captain Billy said through the screw. Little I remembered, as most of it was peed away in the urinal, but I felt an unexplicable sobriety slowing my movements.[77]

---

[77] This whole salami of the screw communicating to Will, I realize now, was not some cheap literary device (also see footnote 56), but rather more symptomatic of his impaired hearing and mental state. In the presence and with the permission of Mrs. Melville, Dr. Salvatore Minella, MD, came down from Ann Arbor and sat between us on a cloudy December afternoon in 1972 as we discussed Will's medical record. This all came about when I asked if her son presented any physical or mental problems that may have caused him to fantasize so extensively about the screw. Of course, I did not mention some of the so-called play-by-play baseball games, as Mrs. Melville was an avid Tigers fan, and I didn't want us to stray too far off base. I was tired after driving most of the night from State College and I almost asked her if Will somehow had a screw loose. Dr. Minella said he received his medical degree from Guadalahara and was board-certified in both otolaryncology and parapsychology, an interesting combination for job security, but a boon to me for addressing Will's condition.

He said, since about five years old, Will suffered frequent ear infections that eventually ruptured an eardrum, thus reducing the clarity of reception. He said some people with hearing loss try to overcompensate by guessing and hoping their end of the conversation is still relevant. Dr. Minella said that at fifteen-years old, Will needed a hearing aid. According to Mrs. Melville, Will laughed at that suggestion as he cupped his hand to the impaired ear to mock the doc. Also, from numerous visits by Mrs. Melville concerning Will's insomnia and sleepwalking, he deduced that Will may have presented classic symptoms of semidelusional deference to undifferentiated psychic emanations (S-DUPE), in addition to an id anomaly he didn't elaborate on. Not quite an aura of paranoia, but in the ballpark. I noticed Mrs. Melville unconsciously put her hand to her jaw to close it when he said this. She asked Dr. Minella if he was implying that her son was then classified as S-DUPE-id and could that have qualified him for a 4F draft exemption, but he assured her that that was not the case and asked her not to get hung up on trying to simplify every little situation. Nonetheless, she mentioned that as a young boy, Will often looked back over his shoulder, but that could merely have been a childish tic. After pie and tea, I said I was very impressed with Dr. Minella's diagnosis and said he was of great help in my decision not to strike from the text all of Will's meandering jibberish from the screw of the Tern. I commented that the screw may have been Will's literary muse, and both of them found that quite amusing, but personally I thought it was an atrocious stretch. Dr. Minella emptied most of his pipe into the ashtray and lifted his bushy eyebrows to say he thought one of his uncles was related to the famous physician-author A.J. Cronin, but he wasn't sure. As an aside, Mrs. Melville discretely brushed some of the errant pipe tobacco off the endtable and said she never smelled tobacco on Will or his clothes when she threw them in the washer. When we gathered at the front door, Dr. Minella removed his dark wraparound sunglasses to present a remarkable case of hyperthyroidism. My eyes nearly popped out, as well. I always wanted to ask a physician if an undescended testicle destined a guy for dictatorship, but I guess that would have been an eye-opener at that moment. While Mrs. Melville wrapped an extra piece of pie (rhubarb) for my trip over to Calumet, I asked the doctor if he felt there was any other human explanation for Will's condition. He shrugged his shoulders and revealed his hands before us like a solemn imam and said, Well, who are we to say? We're only the living. I thanked him for his "profound" thought, asking myself if anyone was home as I watched him slip into his spanking new two-tone

CHAPTER 21

By the time I stepped topside, all memory of Captain Billy's advice was lost in the animated discussion of the crew. Lou lifted his head up from the huddle and waved me off to let me know I was only an honorary member and not privy to their machinations. I bobbed my head in deference to his hand jive and repaired to starboard to see a few islands lolling on the horizon. There were so many of these hiding places on the Caribbean charts, I wondered in the lassitude of idleness how it could take me hours to navigate them on a map with my finger, yet my mind could stretch between the 93 million miles to the sun and back in a millisecond. And even on the Pacific side, there were any number of Costa Ricas where Vinnie's brother-in-law said you could hide and hold off US authorities for untold years and live like an exiled king on pesos a day. Except, I didn't even have centavos a day, yet I was surrounded by suitcases with millions of bucks.

So, here I was in the moral doldrums eluding the middle finger of Uncle Sam, waiting for orders of dubious moral intent from the crew or Uncle directly. I listened at night to the monologue of the screw; talking to a lost bird sitting in my lap; taking advice from a surrogate father; trying to translate Paola's pre-history jibberish; Bud's rambling nostalgia; Les's numbers game; and Lou's snide snippets as sour as a smart-ass teenager. All the while, sneaking a twist of an RC-390 to catch any news about the action overseas. My future didn't go beyond the rolling sea ending on the horizon, no wiser than those illiterate wharf paisanos who told Columbus he was over the edge. I didn't want to surf beyond a scumbled line of blue

---

Skylark. Once again, a highly educated individual talking about faith in things felt but unseen; heard but unspoken.

and white like Vince. He did and got his little butt whipped by the judge who told him ten years at Jackson or four in the Army. Maybe I should have jumped ship with Vin. Either way, he'll be scarred for life. I guess he figured it would be better to throw his body into a foxhole for a year than be molested for seven and out of prison in four with good behavior. Ironically, the abundant lethe on the Tern and the crests of foam it plowed actually did as much as the screw of the Tern to hone the serrated edge of my anxiety about the future. The food was so good, I felt ashamed, imagining K-rations my Dad must have had hunched behind some hedgerow or the MREs of today's soldier. Two over easy; Canadian bacon; filet mignon; pancakes smothered in maple syrup; strawberries; whipping cream; custard; beer and wine from the reefer in the old slave-holding area. I was so bloated sometimes I couldn't even get it up when Paola played ship's mermaid in her bikini at the tip of the foredeck gangplank. I should have gained twenty pounds since we left Fort Lauderdale over two months ago, but I lost twelve. Too much worrying about when all this would end. Maybe Vin made the right decision.

I got bored, then impatient with the crew's aloof exclusion of me, so I forced a dry cough to announce my approach. Bud twisted his head and said yeah, what do you want now?

"Did anyone see Sam this morning?" I stood there for about half a minute with a half-smile to tell them I could take it.

"What?" said Les with an annoying twang.

"I said, did you see Sam the tern earlier?" Again, I folded my arms and waited almost a minute, which reminded me of my interview at the state unemployment office in Detroit when I flunked out the first time in May of 1965. The intake clerk turned his head and acted as if I didn't exist. Why not? He had a job and I figured he was damned if he'd let me get by without some cheap-ass bureaucratic hazing. At least I was sitting down, as about half of the hundred or so in the cramped, hot office milled around for a pocket of smoke-free fresh air, waiting for one of the thirteen seats to open up throughout the all-day affair.

"Sit tight!" he said. "I'll be back."

I knew he went for a fourth cup of coffee, because I could see the shiny bottom of his polyester pants sticking out from the cubicle dividers by the coffee urinal. He had already complained to me, holding his third cup, the coffee was worse than panther piss. So why did he drink it in front of me in the first place? Arrogant schlep!

"I see you flunked—dropped out of Mundane. Never heard of it. Any reason?"

I asked if I had missed this one on the questionnaire, and he said no. Just curious. Then he took my five-page application, which missed asking if I ever slept with a farm animal, and with a condescending curl of an eyebrow flipped it over to the end of his crowded metal desk. He put his hands behind his balding head, then put his feet up on the desk to within a foot of my inferior and unworthy visage and leaned back in his swivel chair.

"You know, my son is getting his Ph.D in American literature from Duke. Ever heard of it?" He didn't even look at me. He looked up at the stained ceiling tiles.

"Yes. It's somewhere near Raleigh."

"Yeah. He's a great kid. Eagle Scout. He worked hard, but now he's on his way. You've heard of Brown. He'll start teaching there in the Fall. I have to tell you, he's the brainy type. Going to be a big success."

I sat there, wondering if he humiliates every applicant with the same insulting trash talk, but I can't say it because I see my application halfway over the edge of his crummy desk, and the slightest effeminate flick of his bangled wrist would brush it into the bureaucratic oblivion of a wire waste basket. So, I said sounds great. I wish him the best of luck. Then he swung around from the window and stared about two feet over my head and picked at an incisor with his pinkie.

"Huh! Lettuce. He won't need any luck. He's all set unlike some of us. Say, wait here. I've got to take a bathroom break. I'll be right back. It's the coffee. Don't touch that dial, as they say on TV."

He stood up hulking over me and I could feel the condescension of someone with lots of time on his hands turn into a lava flow of disgust between his stained teeth as he let out an emphatic rush of dentured air brushing past my face.

I waited it out for twenty minutes, then grabbed my coat and made sure my last picture of this jerk of a bureaucratic clerk was him pissing an endless stream of vanity over the toilet seat. I glanced over my shoulder to see the next two applicants fighting to gain the chair I vacated. Anyway, after two weeks, I finally got a tip from Vinnie's brother-in-law about the Valparaiso job and I grabbed it in a heartbeat.

"Okay," I finally said. "What's happened to Sam?"

Paola stretched her arms and said he flew off early, before anyone got up to feed him. "A good sign he might be getting strong enough to fetch most of his food."

They got up from the deck of this council pow-wow I had rarely seen from them. Usually, they respected each other's territory which boundary took into account the measure of their spittle on the fly, which was often more acceptable on the cheek than the contrail of cerebral insults scarring their exchanges. Once, I saw Bud and Les standing toe-to-toe in the middle of eight of these infamous aluminum suitcases full of dough. Les must have told Bud to take them down the hatch. They were both tight and Bud again called Les a certified public ass and I noticed how the spittle ejected through Bud's loose bridge and landed on Les's green eyeshade, which he often wore more or less as the annoying status symbol of a number-crunching auditor. Les, who was taller but no match for Bud's forearms, responded in a phony professorial accent as to how many Polacks does it take to change a lightbulb? When Bud shouted back nothing could be easier, he already saw his mistake and backed off to resume carrying the suitcases to the old slave-holding compartment below decks.

"What do you know about the equator?" said Lou.

I said it was an imaginary circumference of the earth of equal distance from the poles. I at least retained such trivia from the "D" I got in Geography 101.

"Good for starters," said Les. "Do you know what happens to someone who crosses it the first time? Huh?"

They stood around me. I felt they were after something I may have stolen from them. Maybe an extra serving of New York style cheesecake.

"Well," said Bud. "We've all been there." He thrust out his bicep to show a whitish scar running along it like an engorged vein from curling reps at the gym. It ran right through an old faded tattoo with "Mama" in fancy script.

I was unaccustomed to this modern motley crew moving into my personal space. Like an old lady creeping up on a lacewing to swat its short life into a skidmark on the kitchen doorscreen. "So, what about it?"

Bud said they had agreed that, for me to continue to ride with them and be fully accepted into their privileged association, they arbitrarily moved the equator to the Tern's present latitude.

"What are you getting at, Paola?" I said.

She said it means due to your well-known desire to join the crew as an equal partner-in-crime—ah! it finally came out—I have already consented to the ceremony. I could see the gleam in their eyes, like kids waiting to steal a box of candy while the little old man behind the glass counter nods off from the midday heat. I heard about keelhauling and walking the plank and getting tattooed, so I said rather defensively, so what the devil has this got to do with me?

"It's so easy," said Les.

"What is?" I demanded as a nonvoting participant.

Bud said since it was so strenuous to move the equator, there was no reason for me not to appreciate their efforts and accommodate them by going through the ceremony. And once I got it over with, the better my relations would be all round.

"Isn't this what we strive for in human relations?" said Lou.

"Look," said Bud with a rare facial concession to a smile, "we're not all dental students, so what's the worry?" and the others passed around a mischievous chuckle.

I took a preparatory step backward and flat out told them I know a hazing when I smell it. Paola matched me step-for-step like a fandango partner, but she also swiped at her face like a crouching intercollegiate wrestler and dangled out her arm for contact to start the rubber fall. "It's an initiation. You'll love it and you can tell your grandkids about it."

Lou added yeah, we went through all this trouble to change the world for you. Let's say it's your ersatz basic training rolled up into a pleasant afternoon. You'll save eighty-nine days. Such a deal!"

"Oh, man!" and I backstroked my way starboard in search of Uncle Rob to spare my young cadaver.

Les yelled No! No! You've got it all wrong. There's no goldfish to swallow."[78]

---

[78] Will had good cause for concern. As freshmen at Mundane, both of us pledged for Bhi Kegga Bier, one of the oldest, most maligned, notorious and misunderstood of unofficial fraternities on or off campus. The catalog of atrocities during hazing week would easily overflow ten Eastern Airlines air sickness bags, and if it weren't for the unusual abundance of beer and its efficacy to induce temporary psychosomatic neuropathies, we would have never passed the bar, the ceremonial one at Schreck's on Fourth and Quimm near the agricultural building. Everything went smooth, even the two goldfish each

It was hopeless. There was no place to run or hide like back in Monroe. Was this a drill to prepare me for the long arm of military service? I managed to elude these sudden zombies and pounded on Uncle's stateroom door with the dolphin decal. I pounded and shouted for him to put some common sense, perspective or plain treaty of appeasement on the table to forego the induction.

"Who in hell is it?"

"Uncle, open up. These people want to drag my little butt over the equator. Please open up." I could swear he snickered and chortled his way through "I'm sleeping. Go away. We're nowhere near the equator."

"Come on, Uncle. This isn't fair."

---

of us chug-a-lugged; however, one of the pledges, Peter Malcuzynski, a transfer right tackle from East Lansing, nearly choked to death. Both of us sat next to his three-hundred pound girth and were scared out of our jocks when he turned blue and we were so drunk, we didn't know what to do. Even the house cat growled. This was on the front porch of the frat house, an old wood-frame row house amid others with Afro-Americans barely existing on food stamps. A young woman about twenty (she may have been forty) sashayed over from the next porch, told Will and me to hold Peter up by the arms, then she took a running jump at his two-ply love handles with her left knee slamming into where his diaphragm might be hiding. Suddenly, out jumped the expired goldfish and landed on the carpet and quickly snatched by the house cat. She said she was a midfielder on the Mundane women's soccer team. I thanked her. I still remember her name: Glory B(eauticia) Williams, and sometimes I see her behind me in the cracked bathroom mirror with the others when I shave in the morning, but I can't quite feel her arms around my waist anymore. I remember how she said with a cute pucker of her dimples, you white boys don't know nothin'. She winked at me and later I took her on a few dates after dark, but I knew she was so-to-speak unsurmountable and we fooled around in the back of my Olds 88, but that was all. Mom would have thrown me out of the house. In a different time, we could have fallen hard for each other. She had the most beautiful skin when the afternoon sunlight spilled down her shoulders and arms with her hands hugging a coffee cup at Hazel's All-Star Chili Pot outside Dexter. Several months ago, I called her number and her mother said she was living in Redding with her two kids. She spent a year upstate for cutting her semi-pro footballing husband, whom she said threw back bottles of amphetamines aspiring to the LA Rams suicide squad. She said he had a thing for the Rams horny helmets. Maybe I should have married her.

He must have yawned and mumbled something like fair isn't even in the dictionary. It has to do with where you are and who you are at any given moment. Then he must have fallen back to sleep. The brown bag by the door tinkled with empties when I tapped it with my shoe, and I gave him the benefit of the doubt, as he had with me back in Fort Lauderdale.

They waited for me topside, yucking it up at my expense. I trudged up the ladder, waving my arms to say don't shoot. Bud made a gorilla-like sweep of his arm and said now come along, come along now, matey, like some purser from hell. Lou had a popsicle in his hand and pointed at me. "If you can suffer this, basic should be a breeze." Then Les, the stickler for crooked columns of decimal points, added "That's if you fall under the mock protection of the bell curve like most red-blooded American men."

Even Sam the tern returned to stoop on the foc'scle and secured the best seat. He must have sensed I was in trouble or about to make an ass of myself as he started squawking when Lou tripped me into a ten-foot trough of two-week old rotting fish, veggies and bug-infested flour. Putrid stench stronger than the slitted stomach of a Gulfstream shark. On my belly. Someone kept pushing my head into this unholy stew. Probably Bud. Every time I surfaced, one of them stung my rear with a section of fire hose. I gagged the whole length, then as I got to my knees to get out, Paola shouted, all right now touch the wall, flip and do a backstroke on the turn.

"Through that crap again?" I pleaded.

"No swearing!" said Les.

"Bull!" I retorted.

Right then and there, Lou ordered me to do twenty pushups into the trough, whose six-inch depth required unusual breath control. I finally chucked up the Texas toast and scrambled eggs and sausage from breakfast. It blended in with the stench slop. I think Les kept a Super 8 running to record this humiliation. Someone helped me out of the trough as I barfed the rest of the sausage.

"I can't see!" I pleaded with my eyelids nearly pasted shut from the gelatinous delight like the gummy pus of pink eye.

"Okay," said Paola. "Time to clean up." And she led me by the hand to a large wine barrel. "Step up to the lip and prepare for baptism."

Before I could escape, Bud got hold of my neck and plunged me into a vinagrette suitable for tanning hides. They all must have contributed specimens to the nasty brew. If I relaxed my neck muscles, Bud would think I was drowning and pull me up. On the fifth dunk of about ten seconds, he caught on and added ten more unholy dunks until I lost my grip on the barrel rim.

I wanted to demand why are you doing this to me? What have I done to you? But no one would have been convinced my plea deserved an explanation. Bastards! I thought. All of them. Even Paola, whose polka-dot bikini didn't particularly engorge my appreciation of her.

One of the Filipinos laughed his head off on an Indian River orange crate. He brought a deck chair over so I could sit down for a minute. He came right up to my face and said you look like an afterbirth, man. I said not true with the nonchalance of a pathological liar. The others, whom I had temporarily written out of my will, came up to me to say I was a miscreant swabbie who needed to be punished for not expressing outright joy in the proceedings. An absolute ingrate. How could I? I was coughing up little pieces of rotten entrails I tried not to swallow. I was sick as a dog.

"Back in the car wash, kid," said Lou. "And strip!"

"What the!"

"Don't say it. You're already in a world of shit well beyond this vessel," answered Bud. Nobody said anything.

"Don't worry," said Paola. "You can keep your precious underpants on."

Les and Lou pushed me back down into the trough and ordered me to start crawling on my belly. "Good-for-nothing polliwog," they said together.

Les declared that, because of my insolence toward the crew and poor progress in fully assisting them in the profit motive, I would receive a bonus of two lashes from each of the aggrieved. Eight! God Almighty!

"You're lucky, Melville. It's only a section of a Charleston fire department hose your uncle picked up in a junkyard years ago. It's much softer now."

I received the whipping of my life for transgressions beyond my understanding. Each blow stung worse than the last one and I lost interest in counting after five whacks. Penance. And I really wanted to like these people, but they were making it difficult at the moment.

"*Krutrkrukruk*," mouthed Paola. She was the last one and pound-for-pound was the most punitive in her enthusiasm. "*Clubkparaklukparltru*" and so on.

I think my last resistance was an ancient cliche from Mom's private lexicon. I squeaked, this is the crap for the birds, which she blurted out once over a huge gas bill during a terrible winter in Monroe.[79]

Lou and Bud dragged me out of the gutter and plopped me in a canvas deck chair quite without ceremony.

"Thanks," I bleated. I nearly said, you bunch of Nazis, but I knew it would have ruined Bud's party, so I said thanks a lot.

"Thanks?" said Bud. He raised his arms. "Father forgive us for we know exactly what the hell we're doing." The others got a good laugh out of the blasphemy.

"Stop!" bellowed Uncle. "What on earth is going on here?" I'm sure Melville got a major rise up there in the wheelhouse the whole time.

Les cleared his throat to explain a generous geophysical accommodation was made to allow me to cross the equator and thereby suffer full acceptance by the crew as an equal among whale excrement.

Uncle said hmm! and walked around to inspect the mess on his front porch. Well, all right, but don't ever let this happen again, hear? I heard the crack in his voice when he patted me on the head and I knew he had set me up once again. Was this some kind of preparation to help me crap or get off the pot? He said stand up and then poured a brown bottle of hydrogen peroxide down the back of what he called skivvies as a sort of

---

79   Will exaggerates here. Mrs. Melville never said such as far as I know. She never used foul language. And I was over there at their house plenty during that and other awful winters when neighbors would get together to chat and share the coffee and body heat. Three feet of snow in eighteen hours and five below at night. The only time she came close was in the kitchen once when she burned her wrist badly on a hot skillet full of Canadian bacon. She ran over to the sink and ran cold water over it. She bit her lip and tears rolled out of her closed eyes, lowering her head as if ashamed she was nabbed shoplifting at Gutmann's strip mall, but she never said a peep. And she probably deserved every right to bitch and complain. A young war widow with a son. An RN on nightshifts for years on Blaine Memorial's eighth floor adjusting the drips of terminal patients. Constantly trying to maintain her weight at about ninety-five pounds. Too exhausted to join the girls on the lookout at Sweeney's Dance Club. When Melville's checks started coming in at a thousand a month, a lot of that stress went away and probably spared her life. I was there. Now I do know that Vinnie's Mom, Mrs. Pugliese, swore like the dickens in English and Sicilian. You could even hear it from the other side of James Street.

coup de grace, because it stung like the Sunday admonitions of a rum-crazed preacher. It burned like hell and I didn't yelp for the sheer joy of it.

"All right. Turn to and hose him down real good, and get this garbage over the fantail chop-chop! And don't toss him in my pool."

I should have been mad as hell, but each one came up to me, tapped me on the shoulder and said good sport, you did okay kid, and now you're down to my size. I even heard a gentle round of applause and I gave a big smile while Paola hosed me down by a scupper. She whispered I'm not one of them, but she was and it rued my heart to imagine the gender-hazing abuse she may have hidden for years—far worse than my harmless swim in a trough of rotten putrid fish entrails.

About an hour later, I was in clean shorts and a sport shirt from Twisted Knee CC, sitting on the fore deck or whatever it's called. Sam waddled over and hopped up into the cradle of my crossed legs. Again, I felt privileged he accepted my presence as much as the others now. He squawked, ruffled his long feathers and hopped out onto the deck, leaving a huge gelatinous calling card on my spotless shorts.

"You, too, huh?" and I laughed at the dwindling sunset and my days on the Tern. I already crossed off seventy-three days on the 1960 Skipper's Marine Stripper pinup calendar I stole from the reading room.[80]

---

[80]   I intended to junk this entire part about crossing the equator. I frankly didn't believe this near adolescent diversion actually happened. Will was a dreamer and I knew my work was cut out for me. Even as fiction, it failed to move the story forward like so many formulaic styles with which I grew comfortable from a literary and monetary viewpoint. Reminiscences are so dilatory, and unless a competent hack or ghostwriter can successfully mortise the disjointed and often boring snippets of some famous drunkard or absent-minded has-been (advance or no advance), the reader is right to throw the damn book away (pics or no pics), as I have mentioned earlier. I thought our in-house commercial artist, Mike "Broadbrush" Angelo, could do a nice full-color action-packed glossy cover as a band-aid to hide the weak storyline, but he said he was flat on his back with a slipped disk and in over his head taking on the Van Doren Scuples saga. Life is far too short to listen to a dull fireside chat while watching the embers slowly die down to small crackling whispers in the early dawn. But I was wrong. On a hunch, I called Cliff D. in Mesa and asked if there was any chance he could pidgeon-hole one more visit to Les's place. He said he acquired something called valley sickness and couldn't even get a hard-on, and he referred me to a former nun I'll call Anne-Marie on 43rd Avenue over in Glendale who waited tables at

CHAPTER 22

Late evening, after everything returned to the usual humdrum of radiotelephone knob-twisting and board meetings among Uncle and the crew trolling for dollars, I stretched out on my rack. I wanted to relate the events of the day to Vin, but he was gone and I missed my friend of long ago, who was likely destined for some lonely perimeter in Vietnam to protect what we surely must lose or leave behind as any tourist must do. And I still suspicioned Uncle set up Vin's apprehension at the old Idylwild. If this was the last few months of the Tern's long service to mankind, I could only guess at the connivings Uncle and his crew did on land, where there was a kind of asphaltic traction that made tacking from the authorities easier than lolling around twelve knots at sea. Stubbing my flip-flops on the growing number of aluminum suitcases became so commonplace, I speculated on the number of Uncle's offshore bank vaults.

Rocky's All-Night while looking for a day gig. I sent her three hundred dollars to "visit" Les's place to look for a Super 8 film about this equator thing. She said she finally found it next to the garage in a trashcan simply labelled "Equator" at the bottom of a plastic trashbag full of Super 8 porn films with a handwritten note that said Put out on curb next Wednesday morning. My hunch took a tern for the better. Anne-Marie took it to Cliff who said all but about twenty feet were ruined, but that what he saw of Will actually strapped to a deck chair and covered with gook convinced me that the incident in fact occurred. I sent him an extra fifty dollars and suggested he mix two fingers of tequila with equal amounts of clam and prune juice, and it should be real cold. Anne-Marie sent me a wonderful St. Jude prayer card and a menu from Rocky's if I ever got to Glendale, which I probably will visit before long. I forgot to ask her what she did with the other films.

It was a mystery I would never solve: financial hieroglyphics Les tried to explain once I became a full-fledged crewmember. It was all a wash to me anyway; morally and moneywise. I was an offshore asset, sheltered from military service by Uncle Rob, and I made a private vow of silence about it that some folks back home may have considered as grossly negligent as eating a Good Humor dreamsicle while casually watching a family try to escape from their burning Ford LTD wagon on the shoulder of an interstate, pounding on the fogged windows for a while. It was the good Uncle accomplished which allowed me to tolerate the other junk along the way. I once wrote down on a napkin in the stateroom "capitalist mercy" in block letters in the shape of a suspension bridge drawn between the towering words, "rich" and "poor." When the others sat down to dinner on lobster Newburg, I quickly stuffed the note in my pocket and later flushed it down the toilet. At Mundane, I was never interested in taking Professor Calzoni's seminar "Predatory Economics from Rome to Palermo." My friend, Des Rubinstein, told me it was a great course on theory, but it didn't really teach you the street-smarts of how to reach into someone's pocket and still keep them smiling.[81]

I tossed a bit waiting for the screw to recap the events during the RPM-REM cycle, as I called it by then. The sea was as calm as an empty birdbath around 0300 and the prelude began: *ifyouknewifyouknewifyouknewifyouknewifyouknew.* I lay there somewhat unsettled when I heard the imperceptible rattle back and forth with the sudden swells beginning to rock the Tern like the Titanic steaming two hundred yards off the port bow. I knew I cleaned up the berth ship-shape and couldn't imagine what was the noise. It was so small as to be barely heard over the waves. Almost like a scratching nail on a blackboard. Just

---

[81] Absolutely true. I remember telling this to Will almost verbatim when we bumped into each other at O'Hare after the end of classes in May of 1965. I got an "A" from Calzoni and after taking the final, I asked if he was going to revive his ECON 369 seminar on thievery. We stood around a small circular table with mustard and onion bratwursts and a bottle of beer each. Right in front of us, some old guy in a gray three-piece suit slithered his hand into a woman's purse and filched her wallet. I turned to Will to show him, but the guy was gone in a flash. What a corrupt and talented act of fingerfertigkeit, as my old piano teacher might have said. The guy could have actually played a Mozart piano concerto with those fingers and gained some wider respectability. Will didn't see a thing, yet he said let's try to catch him. Right!

about drove me nuts. The drawer of the antique rolltop writing desk tucked in the corner of the room came into view. It was a pretty piece of furniture Captain Billy must have used many times, and I examined it when I first got the room, but didn't see anything in the drawers.

"This is nuts!" I said rubbing my eyes, because we weren't rolling in swells anymore, yet the noise persisted like knocking at my door. I got up and rolled back the cover and opened each of the twenty-odd cubbyhole drawers until I found the source. All empty. I went back to lay down, rolled over and heard it again. There was a small drawer I overlooked. I pulled it out since it was empty. In the back, there it was. "What is this now?" I sat upright. It was a gold wedding band and I felt uneasy speculating how it got there. It must have become dislodged and rolled around under the buffeting. I took it out with my fingertips and marvelled how smug of me to think I checked every crack with the same methodical boredom I used to study for exams: careless, cramming; a few beers to concentrate. Under the swinging lamp I read the minute inscription along the inner circumference: Lettie Vanderbilt 1911.[82]

"What on earth?" I repeated more from annoyance than discovery. She must have been a guest eons ago and forgot to take it, but why would she have left it unless it got stuck behind the drawer? Surely, the faceless and innumerable crew members through the years, in the scrupulous servitude

---

[82]   Lettie Vanderbilt (1863-1915), born in Asheville; legally unrelated to the Vanderbilts of American wealth fame. She was famous in her own right as an early innovative sociologist who in 1889 developed with the German psychopathologist, Ernst Verruckte, the Maze behavioral technique of self-awareness that laid the framework for the amazing experimental studies of B(ertram) F(iddlewyth) Styckes. An infrequent researcher of mine in Charlottesville, Paul Postumus, found this out oddly in the Vanderbilt historical society collection near Knoxville. Some county census clerk must have misfiled the folder, since Lettie never met the real (i.e., wealthy) Vanderbilts except in this afterlife misfiling. Her own file was empty, save for some faded World Exposition tickets. Even with his trusty cracked Zeiss magnifying lens, Paul saw the scribbled description of her health condition (chronic emphysema; lupus) and referral to the Higgins-Kunkle Lung Clinic near Louisville. The clinic was torn down in 1915, but from next door, a ninety-two year old intubated gentleman scribbled a note to Paul that she was a looker but dying, and was discharged for a vacation cruise out of Jacksonville on a boat with a funny bird's name and never returned.

of the perenially destitute, must have found it and forgot to pawn it ashore. "Have to tell Uncle Rob about this." I tossed it in the air and pocketed it. As I shut the drawer, it jammed until a small piece of stationary fluttered to the deck like a small yellow bird from a sprung cage. I picked it up and held its ghostly onionskin under the swinging lantern. The two words stood out as if it had a voice, screaming out at me from almost sixty years ago. Then I thought out loud, Captain Billy, did you have anything to do with this?

"Help me!" pencilled in a palsied Gothic script. I tried to make light of the horrific message by thinking it could have been written by someone trying to escape the claustrophobic profanity of a jammed pay toilet, but the two words only sank deeper into my conscience.

By the time I tossed the ring in the air again, it was 0400. It caught the moonlight beaming through the porthole. My thoughts went back to Paola's visit to my room and how any flicker in our personal relations was about as stillborn as the meaning of the ring.[83]

After breakfast on the foredeck with a subdued bunch of former friends, now comrades-in-arms, I went around the table thanking them for taking it easy on me.

"You're lucky, pal," said Bud with a mouthful of crepes suzettes. "Your old man told us to make sure we save enough of you in case we need chum bait."

"Isn't that a redundant way to put it, Bud? I joked.

"You didn't hear me. I said in case we need bait, chum." Bud was irked. "For our own ceremonies, we each had to go over the side."

---

[83]   This rings of LaKeesha's discovery of Bud's grandparents' wedding ring back in Monroeville. A verifiable fact. When I saw this part about Lettie Vanderbilt and her wedding ring, I became alarmed at the lack of interplay among Will and the crew and his drifting to a whole new cycle of imaginary characters, ghosts and classical interlopers. It's true that Paul Postumus verified Lettie's existence, but I asked myself, What's next, Will—a double-ring necromantic ceremony? I wanted to be most watchful here, and I hated to play word cop. I knew at Mundane Will favored ice-cold Rheingold, so on a hunch I asked my old friend at the Lyric Opera, Helge Swoops, between rehearsals to purge the numerous passages that he thought made allusions to Wagner's *Flying Dutchman* as well as the ring cycle, which wasn't that easy to ask of a heldentenor broadening his repertoire with Italian opera. I'd invested too much lamp oil and caffeine to let Will's ramblings corrupt my effort to stick to a credible storyline and, with tedious research, make sure that it ring-rang-rung true.

From the wheelhouse, Lou got on the speaker to call for 1300 formation on deck to go over the next portcall in Beaufort. He shouted for all to hear, Hey Will, what's eating you? You act like some ingrate.

"No, Lou. Just tired from yesterday," and I slipped back down the hatchway to my cabin, because there was a deeper and more disturbing sound I heard beyond the ring. If Lettie's ring was there, where on earth was she? And did that matter a pile of beans, since she was a pile of bones all these years?

On the way, I asked one of the Filipinos, Flash, to bring from the scullery the crowbar they used to stir clam chowder. When he came to my room, I asked him to pry open the knotty pine panelling at the bottom of the bulkhead behind Vinnie's old rack. I helped him pry it out and waited. Flash was so stooped down like a spider monkey his buttocks were half an inch off the deck, and his kneecaps were near his ear lobes. I was concerned, because chef told us earlier that Flash was taken off meal preparation due to the runs, and it reminded me what this nubile Asian girl did to Vinnie's hairy chest when she stooped over him at Kiki's strip joint on the outskirts of Mt. Pleasant where I spent a day filing a claims adjustment for Valparaiso. I can never forget how so many applauded for a show that minute-by-minute became so excrementally awful. Flash did it in ten minutes and crawled back out.

"You hiding your girlfriend in there?" as he dragged out a skeleton. My thoughts ran wild with elation over my correct hunch. Flash laughed so hard with his hands covering his mouth, I was concerned his shorts couldn't keep his bowels from soiling my room.

"What's her name?" He laughed and quickly moved his hands from his mouth to his rear end.

"Lettie Vanderbilt," I said. I pulled out her wedding ring and held it up to the sunlight, mesmerized by the circle of intrigue I entered.

Flash stopped laughing. He slowly layed out the skeleton on the deck. Kneeling, his small hands arranged the jangle of bones as if she were taking a nap. The skull was aligned with care; lower jaw reset to meet the upper teeth to get rid of the visage of screaming her head off; leg bones straightened; arms resting on the ribcage. Then he stood over them and crossed himself several times, moving his lips. I never knew an Asian could have feelings like Catholics I knew back home. Could a Vietnamese have the same regard as shown by Flash? They were all the same, weren't they? He stepped back, bowed his head, then noticed the ring held in my fingertips. He smiled again and turned around at the door to say, I leave you two newlyweds alone, and then he laughed with a gaiety that had no sting.[84]

"What is it now, Will?" said Uncle, brushing his teeth over the Italianate marble vanity sink in his stateroom.

I made a bold opening statement. You know, I found Lettie Vanderbilt. He spit and gazed in the mirror. "Will, son; it's too early to start in. So what's your problem. I've got a conference call in half an hour."

"It's about this. You need to come and see it."

"All right, let's not make any bones about it. Who's this Lettie?" I told him he was right on both counts and asked him again to take a quick look.

Uncle still had the wet razor in his hand when he saw the skeleton. He stooped and gently splayed out the ankles so they appeared at attention. "Where did this come from? My closet, again?"

I showed him the wedding ring and pointed to where it came from in the desk.

"Son, Will. I have no idea how this got here. I had the Tern totally cleaned up three years ago. Illegal immigrants around south Miami. They never miss a thing. They even found a bunch of old gold coins in the engine room."

It took a few moments before Uncle began to fathom the mystery and he slowly reached around for the metal framework of my rack to sit down. He cocked his head a bit as if he tried to listen to Lettie, and then gazed at her bones for an answer like a witch doctor who threw them there on the deck.

---

[84] Whoopsie! I'm not too surprised Will could stoop so low here. He told me his last GPA was 1.9. He must have been exhausted at this point. While I found it difficult figuring out Will's wandering, my long-time typist, Gladys Kowalski, bore an even tougher task deciphering his scribbles. It got so bad, she switched to Gregg shorthand to see if she could make any sense of it. Eventually she pasted something together on the light table that seemed to flow as well as the arthritic finger of Southern Comfort she polished off from the bottle I gave her at the Christmas party. The only thing worse than writer's block (WB) is to fall back on a cliche or light-finger a phrase from another's artistic oeuvre. I like to call it "plaguerism," because it's pandemic these days. I'll take pacing the dank halls of a wordsmith's asylum with "WB" any day. Nonetheless, this last phrase (from Lehar's *Golden Days*) was a welcomed indication that Will might be moving away from further unforced errors in the spirit of Wagnerian high camp.

"I guess we're in a dead zone here. Did the screw tell you about this?" He chuckled when he said this, although I could see he was straining when he ran his free hand through his uncombed hair.

"No, Uncle. I was resting here and the ring started rolling around until I found it. The screw had nothing to do with this."

"Then?"

"I came back, because I remembered the other noise—the bones—were somewhere. Flash helped me. See? Over there."

He bent over to see the space the bones came from. He sat there for about five minutes with folded hands, bowed head and the whole scene seemed to really stop him in his tracks like nothing I had seen before. But I knew he wasn't praying. He was an old salt.

"Who do you think it is? Was?"

"Uncle, it's a hunch. Why would she take it off and leave it here, unless someone else did it?"

A knock at the door broke the spell induced by the bones spread out on the deck. Paola poked her head in the hatchway.

"Excuse me, Captain. They're on the phone." I saw her eyes fix on the bones and her jaw slowly drop as if she were ready to expire herself. She mumbled something like *"Ugaharooputcrizur,"* then made the strangest screwball of a pitch I never saw coming: "Can I talk to it? I mean examine it?"

Uncle snapped out of it. "It's dead, Paola. It's a skeleton." Yet the hesitancy in his voice led me to think maybe he thought she could divine something beyond his maritime skills.

"Look, I've got to take care of business. Got to go. We'll discuss this later. Not now."

"Uncle! Your razor!" which I grabbed on my rack and handed to him.

"Thanks. You and Paola work on this. I don't have time for every crazy spook on this ship."

Paola bent down and felt around the darkness of the past occupied by the skeleton, which I now called Lettie with affection as if she were alive.

"She died on the Tern. Look here." Paola pressed out the wrinkles of a dark brocade dress. I showed her the ring. She chanced to slip it on her own ring finger and smiled at me for a long second then took it off. She took a deep breath and sat down on the rack next to me and didn't say a word for about two minutes. I was afraid to break her trance.

"Will, do you remember the Shapiros? Irv and Rose?"

"Sure. They're back at Alice Detwiler. Right?"

"Do you really believe that?" She put her hand on top of mine, and I didn't know what to expect from her. She asked me to swear not to divulge what she was about to tell me.

I sat there in total disbelief as she confessed Irv and Rose were buried at sea. On the Tern. Terminal patients. Weeks to live. Not a snowball's chance. Heavily sedated. It's what they wanted: a beautiful sunset reflecting in their moist eyes as they held hands all the way. Call it a mercy killing, which wouldn't do justice to the nerve it took to pull it off.

"The screw was right," I mumbled. "It was right all along!"

"Don't be silly. It was your runaway imagination. *Bruukrpterp.*"

Another rap on my door punctured my disbelief. Lou walked in as if he owned the place. Little Napoleon going off half-cocked without the cocked hat. He spied Lettie laid out there and said how the hell did she get onboard?

"Sit down over there, Lou," said Paola.

"Look. I had nothing to do with this one, hear?" Lou wiggled his hands in front of him and sat down in the chair by the desk.

I said it must have been one of Captain Billy's guests. Who else?

He squinted at me and said what the devil do you know? A fine family you've got! So your grandfather must have been in the mercy killing business, too. Right, Paola?"

She didn't say a thing. She was busy with an ear a few inches from Lettie's jawbones. "I've told him about Irv and Rose. He has to know now. He has to know how to compartmentalize," said Paola.

"You mean I've got a lot of baggage, don't you?" I said through a veil of anger.

Lou puffed his cheeks and said well, Miss Paola Goldilocks, what a real fine relativistic attitude. Why does anyone have to connect the dots anymore? You would spill it! Go ahead. Why don't you go ahead and publish it like your other psychopaleontologic trash.

"Back off, Lou, and listen for once," she demanded.

During the next hour or so, she defended in clinical whispers some of the sideshows of mercy (her words) they committed over the past nine years. I think I told them they were a bunch of misguided pirates and Uncle was some conflicted seawolf in sheep's clothing. I listened to myself say this, and it was as trite as a second-rate movie review. I had a hard time digesting Paola's version.

"Okay," said Lou. "You can cut out the flowery college stuff around me." His shoes shuffled and I figured he was preparing to use them on my shins.[85]

---

[85] About here in Will's notes, I became very self-conscious that average readers of bestsellers and potboilers are scratching their netherlands saying, Where's the action? And I paid for this book! I'm a cerebral, laid-back guy, and have struggled for years to satisfy their hunger for more than parlor piffle, fey nods and ambiguous handshakes. In spite of his low GPA and classroom challenges at Mundane, Will was actually a very thoughtful and cerebral guy, like myself. For instance, he could have been a real standout on the varsity baseball nine or local Crystal Rock Beer sandlot team if it were not for his hesitancy. That's it! Hesitancy. I've been looking for that word to describe his attitude for fifty thousand words. Eureka! He was always a bit slow on the uptake and a half-step too slow. Coach Burns even said he threw with a sissy arm for a third baseman. Maybe Will was composing a lyric or thinking about an algorithm for this odd contraption he assembled in his basement with a keyboard and CRT (cathode ray tube), a real piece of useless junk. Once, on the way to the DQ on 23rd St., he walked right against the light and I yelled at him, helpless to do anything, like I often am right here and now slogging through his recollections about a dumb boat trip to nowhere—not that the Carib' isn't a nice place to horse around. He was in the middle of the street, busy as hell with rush-hour traffic, standing precariously on the double yellow stripe like a tightrope walker waiting for the wind to die down. I thought he's going to die, because he was inches from his chin and ass getting creamed. If it had been a cattle stampede, instead of side mirrors, both sets of cheeks would have been skewered by horns and trampled into a western hommelette. On the other side, I grabbed him and hugged him—Vinnie often hugged him, too—and said you crazy sonofabitch, you almost got killed. He said he was thinking of something else and was sorry. I said don't ever do that stunt again, because I didn't really like to pick up girls at the DQ by myself. Hesitancy. I said, Will if your mind is somewhere else like that all the time, your body can't be far behind in a pine box or body bag. So I asked his Mom about this problem about no action beyond lip-synching and throat-clearing, spittle and testicular adjustments that the Henry James crowd sucks up with a dusty tome in a cozy stuffed wing chair with a cup of tea by a window and the tapping patter of raindrops racing quietly down to a rotting sill outside. This was during one of my last visits to her; before she started chemotherapy at Lemminghaus in Cleveland. While she got me a piece of Dutch apple pie in the kitchen, I noticed the colorful flyer of clinic services

"Stop it, Lou," she said. "Pick on someone your own size."

---

on the coffee table. The schematic map showed how to get there from Monroe to ultimately Rockefeller Avenue then Cliff Street. I puzzled over the encouraging photo caption from a patient pictured in a wheelchair surrounded by a few friends and family who all shaved their heads in a show of emotional support: "Everyone here at Lemminghaus has been behind me all the way...They have pushed me to take that leap of faith..." I asked Mrs. Melville about my wanting to inject or ad-lib more action into Will's memoirs. She said Why? I said (with selfishness aforethought) people these days get very bored and will probably not buy the book and therefore will not be inspired by Will's search for meaning in his shortened life. "Is it good?" she said. I said yes to both my last scrumptious bite and her tepid consent. She said she was always concerned about Will and Vinnie sitting in front of the TV after school watching Looneytunes and all the celluloid whacking and chopping and dismemberment and double-crossing and, well. Then she put her hand to the side of her face and said "And the blood." I explained to her that, even in color, there was no blood; it was all celluloid, make believe, gratuitous violence, primordial entertainment and that I would try to keep the action as tasteful as possible (She didn't know how my mind was racing ahead with a samurai sword in one hand and an AK-47 in the other and cigar out the side of my mouth with week-old stubble for the remaining hundred pages to sell the damn book. I was getting desperate.) She went to the window and toyed with the curtain between her fingers and told me that several years earlier she noticed across the street some of the Skidmore brood (15, 13, 11, 9, 7, 5, 3, six months) putting a small cat in a hole they dug in their lawn. Their little hands pressed the dirt around the cat's neck. The cat began meowing and shaking its fuzzy little head. She said she immediately thought of Sylvester the Cat and that's when she made the call to the police. One of the cops dove in front of the power mower two of the smaller kids struggled to push over the cat's head. That's when I looked at my plane ticket and asked if I might possibly have another piece of pie and she said how about peach? Eventually, she said well all right, but no blood and I assured her there wouldn't be a spot on those pristine pages other than the finality of little black periods marks. She was a dear, as always, through the years and I really wanted her to be able to relax with my book—Will's story—in her hands in the same wing chair I sat in, with a small demitasse of green tea between chemotherapy visits in Cleveland. I gave her a gentle hug and kissed her hand at the door. I never kissed my own mother's hand. And in the end, that was about all the type of action I could really muster in the book itself.

Then Bud and Les came through the door. I figured they already imbibed their morning ration of tumblered scotch. They pulled up like a couple of bolting horses and saw Lettie relaxed there. "Did we miss this one somewhere along the way?" said Les.

The electrified brass ceiling lamp swung in a gentle arc. It must have survived the refittings and renovations through the years. I imagined it also shone on this very spot sixty or so years ago when Lettie passed away, but how did she die? Why wasn't she buried at sea or taken ashore for proper burial? The lamp knew, but like Captain Billy, it was as mute as a boulder in a chattering stream. She could have been dead for a thousand years, let alone sixty or so. Most everyone back then must be dead by now, so what the hell does it matter? You're gone, you're gone, and I thought it now a waste of time. Lou was right. It was all relative. Paola was right. Compartmentalize! I should have shoved Lettie back in the hole and forgotten about her; but there she was, her mute bones, yet we contended with them as if she might come right back to collect them like a dress she preferred over the one she stepped out in ten minutes ago.

"What did Captain say?" said Les.

I said I showed it to him and he said he didn't know about it and he didn't have any time to deal with it.

"So, let's take a vote and get this over with," said Les.

"My ass!" said Lou. "I never voted for anything in my life outside of a horse race and I'll be damned if I start with a skeleton. Toss the damn thing overboard. We've got work."

Bud turned, poked a finger on Lou's sunken chest. He wanted to say something, but was constrained by a clenched jaw and pursed lips. Lou, who resented anyone with an opposite view, tried to kick Bud in the shins but hit Les instead. There ensued some pushing and shoving, with Paola crouched over Lettie's bones. Lou yelled it's not even a damn corpse.

"Don't you have an ounce of respect for the dead?" said Bud, who was restrained by Les pulling him back by the shoulders. "You don't know the first thing about corpses and skeletons."

We noticed how Bud's lower lip trembled and Lou said, all right, all right and sat down on the edge of my rack.

Paola said why don't you all shut up for once and let her decide. The three men with ample adipose among them to fill out the skeleton stepped back and laughed. Les said, Paola you never cease to amaze me with your lack of compassion for the living, and I braced myself against the rack for a cat fight, but she stared calmly and waited for them to stop the chortle and snicker of latent adolescence. When I saw how they shook their heads to protest in silence, I saw how much grudging respect they really had for her irrational mind. Again, she leaned over the skull and placed an ear where Lettie's breath would have escaped between the silent teeth.

"Nuts, and she calls herself a scientist," muttered Lou.

"Shut up, Lou," said Bud. "We're all in the same boat."

Paola spent about two minutes frowning and even touching Lettie with her ear to listen. Lou, Bud and Les were quiet now, straining with winced eyes and cocked heads to see if Lettie imparted the slightest breath. Then Paola slowly lifted her head and with an intimacy reserved for the living, she placed her hands on top of Lettie's, which were folded together in repose on top of her sternum. She then patted them to comfort her and rose to her feet.

Right then, I drifted back to a war documentary I once saw on TV where a chaplain knelt over a dying soldier. I knew the soldier was dying, because his lips quivered and his face was covered with dark bandages and the chaplain's rosary swung in the breeze almost touching the soldier's chest. He made the sign of the cross, then joined his hands and raised them above the soldier's head. I was around thirteen and infected with the romantic aura of heroism. The scene cut away, and seeing Paola posture over there in her khaki shorts made me question what role I was playing on the Tern.

The seance broke up when Uncle's gruff voice came over the intercom to muster topside. They shuffled past without a word. Paola was last out.

"She's in your keeping now. Put her back there." Paola motioned with her head toward the opening in the bulkhead. "She said she's fine resting there." She shut the door in my face before I could also say she was nuts. She was so sincere in her screwed-up thinking I didn't have the heart to be abrupt with her like the others. And in my rekindled thoughts of adolescent heroism, I still cared for her.

The next day, Uncle stopped me in the passageway. It was the first time I had seen him and the others since Lettie came out of hiding. They were holed up in the COMM room, each at a position wheeling and dealing. I knocked on the door once and Bud opened it a speakeasy crack. He said make it snappy, as I could see the others' backs swivel around their seats, tethered by headsets and patch cords.

"Where is everybody?" I said.

"Busy. Got to go. Make yourself useful and keep a sharp lookout with the flips."

"The Filipinos?"

Bud nearly shut the door right in my face.

Uncle appeared dragged out from the telethon. "Will, I want you to take whoever's bones they are and bury them at sea. Here's something you can say." He handed me a piece of paper with writing on it. "By the way, the Vanderbilts are buried in the cemetery behind Alice Detwiler.[86]

"But the ring, Uncle," and I pulled it out of my pocket.

---

[86] Will, why do you do this to me? He knew I was a stickler for truthful detail. He could have added that he found out later what I discovered from Penny's dogged traipsing for three weeks; but I guess he never got the chance to do that. Melville told him a big fat lie. Penny was visiting her Aunt Bea at a rest home in Florence and I asked her to swing by Mt. Pisgah Cemetery behind Alice Detwiler. It was a rainy day and she said she almost gave up after two hours when she slipped on the wet grass and slid about twenty feet past the last elm tree and there it was. A granite tombstone (incised "Redford B. Vanderbilt and Letiticia W. Vanderbilt") that was ready to keel over from old age and neglect. She said, crapola when I asked her to slip the groundskeeper a fifty to open the graves and confirm this. After she said Des, all this for a lousy book? I told her there was three hundred in it for her. The grave digger, Rufus, was so exhausted she pulled him out of one of the rotted boxes he fell in. He gazed up at her and said jes' folks like us and couldn't tell any more until he broke the ring fingers and handed Penny the two gold wedding rings. "Maisie Doats" and "Dozier Doats" appeared in her penlight glow; the same well-respected Cobb County penitant philanthropists whose three sons served back-to-back life terms in the Georgia state pen. Penny was exhausted and said she certainly couldn't know what Maisie knew, but it was too late anyhow to speculate at two in the morning. On a whim, she took a bus the next day to Biloxi. Two months later, she called to tell me she dove into the recycle bin behind the library after the librarian said she fessed up to throwing out a lot of old trash. Penny gave the security guard ten dollars to help her and between them, she found Captain Billy's leather-bound papers tied in rotting twine. And somewhere in those neglected soiled pages she found mention of the Vanderbilts. "This day, August 23, 1915, Mr. Vanderbilt fell overboard by accident, wheelchair and all, in a rolling sea off Curacao. His wife, Lettie, died a day later after a long struggle with pneumonia and has been stowed below decks until proper arrangements for her burial in the family plot outside Asheville." So, Will was correct in his assumption, eventhough stowage of a corpse reeks

"You'll have to ask Captain Billy how it got here, because I'll be damned if I know." He then patted me on the shoulder and was followed into the stateroom by the crew, a sullen chaingang headed for another lecture.

"What's up, Lou?" I whispered.

"Ask your screwy pal."

---

of mystery in itself. I felt vindicated by the truth, even if it cost me nearly eight hundred bucks to find out who the bag of bones belonged to at one time.

CHAPTER 23

They must have been in the stateroom for three hours in the afternoon. Lou was a real hairpin, and I resented how he liked to take advantage of his size to outhustle me with a wisecrack about my truancy from military service. "Ask you screwy pal." He was so obnoxious I sensed he'd been hurt a lot in the past. Maybe struck out with the girls. Inferiority complex about his high IQ and low stature; a combination for a tyrant. One night as we sat in the canvas deck chairs by the pool, we talked about American League batting averages and he suddenly stopped at Lou Gehrig and said, some of those stupid kids in high school used to call me Toulouse in high school. You know, it could mean "to lose" or Toulouse-Lautrec, the crippled French artist who came up to my shoulders. I didn't ask Lou why. He said then he started throwing punches from the floor and getting plastered after school and then suspended for fighting. He stared at the pool. "Dumb dickheads. I only wanted to fit in." He finished his beer and threw it over the side and got up and said Sorry, I got distracted there. So I knew he was hurt real bad inside and I let him use me as a punching bag. To me it was no big deal.

Around 2030 that evening, Sam nestled by me in a small coil of manila line that Flash made for him. Lately he was cranky and preferred to hang out there after flying off somewhere all day. Why or how he ever came back was still a mystery to all of us. I flipped through a few news items filched from the trashcan under the teletype machine outside the COMM room. Of the eight crumpled pages, four were from wire services about Vietnam and mentioned places like Saigon, Con Thien, Khe Sanh and Phu

Bai ad nauseum.[87] The other four listed stock quotes from various world

---

[87]   My godmother, Judith Chodoff, once said the more you confront your fears, the easier it is to overcome them; sort of withdrawal in reverse. This is the first indication I came upon Will beginning to face going back and turning himself in for induction. This actually came about shortly after committing Lettie to the deep in the body bag which he suspected was a teasing stage prop by one of the crew (probably Lou). Some mental booby trap for a draft-dodger! I chatted long-distance with Cliff D. several weeks ago, and he ragged on about the property taxes in Scottsdale and I said why don't you move to Grand Junction. Same thing but fewer golf courses and a lot cheaper. Anyway, we got on the subject of Will's onboard hazing. "So what about it?" Cliff said. I guess he was pissed I mentioned Grand Junction. He relaxed when I told him about the body bag thing and how Will mentioned a few places in Vietnam. He said Will most likely referred to it one evening when Les and the others drinking and trying to locate on a large quad map some of the wire service references to places over there. I told Cliff to mail Les's notes on this to me, since the call was long-distance, but he said no it'll just be a minute while he dug out a list in Les's own handwriting. He said he wasn't a writer, but said I should add the Les list since a lot of fiction skimmers still want some real names and places to grab their interest. He felt so strongly about it, he told me to reverse the charges. So, after a jaw-breaking ninety minutes of West Texas phonetics, it was done. At the end, I said go to bed and sleep on the Grand Junction move and hung up on him. I hate fillers, but Cliff, with his lowly associates degree from Agua Caliente JC, argued a good point and so here it is, with presumeably grudging consent of the Brown and Shue editorial board, in no particular order to complete Will's "ad nauseum." To some readers who were over there, this may seem like rattling off some place as familiar as a local street corner; to others, I beg your indulgence for other reasons: Ap Bac; La Drang; Ba Gia; Binh Gia; Dong Xoai; Long Tan; Dak To; Ong Thanh; Ban Dong; Phuoc Long; Buon Ma Thuot; Hue; A Shau Valley; An Lao; An Loc; Phan Rang; Xuan Loc; Tan Son Nhut; Can Tho; Chu Lai; My Lai; Bong Son; Hiep Hoa; Kampot; Song Be; An Dien; Rach Bap; DaNang; Plei Me; Pleiku; Vung Ro; Thanh Hoa; Truong Cong Dinh; Hong Kil Dong; Loc Ninh; Lam Son; Suoi Tre; Phuoc Long; Prey Veng; Snoul; Ong Thanh; Hon Da Song Mao; Nam Dong; Long Dinh; Hat Dinh; Long Vei; Ban Hoa Sone; Binh Ba; Kontum; Kompong Speu; Khan Duc; Bien Hoa; Vung Tau;Chan La; Ap Gu; Gung Tai; Olongapo; Kien Long Cu Nghi; Kim Son Valley; Xa Cam My; Minh Thanh; Duc Co; Tra Binh Dong; Ap My An; Vinh Huy; Tam Quan; Thom Tham Khe; Kham Duc; Quang Tri. (Publisher's Note: Although in the field of

exchanges and were heavily marked with a red felt-tip so they resembled the bloody towel from a guy who stopped in for a quick shave and got nicked up to within an inch of his life.

I was reading aloud to Sam one of the reports on some action around DaNang when a shoe nudged my thigh with a light tap to get my attention.

"Hey, sorry for that comment earlier," said Lou.

Amazed he didn't kick me in the shins, I said that's okay forget it. He seemed as tall as everyone else. "Les told me you guys made thirty million on exchange rates today," I said.

"He rounds up. Pretty close. Your bird looks tired. Anything wrong?" He took a long swig from his beer bottle and tossed it over the side, as usual.

I said yeah, he must be getting tired out trying to find his way back home. Paola says he's way off the path.

"And you?" he said to me, grabbing the pages I finished reading.

"What about me?" I suspected he was digging again.

Lou glanced at the pages and exclaimed, damn General Commotion lost thirty-seven cents a share. Damn! He huffed at me as if I were responsible for short-selling, or whatever he called it.

"Asking, that's all."

He mumbled his way past the deck chairs and said you know you wouldn't be here if we hadn't approved of your old man's plan. Sam twisted his head and screeched at Lou, but I was speechless that what Lou admitted snuggled right up to my suspicion that Uncle Rob and his motley crew on the Tern set me up all along as some mascot to carry along for good luck. Anyway, my mind was preoccupied with a midnight rendevous and Lettie.

At 2300, under the swinging arc of the overhead lamp, I sat on the edge of my rack with the piece of paper Uncle handed me. A gentle rap on the door and Paola eased a foot into the doorway like my room was one of her slippers.

"Captain gave me this to give to you," and she handed me two thick black plastic bags.

"*Kloowiprachric.*"

"*Grupsak?*"

"*Grupsak.*"

"*Roolakridtrukbo?*"

---

play, action in and around Vung Tau and Olongapo was primarily limited to catfights and bar brawls.)

"*Purklowirdoof.*"

"Okay," I said. "If that's all there is."

"That's all there is." Her golden ringlets glistened in the light and I just missed stepping on Lettie's foot. I had a perverse impulse to run my fingers through Paola's tresses to somehow prepare me for lifting Lettie's bones in the bag. Paola patted my arm and whispered let's hope this is as close as you ever get to these things. You're lucky you've got a rich uncle who is going out of his way to give you time to think about everything.

I wanted to tell her right there I was so tired of people picking over my conscience like ravens on roadkill over my holiday of evasive behavior. Whether I camped out in Canada or Sweden for the rest of my life or surrendered my carcass to Uncle Sam was none of their damn business.

"Do you want to help me?" I said.

"Orders," she said. "You're on your own."

So I was a novice in this carnival cruise of ambivalent tacking between corruption and benevolence. Right! Start me off with a bag of bones. Like I said, they probably planted Lettie's bones there in the first place. After all, they had me bunked on top of that incessant whine and babble of the screw. And now the body bag only confirmed my growing belief that Uncle prepared me for my own D-Day. I placed the gold wedding ring on Lettie's ring finger with as much reverence as I could muster. I placed her carefully in the double bag. I was so stressed, it felt like there was still the weight of flesh on them as I helped her into the bag. I struggled for a long, drawn-out five minutes to carry her on my back to the fantail where a shimmering veil of moonlit waters danced in our wake. Everyone was asleep, but I still peeked around as I pulled out the piece of paper Uncle Rob gave me. "Lord, as you receive my soul in your keeping, commit my body to the deep, where it will repose until my reincarnation in your glorious kingdom." I never believed in such dribble, which Vin and I sometimes snoozed through at Mundane chapel; but as I recited what surely must have been Uncle's dashed-off prayer and let Lettie's bones slip out of my trembling hands into the deep, I felt alone with not a soul in sight except the belated twinkling of our descendant's eyes above my head. I struggled to keep my confusion from wetting my cheeks like a sudden cloudburst at the close of an otherwise sunny and humdrum day.[88]

---

[88] I am grateful to "Aunt" Judith Chodoff, for deciphering Will's thoughts here. I knew from helping her move last April from her apartment in Hoboken to be closer to some former colleagues in Princeton, that there was on her

kitchen wall a beautiful, ornate doctoral diploma in cosmology from the Pranck Institut fuer Physik und Wahrheit in Quarkstadt, a post-World War II suburb of Heidelberg. I was frustrated with Will's feeble attempt at purple prose (i.e., "belated twinkling...") although to his credit, he didn't swipe Faulkner's "lidless stars," and I asked her opinion of it. She was quite lovely and patient and, as I recall, awfully pretty as a young woman, but when she wanted to make a point, she could spin around her two hundred pounds on a dime in that wheelchair and give you a piece of her brilliant mind. Amid the packing boxes in her small front room, she gently tapped me on the forearm while explaining Will may have flunked out, but he possessed a reasonably perceptive, if not poetic, view of the universe. If I followed her right, the light from stars is from events occurring a hell of a long time ago, but the origin of those events is actually happening in the future (we haven't seen this light yet). Listen, she said, it's like visiting your house in the old neighborhood you haven't seen in forty years; you recognize some places, crumbling steps, thinning hedges, and there's a young couple next door with a baby and you have no idea who they are and they turn the other way before you can say hello. I politely said, I think I see what you mean, and while she talked, I noticed over her shoulder a bottle of beer on the kitchen table and a row of gaily dressed bisque dolls on the shelf above it. So, I said we're neither here nor there, and she said well yeah, we're in the present. In transition. On the razor's edge, but it doesn't mean you shouldn't do your best while you're here. She winced, resettling her heft in the wheelchair and added, think of the present as a present—a nice homonym for you and a nice gift from me. Got it? She tugged on her tubing and rolled her eyes up to the ceiling for a second, and I could tell she didn't want to go on for an hour with this, especially after she pursed her lips and peeked over at the unfilled packing boxes on either side of me. We talked about the kids for a while, which brought me back to Will's passage. By then, we gravitated to the kitchen where she also opened a beer for me. After I got her a new oxygen bottle from under the sink, I asked her from her perspective what was so poetic about Will's prose, which I didn't really care for. She took a sip and said if you look at the whorl of fine hair on a baby's crown, as she said she did when I was a baby, and know anything about spiral galaxies, it's quite obvious where we came from and where we're going. I said I think I see, but lost her there, and I waited for more as she glanced up at the row of dolls above our heads. She was childless and I decided not to go there anymore. She took a long hit of oxygen and said I ought to visit her more. My friend, Will, too. I promised her I would.

CHAPTER 24

"Son, I'd be glad to move you into the big guest room, but we've got a visitor coming," said Uncle Rob the next morning when I asked him for another room. I got less and less sleep because of the damn screw jabbering half the night. At first, it was a nuisance as harmless as checkout lane chatter, but over time it persisted to transmit mayhem far beyond a bench-clearing brawl. Last night, I woke up in a sweat from nightmares of the Tern capsizing and going down in a storm and all of us having one last round of seawater sluice down our gasping throats.

I didn't tell Uncle Rob about the restless night. He would have merely winked and said carry on, son. You know your duties. As the sun rose, it dawned on me that the screw's harmless, monotonous, mechanical and repetitive dialogue was the prelude to my own fugue, variations on my loss of direction and loss of home. The others were familiar with it, but offered scant sympathy besides, oh you'll get used to it. I figured they were part of a much larger clique of nomadic American intelligentsia in on a good thing with Uncle and his specious do-good entanglements. Who wouldn't take the money? And who was I to criticize my protector? If Uncle Rob had been a politician, who wouldn't have voted for him? For his protection and favoritism? Les told me a few days ago that Uncle knew enough high-ups to easily become a successful public servant, but then Les had another kind of diarrhea and rushed to the head before elaborating.[89]

---

[89] When I began this literary caper of editing Will's notes, it bugged me there was so little information on his uncle other than some vague mention of his Navy Cross and the rest home and some private island off Baranquilla. I found Will somewhat of a lazybones for his lack of curiosity. So what did Les tell him about Melville's political aspirations? I guess he didn't want to bite the hand providing

Anyway, last night it was, "*backgetbackgetbackgetbackgetbackgetback...*" and

him safe harbor—as it were—at sea on the Tern. Before I pulled out any last remaining eyebrow hairs over this, my coffee cup led me to the dank fluorescent-lit basement of Brown and Shue, where the tech editors and ghostwriters were incarcerated. I would rather pick undigested corn kernels in a pigsty than suffer the neurotic deadlines under which they must survive. I asked my good buddy, Diebold Krantz, if he could use some of his ancestor's (he was one-third Cherokee) skills to track down Melville's background. Dee burned himself out on the fifth floor shelter of padded cubicles where researchers, homeless stringers, dopers and romance hacks hung out. We always got along real well, probably since I never asked him about his personal life. Weather, the Yankees, the lunch menu around the corner at Gruntz's Cafeteria. Maybe where to get cheap theater tickets. He could see I was upset and he lifted the withered right arm of his bony one-hundred twenty pound frame and said, You bet. Two weeks later, I went down to see his desk piled high with open boxes. Someone told me he was run over on the East Side and was in a coma at the hospital. Good old Dee. After rummaging his desk drawers, I found a manila folder labelled "Melville." Bingo! It was about two inches thick. I visited him (I should say his body) once at the hospital. I really choked up when I put my hand on top of his. It was as clammy as a slab of black marble. I said, Dee I'm so sorry and thanked him for the folder on Melville. A nurse fumbled with his IV on the other side of the bed and I said out loud, Dee I love you, man, and I didn't give a rip if the nurse heard it. The attending physician came in and stood by Dee's bed. The clipboard with Dee's chart was a single damn sheet of printout with a few lines on it. He told me in a thick accent I caught up with there was little chance Dee would ever regain consciousness (let alone see Will's book, I thought). Out of some cynical and hopeless desperation for Dee's wellness, I wrung my hands and asked him what if someone tripped on the powercord to his ventilator, would it get him discharged and out of his misery? The resident's forehead broke out in a dozen wrinkles as he intoned, this is a serious matter of life and death. I said you're right and left him shaking his head at my sudden concurrence. Some time later, after Dee was cremated, I overheard two coworkers I never met before chat at the next table in the cafeteria say Dee was hit by his long-time live-in girlfriend, who was then whip-lashed from behind by Dee's former live-in boyfriend. The creamcheese bagel nearly dropped out of my mouth as I asked them what else. They said everybody knew Dee gave it and took it, if I knew what they meant. They said it was no exaggeration Dee exhibited in the building the biggest schlang, which was sixty-five stories and fully occupied. One of the gals held it took me the usual quarter hour to decipher that syncopated whine into plain language. It could have been interpreted by anyone in a far different

up her hands about a foot apart and her words sailed through them like extra points through the goalposts at the Polo Grounds. Always the last to know. After a few hours, I could still see Dee sitting at his desk in the basement and I fondly remembered his courteous smile and kindness to me, and I still loved the guy, even if he was dead and in a totally different closet. Anyway, after wading through the list of tonnage sunk in the Pacific Campaign; a laundry list of service medals in addition to the Navy Cross; four patents on a submarine hull design and surface coating, with everything blacked out except the title and extract, as well as one for a licorice extruder and copies of licensing agreements with several major confectioners such as Neptune Candy Company; a list of 235 Child's Garden of Learning Centers for the handicapped; Goob's discount chain; court documents pertaining to his defense in State of California v. Claire Dibble Temps, infamous for providing female escorts to relieve short-handed union shops; the Bait and Switch Deep Sea Fishing Rod System used by charter fishing boats from Ketchikan to Portland, Maine; copies of deeds for thirty large office buildings in twenty-five states; a list of the hospice care facilities (e.g., Alice Detwiler); Come Clean Detoxification Centers (subsidiary of the American Polygraph Corp.) and so many other fascinating profit sources, I got constipated sitting there for hours in sheer disbelief, recalling how Melville was at one time totally broke and picked up for panhandling near Pensacola after the war. I focused my interest on his political activities, which literally took all of two pages of Dee's folder. Nothing. A long list of phone numbers with a (D) or (R) after each name. I recognized a handful of them (e.g., Wilson, Jackson, Raybourne; Cuccaro). I chanced to call two of them for some odd verification. Someone answered with cultivated modulation, Senator Raybourne's residence. No, he is currently at a fundraiser. Is this the office of Senator Cuccaro? Who the hell is this? I held my breath. Who is it? If it's you, Bobby, you're dead meat. He spoke with such projectile force, I thought I was Bobby, hung up and poured a black coffee to settle my nerves. I mean I could see blood oozing through the little speaker holes. Other than three meritorious UN citations for refugee resettlement contracts, there was correspondence on Melville Corporation letterhead to the US State Department declining an ambassadorship to Ghana in West Africa. It was probably better Will didn't wait for Les to wipe himself and tell him about this ball of wax, as it wouldn't have moved his story along much; but as his editor, I needed to find out for the record, since I've always been a persistent and unapologetic fan of the facts over modern storytelling.

way, but to me it had an urgency this time I could no longer ignore: Get back! After four months of self-imposed exile, I was bored with the selfish luxury of excluding myself from the mainstream of events back home. That dream woke me up in a sweat: a howling storm; trees across downed sparking powerlines. When I got home, there was nothing left but the staircase. I saw Mom in her flowered nightgown trip at the top on that edge of carpeting I always intended to tack down. She tumbled all the way down. I tried to run to help, but my legs got so heavy I could only watch her in my guilt and inadequacy as she hit the bottom step. Then she suddenly got up, brushed herself off and walked right through me into the dining room where her friends from the book club gabbed around the coffee table. She didn't even recognize me. That hurt, and I missed her a lot.

"Will, get your butt up here on the double," said Lou over the intercom. That order woke me up from the semi-conscious epilogue to my traumatic dream and I quickly suppressed it with the other bad ones as I jammed my wallet, pen and pocketknife into my khaki shorts.

We lined up. Uncle, in his white polo shirt, white shorts, white deck shoes and socks, white baseball cap and gleaming white teeth seemed at once to be there and not there in the brightest morning of the entire voyage. He held up his hand as if to declare, I am the way, which was an overplayed and ambiguous entrance, since the golden sparkle from the frame of his aviator glasses and heavy Rolex watch enriched his attire far beyond that of the humble carpenter.

I bumped Lou next to me as I looked up at the steering wheel. "Who's driving?"

"A piece of string. Don't worry."

"Mr. Vice?" said Uncle.

"Here, sir," said Les. I peeked over at him to see if he was steady on his feet. Almost.

"Mr. Shill?"

"There, sir?" said Bud. He leaned on my left shoulder, sad stunk drunk.

"Mr. Melville?"

"Present, sir!" Uncle didn't acknowledge me other than to keep his eyes glued on his clipboard.

"Mr. Lewis?"

"Everywhere, suh!" said Lou with righteous enunciation. He steadied himself on my right forearm with the tenacity of a child waiting to cross the street.

"Ms. Paleo-Tosti?"

"*Krukpuk*," replied Paola. She wore the spaced-out smile of a good time. She must have enjoyed a book, to my regret.

Uncle cleared his throat of a persistent frog to announce the Tern's last gig. He sighed so deep, he began coughing like a chain smoker.

"No penultimates?" asked Lou.

"Nope. This is it." Uncle motioned to Flash to bring over a canvas deck chair. "My knees are shot."

Paola laughed out loud and said it was his rotator cuffs last year.

"Nope."

"So what happens to the Tern?"

Uncle said he accomplished all he intended with Captain Billy's vessel during the last nine years. Each one took turns clearing their own pipes as they sat around the table across from Uncle. Their complicity showed in lowered heads and a silence that felt more profound than the soft breeze fluttering leftover napkins in the center of the table.

"The scrap heap?" asked Bud.

"Nope. There's some lawyers in The Loop who want to take it to Saugatuck on summer weekends. They wired the cash already."

"So this is it, then?" asked Lou.

"Yep."

"So we go home?" said Bud.

"Yep. Don't worry," said Uncle. He doodled on the clipboard and tore off a caricature of each one. He passed them out. "Here. These wanted posters should keep you out of trouble."

Bud grimaced at his distorted features. "If I remember correctly, you once said this must be the work of a hedonistic onanist, right?"

"Yeah," added Lou. "You used your hands. I saw you."

Uncle almost fell back off his chair with a rollicking chortle. "Bud, you're dealing with forces of language you know nothing about. You must have repeated the fourth grade."

"Okay," said Bud. "It was the sixth grade." He pulled out his deck of cards and started shuffling. "Okay, would it be classier if we called you an epicurean, huh?"

"Yep." Uncle cleared his throat and said, my word, this is an inauspicious occasion; the gang of four to carry out our last mission of remunerated mercy. One last guest to close out the illustrious log of the Tern.

When Uncle couched the deed at-hand in those evasive terms, I sensed yet another nefarious folly. That was about as high-minded a mental description this acolyte could give it. I was up to my waist in this humanitarian muck and not a one of them had the slightest inclination to reach over and pull me out. So I faked enthusiasm and clapped politely with the others when Bud said Captain, would you mind hot-wiring the intros.

"Noted," said Uncle, who tapped the beer can in his hand with his chunky UofM class ring. I never saw him do that with his wedding ring, which he must have worn in silent memory of his deceased first wife and child. He tossed the clipboard to Flash, sitting next to Sam on the foc'scle.

"What the heck!" said Lou, scratching the dark mole on his neck.

Uncle pulled out a glossy photograph from the sheaf of papers in front of him and held it up. "He's sold twenty million albums and once we're done with him, he'll be worth more than ever."

I said, Yeah he'll be worth more dead than alive. I said this with such spontaneous enthusiasm that the others sat up and glowered like gargoyles down at me as if I were the only Negro parishioner at lily-white St. Luke's Thursday night Bible study back home.

Above the disparaging nays and outright boo from Bud, Paola said to me, you're not funny, you know that. Don't presume that we don't know what we're doing out here. This is and has always been a venture of the highest moral purpose. Otherwise, we wouldn't be here in the first place.

Down into the table surface rippled my own vacillating reflection confirmed in spite of the show of camaraderie and crossing "their" equator and all the other junk, I was still an outsider on the Tern, which only magnified my isolation from home and friends by dodging the draft. When Paola said how about looking at me when I'm addressing you, Sam squawked and answered for me.

Uncle sat there in silence and let it all pay out like reeling in a big one on an eighty-pound test line; one last series of fantastic leaps and soundings for the camera until it's gaffed onto the deck, defeated. Les patted me on the back, but I knew this was about the end of the good times; and I vowed inside to be an obedient swabby until the Tern dropped anchor for the last time.

Bud quietly put his playing cards away when Paola spoke about high moral purpose and asked Uncle what's the deal with Jimmy Hank Cullipher, an early rock-and-roll superstar of the mid-Fifties who sank from the scene around 1958 extending his career on tour as a cross-dresser covering other's chartbusters.

Uncle Rob tugged on his toy cap bill and claimed that old Jimmy Hank was a mess. Elevator drugs and deep gully hootch. "We treated him at the Beverly Hills Come Clean location. He escaped one night. We picked him up an hour later swivelling his hips stark naked at Third and Olive in Burbank."

"So how does he get here?" said Lou. "I've got a footlocker full of his LPs. Is he bringing his guitar with the diamond-studded frets?"

Uncle glanced at his platinum Rolex, which gave me a headache from its brilliant reflection of sunlight. "You'll see. His agent, Spade Hill, asked me to get him sober to resurrect him and his career. Sort of a second coming."

Les said Cullipher (aka JHC to his fans) was a shadow of his former self, "but we'll bring him down from that mountain of snow and have him back into the limelight."

Uncle said all right then. Let's turn to. I don't want Mr. Cullipher to think we're running a banana boat. Flash, let's clean up all this guacamole mess on the deck."

Sam knew better. He took off for the afternoon. Then Uncle turned to me and said "Will, let's talk."

I followed him up and into the COMM room, where Uncle said he was missing some tape recordings from the library. He stared at me. "If you happen to see them, Will, do me the courtesy of letting me know. And, by the way, if you ever have a desire to write about your adventure here on the Tern's last voyage, I'd like you to leave out the stuff like the Shapiros and Jimmy Hank. Treat this sailing sort of like bootcamp; something to remember but not write home about beyond love and kisses. Got that, son?"

"Sure, Uncle Rob. Sure." I said I had no idea where were the tapes.

"Okay?" he said with a drumroll of fingers on an R390 console.

"Sure, Uncle Rob." I think he could sense by my quick formal response I was half-truthing, because I did take some, but I saw Les and Lou also snatch several from time to time.

"Son, your mother called last night from Monroe." My wandering half-truth eyes focused right on his. "She told me not to tell you this, but I think you have the NTK."

"Damn!" Before I escaped many weeks ago, which seemed like years without the usual reference points of streetlamps and short-skirted girls instead of endless waves slapping the side of the Tern's hull, it suddenly dawned on me that

"Have you no honor? Have you no shame, my son?" said the older knight.

The two knights, one younger, angular and headstrong; and the other, avuncular, gray and slumped in his saddle, met on the green grassy lea overlooking Castle Glans, glistening in the morning mist with its prominent, crenelated tower thrust to the heavens in erect obeissance to the glory of days past and those yet to come.

"Alas, neither, Sir Goode," said Sir Reynard, vacillating in his saddle. "I have lost the way, and to meet you here in honorable, if dubious, combat is to have surely lost the way."

"Sir Reynard, you are a true scoundrel befitting of a right good tongue-lashing." He leaned forward in his suit of aged armour, dabbled with the crimson patina of long-past glory. "I say, raise your visor when I address you."

"Ho! Sir Ivan. A tongue lashing? Nay, not by you, but your good wife, Lady Mouthbutton. Now that would be by jove a fair offer."

"I am not Sir Ivan, you insolent cur. It is I, your father-in-law. Again, I say to you, have you no honor; no sense of duty?"

"Sir Goode, those merits I lost on the field by Antioch, as you well know. It was there I lost my faith, my faithful steed, Oreck, and my faithless wife, your daughter, Lady Eliza."

Suddenly, Sir Goode's mount reared up and dumped him up onto the damp turf with a resounding clank and screech of metal. Sir Reynard quickly dismounted and approached.

"Son, I have fallen on my arse. If this be my fate on this fine day, I say lend me your once-honorable hand that I may remount to smote thee for your unforgiveable indiscretions."

Sir Reynard pulled his father-in-law up from the ground and henceforth gave him a rude push down from where he once lay, saying, "forgive me as any good Christian soul would do and I shall forego the final unforgiveable indiscretion of lopping off your head."

"Aye, my son. As a true Christian, that I cannot entertain. You may sit erect and proud like the gorged cod of an urgent horse, but you will never see the morrow, lest it be from your curious skull, eyeless and utterless atop the tip of my pike. Now, be a good fellow and pull me up."

Sir Reynard commended his elder adversary on making an impressive point, and proceeded to pull him up once again, and with discrete care picked the tufts of grass shooting from his clanking arse.

"I commend you also, Sir Reynard, for giving me anon the chance to forgive your sins with one blow of my excelsior blade."

Sir Reynard assisted his aged opponent up into the saddle and rambled back to his own mount before the old man could think to rush him from behind.

"There is still time, my son. I beg you reconsider another path to end this madness."

Both men retreated sixteen rods to the end game for one of them. They dug their heels into sweating flanks and flew like the wind towards one another.

Sir Goode fell hard once more to the sod, and once again the younger one stood over him with sword unsheathed. The elder was in sheer agony from the jolt that dislodged his honor and helmet from his gray visage. Sir Reynard peered around his latest conquest and recited the long soliloquy of a sullen rascal.

"Must you stand there and bore me with such gibberish as I lay dying? Have you no final shame before God?" The penultimate words of Sir Goode were tinged in bloody froth, as the playful prattle of hawthorne and holly from the forest glen echoed in his ear.

"There still be time, my son. Confess your wastrel ways and repent or hasten my journey at this final curtain call to our Lord's heavenly kingdom."

Sir Reynard lifted his encrusted sword. "Sir Goode, good night," and with the tip of his taut tongue touching his nose, raised his sword and thrust it down through the throat of his father-in-law with the glee of a mad dog deserving no less than the devil's own naked applause.

Gone was Sir Goode; Goode no more. Sir Reynard removed his battered helmet, breathed deeply the mellow mew mist and exclaimed, "Surely have I lost the way once again, and I shall only find it whence I am prostrate as you, dear gone Sir Goode, with a sword pinning my gorge to a bloody clod of sweet earth."

Toward evening, I sensed that my mood swings from buoyant delight to total dismay at my impressed freedom on the Tern finally had finally become unacceptable to Uncle Rob and the crew, especially after my outspoken unmasking of their last so-called mission of mercy.

Uncle broke open two German dark beers from the small fridge under an R-390 pos. "Son, I'd venture to say you're bored senseless. Right?"

"Not really, Uncle Rob. Maybe tired, but not bored," I fibbed once again.

He took a long swig. "That's horse manure. Right, son?"

"Yeah," and I took a longer swig.

Uncle winked, pulled on the ridiculous, shiny toy captain's hat. Well, it'll be all downhill from now on, son."

"Yeah. I know."

"What?" He took off his toy hat.

"I feel I'm in the way, Uncle." I brushed a hand through my hair, which the wind and spray coiffed to resemble the mop Flash used to swab the deck at sunrise.

"How so?"

"You know, with the kind of stuff going on here and what's going on at home and in Nam."

Uncle fanned the pages of an old issue of *Midwest Spearfishing*. "Yeah, it's very confusing for kids these days." Back when I got out of college during the big one, there was no choice with an enemy at each end of the block. You served or you were called a traitor and punished. You know, classified as lower than whale shit.

"What about conscientious objectors?"

"Pure nonsense," he replied. He looked over his shoulder at the huge stuffed swordfish frozen on the apogee of an arching leap. The brass nameplate under it was dated November 12, 1939, caught off Key Largo by Senator Bob Claghorn (OK). "Huh!" he said. "I didn't know they spearfished in Lake Superior." He chuckled and flipped it aside as if it were a comic book. He folded his arms on the table. He told me how a childhood friend raised in a Quaker family near Goshen was unmercifully chastised for exercising his religious beliefs.

"Yeah?" I said.

"I lost track of him when I was sent overseas. After the war, I visited a cemetery outside Terre Haute to pay my respects to a buddy who served with me on the Cuke. As I got up after brushing some leaves off his tombstone, I turned my head for an instant and there he was, two plots away."

"No kidding."

I found out from his brother that he joined the Army and drowned before he could reach the beachhead in France. I was shocked. I didn't think he was capable of making such a courageous decision, and then dying for it.

"Yeah?"

"Nowadays, it's no big deal for an agnostic to get away with stabbing a believer in the back."

"Isn't that sort of strong?" I said.

"Hell no, son. The ones getting away with murder back home are defended in their right to do so by those who are actually getting murdered overseas.[90]

---

[90]   Will, Will, Will! This stuff went on for another thirty pages in Will's notes, and I said to myself this mindless, irrelevant rant has to cease. Back at Mundane, he took my advice for once and dropped Philosophy 101 in the first week. You could argue till the vultures came home as to who was right or wrong about the war. It sounded so juvenile and disingenuous, I thought he was turning into the kind of self-centered narcissist I'd never want to meet. I threw out only those pages which I relentlessly marked up so heavily I could no longer read them. He wrapped himself around quite a flagpole of indecision, and his story is more or less idling on random, almost adolescent, comments and I've decided to step in, put my shoulder so-to-speak under his arm, and carry him over the last hundred or so pages until this misadventure limps across the finish line. I've perused his notes to the end and can't in good editorial conscience let the reader suffer any more of this reaching for a moral lesson, prepubescent profundity or whatever the hell you want to call it. In particular, his handling of characters is tantamount to seeing your mother walk toward you on a familiar old street and pass right by you as if you didn't exist. Not even a hello or small chat; or even a rarer moment of illumination later when you turn around and walk after your mother and tap her gently on the shoulder only to realize she died three months earlier. And what happened to the lights, camera and action? This thing is coasting on fumes and it upsets me to no end. So sorry, Will. I love you like a brother, but here's where we part ways. Call it an editor's mutiny, but what he

225

I said it's a really screwed-up situation. Uncle drained his stein and said you got that right.

A few days earlier, Uncle Rob, who continued the habit of answering his own question, passed the Old Bay seasoning and asked me flat-out why I didn't want to serve. I took a bite of my crabcake. He answered that it really comes down to peer pressure. If your neighbor's house is on fire, you're going to help him save his to save your own. It's a social fabric thing, and more of a gut reaction than a moral choice. Les butted in and said I should have stayed in school, to which Paola responded *frublagickurruplikejlrposptagbeltch.* Uncle said she meant the home will continue to burn if you don't do something.

"I think I understand what you all mean."

Lou said you don't get squat, kid. Look, if you see someone drowning and you can't swim, you're a flaming asshole if you jump in. It's not in the dive, but in the preparation for the dive that you succeed.

Bud, whose ears turned a curious crimson red when he even looked at crabmeat, cleared the table with a rare gem that must have tumbled in his

---

has in store for his characters is totally unacceptable. I didn't mind doing your term papers and crib notes back at Mundane, but now I've got to make a living entertaining a most disarming, impatient and demanding readership and it's far more challenging than getting a sleepy tenured French professor's scribbled "vu" ("seen") to get through the class. By the way, my impatience and urgency to finish off this rambling nonsense of an adventure is probably due to my daughter Rachel's illness. She'd been feeling out of sorts and missed two weeks of school. We took her down to Hopkins and the specialist (oncologist) told us she has a rare form of multiple myeloma. It's advanced. My God! Roberta and I about went nuts. Our dear sweet child, Rachel. Dying? My own flesh! Why? She's just a child! I feel like I'm dying with her and I told the doctor I'd take her place in a heartbeat. I can't begin to tell you how beautiful she is. You wouldn't believe it anyway coming from a schlepping wordshyster like me. You see, she's not a bunch of words on a page. She's real. You can put your arms around her and find infinite and everlasting joy in her warmth, her smile and the way she looks at you and wrinkles her little nose and laughs with such gaiety and innocence. And an ebullient confidence I could never attain. You can practically see God, except she's more beautiful than the old man could ever be and right now we're praying for a miracle. Please, God; please don't take away my sweet Rachel. Let it be me. I sincerely apologize to the reader for this unacceptable intrusion, but I feel you need to know why I have such an urgency and distraction to finish Will's story.

mind with some of the rocks in his head over the years: "Right! Inanity is only one letter removed from insanity. You're a damn fool if you go in the Army."

Uncle raised his eyebrows and jumped on Bud. Mr. Shill, there's nothing senseless or nuts about defending your country. We all knew from Bud himself that his younger brother died in Korea. Bud drained his beer mug in slow deliberate gulps and I could tell the party was over with all this casual yet uncomfortable interrogation.

And as if I hadn't had enough, I lay in my rack and the screw of the Tern squealed *IcanhackitIcanhackitIcanhackit* until I finally got a few hours of restless sleep.[91]

---

[91]   With this business of the Tern's screw, Will may have stepped on more than the dog excrement we both navigated on the Quad at Mundane when late for the lecture, "Acoustics for the Tone-Deaf," at Aeolian Hall. This was before he took an academic dive. It was taught by physics Professor Sigismund Saxe, a really nice old guy who looked like a snowy owl with his hunched back, wire-rimmed glasses and little beak of a nose sticking out of the fluffy white shock of beard and hair. A very pleasant fellow as he shuffled before the chalkboard like an impotent, absentminded grandfather. "Siggy" once told us during a break that as an undergrad at Pomona he made a few bucks playing the violin for Rudolph Valentino for mood music during love scenes. Will and I shared a good laugh over it until someone later said old Siggy was slipping it to a quiet coed in the last row whom I'll call Penelope Arcade to protect her precious 4.0 GPA and those delicious honey blond tresses dripping over her stuck-up profile and incredible balcon as she looked out the ivy-choked window. Around this time, I noticed how the old mimeograph machine down the hall from the classroom kept telling me *buggeroffbuggeroffbuggeroffbuggeroff* so distinctly I became quite self-conscious everyone else might have also heard it. Even a few weeks ago when I popped into the repro room on the fourth floor at Brown and Shue, I was annoyed by the foreboding of the Xerox model GL1B copier with its easily recognizable *gotchagotchagotcha* as it spit out reams of someone's furtive attempt to print flyers for the Mom's Club or a *Playboy* foldout. Again, back to an incident that Will described in his diary: if you repeat something long enough, it becomes unintelligible. Of course there are exceptions such as Will's overall story, which upon first reading could be considered unintelligible mumbling. One really needs to reread it in paperback for no other reason than to spend a dollar on something more intellectually nutritious than a Clark Bar. From the shower squish-squash of flip-flops to the buzz of a defunct starter on a Fleetwood

CHAPTER 25

The night Jimmy Hank arrived, I was on deck on my back looking for the faded star cluster known as Pleiades. It was so much easier to see from Mom's backyard after she turned out her bedroom table lamp and Billie Caroline and I held hands on the glider. We could see them looking down on us as we swung back and forth between kisses.

When the flotilla of assorted boats nestled up to the Tern, we were soon boarded by a ragged assortment of ten retainers, bodyguards, physician, lawyer, make-up artist, advanceman, personal trainer and business manager. I got this from Lou, who stood next to me and Bud as we watched them climb up the ladder to the quarterdeck. Then Jimmy Hank came up last and looked more disoriented and ambiguous than Pleiades; faded, holding onto the arms of two bodyguards who showed no emotion in dragging him over to meet Uncle Rob. His dyed platinum bouffant

---

convertible, Siggy opened our ears with his quaint, if somewhat hair-brained, explanations and translations of fugitive, if not furtive, mechanical noise, and his equations were impossible to follow. He often referenced *The Secret Language of Machines* (V. Sokolov, 1950 Novosibirsk, USSR, translated by Klaus Diesel), an 800-page monster companion to a set of ten 78-RPM discs of baleen and ship sounds and extraneous white noise otherwise unintelligible on first-hearing and often regarded as wasted energy much like flatus, cocktail chit-chat or dugout chatter, itself a mystery to most people unfamiliar with baseball. Although not part of this story, Will made note of a heated argument between Lou and Paola over whether such mechanical language predated paleolithic tongues. Paola uttered *trukburgorgrah*, and Lou responded *clickpurrbuzzcreecree*. Bud yelled knock it off you babbling nincompoops and went over to physically break up what he later said were the underpinnings of Lou's deep sexual frustration.

flopped around like the tail of a squirrel in heat. The dark gold-rimmed sunglasses kept slipping over his saddleback nose and his jaw was askew as if he were ready to sing one of his old hits like "A Million Bucks" or "Annie Take Me Back." As a kid, I vaguely remembered the days when he juked and hip-faked his way to the top of the rock and roll music charts.

"Mornin', cap," he mumbled to Uncle, who said welcome aboard JHC and returned a crisp naval salute to the drunken swipe from our honored guest. After the exchange of howdy-do's, he was hustled off to the guest stateroom. About five large trunks with red white and blue stripes were carried by the so-called bodyguards, halting every few steps while JHC stumbled forward on his manager's arm. Les's jaw dropped when he saw this charade.

"You mean that's—that's what's left of him?" said Les.

Paola nudged him in the ribs and told him to keep it down. "This is the last one."

I asked her what she meant about that and she squinted at me and my naivete. She said there goes the last in a long procession of guests on the Tern.

"Like Irv and Rose and the rest?" I said.

"Not at all. He's here for a short rehab physically and career-wise according to his manager."

I thought Lou was more to the point when he said something like, the farther out I live my inconsequential life, the closer I feel the immense warmth and nearness of those who have passed. He could get real obtuse, but I think that's about what he said, and Bud turned to him and said what in hell are you whining about? And he quietly put his arm around Lou. What Lou said was sadly more prescient than anything I recalled during the whole voyage.

After the commotion of boarding JHC and his clutch of muscle-bound hangers-on, I spotted one more of those aluminum suitcases on the way down the ladder. As I lay in my rack, I could hear the faint strumming of an acoustic guitar through the bulkhead and could imagine his long bony fingers palsy their way across the frets trying to recall the past glory and tumult and hype of a starry career entertaining screaming kids and bewildered parents. Then it faded away. Lou told me before we broke up on deck that he attended many of his concerts and even got his autograph once. His eyes really lit up when he mentioned that and shaking his hand and touching his rhinestone-studded jacket. Lou also said JHC was about six feet four in his shitkickers and he actually stooped down to shake his hand. I could see Lou was deeply immersed in this guy's career. He even showed me a picture of him and his stage hero dated July 1954 at Queens Stadium. Bud interrupted Lou and said the guy was all washed up; an old fart on drugs. Lou got very agitated and tried to kick Bud in the shins, saying his idol was making a comeback and would show them all who was boss. And this was after Bud put an arm around him earlier. Those two guys. Then the screw interrupted my thoughts with *thefixisonthefixisonthefixison* and I had a comet-like flash of a dream where Jimmy Hank was this huge pinata and people hitting it with sticks and dollar bills flying out of it all over the place in a funnel cloud and the next minute it was in shreds like a faded torn poster slapped by the wind against the urine-stained doors of a shuttered movie theatre. I awoke in a sweat, but the next few days didn't prove out the screw's latest prophecy, and I could relax to think its monotonous hearsay was the fugitive sound that harmlessly annoys and distracts a freighted conscience such as mine.

Next morning, Uncle Rob told us all that everything was moving along as planned. "As I told you before, JHC is onboard for recuperation of his body and the resuscitation of his career."

"He's a mess," said Les.

"Shut up, Les," said Lou. "He looks great, just like he nailed it in his last album, *Looking Up Love*."

"Stop it, Lou. How the hell do you know?" entered Bud.

Paola tapped her coffee cup with a spoon and said JHC mumbled all night, reminding her of a hunkered group of aborigines near Ayer's Rock she said she recorded in 1961 on a Halfebright scholarship.

Lou admitted he once sneaked past a bodyguard and touched JHC's sequined robe. "I swear to God he's the greatest. He remembered me! Can you beat that? Out of all the thousands of fans. Little me."

"No kidding," said Bud in mock disbelief.

Lou scrambled up and across the breakfast table and threw himself onto Bud who had a bearclaw stusffed in his mouth. They both fell over and onto the deck. "These two are such buddies," said Uncle, who walked over with Paola and pulled off Lou.

"Don't touch me! Any of you! Keep your hands off me!" Lou demanded.

Uncle Rob raised his hands in benediction and said Lou, you're the greatest. We love ya.

CHAPTER 26

On the third night since JHC arrived, we relaxed on deck mimicking the calm sea about fifty miles off New Smyrna Beach with small talk about nothing in particular when Spade Hill was bumped and prodded into view by his reclusive client who demanded his meds. "You're late Spade. Where's my pills? You get them right now or I'm outta' here. You hear, boy?"

Uncle told us that Spade had told him tried to dry out, clean up and otherwise get Jimmy Hank back among mammaliens. My doubts lingered after the screw prompted my pinata dream about our guest, not to mention the sleazy appearance of Mr. Hill in his baggy pants, wraparound sunglasses and greaseball hair he combed back and forth every few minutes. Bud told me it wasn't his own hair and he paid a fortune for the rug, which had an obsidian sheen that made wet asphalt look dry.

Lou waved and shouted Hey Jimmy! and got both of them to flip a switch and greet us like we were fans around the blinding stage of a sold-out arena. He managed to stumble over to us and close-up he exuded an evanescent graciousness and innocence that surprised the hell out of us as he shook our hands and said, Hey how are ya, good to see some of my fans back again, and he winked at Paola and gave her an awkward peck on the cheek that made her speechless for once with the sheepish smile of the teenager she might have been at one time. When he shook my hand I mumbled Jesus! He snapped his long fingers and aimed them like a pistol at Spade. Hey, Spade, go back and git my guitar and some glossies for these folks. I'm feelin' good and I'm gonna' hit a few licks for these kind folks. I looked over at Lou, who was as excitable as a kid skipping classes in high school. Bud and Les stood behind us with Uncle Rob chuckling in amusement. Even Flash and the other Filipinos, off to the side, jabbered away in Tagalog at their good fortune to get a free show. Bud told Spade he should have kept the rest of the entourage onboard as the 8x10 presigned photos were passed out, but Spade said, Nah, they're better off in Miami for a few days. He said this with a hesitation that made me wonder if this whole thing were planned, because JHC, in his white terricloth bathrobe, seemed vulnerable without a crowd around him. Maybe it was the eerie incandescent glow from the moonlight off his robe. No, no. I insist, he said holding up his hands. It's okay. Jimmy Hank'll be fine.

Jimmy Hank blurted out, you damn well know I'm good to go, Spade. Let's hit a few bars boys, and he turned around to his original backup musicians, the Johnson City Headbangers and the Milltown gospel singers, who were not there. "Well, I guess there's no room for 'em anyhow," he said with a laugh and raced through a crisp atonal chord progression that floored us.

Lou said, "I told you he was back."

Jimmy Hank was back! He went through a half dozen of his familiar chartbusters from the mid-Fifties like "Smoky Motel," "Heartbreak on the Radio," and "Trailer Park Party." It was near sacrilegious how his legs gyrated in that apostolic white robe like eggbeaters in whipped cream. Lou inched his way right up to Jimmy Hank's feet. His famous falsetto broke through with chilling effect and he didn't appear to flub a lyric. We clapped and cheered with the enthusiasm of a much larger crowd as it resounded off the dark moonlit water lapping around us. Quiet and waiting as it always did. Especially out there. We were all getting on a good beer-wine buzz. Uncle Rob came over and said, son are you having a good time? I said sure thing, dad, and then quickly said sorry. He put his arm around my shoulder and tossled my hair and said don't worry, it's okay and then moved over to Paola.

Then it happened. Spade whispered something to him and Jimmy Hank hopped his lanky frame onto a plank atop the gunwale opening we all used to extend the gangway to the pier. JHC took a step back for leverage into the next bar and fell overboard. I know what I saw.

We all jumped up and ran over toppled wine and beer glasses. He flopped his arms around in the moonlit water that was as calm as a cup of cold black coffee.

"I can't swim," yelled Spade, but I know what I saw. "Somebody get him!" he shouted.

Uncle Rob was first in, then Paola, then Lou in quick succession. Then Flash jumped off the gunwale. I couldn't swim and Lou's advice earlier alerted me to my inadequacy. Les pursed his lips and dropped his head and I knew he was a nonswimmer, too.

Spade leaned over the gunwale, yelling to Jimmy Hank, "Let's hang on, Jimmy. Hang on!" The cluster of three diamond rings on his left hand glittered as he shouted, then screamed, Save him for God's sake.

In the great discomfort of my helplessness, I watched over the side as the Tern pitched and awed at our dilemma. JHC bobbed up once and then went down like a torpedoed merchant vessel in old movie newsreels with his guitar held up in a defiant gesture like the bow of a sinking ship. Bud and Paola surrounded the spot where Jimmy went on to his last performance. Olives bobbing in a dry martini; they were drunker than stuffed olives and shouldn't have been in the drink.

Uncle Rob suddenly popped up like a cork from down under. The surface was like a stage spotlight, but underneath was as empty and black as a starless night. He shook his head from side to side and thrust the guitar in the air.

"Get out of the water!" he yelled. "Now!" He swam over and collared Bud and Paola. "Get out!" he yelled at them. They swam about thirty yards back to the metal ladder lowered the day before to transfer Jimmy's entourage. They were exhausted and coughed up seawater, shaking their heads, groping for the railing to pull themselves on deck.

"Where is he? Where's my Jimmy Hank?"

Bud and Paola shook their heads and clutched the railing to watch Uncle Rob, who collared Lou by an armpit, slapping the water with the guitar until it broke into pieces.

"What's he trying to do?" screamed Spade. "That guitar's worth ten thousand dollars."

"Shark," said Paola.

"What?" winced Spade.

Uncle tugged Lou in tow to the ladder, where Bud and Flash pulled him out of the water and I guess what was left of Lou. I could see in the dark something was gone. His legs were missing. I wretched and was ashamed that I wretched and that I couldn't have tried to save Jimmy and now Lou.

"Get him up on deck. Hurry!" said Uncle.

They laid him down on some deckchair cushions. His legs had been shorn by a shark. Why his legs? They weren't much to begin with.

"Come on. Tourniquets. Give me some shirts," said Uncle, fighting exhaustion in gasps. Flash ran up with some white galley towels that Uncle knotted together and tied around Lou's little thighs.

"Bud! Some line. Quickly," said Uncle.

Paola cradled Lou's head. His eyes were alert and he looked up at her in great anticipation. "How'm I doin', doll?" he muttered between his chattering jaws.

"Fine. Fine. We're taking care of you, Lou," she said. She brushed the palm of her hand over his forehead and breathed in small, imperceptible gasps like a small child with a skinned knee.

"Thanks, Bud. Tie the other one. Quickly."

Bud and Uncle applied pressure to Lou's thighs. My jaw trembled watching blood leak slowly through their fingers.

Les knelt behind Uncle and put a hand on his shoulder. Spade slumped over by the scene of the event, unmoved and probably in shock. I knew what happened. He didn't look up. Yet in the ten long minutes after I saw Spade grab Jimmy's ankle and push it back off the plank, I began to wonder if, after all, he wasn't trying to catch his falling star.

Bud mumbled in a low controlled voice across to Uncle, Where's Jan Peerce when you need him?

Uncle whispered back, "Knock it off, Bud. One bird's enough for now."

I didn't know who this Jan or whoever was or what the hell Bud talked about until later. Uncle shook his head and pursed his lips within his white scruffy beard.

"Come on, Lou. Come on Lou," pleaded Uncle.

"How'm I doin', captain?" Lou's voice was fading.

"Great, Lou. Great," responded Bud, holding one of Lou's little hands.

All of a sudden, Lou sat up in a thrust of energy. His eyes had that sharp stare I was so used to when he thought of kicking someone's shins, except he wasn't going to do that now. Ever.

"Lift me up! Lift me up for God's sake," he shouted.

Uncle and Bud held his legs while Paola and I struggled to raise him up by placing the nape of our necks in his armpits.

"Higher! Higher!" he moaned. "Great! That's it! Thanks," and his torso relaxed.

Then Les, who stood right in front of us like he was hunched over to take a group photo, shouted "Now you're standing tall, Lou." For that brief moment, Lou was now taller than any of us. His chest pressed into my right ear and I could hear his heart pounding away and then it stopped just like that. Lou's head dropped onto his chest like the head of a child's ragdoll when it's tossed back into the corner of a crib.

We laid Lou back down onto the cushions. His body gave a stiff jolt and that was it. We were all around him on our knees.

I had never been so close to Lou when he was alive, but I was there on my knees. I slumped back onto the deck and felt a strange wave of relief that I got to hold him up in the end. The Tern's deck was a real stage, unlike my flubbing a Biff Loman audition at Mundane's Sandburg Playhouse and noticing the sparse audience drift away from the corner of my eye.

Paola went back to patting Lou's hair with her hands. She may have discovered some silent phrases for her ancient vocabulary, but I had no idea how she could write them down. I remember that Bud volunteered the profanity for the rest of us. "Aw, shit!" and he lost it after that, prostrating himself next to Lou. I guess he muttered for some kind of forgiveness. Uncle rose to his feet and heaved a lengthy sigh of exhaustion. He shook his head and said, "Sorry, Lou" and I wondered how many shipmates he had to leave behind. I glanced up at him and he looked around and then at me and winked and clicked his tongue against his inner cheek. There was no joy in his face. No zest. Nothing. Blackness in a full moon and eight bells for Lou.

CHAPTER 27

Around 0700, Uncle and Spade Hill were the only ones still standing. Barely. The rest of us sort of crawled away to separate corners on deck while Flash and his two compatriots placed Lou in a large black plastic trash bag then layed it onto a large swath of canvas, sewed up and set aside on the quarterdeck a few feet from the portside ladder. Then they came up with two plastic buckets from the galley and swabbed the blood down and out the scuppers. My spirits lifted when I saw Sam in the coiled manila-line nest. He was missing for three days and I was glad to see him back in his usual spot. If Sam came back, could Lou be far behind? What other foolish thoughts would come from my despair? The previous five hours were a dense fog. The clear night sky; the moon shining like a new silver dollar; the calm sea, but the details escaped me much like the night I was delivered to Fort Lauderdale. Lou's body was wrapped up over there, yet he was still among us because I thought he could still be alive. I was so exhausted I almost saw him kicking inside the canvas shroud.

Uncle and Hill talked a few minutes. I don't know if Spade had an actual hand in Jimmy Hank's demise, but I recalled that in death JHC would be worth more dead than alive in his second coming. Uncle Rob, I believe, had nothing ulterior to do with this, except he provided the scene of the crime or event. Mr. Behind-the-Scenes, just like with the Shapiros and probably lots of others, but who was I to judge and condemn his circumstantial involvement. I didn't really have the facts, as I didn't have them in school and that's how I got on the Tern.

A boat bow bobbed on the western horizon. Spade grabbed Uncle's forearm and dropped his head on Uncle Rob's shoulder. Uncle cupped with care the back of Spade's head with his hand while Spade's body gave up an aftershock of emotion. Then he fell into a deck chair to wait for his lift back to Miami. I got up and watched Hill stumble down the ladder later without the pushing and shoving he must have absorbed in JHC's heyday. Maybe later, he wouldn't have the hassle of concert dates, security, dopeheads, pushers, groupies, booking agents and all that rabble to deal with now that JHC had ascended and was ethereal and ready for that second coming on tapes, LP albums and assorted memorabilia. Profiting off someone who didn't actually exist. Spiritus sanctus ad valorem. JHC Enterprises? Jimmy Hank Cullipher Entertainment? Whatever moniker Hill decided on.

Uncle came over and announced the burial at-sea for noon. "I'd like all of you to freshen up below and be up here looking sharp to say goodbye to Lou."

"Aren't we taking him back for a proper burial?" asked Paola.

"Paola, Lou is one of us. We're responsible for him. He has no one else. He's not going to be decked out and powdered up and..." Uncle's eyes drifted out to the horizon for a moment. "It's our duty. Les, you take care of the legal stuff later."

Lou was so small now, resting on a metal serving cart used for dinner in the stateroom.

"Go ahead, Captain. You say it for us," mumbled Bud.

I was so wrapted up in Lou's presence, I scarcely recall Uncle's parting words. Something like tall in our hearts, and then he did the strangest send-off I never heard. He hummed a short, vaguely familiar tune. I looked at Bud, his head bowed like the rest of us. He had a cynical grin, closed his eyes and raised an eyebrow when Uncle started to hum a bit off-key, but I knew he took Lou's departure hard. Some days later, I passed him sitting in a deck chair and as we chatted for a while, he kept rubbing his shin. Uncle later told me the name of the piece (Navy Hymn) and said he forgot what he wanted to say right after the first few lines and he didn't write it down ahead of time. Flash must have put something heavy in the bag below, because after we all touched the bag and pushed it off the caddy, the bag and Lou sank like a rock with hardly a ripple. Lou would soon be right back at JHC's feet and that didn't have to be but it was. Maybe Lou was happier there, but for days thereafter, we felt his presence and peeked around where he used to hang out and touched his favorite deck chair when we passed it and brushed up against the passageway he backed up against to pass us. Before I went below for the night, I spent an hour at sunset with Sam, who hopped out of his coil of manila rope and plopped into my hairy nest of crossed legs. I will never understand how he confided in me, and I don't think anyone would ever believe this kind of behavior could exist for such a solitary, no less migratory, creature. I should probably have never mentioned it in the first place. It was tough enough recording my thoughts about Lou's passing. And for once, the screw was dead in the water and silent.

The next morning, Uncle said "Son, would you mind sitting at Lou's position? As a personal favor?"

"But why, Uncle? You know I've got to get back or move on or do something."

"Yeah. I know." He glanced around to the empty R-390 position. The one with two thick Miami telephone books on the seat. "I'd like you to take over Lou's slot. It would be for a few days. I'll have Les show you what to do. It's easy as pie. Will you?"

I knew he knew I had no other place to escape to. "But you know I have to go eventually."

"We all do, son, sooner or later. This is the Tern's last voyage and I'd hate to lose another shipmate just now." He pulled on his toy captain's hat. "Come on over and sit down for a second." He put his bronzed arm around my shoulder and took off the phone books and set them on a shelf.

"What the devil am I supposed to do for God's sake?" I was working on my fourth month of absenteeism and getting roped into shipping over, as Uncle referred to it.

Uncle raised a finger and eyebrow at the same time. "Sorry, Uncle, but what am I supposed to do. I'm not an accountant," as I spied the small green metal index card box and necklace of numbers hanging from one of the tuning knobs.

In an hour or less, Uncle Rob showed me how to transfer funds from one account to an offshore bank somewhere in the Caribbean (that much he told me). I said it's like taking the money out of the US to hide it from the tax collectors. Uncle glanced at Les, who came into the room and sat to my left.

"Sort of like your invite as our special guest and inductee on the Tern, eh?" he said with a snide lisp that took up where Lou left off.

"Okay, okay. I can hack it," I responded in a huff. "So, what's the bag for anyway?"

Uncle chuckled as he left us and said, "Heavy seas and boarding parties."

"What?"

"Vomit and, if we're raided, dumping overboard everything you see in front of you." I laughed for the first time since Lou's burial until I lifted the bag and felt the sixty pounds of lead at the bottom. Lou couldn't have weighed much more. With Lou around, it was like sitting on a three-legged barstool; a triangulation of entertaining uncertainty. No more, but I missed that.

For the next ten days, I twisted some knobs on the RC390, waited for the right pegs on the control windows and rattled off alphanumerics that made no sense to me until, after I'd done about 150 of them, Les said I didn't have the NTK, but he relented once and told me 4ZKCLA390CURA7639-4 was a transfer of $3.9 million from four accounts in Kansas City and Los Angeles to an unnumbered account in Curacao, except the account was actually somewhere else and he wouldn't say. He held up his hands in front of my face and said, Look, no dirt, no ink. Kid, this is all legal. He tapped out every word with his index finger on the desktop: "Every single lousy transaction," Thank God the tax code is both muddled and munificent.

"Say that again?" I didn't like him showing off his vocabulary like some smug graduate assistant. I'd had enough problems with Paola. Les almost picked his nose right in front of me. And I added in my fatigue, "What about the Shapiros and the others before them?"

Les stared straight ahead at the blinking lights, then turned to me and took the same finger and pressed it firmly into my sternum. "You know, kid, you're something else. Do you know that? You should be so lucky to have someone like your uncle to give you the best gift a young man on the run could ever ask for: sanctuary."

I swallowed hard. Lester Vice was not the flunkie he masqueraded as.

He pounded the desk with his fist this time and said, "And as for the Shapiros, it was freedom from years of excruciating pain." He got up, walked around the COMM room, then said, sorry, you got me going there. Sorry, kid and softly shut the hatch behind him.

Bud and Paola were busy at their positions, but I know they heard every syllable and I felt humiliated as if I'd been chewed out by some drill sergeant I'd seen on a late-night movie on Channel 5. Bud put his cans, or headphones, down and leaned over toward me. "Now you know who's second-in-command."[92]

---

[92] Voila! See what I mean? This chapter is where I took over. Notice how seamlessly it continues the story without any sense of trite intrusion. You wouldn't even know the difference if I told you—which I have. It does ramble on, but now with more credible dialogue and action. When I perused Will's notes—and there were still five unopened shoeboxes—mostly on the deaths of Jimmy Hank Cullipher and Lou—I could see an impending trainwreck like watching a saboteur tear up the rails on the wooden trestle around the bend. Strangely, the violence back at the cafe in Kingston and the attempted boarding by rogue local authorities there didn't affect Will as much. I think the fatigue and impulse to leave the Tern reduced his writing to the barest of scribbled notes. At times, I flooded my "headlights" with eyedrops, slugged down a black coffee and even used a little magnifying glass from one of the girl's botany kits, and still I could barely fathom his scribbled words much less plumb his thoughts, for which sonar would not have been much better. Look, here's an example—and this is only the beginning of the end for the rest of Will's story, and you can see why I stepped into the batter's box like any well-intending editor:
"0700: Lou is dead. Can't believe it. All a blur since. Hard to comprehend, like a bolt out of the blue. Same for the others.
0800: Flips cleaned up deck of blood. Have gone "nowhere" in almost 4 mos. What am I doing here?
0833: Spade Hill leaves. What a sorry-ass messed-up guy. Hope UR not a part of this mess.
0914: Sam the Tern dropped in and took off right away.
1203: UR visibly shaken; can't finish parting words for Lou; humming a tune. We dump Lou's remains over the side. We're all very very sad about this. Bud taking it real hard. Lots of emotional pain.
1540: Tomorrow morning headed due Key West and parts unknown; typical of UR's far-reaching empire. Not doing my part here. Must go where I feel needed. Miss Vince and the others.
1615: Should have jumped in and tried to save Lou. He and the others were all stinking drunk and beyond helping.
1810: Not hungry. Paola visits me. She's still devastated. I hold her close. Lou's death has hurt her a lot. I love her, but can't tell anyone how close we've gotten. Especially the others. UR probably knows—like everything else.
2010: UR and LV show me how to run Lou's old position. Creepy as hell; the America I never knew existed; millions at the push of a button.

CHAPTER 28[93]

2115: LV chews me out real good. I deserve it. Really none of my business to question their ethics or means.

2205: UR offers to fly me to Toronto to take over Lou's job after voyage. I respectfully say no. UR said he didn't think I would take the offer anyway. He seemed relieved.

2311: Screw strangely quiet. Why?"

[93] Sonofabitch! Some shitheel on the eighth floor got hold of my draft and I got a friendly visit from Rory Parker, the nephew of our senior editor, Royce Butterworth. Rory's a chubby 26-year old recent grad from Harvard. He waddles around like he's playing a cello all the time. He's okay, but he can be such a pain in the ass leaning over my shoulder and dropping bagel crumbs onto my desk as he suggests some rewrite I fretted over for an hour. I told him there's a great two-year workshop in Iowa. He said he'd rather stay on the editorial side at Brown and Shue. Anyway, I ushered him out to neutral ground at Gino's on Third and Chase where I tried to enjoy a Reuben and beer and watched him slobber through linguini alfredo with a mountain of Parmesan on top. He said he was "crafting" an historical romance about medieval knights. I said I had edited quite a few "hysterical" romances and offered to read it over, and he said with an upturned eyebrow that he would never think of intruding on my time. I could tell he was somewhat put off by my mispronunciation of "historical." Halfway through, he sneezed some of the cheese across to my plate and I said to hell with the rest of the Reuben. He liked what I'd done so far with Will's story—he called my effort "assembling" like I was some stupid schlep putting bumpers on a Buick in Flint. He wanted to know why I refrained from using more visuals like describing the sea waves, the weather, the hors d'oeuvres, the clothing of some characters and whether they played footsie under the overhang of the red-checkered tablecloth. You know, I should have said sounds like a great idea, Rory, and I'll get right on it, but I saw a rare opening in his sophomoric

One afternoon after classes, I washed the dishes in the kitchen. It

pomposity as he forked the cheesecake and I said what the hell for? I can't waste my time on details you can read in fashion mags and the National Geographic and Funk and Wagnalls. It's the human landscape and it's psychological impact I'm after. I said Will didn't mention it; so why me? Rory got a little more miffed and ordered a screwdriver as an apertif (what class!) and inquired, well isn't it what we're paying you for—to massage the text so it will appeal to a large audience? I swear I almost stood up and called him a jerk-off to his fat little frat face, but I knew it would get back to his uncle. So instead, again I bit my tongue and said, yeah, sounds like a great suggestion, Rory (you little twerp); let me see what I can do. What seemed like twenty years in this business and this kid right out of school telling me what to do. I coughed into the phone the next day and called in sick. All right; granted I teased him a bit, but what's this business coming to with another illiterate boy wonder with a business degree? I'm not sure Rory could even ace the **Reader's Digest** vocabulary quiz. Maybe everyone should publish their own stuff and relieve me of suffering any more of this literary slipstream existence. When I got back to my cubicle the next Monday, Brenda, Butterworth's executive secretary, told me he wanted to talk to me (i.e., talk down to me, since every visitor sat well below the front of his massive mahogany credenza of a desk). "How's tricks, Scott?" like I was a plagairist or scrivener of shortcuts to meet his deadlines. I said everything's going well and was ready to shake his hand for the first time in six months, but I sat down when he kept his shoes propped up on his desk in front of my face and his hands locked behind his powdered pate. "Scotty, how's the Melville thing coming along?" I said fine. A bit tedious, but fine. I then noticed on the side of his desk a stack of about fifteen books rising up in a broken column from the polished faux marble linoleum. "Two things, Scotty." Yes, I responded like the first Labrador ever to utter a human word. He said Claire Kendall is off on maternity leave and I responded Yes. He said someone needs to finish the last installment (**Ciao! Ciao! Carmina**) of her trilogy on the Scudero clan. I looked at him for a reduced sentence, but he said Good, then that's settled. Anything else? I said. He pointed his gold-plated Waterman fountain pen at the books. "Rory suggested you may want to dress up your Melville thing. You know, a little more wave action, flesh tones; perhaps a bit of gratuitous sex. The stack should help you sharpen your efforts." The little SOB ratted me out. "Can do, Scotty?" In my mind I heard a "Hike, hike" and sort of stared at him and let him run right by me like the all-Ivy League fullback he was twenty years earlier at Yale. "Good. Thanks a bunch, Scott. I knew I could count on you." Then he happened to be the anniversary of my Dad's death and Mom wasn't taking it too well this time. She strayed around the front room, straightened his framed photograph with her slender fingers and then parted the diaphanous curtains at the front window, waiting for someone. I guess she never quite accepted that he wouldn't come bounding up the long brick walk to the front door. I didn't say anything, but I banged a few dishes to try to distract her and eventually she came and sat down at the formica table. I heard her sobbing into a dish towel and I said Mom, look, cheer up. It's going to be a beautiful day. Please stop crying, Mom. She looked at me and said I can't. I'm trying. I put an arm around her little shoulders, then went into the other room to call Mrs. Pugliese to come over to cheer her up. She was good about that. Mom told me a long time ago that Mrs. P's first husband, Freddy, was killed in the Heurtgen Forest somewhere over there, but she managed to find a nice guy on the line in Saginaw who turned out to be a good stepdad to Vinnie. She pushed right through the back door and said "Hi! Pazza" and put some coffee on the stove.

"Why do you keep calling me crazy like that all the time?" I said over my shoulder with a laugh.

"Because I love you like my own son, and I know you and Vinnie are up to no good." She was a tough little Sicilian lady who must have been a dark beauty in her youth. Even in that mournful black dress she always

---

propped himself up and reached an arm out to shake my hand, but actually he was headed for the intercom and asked Brenda to bring in the shopping cart for the books and escort me out like I was there for a parole board hearing. I think I schlepped out with a leg-irons shuffle. Now, do you see why I've got to knife the hell out of Will's story, or I'll get the axe. You can see my real frustration in this cheap stab at metaphors. Sorry. At the bank-vault of a door, Butterworth boomed, And Scott, don't forget the blue dolphins leaping joyfully out of the warm emerald green Gulfstream waters. I said Right! boss (and a nice big emerald green weenie leaping joyfully up yours). I should have never left my copy ad job with "The Three L's" (Lowey, Lang and Liebowitz). Stuff no one reads, even on the toilet. As if it wasn't enough harassment, I got off the full elevator and Craig Collingsworth, the rising (flaming) star of a junior editor, popped up out of nowhere like a trip-wired booby trap. A real jock with the perennial moist appearance of stepping out of a gym shower, he patted me on the shoulder to squeeze by and piped, "Pick'em up and put'em down, old man; pick'em up and put'em down" for the benefit of the crowd. May his soul rest his soul.

wore, her main attractions still announced themselves with unspoken ardor and longing.

"Mrs. Pugliese, they haven't caught us yet. I mean..."

"You two better watch out or they will," as she sipped her coffee and pointed a stiff finger at me.

As usual, she got Mom calmed down pretty fast, patting her hand, giving her a big smooch on the cheek and pushing the cup of coffee in front of her. The washer by the broom closet spun around and their conversation faded in and out until Mrs. Pugliese turned to me and said, "Will isn't that right? You live through others." I said I didn't know. I guess so. She said you crazy not to think so.

This thought barged into me as I sat there in a daze during some afternoon downtime from the COMM room. Sam died right there in the cradle of my legs. Coming a few days after Lou's death. He didn't say or do a thing. He just sat there and when I looked down at him after watching a ship on the horizon and talking to him about it, he stopped moving forever. How do you live through a bird? I stroked the top of his head gently with a finger, but he was gone for good this time. My eyes welled up as I looked down at his lifeless body. I didn't cry for Lou and I felt ashamed about that, but here I whimpered for a bird, this pet, and was not ashamed. Lost like me. I was closer to Sam than Lou or anyone else save for Mom. I guess that's why I recalled what Vinnie's mom said ("You live through others"). I carried him down to my room and asked Paola on the intercom to come by.

"What is it, Will?" she said with hands on hips, then she saw Sam on my rack and went over to see him. She was stronger than I could ever be, which was one reason I grew so fond of her. She muttered something like our first child and shook her head. I thought she was about to shift into her paleolithic mode due to the emotional scene, but she didn't.

"You upset too, huh?" I said.

She stared around at me, ready to accuse me of a crime, then pursed her lips, brushed by me and said let me get a box and twine.

Uncle Rob must have heard on the intercom, because he knocked and came in. "Sorry, you two." He moved between us and said, "Must have been an old bird."

"More like he couldn't find his way back," said Paola.

"Whatever," said Uncle who left us alone.

Together, we lined the large white cardboard shoe box with toilet paper. At least, our hands worked well together. I handed Sam to her. She placed him in the box. I moved to touch his tail feathers sticking out a bit. She gave a deep impatient sigh, tapped me gently on the wrist and said, Will, I'm good at this. She bent over and kissed the bird on the head and then closed the box. She made a nice bow with a run of satin ribbon dangling from her pants pocket and tied it on top and said, now you can finally find your way home. It was hopeless for us. Topside, I said, go ahead, and she leaned over and dropped the shoebox over the side. I didn't have the courage to do it. White towering clouds scalloped the horizon. Everything bright as hell and I was still in the dark trying to find my own way back. For the few moments that Sam's box floated out beyond us, I wished he could have busted out of there, perched on my shoulder and flown away with me to Copenhagen, Malmo, Stockholm, Toronto or...they were all far off his migratory route in life, and probably mine, too.[94] Les and Bud strolled over from starboard and said they were sorry about Sam. Paola turned and walked away. I said Thanks. It's okay.

On the last day of catching up on Lou's accounts, I swivelled around and asked Les, Look at this. What's it all about? He poked his green eyeshade up a notch and in a split-second said Nothing. The usual. Then he cocked his head with that dubious stare-down he whipped on me when I didn't have the NTK.

"So what's it to ya?"

"It's a transfer from Biddlowe Construction in Las Vegas to one of Uncle's offshore bank accounts. I've read a lot about these guys. They're into all sorts of stuff—mostly illegal."

"Have they done anything to you lately?" he retorted.

"Well, no, but the point is they're..."

"They're what? Tell me, bright boy." Les had grown quite impatient with me since Lou's death. Maybe he missed the shin kicks. Maybe he looked for a replacement with whom to jawbone. I made a few similar transfers before (such as the Flagrante Brothers' Roulette Enterprises in Reno) and suspected Uncle Rob was up to some simian business.

---

[94]   Not true. In the Spring, the Arctic tern migrates North to breeding grounds including Scandinavia. In early Fall, it flies back South to Antarctica, over ten thousand miles away, where it winters. As for Toronto, you could take nearly any "bird" (e.g., American, TWA) or Greyhound to get there.

"Do you want me to spell it out for you, college boy?" exasperated Les, slapping his hands on his thighs.

I said no it's okay, it's okay, but he insisted.

"Good. Here's the deal, okay? Listen. For example, Bobby Biddlowe builds hi-rises for your uncle on the West Coast. Say his accountant has a very stubby pencil and submits a final bill for ten million for labor and materials in change orders and add-ons which your uncle never signed—wink-wink--and refuses to pay. So Bobby eats it, declares a loss on his taxes and and slips the hidden ten mil to your uncle's offshore account for safekeeping. Do you follow me?"

"Nope. Impossible. Pure nonsense. If this is a pre-wash cycle, I don't get it."

"Yeah. You could call it that."

"First of all, where did Biddlowe get the ten million? Out of thin air?"

"Look, he's in business. Obviously, you never worked on the loading dock at Sears and Roebuck? We're talking about five balls in the air at once and paper flying all over the damn place. Lots of money falls through the crack. Look, right now I wish to hell I was a contractor over there in Vietnam."

"Les, come on. You can't hide money like that from the authorities. Anyway, what's in it for Lowebidd?"

"Of course you can," said Lester Vice in a flat, uninflected voice that could have come from a bored judge or back-bench bureaucrat. "You uncle gives it a second rinse in his various business pursuits and Biddlowe gets interest and a line-of-credit. You know; a marker." Les rocked back in his chair.

"Shenanigans, Les. I'll stick to Monopoly."

"Don't get the wrong idea. This is a very small part of your uncle's business dealings. It's more of a favor to an old Navy buddy." Les held up two fingers within a hair of each other to emphasize the laundering part. "Ultimately the money goes to purchase real estate, medicine and food. Lots of stuff the less fortunate need. In the end, it's very clean, respectable and everyone's happy. Remember those kids on the island?"

"Okay, I see. Like a modern-day Robin Hood."

"Yeah, except your uncle's no robber and no hood; so do me a favor and don't tell him we talked about this."

"Sure, but one thing."

"What?"

"Isn't all this stuff cheating?"

"Cheating? Maybe you should have thought of doing that back in school. Listen, you uncle's the most compassionate and caring individual I've ever known." Les enunciated this so slowly, I imagined him putting each magnetized letter on a refrigerator door.

I stopped talking and dipped my head in agreement.

"Good. Let's finish up and have a beer topside." He reached over and gave me a pat on the shoulder.

On deck, I watched Uncle lean on the rail and look out at nothing in particular. One of the few times I saw him alone on the entire voyage. Lonely. I figured he gained a lot of wealth and a lot of attendant problems babysitting all of it. I knew he also lost a lot: a wife and stillborn infant son; one divorce and another in the oven; no family; no port to call home; forgotten war hero; old shipmates died and still calling from the steerage of his conscience. Adrift. I figured he did his best to keep the scales balanced. I finished my beer and walked over to him, said Hi! and put an arm around his shoulder.

"Say, Will! How's everything?"

I clicked my tongue against the inside of my mouth like he did from time to time and said, Fine, Uncle Rob. Fine."

CHAPTER 29

On the way down to Key West about thirty miles off Miami, Bud, Les and Paola regrouped in the wake of Lou's and Sam's deaths to hold a deep sea fishing contest. Les said they always managed to squeeze one in near the end of the Tern's annual voyage. This was the ninth and last trip in her resurrection with Uncle Rob at the helm. On the fantail, I noticed early on four metal holes in the deck and now I knew what they were for, as they dropped into them the steel poles of canvas deck chairs. They harnessed themselves into the chairs and Bud turned around and asked if I was in.

"Don't get it," I said, watching Flash hand each a heavy fishing rod and stooped over to bait each hook.

"Take the fourth chair over there," said Les who had already cast his line. I hesitated to respond until Bud said Come on, take Lou's chair. He'll be glad you did.

I said if I know Lou, he would be pissed, but Bud said sit down; Flash will help you with that harness. "Your uncle said he will stake you to five hundred. It's winner-take-all, pal," and he let fly his line among the blue dolphins leaping joyfully out of the warm emerald green Gulfstream waters.**

**(How's that, Mr. Butterballs?)*

After about five minutes, Paola's pole quivered like a divining rod. She hooked into something big and fast.

"Marlin!" yelled Bud. "Let him out. Let him run," he shouted. "Now, put your boobs—back!—into it. Yeah! That's it! He's out there looking for the back door. Don't let him out, girl."

"I won't," she strained.

"Here, let me give you a hand," said Bud.

"Let me be," she demanded.

"Okay, okay. It'll take you about an hour to bring him in. Ruff-ruff," muttered Bud.

Uncle Rob yelled from the bridge, "It's a beauty. Look at him leap."

Half an hour later, Bud landed two large bonitas and joined Les, who managed to reel in a barracuda. I hooked nothing and offered to spell Paola, who grunted with each flex of her rod. She said I don't need your help. Thanks anyway.

"Why not, then?" and I knelt next to her grunting. It was the only sound besides the waves and breeze flapping the pennants behind us on the bridge.

"You don't understand, Will."

I retreated and joined Bud and Les.

"Women," said Bud.

I waved to Uncle and motioned for him to join us. He pulled on his toy captain's hat and adjusted his aviator sunglasses. "Can't. Visitors."

Bud, Les and I stood up and saw on the horizon two speedboats slicing through wavecrests toward us.

"Not again!" I complained.

Les raised his arms to stretch and said when they come at you that fast, it's usually for folding money.

"What do you mean, Les?"

"Relax and act natural. We're outgunned."

When Bud said to hell with this, Les grabbed him by the forearm and told him, relax they only want their money back. Paola was portside working on the marlin leaping at five hundred yards, breaking the surface in an explosive display of annoyance at the piece of metal hooked in its lower jaw.

Ten minutes later, the two speedboats idled about one hundred yards to starboard. Spade Hill was back for an encore flanked by four of his entourage dangling machineguns along their legs like they were ready to piss all over us.

"Captain Melville," blurted Hill into a bullhorn. "How is everything?"

"Oh, peachy, Hill. Out of fuel?" he bullhorned back.

Spade snickered and said no, I forgot something when I left your tub.

Bud couldn't hold it in and cupped his hands around his mouth to say Yeah, your boy Jimmy Hank. For that crack, one of them sprayed the water between us with a semiautomatic. It was not a stage prop. Paola jerked her head around and shouted I'm not letting go.

"Not nice," shouted Hill, wagging his finger at us.

"You mean the suitcase?" said Uncle Rob, who came down to join us on the rail.

"You got that right, Melville. Where's it at?"

"Give me ten minutes. I have to dig it out of the hold." Uncle threw a submissive wave at Spade, who said Okay, asshole. Hurry it up, and then pointed to a spot close to the Tern where another spray of bullets shattered the surface in angry white geysers. One round got away from the shooter and slammed into the storage box next to Paola and left a hole the size of my fist. I dropped down for a moment and thought that the Tern's crew engaged in a lot of scuttlebut, but never once called the old man an asshole. The nerve! Uncle grabbed Les by the arm and disappeared down the ladder to the stateroom.

Paola was really grunting now and I wanted to go help her, but was afraid Hill's straight shooters would let their weapons get away from them again.

Bud shouted to Spade, "How is everyone taking your boy's death?"

"What?"

Jimmy Hank's death?"

"Haven't reported it yet. Still putting together the promo package." I could sense Bud wanted to tell him what if we spill the beans. I whispered, "Bud don't. It was an accident. I saw it. An accident."

"Accident my ass," he growled.

"It's been twenty minutes. Where the hell is my money, asshole?"

Several minutes passed before Les came up with the aluminum suitcase and held it up in the air. "Familiar?" he yelled over the waves.

"Oh, yeah!" shouted Hill. "Be right there. No tricks."

A small rubber outboard dropped down the side of Spade's boat and bobbed its way through the eighty yards of rippling, agitated water. Not as stunning as Paola's marlin leaping high above the waves. Les tied a manila line around the suitcase handle and lowered it over the side. When it was handed to Hill, he shouted into the bullhorn, 'gonna count it first. He spent about ten minutes and then popped his head up. "It's here. Thanks a load."

"You're entirely welcome," said Les. "It even accrued interest." Les elbowed me in the side in a movement with as much communicative value as a kicking fetus.

"I noticed that. Where's Melville?"

"He threw up. Ate something bad," shouted Les.

"Too bad. Give the good captain my best."

Les mumbled from the side of his mouth, And I trust Melville has given you his best.

I stood there wondering what kind of damn slow-motion movie scene was this from; then I peered over at the huge hole that the errant round made to confirm that this was not a front-row seat in a dollar rerun movie theatre. I started to shake all over like I jumped into a cold shower after a long Saturday night at Martin's Tavern outside Ann Arbor. I said thank God we'll get out of this alive when Bud shouted over, Hey, Spade, they say if you live long enough you'll die.

"Oh no," I said.

Spade smiled and lowered his head to figure out what he thought he heard. It made no damn sense to me. Then he laughed heartily into the bullhorn and said, Very good, asshole. He grabbed a weapon from the guy next to him and we all ducked down as a five-second burst flew over our heads and ricocheted in a rage of whining metallic thuds behind us. Then he emptied his mouth around a cigar and said Bye-bye for now. See you later.

Their outboards cranked up and Spade glided away in leisure like some schmuck strolling out of a casino in Las Vegas with his grubby fingers walking through a wad of hundred-dollar bills.

Just as I said why is Uncle Rob all of a sudden sick, he appeared topside in his wetsuit. It was wet and I guessed he'd taken a shower. He breathed heavily through a sardonic grin behind that white hedgerow of beard.

"Whew! One time too many. Never again," he said between deep sighs of exhaustion.[95]

---

[95] Not bad so far, eh? You wouldn't believe what Will left me to work with here (I'll show you in a second). It's as if nothing ever happened. Another hum-drum welfare day. I mean, what else do the unemployed do half the time but daydream? He actually said he merely imagined what would happen if JHC's agent ever returned to, say, retrieve a suitcase full of money he left behind. Frankly, I'm not convinced this whole scene wasn't more than an idle fabrication of Will's to distract him from boredom and the angst someone from the Army was after

"Well?" said Les.

---

him for not reporting to his draft board. He mentioned he was prompted by the sound of the Tern's screw (which I have never fully bought as the truth from Will) rolling over phrases like *Heretheycomeheretheycomeheretheycomehere* and *incomingincomingincomingincoming*. Once again, I endeavored to separate myth from fact. I know you're saying, not another investigator, please; but I feel strongly that special recognition is due those who help us to clarify the fiction in our daily lives and polish the little stones of truth shining at our feet and show the way to a clear and bright dawn of self-illumination. So, I called an old buddy of mine from high school, Drew Moody (his real name) last August. He was Phi Beta Kappa and summa cum laude at Northwestern and whizzed through to rip and read an MA in journalism. He told me once on a commuter train through a white-out near Evanston that he wasn't interested in the standard strictures of reportage (i.e., What-Where-Who-When-How—and Why for the opinion editor) as much as creating a good salable entertaining story for readers who, heaven knows, get enough facts thrown at them when they pay their Winter utility bills in the cavernous chill of the basement annex to City Hall. For several years now he's been a well-paid stringer for the *National Inquisitor* and I'm certain most people have read his stuff, which can prompt an enormous range of emotions from pure pity to downright tight-fisted rage sufficient to coax you to buy the latest issue along with the Pepsi and bag of potato chips in the check-out lane. He is also a very talented cartoonist and has a syndicated strip called "Drewsome" which you may have seen in the Charade supplement to the Sunday newspaper. Anyway, I propositioned him with three hundred dollars to go up to Saugatuck and check out the Tern, which by then was in the hands of those two lawyers from the Loop. They let him check out the yacht thoroughly and after two hours, he climbed down (it was in drydock) and said he couldn't find any evidence of such an incident about Spade Hill's attack. Drew mentioned these guys wore matching embroidered pink shirts by Viviani open at the neck, matching gold ropechains around their necks, matching powder blue slacks and Birkenstocks. They were at once quite proper and friendly. Drew asked if they were twins and they responded in unison, "Of course not, silly," and Drew decided to say well, thanks a lot and good-bye right then and there, as he was raised on a pig farm downstate beyond Peoria. They called after him and he rolled down the window and they pulled out the necklaces from their shirts. They said, by the way we found these rounds lodged in the bulkhead to the bathroom when we remodeled the yacht. They told Drew they playfully whip them out at cocktail parties to engender conversation. They allowed him

"Well?" repeated Bud.

"Well?" echoed Uncle Rob through the crack of a sardonic smile.

There was a five-second gap of silence like the hum of an erased tape recording. I could almost hear Sam's wings flapping as he strutted about the foc'sle to sit in my lap. Then the trio of old men burst into rolls of laughter that were not canned or rehearsed, but pure, spontaneous, infectious and lifted up from their bellies and sifted down in triumph through despairing

---

to take a picture of them together, holding up their shell-case pendants. When I got the photo, I felt near humiliation and then instant vindication that once again, Will's notes reflected a true and factual adventure, screw jibber-jabber be damned! I felt my effort wasn't just another childish romp in the sandbox of someone's mind where the distinction between fact and fiction becomes blurred even for someone in his/her early Twenties. For the record, here's an excerpt from Will's notes on this incident. Obviously, I teased out some transitionals here to make it flow:

1000: fishing contest goes on as planned.

1023: Bud and Les quickly land two beautiful fish. They're not satisfied, but sit down and pop two Lowenbraus.

1043: Paola hooked a huge marlin portside; it's way out there and the spool whines like crazy.

1058: We leave her alone. She says she can handle it.

1205: Danger. Two boats come close. Guns shown. It's that jerk, Spade Hill. He wants his suitcase back. I feel sort of sick to my stomach at the threat of gunfire. The bloodshed in Kingston settled in my mind a while ago and I think I can keep it down my cheese burrito.

1216: Uncle says he'll get it. He and Les go below to get it.

1231: Les hands over suitcase. Bud almost gets our heads blown off after saying something like may you live long enough to spend it, shitface.

1240: Uncle reappears. Exhausted. He said watch now.

1253: See two speedboats receding toward horizon and Florida coast.

1253: Can't find boats. Disappeared like two rocks.

1302: Uncle comes down from bridge with binoculars; tells us he snorkled under and slapped some plastique with timers on the hulls. Says they never knew what happened. We all cheer. I'm in disbelief and awe, and have renewed admiration for his courage. I'm sure Dad was like him, but I worry about my faith in Uncle. Thought he was an ordinary laid-back businessman. Strictly business?? How much retribution is kosher? For two mil? For ten dollars in the left pocket? Anyhow, we were alive and they were dead.

tears of past regrets. I'm sure Paola would have been incensed how they bypassed her desperate research into the earliest humanoid utterances, held on to each other and chortled and wheezed for breath and ached for three solid minutes without saying a word but understanding what Uncle was about to say, eventhough he didn't have to really explain anything.

They struggled to gain the table, plopped down and started in again until they held their sides like broken ribs and wiped away tears with the backs of their hands. I stood off to the side and laughed along, for this was a club of which I was an honorary member, but one to which I could never gain entrance.

"Boys," Uncle raised a hand "and I think we're still boys." Boys never wept for joy like that and soon the cleared throats and aftershocks of hilarity at an inside joke subsided from sheer exhaustion.

"So what's the AAR, captain?" said Bud flat on his back.

"They never knew what hit them." He found half a tank, strapped it on over Bud's wetsuit hanging outside the COMM center hatch and grabbed a mask and fins and slipped out the sliding glass door of the guest suite.

Just like Kingston, I imagined.

"I could have snorkled over, but they may have spotted me."

"I didn't know you had explosives onboard," I said.

"Well now you do, and now they know—knew," as Uncle jerked his head toward the horizon not quite attained by Hill's boats.

"So, where's the dough?" said Les, who wrinkled his brow and reanimated his usual self.

"I put a beacon on one of the hulls. Might pick up the signal. Might not," said Uncle.

"That's a mil point three, captain," said Les.

"I know. Consider it ransom."

"What?" objected Les.

Flash handed Uncle a towel through which he mumbled, Les, Les. You can shake it out of another tree. Don't worry.

"I do."

"Well don't," emphasized Uncle Rob.

Again, I sat down with them in awe of what Uncle had done. He was an old man, to boot. He was bigger than life as I looked over at him. I felt both comforted and humbled by these two courageous brothers: one at peace above me, and one so-to-speak at war in front of me. Yet, I worried about a cold-blooded determination beneath all the jocularity and absurd toy captain's cap. That arm around my shoulder, wink and grin and click of his tongue against his cheek. Was this the kind of person I should emulate? I knew I didn't have it in me.

Uncle came over to me and gave me a big hug. I gave him one in return and said you're the greatest. I said it without compunction or hesitation and I said it from my heart.

Suddenly, Flash yelled across to us, Missy she dead.

We must have left her alone. We stumbled portside where she was slumped over in her chair.

"Was she hit?" said Bud.

The pole was still in her hands. Uncle placed two fingers to her neck and took a deep sigh. "There's no blood. She's pooped out," he announced.

"Thank God for women," said Bud, who patted her hand and whispered come on sweetheart, it's over.

I wrung out a wet washcloth and placed it on her forehead, brushing back her golden curls so they draped her bronzed shoulders like a comforting shawl.

Les came up the portside ladder. "It's a beauty. Must be eleven feet tip to tail."

That's when Paola came to her senses. I held her hand, because I knew she would withdraw it as soon as she regained her strength. She said, "Did I win?"

CHAPTER 30[96]

(I'm still in charge here.) I've been worried all along about this: Will's obsession with the fugitive noise of the Tern's screw got out of hand and, I venture, drove him out of his mind for a while. Who wouldn't with the government goonies on your tail? A few months ago in a rush to Grand Central, I ran a yellow-red traffic light just missing a blaring ambulance and worried for the next ten blocks that the car following me was a psycho or unmarked cop car. Perhaps it was the modulation of ennui and anxiety he mentioned about his flight from military servitude inducing this behavior. There was a block of roughly eight pages of scribbles, transcriptions or translations of the screw's noises into messages he perceived as revelations on what to do. For a few lines, he even reduced these "messages" to wavy lines (and he squiggled a bunch on several pages) which he described as sea waves, and he even measured the distance between them. He then had the unbelievably delusional audacity to theorize the screw could be transcribing what the sea waves were telling the Tern's screw, which in turn was passing it on to him. This was some crazy garbage I was not prepared to divulge to anyone, and I almost dumped it in the trash compactor. This was otherworldly sci-fi stuff and far beyond anything Paola was into; but then again, I wondered half-asleep in my chair: If inspiration doesn't come from the sea, how can we describe it coming from our thoughts, which are infinitely more ephemeral than a drop of water? Listen, a mazurka is telling me something, but I can only feel it. Waves of arpeggios. I don't know. One late afternoon last September at Coney, I walked alone barefoot along the scalloping tide and thought about Will's stupid obsession with the sea and the screw. He must have been one sick puppy. Yet, as I turned away and started for the boardwalk, I heard my kids playing in the surf behind me. Who knows? Maybe the greatest human expression is the unspoken love of a mother's heartbeat to her unborn child. Anyway I said, okay, I'll sit down for once and look this crap over and try to salvage a chapter out of it. Obviously, Will tried to express some deep emotional or traumatic

On the way down, the coast lit up at night like a debutant's diamond

process that left him speechless and most impressionable. I must have stayed up all night at the office with a carafe of cold coffee some idiot dunked a cake doughnut into, trying to decipher at least three thousand words out of this mess. Roberta finally woke me up at five in the morning to ask if I was all right. I said sure, sure. I decided to stay in town because of the snowstorm. I lied to my wife like some schmuck banging all three secretaries at the office. Right! And for a book deadline, no less. Yeah, boy do I love to screw those deadlines behind my wife's back. Anyway, the only other time I ever got this pissed with Will was at Mundane. For a time there during his academic nosedive, he'd go around humming a tune more than actually talking with me. He went incommunicado on me, his best friend. I thought, silence is not golden; it can eat you up. What do you think, Will? He hummed. Hey, what's up? He hummed and even whistled. Several times, I grabbed his arm and said what the hell are you humming? I can make more sense out of a jukebox. He'd rattle off some name like "Sherbet" (I told him, it's Franz "Shoobert"). He really put his head up his ass then, but I still regarded him as my best friend—even with the humming, which actually may not have been half as bad as all the anti-government spouting and shouting erupting around campus like a travelling morality play. I'm struggling with this guy who's losing his marbles big-time. How in hell do I finish this book I promised his Mom? It's not about the apple pies cooling on her windowsill, because I always regarded her as my second mother. She never ever questioned why I hung around her place all the time. I knew she saw me many times late Saturday nights pulling my own drunken mother up our front steps. Not a word! Not a peep! One early Sunday morning around three, we almost made it through the front door when Mom threw up all over the damn place; the mail box, the railing. My clothes. Mrs. Melville peeked out the door in her bathrobe and looked over at us. "You okay, Scott?" she whispered. Am I okay! It was my own drunk mother who was not okay. God, I loved Will's Mom for that. When I got Mom inside and settled her into the frayed wing chair by the bulky Muntz TV and cleaned up the globs of pizza with a warm damp washcloth and put the soft baby blanket around her, I kissed her on the forehead and gently poked the loose strands of dyed hair behind her ears. I dumped myself into a chair across from her to watch out for her. I whispered I love you, mom, and I wept for her and my dead baby brother. I won't get into it any more than other than to say my mother was a saint. And I regarded Mrs. Melville as the saint two doors down on James Street where I grew up. And I said, damn it! Even if my friend Will goes off the deep end in this world, I'm at least going to try to rescue him in necklace sparkling across the room through a haze of smoke and lights. That's the last time she let me hold her hand. She had been out of sorts after reeling in the high-flying marlin. She showed us up, but she didn't gloat about it. She preferred to sleep in her reserved room instead of the much larger sleeping quarters with Bud and Les, eventhough she had a lot of curtained privacy there. I heard her retch in the morning, but then we all came down with some food bug at that time. Even Uncle Rob tossed his cookies over the side and one night he threw up at dinner. He was peeved at the chef standing nearby with tongs at the ready to serve spare ribs and his spicy Dagupan City pineapple barbecue sauce.

"Chef Felipe," said Uncle Rob, "I want you to throw out what's left in the reefer. I don't want to take this yacht into the sunset embracing a toilet bowl." He wiped his beard with the end of the tablecloth.

"Yes, boss. It's all good. Never problem before."

"I understand chef. This is worse than Christ's last cheeseburger. I feel the runs coming on." He pushed back from the dining table, pinched his nose and said chop-chop.

"But it's okay, boss." The diminutive Filipino in his spotless white apron and toque that got him up to six feet smiled in confusion. Paola once told me he was on every voyage she could remember. Uncle Rob would fly him in with Flash and his younger brother, Angel, from Manila for the

---

literature—as if a book lived a life of its own! All right. So, I have to put bread on the table, but I also have a greater obligation to Will's Mom. Much greater. By the way, on a whim, I sent Will's notes transcribing the Tern's screw noise to Dr. LePage at the Navy office up the Potomac River. A few days later, some guy called me and said, "Where did you get this?" I said I edited notes from a friend and planned to have it published. After a breathless pause and a few weird clicks of the phone, he said, You don't want to do that. I said what the hell for? And he said It's classified encryption. Where are you now? I heard another click and then I got panicky and hung up the phone like a hot tamale. It's a good thing I called from the phone booth in the back of McGuffey's on 12th Street around the corner. And I didn't go back to Terry's place for several weeks. Anyway, here's a small sample to show you what the devil I was up against:

LosinghrLosinghrLosinghrLosinghrLosinghr...
GivitupGivitupGivitupGivitupGivitupGivitup...DiefurDiefurDiefurDiefurDie...
BakgoBakgoBakgoBakgo...VerdoVerdoVerdoVerdoVerdo...
SemprSemprSemprSemprSempr...WardcoWardcoWardcoWardco...
FaycitFaycitFaycitFaycitFaycitFaycit...(ad nauseum).

three- to four-month annual cruise and no one ever got sick, even with the wild pig stew and monkey meat sticks and other jungle jive he concocted.

"No mas," Uncle responded.

"No home run this time, chef," said Bud across from me. He rubbed his stomach and excused himself, adding, "Captain yank him. We need a closer to stop the runs.

"What's he talking about?" I asked Les.

"The nausea has Bud off on a tangent in addition to his normal delusions. He means in baseball you need a relief pitcher to come in from the bullpen to save the game. Sabe?"

Uncle raised his voice and said no wonder Miss Paleo-Tosti is sick with this garbage. He saw Bud rush to the head down the passageway and asked if the rest of us felt the same. Then he turned and said, and how about you, Mr. Cookietosser, but Les was already in midstream, grabbing the empty wine chiller and retching his food at the far end of the table. Then I upchucked into my oversized linen napkin.

"My word," said Uncle. "That's faster than the oysters Rockefeller we ate at the Waldorf last Christmas."

Flash and the seldom-seen Angel spent the next twenty minutes clearing away the regurgitated carnage with a slop bucket. They reset the table and it looked as if we were retaking scene two. We reassumed our spots thirty minutes later, passed around a two-liter bottle of Scheissbach seltzer water from the Taunus Mountains and relaxed. Bud heard snickering at the hatchway and pushed away from the table to go after Angel. Did I catch Uncle Rob slip a wink and nod to the chef? It was too far to tell.

"Try to poison us you little devil," Bud blurted out through a tight grimace.

Uncle grabbed his arm and said you'd rather have MREs from the safety locker?

Bud pulled back with a porcine grunt. Then he shouted over Uncle's shoulder, Why don't you try pierogis next time you little ape? On the way back to his seat, he brushed up against Captain Billy's portrait and dislodged it from the bulkhead. He said Sorry, Captain. Let me help you.

"No, Bud. That's all right. The old man needed to be put in his place for once and anyway I intended to reframe him," said Uncle stooping down to collect the glass shards.

I came over to help Uncle and looked down at Captain Billy, in that stiff Victorian posture, and was sad he was so broken up over the last voyage of his beloved Tern.[97]

---

[97] Two weeks ago, Cliff left a phone message with our receptionist: Call me! Urgent. Wire $200. Captain Billy's alive! I contended with enough mental anguish slogging through the last box of Will's meandering notes without someone like that bird Cliff pawning off more lard to slap between the covers of this dagwood sandwich of a novel. I called him back and said, Hey Cliffie, thanks a lot but I don't need any more help unless you want to donate my next Bel Air payment. No Des, no, he said. I know you're draft is almost in the can (I thought, ouch! How right he is), but I found a real gem for you this time. It's an old lacquer cylinder recording of none other than Captain Billy. Really! Cliff, I'm trying to put this thing to bed, but he rambled on how he flew in from Phoenix to attend his ex's father's (Jack Bowersox) funeral in Hackensack and when the funeral director told everyone Jack wasn't quite ready to view anyone, Cliff stepped out for a quick drag on a cheroot. If I knew Cliff, with those two titanium rods in his back, he probably popped some percocets to dull the pain for the rest of the afternoon. He said in the alley he noticed an open trash container under a sign in a cruddy window: Pollard's Novelty Shop—Tradesmens Entrance; and since he was a professional dumpster-diving gumshoe, he jumped in, kicked around some Made in China boxes and spotted a dilapidated cardboard box with heavily faded lettering on the side almost reading "Edison, Menlo Park." He said when he later went back in the showroom when Jack was decent, "she" came up and poked him in the ribs and said the least you could have done was take a shower after your flight. Look, Cliff, some other time Wait, Des, wait. So I opened it up and found five of these dusty old cylinders, one of which cracked to pieces as soon as I picked it up. Hurry up, Cliff. I've got to take a dump now. Okay, Des. So I was able to salvage one. The others were already busted and, damn Des, this thing must be worth a fortune. I used my fingernail to pick out the faded paper label inside the cylinder and it read October 29, 1889, Edison recording of Captain Wm. Melville aboard yacht, Red Hook N. Jersey. When I told him he should have picked his nose instead, Cliff said What you mean? I said you probably detracted from the value. Your booger cost an extra hundred thousand at Sotheby's. Anyway, Cliff, Edison never took the recorder out of his lab then. No, no, Des. I took it to Vorhees Labs in Camden. They got all worked up and were very helpful. They cleaned it off and actually played it on one those old gramophone things with the horn. Cliff! Des! Cliff, later! Got it? Des, listen to this. Ready? "Mary had a little lamb (a high squeaky voice in the background

Shortly after we anchored off Key West two days later, Paola suddenly

yelled, no dumbhead; somebody already beat you to it) Captain William Billy Melville, proud skipper of the yacht, Tern, in Red Hook New Jersey dedicated to my family and friends and future descendants whom I trust will sail my good ship in fair weather and foul through profit and loss for this great nation of ours...harrumpf! I'm a yankee doodle dan...(squeaky voice yells get the loon out of here)". Did you hear, Des? Yes, I said. So where's the cylinder now? We can pay off both our cars. Well, you see, the guy said he thought it was Edison's voice in the background and then they said they wanted to keep it for their collection and offered me thirty bucks. So? So I tried to grab it from them and the damn thing broke into a hundred pieces. I pulled their tape off the Ampex and they proceeded to kick me out of the place. I took a deep breath and said listen, Cliff I'm getting sick and tired of this thing. I glanced at the red circled date on the wall calendar and said So help me, Captain Billy, I'll kill you off like those other darlings. What, Des? Cliff, why do you bother me with this stuff? I could hear the cars racing by in the background. Listen, Des. Just trying to help. You do know this is Will Melville's real-life story, not yours and you should not take it upon yourself to intrude or corrupt it by exaggerating your own self-worth. Whoa! Stop it, Cliff! Look, I can get rid of you, too, you know. I bit my tongue and said to myself, Cliff's a real person, you idiot. There was more dead silence and I thought he'd walked away and left the phone hanging in the booth. Scott, I think you'd better cool off, pal. Right away, I apologized and said I was beside myself and confessed to worrying about my daughter, Rachel. Cliff said okay Scottie, okay. I understand now. Scott, try to pull yourself together. I didn't know. Sorry. I said I'm sorry I got short with you. Don't worry, Scott. You're all in my prayers. Don't ever discount the prayers of an agnostic, eh? Yeah. Okay. I got a little chuckle of relief. He even gave up on Gautama. Cliff said we've known each other for too long to let a lousy phone call get between us. Okay, bud? Okay, guy. Don't feel so down on yourself, Des. You're a great editor and super ghost writer. Listen, would there have been a Beethoven without a Bach? I said What? Des, would there be a Will Melville without you? Cliff, please don't. Please. I'm a schlepping sconce hanging out along a dark hallway in this fifty-story monolith trying to shine a little light on someone. That's all. Okay, Scott. I believe in you, guy. I really do. Listen I gotta' run. Tell Roberta I said hello. Thanks, Cliff. I glanced over at the caged prison-style wall clock and also told him I needed to attend a meeting at noon with Butterballs. How could I have been so crass with Cliff, my best researcher? I wired him $300 for his flight back and his prescriptions at Rectalls in Newark. He said when he got back they hit packed up and left. It broke my heart. When Lou died, he went to a better place. When he was around, it felt like sitting on a three-legged barstool with that air of uncertainty, especially when he got in someone's face. When Sam died, he finally found his flight path. When he sat in my lap, my hopes were uplifted and I felt anointed as someone special. JHC was already gone in his rhinestone leotard. Spade Hill had it coming. We could have all been killed. When Paola left, she was more beautiful then ever—and alive. Breathing; brilliant; fidgeting about this and that. A perfectionist. She wasn't going to a better place. She wouldn't say. I only know when she left, it would be like her dying slowly out there and I could do no better than suffer inside, because there was no finality to it like the famous painting of a bird knawing away at some guy's liver. With her around, the deck felt solid under my feet and I knew exactly where my heart was, and I never felt more enthused about confronting life head-on than with her in my arms. Now she was leaving and taking a part of me with her.

The Tern was stillborn in the water as we lay tethered by its iron umbilical linking it to the sandy bottom sixty feet below. I say "stillborn," because underway there's an exhilaration that defies gravity. When you're in desert boots clopping along the broken sidewalk or chewed-up macadam of a strip mall parking lot, you pretty much know you're headed for something like a red pop and pepperoni pizza. Out here on this other planet, the undulation of waves often lifts the spirits to convey a sense of buoyant freedom that our next port of call is limited only by the stars and ocean currents instead of beebee-gunned stop signs and cheap gas. I don't know why this abortive word surfaced in my mind when I found out about Paola's leaving, except the screw rumbled some jibberish I blocked out with my ears sunk deep into my pillow.

There was no going-away party, ship's party or any other parting. Another day for Bud and Les topside at their lucrative positions in the COMM spaces. Telephonic slot machines that always paid off. I knew

---

an air pocket over Salt Lake and the stewardess knocked out two of his teeth with her elbow. I sent him another $200. I felt terrible. I almost lost a friend over Captain Billy whom I resurrected into some damn fictional walk-on. Editing and rewriting novels for the masses has been my so-called metier for what seems like a long, long time, but every once in a while I'd like to grab a sledgehammer and drive a wooden stake through some of those characters. Thank God I can see that locomotive light from this one coming at me. Hit me, baby!

those odds, because I sat down when Lou left his seat at the table. The dice were so loaded in our favor, it wasn't worth throwing them.

I peeked in through the crack in Paola's hatchway and asked, Do you need some help?

"No thanks. I'm all right. I can deal with it."

"Can I come in for a second?"

"*Vakrup.*"

"*Gorpchukreckrah?*"

"*Borkorgrakreshcrolpdakmok!*"

"*Druk?*"

"*Druk!*"

I can't describe in plainer words how I felt when she wouldn't even let me get close. She relented to let me carry her heavy canvas seabag around as she said good-bye to the others.

"Lots of luck to the virgin queen of the Tern. Take care of yourself," said Bud. He turned in his chair after he said this and looked right at her for once, and then at me over her shoulder. His voice carried a buggy-ride quaver as he tried to come up with something pithy, cute, and unrehearsed.

"I wouldn't expect anything less from you after nine years," she replied. Then she grabbed him in a headlock and he said Stop it! You're hurting me. Submission! You win, and tapped out on her back. No one could ever got close to Bud like that, but she did. The tough old Pole.

Les already stood by for his parting shot and internal punishment, because they were a lot closer. He removed his green eyeshade and tossed it on his desk. "Sure you won't stay. We can't handle all the traffic alone."

"Tell me another nursery rhyme, Les. This whole thing is a corporation. A legal person. Right?"

"What's that got to do with anything?" he said.

"What's it about is that that fancy registration certificate on the bulkhead behind you has more right to life than some Mexican trying to cross the Rio Grande. Right?"

"Come on. Not again. You don't mean that, Paola. Of all people, you should know how many we've pulled from the gutter; fed them; clothed them; educated them. Made them whole."

"Not nearly enough." She leaned forward as if to spell out each word for him.

"Right. So, we'll get to them in time. Right?"

"You just keep juggling the books in their favor."

Les said Gotcha, reached out and gave her a hug before she could defend her space.

At the hatch, she threw them a kiss.

"Write!" shouted Les as she walked out.

Bud said find someone to take care of you.

"Not a chance on both counts," she replied.

On the way to the bridge, she gave a quick hug to the three Filipinos. I dragged the seabag around her and heard her tell chef he outdid himself on that last dinner.

"I've got to say good-bye to your uncle," she said in a flat, unmelodious tone that told me to wait outside.

Twenty minutes later, I stood at the bottom of the ladder, waiting for her next to the small cabin cruiser tied up to take her away. She stepped down. She glowed in the full sun more radiant than anything I had ever seen.

"I can manage," she said matter-of-factly and passed right by me like I was a dog's least favored lamppost.

I didn't know whether to feel devastation or shame. They all must have seen her do that to me like gargoyles from their vantage up on the rail.

"Can I see you again?" I said over the rev of the twin outboards.

Paola stood up from checking a shopping bag and turned around. "Maybe. Some day. I don't know. Call me."

And in that full blinding sunlight sequestered by the waves, I saw her vanish into the blue-green stitching of sky and sea and stood speechless in the shadows of deep sorrow.[98] [99]

---

[98] Whoops! Easy on the mayo, 'tweethot. This passage is another instance where I saved the patient. It's grafted from an earlier note Will made about Paola and replaces "Paola grew on me ever so slowly, like moss along the stones of a dark forest path, and I sensed I would slip and fall at some point." This was one of many pitiful descriptions I felt the need to mercifully cut. This kind of trite, metaphorical abcess was throughout Will's writing. My red pencil was essentially a scalpel and many a bloody page simply expired on the light table. I cut so much, it reminded me once of how my granny babushka used to sit on her sprung hide-a-bed sofa chatting with mother and all of a sudden, for no reason, she would stop and look over at me tying my shoelaces and declare like a palmist reading my future along the frayed long threads of her old Balochistan rug, My God, dear, your Desmond should be a surgeon. Every time Roberta and I and the kids visit her mother, I think of granny with fondness as my inner eye wanders through the worried threads of that fine antique rug.

[99] On a more paramount subject, one more last nail while I've got Will up here (and I apologize for keeping you hanging on). Maybe it's due to my latent jealousy of Will—on double dates, he'd wind up with the prettier girl, although I often got some pretty darn cute and even sexy ones once I looked beyond their spectacles and lack of lip liner and such—and a momentary swashbuckling sense of self-importance, but there were numerous naive and icaristic passages I literally cut to ribbons. Remember the scene back at Bill's Place outside Ft. Lauderdale? I took a chance to slip it past Butterball's puritanical pulpit by leaving in Uncle Rob's inebriated rant reducing everything to self-gratification or intercourse with conception aforethought (although I personally believe a lot of manipulative lurid foldouts of titilating female pulchritude eventually lead to pregnancies) simply because it is still taboo even to this day (1973) in the vast morass of mainstream literature. And I wanted to steer Will's memoir away from the fringe lit market of downright lascivious and gratuitous perversity. Of course, it may well have been I flushed out some latent prurient side of his nephew, Rory Parker, who was assigned as my first-cut man on this book—like I really needed the brat in my corner while I beat up myself in this ring undercard of redactive retribution. Anyhow, I wanted to let you see for yourself in the following passage how I eventually trashed Will's "head in the clouds" adolescent and quasi-philosophical mooning I thought plainly inappropriate and even dyspeptic to the perceptive and voracious reader. You can't use characters like fingerpuppets

and have them babble on like a cheerful four-year old playing in a warm column of kitchen sunlight while intermittently banging the hell out of a cooking pan with a wooden spatula:

(At Kelly's Bar and Grill in Tampa) For all his business acumen, I was still dumbstruck how Uncle Rob could sit down in a bar and drink like he did. Earlier in the day I dragged a burnbag of shredded transactions past the COMM room when I overheard Uncle and Les chat more fantastically than the Tern's screw ever did to me. Snatches like "fifty-three to Hamilton; twenty to San Juan C5 account; eighty-five to Zurich and take back twenty for Tony in Bayside" and "The hospital in Belize should be ready by October...Les, squeeze them for August I promised El Presidente." So here I was next to him at Kelly's:

"All these scientists and stargazers looking for signs of life in the universe. You don't need a Ph.D in Hilbert Space to see there's hundreds of aliens from other planets in any apartment building."

"You're drunk, Captain. How many have you consumed so far? Who's this guy Gilbert, anyway?" said Bud.

"Not enough," said Uncle. "Look; you might live in 2A and listen to Bud Powell and be late on the rent, and the tenant across the hall in 2D might put on Clara Haskil and clip coupons. And that's as close as you two will ever get, because you're light years apart in everything else except maybe Saturday morning on the elevator when he says, Hi! They say it's going to snow tonight."

"Look Captain, I'm sitting here at Kelly's five feet across from you and I don't know who or what you're talking about. You're in outer space, am I not right?" said Lou above the edge of the plastic tablecloth.

"See!" replied Uncle pointing the orifice of his imported Rheinschatz beer at Lou. "What did I tell you?"

Lou was hotter than a handful of chili peppers. He clambered up from his chair to the middle of the table and announced, I want to say before everyone on this world stage at Kelly's I never ever said to Captain Robert Melville, Captain you have your head up you royal ass. And therefore, I owe you, Captain, no apology for ever having said in public before you have your head up your royal ass.

Uncle Rob laughed so hard he sprayed a passel of suds in Lou's direction and fell backwards. Les broke his fall, but then must have exercised a change of heart. He shrugged his shoulders, looked away and let Uncle finish his descent onto the chipped particle board Kelly was too cheap to tile over.

CHAPTER 31

Rachel, my dear sweet daughter, died yesterday at Johns Hopkins. I am so heartbroken I want to die. I tremble before her magnificent courage. God! She was a fighter. We all drove down a week earlier to be with her for two days, and Roberta and I planned to bring her home. Roberta whispered to me when she got a call from the hospital. "Honey, they said we should come back down now." The kids were excited about getting another unexpected school break, but they settled down when we told them we had to pay another visit to their sister. Aaron had an inkling of what was really going on, and on the way down I could hear him in the back seat answering Becky's wandering queries about her twin sister as she pressed her upturned cheek against the window at the fleeting array of billboards, liquor stores and gas stations. She stood up for most of the trip. A part of my heart, my soul, has been torn away from me. God, why don't you just take the rest of it and be done with me? Come on! Aaron did a real nice job covering for me when they wanted me to answer a question. My mind was way out there and often Roberta took her hand off the steering wheel and felt over to put her hand on top of mine. It was warm. She's so strong. She's always been much stronger. She said, "I'll drive down. You get some rest."

I reclined the seat a bit and somewhere near Essex my thoughts swirled around the only thing I ever memorized at Mundane. It was around the time Mom lost the baby and then herself. If for no other reason than that my middle name was Scott (a suggestion from Aunt Judith), I audited a summer class on F. Scott Fitzgerald to inflate my youthful aspirations of becoming a novelist. He said something like, the real test of a first-rate intelligence is to be able to have the ability to hold two opposed ideas in your head at the same time, and still have the ability to function. For example, you should be able to see that things are hopeless and yet be determined to make them otherwise. Rachel's dying and my struggles editing Will's notes overwhelmed me at that moment and I turned my tears towards the window. How in God's name could I make anything "otherwise" now? Roberta nudged me with the tissue box and said, Honey, blow your nose.

Little Josh, all four years of him, also stood a good part of the way when he wasn't flipping his oversized alphabet picture book. He poked his head over it once and asked his older brother, who does God pray to?" Aaron said I don't know and tapped me on the shoulder.

"What? Not another question?" I begged.

They both responded with a noticeable pitch between them, Who does God pray to? I turned around and must have stared out the rear window for an eternity, preoccupied with the way God was neglecting our sweet Rachel. "Daddy? Huh?" I managed to put on the brave all-knowing game-face of a parent and said That's a very good question, Josh. Let me find out the answer for you, okay?"

"Okay," said his little voice and his tossle of curls flopped back down into his book. He had that much faith in me. I love him to death. Becky turned around and said Joshie, Daddy knows everything, don't you Daddy?

"Sure, sweetheart," said Roberta.

Once I tried to make a little extra income early in our marriage by teaching an evening composition class at the local junior college up in Albany. I worked two jobs to boot and then dragged my kiester three nights a week up there until ten-thirty. I was a stranger to my own kids. They thought I was someone who took out the trash on Thursday night. Some of those students (one was seventy-two) would throw questions at me like I was a moving dartboard, and I used misdirection to get by a lot of them: "Let me get back to you on that." "Excellent point." "What do you think about that, Miss Murphy?" Real sloppy backhands into the taut net of plain ignorance from my side of the court. I let them take an extra long break and rummaged through some of my scribbled notes I could barely read as they straggled back in from the dim hallway. I passed them all. And here, years later, in the backseat little Josh smashed an ace right by my snow-white tennis shoes. I felt a secret inner pride at his precosity, but it also reinforced my deep feelings of inadequacy, especially when I struggled to read a story to Rachel by her hospital bed during our previous visit as if she were going to sleep to go to school the next day.

We decided early on that the kids should be there at the end and promised each other to put on our best faces to let them know they shouldn't be afraid. We didn't use "death." They should know about words like "movies," and "amusement park" and "zoo" and "the sandy beach" and "birthday party." Not "death."

"She's sleeping, sweetie," I said to Becky, as we stood around Rachel's bed. I had asked the doctor if they could please take away all the damned tubing and stuff so Rachel looked like she was happy and asleep and not some inhuman extension of a mumbling machine.

I lifted little Josh to give Rachel a kiss. "All right now. Let's give the sleeping princess a big kiss goodnight." He must have weighed over thirty pounds. When I put him down, he said but that's not the sleeping princess; that's Rachel. I lost it and said you're so right, Josh, and had to hand him to Roberta on my way out to the men's room across the hall. I locked the door and turned on both faucets. When I finally collected the pieces and dragged my body back to the room, Roberta finished what I couldn't. Becky said are we coming back next week? We'll see what the doctor says. Aaron was subdued and I knew he saw me struggle and I was hoping he would cover for me. He wanted to wear a dress shirt. Roberta helped him with one of my old ties. He's such a good kid.

Okay, let's all say goodnight to Rachel like last time. Then, Roberta gently ushered them to the small alcove of sofas and chairs two rooms away so I could be alone with my little angel. Roberta kissed me and closed the heavy door behind her. I sidled up onto the bed and embraced my angel in my arms. I was tired of praying to God and to whomever God prayed to. I brushed my fingers through her fine blond tresses and caressed her cheek and kissed her forehead and wet her delicate gaunt face with tears that were waiting in the wings for a long time. I lost track of time until Roberta tiptoed in. "Honey, you have to watch the kids." They can wait a minute. If there's one thing I was grateful for to an uncaring God was the chance for us to be together with Rachel as she finally let go of us. I thought, God's plan?—bunk! I almost thought my angel waited around so *she* could say bye-bye to us. Alone. And to thank us for giving her life and helping her on her way to heaven to wait for us.

The next morning, we thanked the staff; especially the palliative crew. One doctor assured us Rachel had been very comfortable and in no pain.

I shook his hand and said, Thank you very much. She was magnificent, wasn't she? He hesitated, looked at me and then over to Roberta and said, Yes she was quite magnificent.

Roberta said, honey I want you to drive us back. That helped a lot.

As we got ready to leave the motel, Rabbi Schnitzler called from back home. Right to our room like a guided missile. "How do you know?"

"Your brother told me."

"What can I do for you, rabbi?"

He informed me—reminded me—of the twenty-four hours. I had a knee pressed down hard to close a suitcase. "I'm familiar with it."

"I am so glad I caught you in time. In accordance with...It is written"

"Rabbi, please let me interrupt. I haven't been to the temple in years."

"Nevertheless, it is written..."

"I know. I know, rabbi. There's a lot of stuff written."

"Please, if I may finish," the rabbi insisted.

"But we're all off-script here right now. Anyway we've decided to have her cremated."

"But you can't do that! You should know that and I strongly advise you to reconsider. Look, why don't you let me help you? I can handle the details from here. Say the word. I'm here to help you. Anytime."

"Look, rabbi, check-out is at noon and we're running really late. With all due respect, I'll talk to you later.

"Later? What kind of a mensch is it with you?"

"Rabbi, a mensch I'm not."

Brushing my tracks to throw Rebbe Schnitzler off my trail was nothing compared to the ill and fickle wind of employment I pushed against on Monday when I "reported for duty." I no sooner sat down to the mess in my cubicle than Rory poked his freaky Cheshire face in the doorway and said, Welcome back, brother Rubinstein. Uncle wishes to see you pronto.

"Well, thanks a whole bunch, brother Parker. My word, do I see a shoe untied?" He always wore tasselled penny loafers, and I felt better after he gave the slightest inclination of obeissance bowing forward to peek down at his shoes.

"Okay, Scott. Just to forewarn you, the old man may have some unfortunate news for you."

"What?" as I sharpened my last two red pencils at Brown and Shue to draw him out.

"Come on, Rubinstein. Let's go."

At the door, Rory opened with Uncle, here's the guy.

"Rory, cut it out and go sit down over there," said Butterballs. Butterballs charged into me with an off-tackle trap play for missing the final extended deadline of *If Stalin Had Lived*. I told him I was absorbed with finishing up transforming Will's diary into the *Screw of the Tern*. "He was my best friend and I think it's going to be on the next Times bestseller list."

He actually picked his teeth with that filthy gold-plated toothpick in his ashtray. "Scotty," there's no love lost in this business." He sighed and added we're all prostitutes in this trade. You and I both know it. I've picked them up and layed them down like the rest of you."

I wanted to say, the hell you have. "Isn't that a rather jaded viewpoint?"

"And frankly it's getting to be a bore as your pimp while you dilly-dally with this screwy draft."

I could see it coming. That light at the end of the tunnel was the old Butterballs express, not the end of my work on the *Tern*.

"And another thing. Where the hell have you been for the last three days screwing off?"

I was determined to take this like a man with all the sobered-up dignity of a gunnery sergeant on his third bust to private.

"My daughter died over the weekend and I thought it would be sort of nice if I was there to be with her."

That caught him up short enough to break his stride and slow that scoring drive into the endzone of his former gridiron glory days.

"Well, I see. Sorry to hear about that. My condolences to you and Roberta," he said with the intonation of someone mumbling through the daily Dow-Jones.

"Thank you."

He started to feel around his desk drawers—as if he didn't know where the dingus was.

"Ah! Here, Scotty. This is for you. Go ahead. You can open it."

"Thanks." What else could I say, with bill collectors nagging me every other day? I knew from talking with Jhonny Carbonara, who had minor sales success with his Giacomo O'Keefe detective series, that inside there was a kiss-my-ass goodbye check for five thousand.

"Scotty, I really wish we could keep you. Really. But we've got to let you go. Times are rough. It's the bottom line, not you. You've been great."

I sat there and thought: brevity is the soul of shit.

Butterballs got up and reached over his massive mahogany mesa of a desk and said, It's been fun, Scott. Really. It has. Gonna' miss you, big guy."

I got up, took the envelope and left his hand hanging out there for a second until he retracted it like he'd had it on a hot stove. Rory trundled over to open the door—the nicest thing he ever did for me. As I passed close by, I moaned in his ear, "Save yourself," much like the poor inebriated Ph.D in chemical engineering often said to me as I passed him standing outside the mission soup kitchen with his ten-year old daughter; except that I didn't give Rory a dollar. I also permanently borrowed the *Tern* draft. What the hell. It was mine. The front desk security guard approached me with that ham of a hand on his holster and said, hey what chew got 'dere, pal? I said, trash and he said that's what I tawt; you can go. Amazing—this guy. He carried a gun and stared a lot. I wagged my head. As I pushed through the heavy brass-plated revolving door, I felt so relieved to be out from under the overseers at Brown and Shue that I made a snap decision two blocks away to let Will himself take over for a spell, since his notes seemed to flow pretty well at this point—almost like the way I helped him string his sentences together at Mundane:[100]

---

[100] (I, Will Melville, feel so humiliated and lost at this point of the journey, I don't think I could ever use the word "I" again, because I have been so unforthcoming with myself and to whomever may read this diary down the road. I'll try to be as dispassionate and objective as I can from hereon out. I'll try and switch to the third person so I can sort of step back out of my skin. It might help. I haven't levelled with Uncle Rob or the others; I've let Mom down flunking out of school; sometimes I felt so small standing before my fallen father's photo on the fireplace mantel; I've abandoned my friends by what I see now as a selfish act of sophomoric defiance in the face of social responsibility by evading the military draft and seeking the sanctuary of my Uncle's dubious altruism.)

Will took a break from the "money machine," as he called the COMM room wherein Uncle churned tons of money the same way the Tern's screw turned out tales of Will amid the school of porpoise racing alongside every day.

"Mister Will," said Flash, who came up from the engine room," you please help me with waste cans from the scullery, okay?"

"Not again," said Will, struggling to escape lethargy. Ten minutes later Will, Flash, Angel and chef Felipe were tipping four corrugated metal trashcans of food waste over the fantail. As they finished the last can, a small dark brown glass bottle bounced out onto the deck. Will picked it up ahead of the quick grasp of chef Felipe. The torn label read, syrup of ipecac. Will stood there with his jaw dropped.

"What's this doing here?" he asked the chef.

"It come from medicine chest. Here give it to me." Chef reached over to grab it, but Will pulled it out of reach, saying I know what this crap is used for.

"No, you don't," said Flash.

Will evaded their flailing arms as they laughed half-heartedly at his escape down the ladder to Uncle Rob's quarters.

"Can I come in, Uncle?"

"Open the door, son."

Melville was at his small wooden desk where his father, Captain Billy, sat many years earlier. "With you in a minute. He licked the envelope closed and jabbed it in and out of the postage meter.

"Uncle Rob, what's this all about?" as he handed over the small bottle.

Melville held it up, raising his eyebrows and making the usual sharp clicking sound with his tongue against his back molars. "Looks like a bottle of vanilla or Cajun hot sauce. What about it?"

"Uncle, come on. It's ipecac. We used it all the time at the frat house on party crashers."

"So, did you bring it onboard with you?"

"Nope. It's from the scullery."

"Hmm," remarked Melville, who now sat up in his chair with renewed interest. Will wanted to sit down, but he sensed the hardening glare of Melville's eyes trapping him where he stood.

"An anti-vomitive." Melville leaned forward to parry like a wheelchaired fencer.

"No, Uncle. Come on. It's used to make people vomit. Throw up. No joke."

"Just kidding, son. Have a seat. What's with this ipecac stuff?"

Will reached for a chair, not taking his eye off Melville; seeking an answer from his posture before the words spewed forth.

"Uncle Rob, there was no bad food the other night, was there?"

"Why on earth would you think that, Will?" He leaned back in his chair and locked his hands behind his head.

"Because Bud and Les and me and even you recovered pretty darn fast, and I know how this stuff works from college."

"Melville folded his arms across his chest. "I hope it isn't all you learned there," as he forced a laugh.

"And, Uncle, I know you can be a real practical joker sometimes, but it's okay. I can take a joke like the next person."

Melville said "What do you think? Would I play such a low-down rotten trick on everyone? Melville cleared his throat, rubbing his fingers briskly through the white stubble of beard. "Will, son, I think you're listing badly here."

"Well yeah, Uncle, but why did you do it for Christ's sake."

Melville shot out his hand like a traffic cop.

"Sorry, sir," said Will.

Melville then asked Will, "Was everybody sick as a dog?"

"As far as I could tell. Yeah."

"What about Ms. Paleo-Tosti? I didn't see her barfing up her innards like the rest of us."

At first, Will didn't seem to understand the question. "No, but."

"But what, son?" said Melville.

"She didn't, but I know she was retching for a couple of days before..."

"Before what? Before my little diversionary tactic?"

"What do you mean?"

"There's usually a motive good, bad or indifferent for everything except maybe the rolling of the sea." Melville looked down at a worn spot in the royal blue carpet and mumbled into distraction. He regained his senses in a few seconds while Will waited like an accused in the trial docket. "Will, son. Listen. Why do you think Paola didn't join in the fun?"

Will scratched his head. "Because she didn't get any on her food. She was throwing up in the morning. Bud and Lew told me about it and I said she must have eaten something disagreeable."

"Because I told chef not to spike her food." Melville leaned forward and put his hands on his knees to support his delivery.

"So, like I said, it was another practical joke, right?"

"You still don't get it, do you, son?"

Will suddenly stared down at the carpet around the same spot sought by Melville.

Melville cleared his throat again. "I couldn't let Bud and Lew in on this one. I didn't want them to suspect what you should know by now."

Will felt a complicit chill brush the fine hairs of his forearms and snake along like a silk scarf up and around his neck. "Go ahead, Uncle. You tell me what's going on," he said with despondent resignation.

"Okay, I'll tell you. Morning sickness. Know what it is?"

Again, Will lowered his head and then put the palms of his hands over his face, shaking it in a slow arc back and forth as if he had an abcessed molar. Then he mumbled, "Yeah. I know what it is."

"Now do you understand why she left. Do you?"

Will wiped his eyes with the back of his hand. "Yeah. All right, but what's it got to do with you? It was between me and her." Will coughed and forced himself to sit up, then stand before Melville like an accused before a magistrate. "She's single and all that and it was her choice and I fell in love with her."

Melville raised his voice. "Right you are, Will. It was her choice. She's single, intelligent and beautiful and vulnerable and you two fell in love and—for God's sake—she's my stepdaughter." He pounded his fist onto the desk, rattling the spoon in his empty coffee mug. "And I asked her to leave the ship so she can make whatever choice she chooses, and so you can make your own decisions before this old lady sinks to the bottom of our collective memories. Here, take this." He withdrew a crisp white handkerchief from his pocket and handed it to Will.

Will unfurled it like a flag of surrender and wiped his eyes. "So, you're the reason she left. You kicked her off the ship," he muttered in a last gasp to reduce his sentence.

Melville took a deep breath and glanced at the small picture frame in the corner of the desk with no photograph looking back at him. Black emptiness. "You're dead wrong, son. You're the reason she left. I knew something like this would happen."

"The one bright thing in my life and you threw her over," said Will, suddenly shifting direction like an ill wind filling his sails. "Why didn't you tell me all along?"

"I should have an answer for that. Some things are better left unsaid." Melville glanced over at the other tarnished, silver-framed photograph of a group of men, haggard, smiling into the camera one last time; crouched and standing in front of a submarine conning tower.

Will suddenly rose from his chair. "I've got to get out of here. I should have never have come here in the first place." He walked towards the hatchway.

"Son, look. Please sit down. Come on," pleaded Melville, as he pawed the air for reconciliation.

Will wiped his eyes with his forearm and turned around. "And for Pete's sake, please stop calling me your son. I'm sick of it." He stepped into the passageway, then looked back at Melville.

CHAPTER 32[101]

Melville clicked his tongue against his back molars, shaking his head; staring out the porthole at the irony of the calm anchorage he chose outside Tampa Bay. "Crush depth," he mumbled. "Guess it was too good to be true."

"What did you say?" Will sneered.

"Crush depth."

"What's that supposed to mean?"

"You wouldn't know about those things. You don't have the NTK."

---

[101] After Paola left, Will lost the desire to continue on. It was strange his very own name would to hang on his conscience. Around midnight, after the lengthy chastisement from the screw (*ingrateingrateingrateingrateingrateingrateingrate*) as Melville weighed anchor and repositioned the Tern in the harbor, Will scribbled his name "Will-I-am" on the roll of toilet paper, wiped himself, flushed and wrote it off as a play on turds.

Around 0600 after the previous day confronting Melville, Will put everything but his razor in his bag. Bud knocked on his door.

"Your pop—sorry—uncle would like to see you."

"Okay. Be there in a minute."

"You know, you shouldn't have talked to him the way you did yesterday."

"How did you know?"

"Because me and Les heard it through the bulkhead. Who couldn't?"

"I guess I didn't mean what I said."

"He's the one you should be telling that to, right?"

Will paused tying his shoes and wagged his head in agreement.

Ten minutes later, Will knocked on Melville's open door. "Uncle Rob, can I come in for a second?"

Melville was on the ship-to-shore phone and waved an arm for Will to come in. "Be right there. Damn it; lost the connection." He turned around and saw Will

God is great. God is good. Now we thank him for my old job back. I

---

standing by the doorway. "Come in, Will; come in. And don't call me sir." He pointed a finger in the air. "Remember, I'm your uncle. When you've been at the helm as long as I have, you get downright personal sometimes with the crew."

"Yeah, I guess so. I'm here to tell you I'm sorry about yesterday."

Melville asked him about the bag topside he nearly stumbled over. Will said it was time he get his shit together. Uncle again raised his finger to check Will's choice of words.

"Listen, Will, why don't you stay on a bit longer? You've got a snug harbor here. I'll get you a deferment."

"No. The last four months were enough of a deferment."

"Well, how about some place in the business. You pick the city."

Will moved his head like a lowing cow at an opportunity for which most guys would give either testicle. Melville scraped his chair along the deck closer to Will and asked not more than three feet away, well, what on earth do you want? You name it.

"I really don't know."

"You mean when you find it, you'll know it."

"I guess. I don't want it given to me."

"Okay. Would you sacrifice yourself for it? We might as well get to the heart of the matter."

"I don't know. I might."

Again, Melville looked above Will's head at the framed group photograph of his last crew. "I see. I suppose that eliminates me from consideration," he said with a deceptive smug and chuckle. "How about a ticket to Copenhagen. I'll set you up over there for the duration."

"Nope."

"Sure?"

"Sure."

Melville rubbed his beard with both hands and blew out a deep breath. "Well, I guess you've got to crap or get off the pot some day. What'll it be?"

Will leaned forward in his chair and folded his hands together.

A passing yacht smacked water on the Tern's hull. Annoyed, Melville closed his eyes and muttered, jerk. They should take his license away.

"Like I said yesterday, I've got to go back."

"What for? What about your mother? Have you thought about her?"

"I've made enough of a mess here. I can't study anymore. I can't do jack-zip. Mom's sick and I don't know where to turn."

277

know this twangs pedestrian, from the red dirt of Tuscumbia (pop. 8901)

"What's wrong? All this capitalist caper stuff not your cup of tea, eh? Too much too soon?"

"No, Uncle Rob. I know you've done a lot of good stuff, even if it's confusing some of the time."

"Tell you what. At least do your mom a favor. She's worried sick. I'll get you to Toronto. You can cool your heels there. No one will bother you. I've got a penthouse at the Orlofsky. Don't do anything stupid until you're convinced about what you need to do. Then, as they say, go balls to the walls."

"Yeah. I suppose so."

Good. Then you'll take my offer."

"No. I meant you've got to believe in what you do."

Melville pressed his hand to his forehead. "Will, at least give yourself the benefit of the doubt, okay?"

Before Will could say no, Melville said yes, good. Then it's settled."

"Thirty days?" determined Will.

"It's a deal."

Will looked around at the wall charts as he walked around Melville's quarters. "The Tern has served us well,"said Uncle Rob. He ran his stubby fingers along the grain of the small circular table with a golden sextent inlaid in the middle. "You'll never know how many times your grandfather and I have saved her from the scrapyard."

"What about Bud and Les?"

"Oh, hell. Those two swabbies. They'll do the same old stuff for me back in Scottsdale and Monroeville. I'll have to show you their recreation rooms some time. They're like underground bunkers." What? I'm flying Flash and the other two back to Manila tomorrow. They've been great company all these years. I've set them up back home."

"What about Paola?"

"You should ask. Not sure. If I knew, I wouldn't tell you anyway. She's real bitter at you. She likes you a lot, too. Maybe she'll get over it. You kind of let me down there, you know."

"I know." Will jammed his hands in his pockets.

"Take your hands out of your pockets, sailor!" joked Melville.

Will glanced up at the group photo above the door. "What happened to these guys?" he ventured to change the subject.

Melville cracked a half smile and let in a brief snort. "They're in a better place."

"Sorry."

to the secular sidewalks of Hollywood (pop. 190M), but I could now
hold up my head a bit higher than the serrated edge of the Help Wanted

---

"It's okay, son. I keep in touch with them all the time."

Will looked around and said did I leave anything? Melville said you bet you did:
a part of yourself. He drew in a deep sigh, then clicked his tongue against his
back molars. "She'll always be a part of me. Every ship has been a part of me,
but this one has been special." He stared off toward the open porthole through
which filtered the reflecting the light off the water and faint laughter from a
passing boat.

"So where are you going from here?"

"Do you know what it means to run silent, run deep, son?"

"No."

"Well, if you don't know, I'm not going to tell you, because you don't have," and
he pointed to Will.

"The NTK."

On deck, Will shook Bud's hand, who then poked a finger on Will's chest. "All
you gotta' do is keep your head where the sun shines. Be good! Cleaned up
enough, Captain?"

"Not nearly," chided Melville.

Les took Will's hand with both of his. "Call me if you need to set up a retirement
plan."

"Don't think I'll need one for now."

"You young punks think you'll live forever." Les raised his chin with an envious
grin.

"Sorry Lou's not here," said Melville. "He'd have us all hobbling about." They
paused for a brief communion of chuckles, then cleared their throats. The waves
against the Tern and the penance flapping overhead filled in the next few seconds
of silence.

Melville bear-hugged Will so hard he squeezed moisture from the corners of his
own sea-filled eyes. Then he whispered in his ear don't worry, son. Something
beautiful is going to happen.

"You're repeating yourself, but thanks anyway, Uncle Rob."

On the boat alongside, Will looked up and waved one last time.

"Don't forget to tell the driver to go to hangar 12A. Got it, son?"

"Got it, Dad," he shouted back.

The three watched the boat recede into the distant thin line between water and
wharf until it was the size of six-point type on some wet windswept page of a
paperback floating toward a rain-swollen storm sewer.

pages as I trudged back to Brown and Shue. I was on unemployment for three weeks. Registering at that charitable zoo for the royal pittance of eighty dollars a week plus the two weekly bags of food at the ghetto store across town kept us from starving. The humiliating sense of worthlessness permeated the place, and it's something I never want to suffer again. The only thing they could have done but didn't was order me to drop my drawers to stick a curious bureaucratic finger up there to see if it hid a load of undeclared income.

Anyway, I went in and lined up with about two hundred other workless wonders to report I didn't find work, when I felt my left wrist. I forgot my gold Bulova in my desk drawer at work. Then I remembered they locked my cubicle door and handed me a paper bag with "Rosenberg" scribbled on it and escorted me out of the building. I walked twenty blocks to my old building and briefly hunched down within a small group of Haiku novelists from Japan to get past the entrance security guard. I peeled off too soon and he yelled, Hey! Whatchoo doin' back here. Yeah! You! I told him there's a car illegally parked out front, which was enough to get me on the elevator as he grabbed my coat sleeve and tried pulling it through the closing doors.

On my old floor, I sneaked around like an escaped convict until I got to my cell. Mel and Sid, two ghost writers I knew from the fifth floor were shoehorned into my cubicle.

"Hey, did you guys see a gold watch in my drawer?"

""Hey, Scott, you look like hell. What happened?"

"Butterballs fired me a month ago and took my watch."

"What's new with him. We didn't see it. Anyway, We don't exist anymore. No recognition. Zip. That bitch Paige Turner gets all the recognition and rubles."

"You want recognition? They need a sandwich board in front of Zoster's deli. Gotta' run."

Brenda buzzed me in after I said It's Clark Kent, but as soon as she noticed she wasn't Lois Lane, she reached under her desk and rebuzzed for security. I bruised her personal space and pushed the intercom.

"Hey, Royce, I want my gold Bulova back."

"Say Scott! How's it going? I'm in a meeting. Sorry."

"I want the watch back, Butterwort."

"Look, I don't have your lousy watch. Anyway, you've been written out of here. You don't exist. Beat it or else."

"Well, screw you, Royce, and your phony baloney papered you-know-what."

I was rudely escorted out by two plainclothes guards I recognized from our Jackson Heights typesetting plant. At the elevator, little old Ruth Eddy Chadwick floated down one side of the hallway through the sunlight like a ghost of a gothic novel. She came over and placed her palsied hand on my arm.

Ever since my first days on the job, Ruthie seemed to wander around the building like a long-retired secretary visiting on a day-pass. Not even the bully bosses on the forty-third floor bothered her. She was still sharp, because when I often stopped to chat with her, she would suddenly frown upon glancing down the hallway over my shoulder and excuse herself rather abruptly.

"Scott, it's so good to see you again. Where on earth have you been? I'm so sorry to hear about your daughter."

"Thanks, Ruthie."

"Anything I can do?" She turned her head up and fiddled with that everpresent Woolworthian strand of pearls.

"No, Ruthie. I came back for my watch and Butterworth threw me out."

"What do you mean came back? Aren't you still on the third floor?"

I smiled and said, no, it was a long story as they pushed me onto the elevator. Then she stuck her slender arm between the doors and said, "Wait a minute. You two can go back to work," as she tilted her head toward the hallway.

I was confused as hell as she led me out of the elevator. For years, she only carried the key to the men's room. Where did she get off all of a sudden?

"Let's have a coffee and tell me about it."

Sometimes you pass someone and they're a blur for years and you miss the details. Now that we weren't two tramp steamers passing in the fog, I noticed the fine patrician lines radiating from the corners of her eyes and firm mouth; the well-tailored fit of her plain dress; the balletic grace of her small hands; the gray hair brushed back into a neat, business-like bun.

After five minutes of keeping my recent tragedy to a Snickers-sized sarcophagus, Ruthie reached over, patted my hand with end-stage care and said Scott, you wait here; I'll be right back. She rose and with the sweeping turn of a debutante she walked straight to the elevator. I rubbed the hand she patted. Little Ruthie was an imposter all those years and I felt like that down-and-out Ph.D standing with his little girl in front of the soup kitchen waiting for a handout. I raised my voice and said Ruthie, what do you do here? Really? She casually waved her hand in the air like the flutter of a dove's wing as the doors shut and said Oh, I work here, and I wondered if she turned pumpkins into golden coaches. When I apologized to her earlier for rushing past all those years (to escape to the sanctuary of the men's room), she said Don't worry your head off, dearie; you're fine. Half an hour later, she came back and sat down.

"Well, that's settled, Scott." She smiled at me and conveyed a maternal grace I hadn't felt since before my own mother fell off the wagon when I was in high school.

I sat stunned as she handed over my Bulova and said Scott, you come back Monday. Then she patted my hand again.

"But I don't understand, Ruth. How did?"

"Oh, it's nothing," she said, shrugging her petite shoulders and taking a last sip of coffee. "Don't you worry your little head off. That nephew of mine thinks he can do whatever he wants." Then she got up and shook my hand as if we just signed a treaty in the Hall of Mirrors.

"How did you do all this?" I mouthed.

"That's my secret," she winked again. She turned back and tossed me the red key to the men's room. "Keep it. It's yours," she said floating down the hallway and fading into the late afternoon sunlight.

"Ruthie," I shouted, "I don't know about all this, but your a doll! Thanks a million." And I never bumped into her again, as if she were a one-line walk-on character in a paperback from those two ghost writers who took over my old cubicle.

CHAPTER 33

In closing, I feel more conflicted than if I were an informer at Auschwitz. Sorry. I don't even have the moral right to be so disrespectful. I wasn't there. I mean, I've fumbled through the last two shoeboxes (they're in my '56 Bel Air trunk under two tangled jumper cables), battered from mishandling and look like little pine coffins of what I believed all along were the figurative remains of my best friend, William H. Melville. Mrs. Melville once explained to me over washing dishes in her kitchen sink that the "H" stood for Herman. I said to myself, no; not even close to a cigar. She laughed and explained in a rare flippant moment tossing back her head how she was overdue with Will and barely finished *Moby Dick* (of all the books) where she abruptly picked Herman after a restless and delerious night at Cranford Memorial when she and four other women struggled like buggy-whipped mares at dawn to deliver more than clinking milk bottles. Among the wailing chorus of mothers-to-be, hot water rattling the radiator and the swoosh of the white whale breaking water, she said she heard in the damp thick air of expectancy, *callmehermancallmehermancallhermancallmeherman*. I also got a chuckle when she gazed out the window at the windblown sifted snowfall and said she hoped her choice of Herman would rub off on her newborn. With my tongue marbled through the last forkful of her warm apple pie, I praised his (scattered and dishevelled) reminiscence on the Tern, and told her I did my very best to make it a tome worthy of something written by Herm baby himself. But in my heart I knew I betrayed her and Will's memory with the self-serving cynical intrusions I used to bastardize Will's story and make it my own sort of mea culpa to escape the drudgery of whipping into shape an unending line of worthless manuscripts, waiting to strip them down and send them scurrying off to a common chamber of rejects, and then shovelled like cadavers into unmarked ashcans on the delivery dock behind the building. In the end, when even Ruthie tried to save me, I blamed Butterworth and the others who ran the business upstairs at Brown and Shue; but as I looked up at the building while waiting for a bus across the street, I knew I was solely at fault for the miserable fate of a lot of innocent and decent literary aspirations.

In her bright kitchen with the snow outside swirling like delicate shrouds of white lace, Mrs. Melville handed me a last hot cup of tea, holding it in her fingertips like a rare porcelain chalice and placing it before me. "There, Scott. You can't leave without a cup of hot tea, can you?" She turned to get her cup and paused to place her hand on my shoulder for support, but I knew inside she wanted to say more. She told me she finished her last chemotherapy treatment at Birgit Lemminghaus. I stole a glance at her as she talked about the ordeal with a childish sing-song lilt. She lost so much weight, her face was drawn in waneful expectation and a waxen lustre that brought out a surprising inner glow far more beautiful than the fullness of her cherubic expression for years. I thought, Captain Melville, if something beautiful is going to happen, why can't we make this courageous woman whole right now? "Look at my hair. It's a mess," she chided, running her weary fingers through thinning gray strands. I said you look terrific after all that treatment, and she acquiesced in my obvious deceitfulness, and I sensed how small it is to pander to someone who understands the true odds. Right there, I wanted to start a book about her; a testament by which I could remember her unwavering kindness to me and belief in Will, whom I so selfishly maligned in the *Tern of the Screw*.

I told Mrs. Melville—and I never had the temerity to call her by her first name (Mary)—that the book was in production at Brown and Shue and would be in the bookstores by Christmas. She was overjoyed and exhaled, "Finally." I received a delicate hug and felt like the spent seed of Judas. I didn't have the courage or human decency to impart the truth that I swiped the manuscript from under Butterball's uncaring schnozz and tried to find the money to publish it myself.

After tea, she took my hand and led me to the front room to show me the framed photograph of Will next to his dad's.

"Isn't he handsome. Just like his father," she said. Tears welled like diamonds in her eyes as a sudden ray of sunlight burst through the flurries outside and filled the room.

"Mrs. Melville, you can't give up hope. I know he's out there," I said so many times to her since the Fall of 1969.

We sat down on the sofa across the room. I felt humiliated that I had ended Will's story the way I found it in the last shoebox—leaving the Tern and waving good-bye to Uncle Rob, Bud Shill and Les Vice. Only the facts. Screw the facts and my slavish obsession with their punctuation. And I couldn't find the wherewithal to give Mrs. Melville the sympathetic denouement she so deserved. I knew more than ever I was a hack editor and had no business sitting there except for the fact she begged me to write Will's story. And here I begged her to hold on to hope that by some miracle Will would walk out of the Central Highlands from whence he was dumped like a piece of clay years ago and knock on the front door, blowing fluffly snowflakes off the sleeves of his crisp green uniform.

"Have you heard any news?" she said.

"Nothing yet," I said. "But I'm checking every day with the Army."

She sank back in the sofa and closed her eyes, and I almost thought she was ready to die right there with hope heavy on her heart. Will had been missing-in-action (MIA) for four years by then in that misbegotten jungle for good 'ole Uncle Sam, and I didn't have the nerve to tell her I hadn't checked on Will for several weeks. I looked down at my hands in shame. This was the last time I saw Mrs. Melville before she could no longer manage by herself. I spied a colorful pamphlet from the Camelot Hospice near Hillsdale with models yukking it up around an indoor pool in a photoshoot P.T. Barnum would have been proud of. I knew things were on the downside after she came back from Cleveland, because the apple pie was store-bought, gooey with corn syrup and tough slices. When I complimented her on the pie, she looked up at me from her cup of tea and said, you can't fool me, Scott. You know it came from the freezer section; and we laughed about it. "Next time you come with Roberta and the children, I'll have two of my own ready for you." After Mom died cracking her head on our iced-over front steps in 1968, Mrs. Melville practically gave birth to me with open arms. Sometimes I feel like I was born of two mothers. I could go on, but words here would make less sense than a shaman tossing twigs to the ground on a moonless night. I cried on her shoulder at the door. I couldn't help myself.

"Now, don't you worry, Scott. He'll show up." She held on to me with all her remaining strength, and I privately felt she was talking to Will;

and, in a way, I was his understudy, standing in for him and crying on her shoulder back from the dead.

I wished I could have died right there in her arms and been resurrected as Will, her own son. And in some abstract, deluded and desperate way, I wanted to achieve that, even if most ignobly as a character in the *Screw*. She waved to me from the fluted archway of her front door. I threw her a kiss. "Be back in a week," I cheered.

As I pulled up to her house late afternoon the next week, two medics rolled her out the front door on an ambulance gurney. Before they lifted her into the van, I said I was a family friend and wanted to wish her the best. When I placed my hand on hers, she turned her head my way, opened her eyes and gave a weak little smile.

"Don't worry, Mrs. Melville. I'll be here when you get back."

She raised her thin eyebrows and I think she said through the plastic oxygen mask, "Will, is that you?"

"It's Scott, Mrs. Melville." I pressed my lips together to stifle my emotions, because I never thought I meant that much to anybody.

She died three days later. I drove down in a rental car from the airport and knew there wasn't much time. I lifted the bedroom window I used before to gain access to the attic. I stole her photo off her bedroom wall and now have it in my den along with those of Will and his father from the fireplace mantel.

Just a bit more and I'll be done with this wrap-up. You might say I overstayed my welcome when Mrs. Melville's estranged sister, Eunice (Rusty) Box, swooped down from Saginaw to take care of the funeral arrangements.

"I'm one of Will's and Mrs. Melville's old friends. I lived two doors away," as I hung up my raincoat on its usual hook in the hallway. She said that's nice, as she hung her's at the end of the closet and turned her back on me. "Can I help in any way?" with my ballcap clutched in my hands like I needed a handout. That's when she finally eyeballed me from head to toe and said, "No. I think we can manage," through a clenched truckdriver jaw and sniff of air. I whispered to Roberta at the funeral, if I can ever get enough cash together to publish Will's book, I'll sign it, "To Mary Melville With Deepest Gratitude, Your Scott" and bury it next to her and her husband's tombstone at Fort Sheridan.

A few days before I finished editing Will's notes, the other jackboot dropped at Brown and Shue. I was determined to craft a fine ending to his adventure on the Tern, but I dropped it for a while on unemployment and then got picked up by a small press across the river writing balloon captions for the Heartstone imprimatur. Mel got me the job and that was real nice of him. I also got odd jobs transcribing court testimony tapes at thirty cents per page. What a circus of sophistry; the truth be taffy. One night after Roberta got a small raise as a receptionist at the Wortzinal Center for Skin Diseases, I was in the basement sweeping up sawdust from one of Aaron's Boy Scout projects when I saw the manuscript hanging like a surreal speechless tongue half over a shelf between paint cans. After we put the kids to bed and I kissed Rachel's small picture in the silver locket on the chain around my neck, I put the trash out and went back down to the basement and spent an hour flipping throught the *Screw* draft. It actually wasn't that bad a read. I was much more at ease sitting there on a wooden stool by the tool-strewn workbench than slaving under deadlines at Brown and Shue; and the pure naivete and awkwardness of Will's expression I now found somewhat charming and even hinted at touches of really good prose for a young man who flunked out of college twice.

I set aside about sixteen hundred dollars, most of it from Roberta, to find a print shop, as I knew I would have been summarily shot at sunrise with the book over my heart if I hanged on at Brown and Shue.

"Hon," said Roberta one day after Mrs. Melville's funeral, "why don't you find out what happened to the others?"

Now that posed a real condom for me, because I barely retained enough energy to whip the thing out before it withered on the vine. Of course, she was right. So, I called Cliff in Grand Junction (he took my advice) to help me put some bunting on the fate of Bud, Les, Paola, Melville and Will himself. Incidentally, I was still shook up when I first learned that Will never did get to Copenhagen or Toronto to hide out from Uncle Sam for the duration. When he left the Tern, I thought for sure he would skip the country. At first, his name was misspelled as "William Marvell" in one of the obscure weekly inserts of soldiers killed or MIA in the *Free Press*. I called the society page editor to have it corrected. Will must have turned himself in for induction, and I was somewhat relieved to see he at least got off the dime and got his life back on track, eventhough it no doubt may have cost him his life. He must have asked for another tour of duty over there. He didn't show up with the POWs that came home last year. I don't know. I should have kept in touch with him no matter what, but somehow I didn't. I couldn't. The Army didn't even know where he was.

Since Roberta always had better sense, I told Three-Fingers Clementi to hold off his press until I could track down at least the crew of the Tern.

"Mr. Rubinstein, gotta' keep the press running. Give you thirty days."

"Why thirty?"

"Because I know you self-publishing types. You won't do a damn thing for twenty-nine days and then spend half the last day trying to take me to lunch. I don't need another club sandwich with onion rings. I need new shocks and a best-seller in that order. If it bombs, I can still drive to the store for bread and milk."

Once I got the addresses, I dipped into the printing funds because I wanted to meet these people to allay any doubt beyond my research that they were the real thing instead of figments of Will's imagination. Some days, I really had my doubts. For one, they all sounded like they sang off the same sheet of music, but maybe that was the way Will synthesized their speech and thought. I could have called them, but they wouldn't really have known me and vice versa. Many times I impersonated my mother and aunt on the telephone to shield them from harrassing bill collectors, so I knew a voice on the phone could be as elusive in intent as say a thief uttering "as Christ is my witness" in a crime novel.

I had a real nice chat with the real Les Vice in Glendale. It's always nice there in February. He was quite the gentlemen and appeared as he did in Will's notes, except for the long mermaid tattoo long his left forearm. He told me to meet him at Nina's Taqueria, because his house was a mess, although his intonation sounded a bit hushed and secretive. One of his dogs barked in the background until he yelled, "Thunder!" I left some of the physical details by the wayside, since I felt it was way too much to convey the image of a character so fastidious about his appearance and making arithmetic errors. I noticed how he sometimes quickly rubbed his fingertips while reaching for the salt, and how he almost held the receipt of his tab at the edge up to the window as if to confirm it was a genuine hundred dollar bill.

He asked me if I was a friend of Will's and I said more or less, Les. I asked him several questions about Will's time on the Tern, picturing in my mind one of Cliff's break-ins at Les's mansion.

"No, I really can't discuss business with you, except to say that Mr. Melville was and is still very active in philanthropy."

He confirmed that Lou died on the cruise, but gave no details. "He's gone and let's leave it at that." He didn't hesitate to give me Bud's address, which jived with Cliff's notes.

"What about Paola's address?"

"I'll send it to you. Don't worry."

He said the Tern was a beautiful old yacht. His words fell off in a wistful sigh sipping from his wine glass, and he slowly turned the salt shaker again and again with his fingertips like it was a radio tuning knob searching for the right tone and frequency with which to respond to my questions. And I pictured him in the story turning the RC390 knobs.

"Captain Melville, where's he?"

"Captain Melville? He's off somewhere. He's a moving target to a lot of people. Probably the greatest American I'll have ever met."

"How so?" I asked.

"For someone to recover from the kind of combat wounds he suffered and then build an enterprise out of pure nothing and then to keep giving to his country like that. And to think, years ago he was picked up once by the cops for vagrancy in Pensacola." I watched the fork as he held it suspended between the plate and his mouth. "There's a handful like him. A rare bird."

"What about that scene with the horse at Bill's Place?"

"What horse?"

"You know, in the hurricane."

"Oh yes," he strayed. If I hadn't looked straight at him I would have missed his eyelids flutter for an instant. Maybe a memory tic of some kind. He said he wasn't there, but back in his hotel room, and the next morning everyone suffered hangovers and didn't want to talk. He laughed with restraint and repeated, "that young kid sure had a good imagination. Should have been a writer."

I asked him what he thought of Will classified as missing-in-action since 1969.

"Yes. I had heard about it. Very sad. Funny how Melville always referred to him as his 'son.'"

When I asked him about the incidents with the Shapiros and JHC, he almost choked. He expectorated a cud of quesadilla on my side and mumbled in profusion, I don't know how Will got that. Nothing like that ever happened. When I mentioned some passages about the transfer of funds, he said, look wait a minute Mr. Robertson; Will sure congered up a good one there. After a few minutes of banal banter and a large swallow of wine, he flicked his wrist to check his watch, wiped his mouth with a napkin like a priest at communion and raised his hand for the bill. I was only halfway through my chicken burrito. "Really sorry, I forgot I have an appointment I'm late. Gotta' run." He shook my hand with a wink and whispered, say why don't you send it to me and let me check it over for accuracy. You know, Will was a good kid, but we all knew he had problems. That was obvious from the day he came onboard. I raised my eyebrows in confusion. He said, by the way, is this a work of fiction or what?

"Sort of," I replied. "Is there anything wrong in your opinion?"

"No, no," he insisted. "You've really got to check your facts. Did you check all the facts? Will was so confused."

How in hell was I able to check the facts if he didn't want to confide in me. I had the urge to tell Mr. Vice, you're all facted up.

Les shook my hand again at the entrance and he got into the longest chartreuse limousine I'd ever seen. I asked him about the screw noise. He said, yeah, it was noisy as hell, but never made the kind of crackpot conversations Will talked about. He had problems, you know. We all knew that. Les rolled down the window and asked for my phone number at the last second. I gave it to him like a damn fool with the uneasy feeling I had just abetted the escape of a fictional character into the real world.

Roberta called me two days later. Frantic. "I went out with the children to Ginny Wu's pizza and when we came back the garage door was wide open. She could tell someone snooped around. A few drawers were not shut. Closets opened; bed covers pulled back. Nothing trashed. a respectable break-in. When are you coming back?"

"What about the basement? The manuscript?"

"It's not there."

If it was gone, the last two years of my slavish devotion to Will's memory and Mrs. Melville's wishes would have been a mere fiction. My life would have been hearsay. "Keep looking!"

"We will, we will. Where are you staying?"

A few minutes later, Roberta called back. "Honey, Aaron has something to say to you."

Aaron, who would be nine in a month, confessed he borrowed the box and took it up in the tree house in the old live oak in the far corner of the backyard. "Sorry, Dad. I wanted something to read besides *Boys' Life*.

I won the lottery and chastised my son at the same time. I said don't worry, son. It's all right. It's okay, but please let me know next time?

Roberta said someone from Brown and Shue called the day before to ask if I took home the manuscript. Mel called her earlier to say someone ransacked my old cubicle. It was a total mess.

I whispered, "Les. Out of the bottle," into the phone.

"Who?"

"No one, dear."

As the Boing 747 dropped urinesicles from thirty-five thousand feet over wheat fields near Topeka, I reclined my padded window seat and imagined the pilot describing another scene below: Ladies and gentlemen, looking out your cabin window you can see what's left of this part of the country. Total devastation. Believe me, there's nothing left down there except a few stray dogs and mutant barnyard animals. Notice the huge craters on the horizon left by those nukes. It was great while it lasted. What? About two hundred years. At least you can say you were there and saw what you gave away. God bless the America we knew and loved. May she live in our hearts and minds forever and ever, amen. The overhead seatbelt sign flashed: Now let us pray for our children's children.

I flipped through a magazine and wondered about Les Vice telling me what a wild imagination Will had. Was he on the level or lying through his crooked mottled teeth? I wasn't there, so I could only go on my faith and confidence in Will, my best friend. I believed everything he wrote down, in spite of a lot of purple prose, mixed metaphors and other dirty laundry in a young writer's hamper. Les's brief testimony contradicted so much of Will's story, it reminded me of the time Jacques Taitois, my visiting European history professor at Mundane, peered around the classroom with the most arrogant academic sneer I'd ever seen after I asked him as a joke if he was a "revisionista." He got real testy and said, just because *you* in this country have free speech doesn't guarantee that everything you say is or even has to be the truth for the rest of us. He thrust his arm out a bit higher than Hitler used to do and pounded on the desk until my pens rolled off, shouting to the other two hundred in the hall, and you're not obligated by the powers that be to tell the truth. And you can print that, too. Little did I know how that dramatic reference to libel coaxed me into the arcane field of editing manuscripts for brevity, correct punctuation and other junk having little real effect on a good profitable story filled with trapdoors of untruths.

Especially after Roberta told me about the break-in, I was so mixed up I had a vague uneasiness that, if Les was behind it, he may have tried to correct a largely flawed version of what happened on the Tern, thereby morally justifying the illegal intrusion. I only say this, because I maintained such high hopes of getting at the truth these last eighteen months it cost me my job. I let everything else fall in a pile over the side of my desk where *Stalin* was buried.

When we landed in Pisstburgh, I rented a car and drove through a driving downpour to Bud's house in Monroeville. It was an unremarkable clapboard bungalow save for the tall ham radio tower looming in the backyard. I thought that jived with Will's descriptions of Melville's communicating the transfer of millions over the airwaves. I knocked on the buckled aluminum storm door for a couple of minutes, then snooped around the side for an open window. Little Clarisse did a nice job of getting in. There were only a few small pry marks in the wooden frame of a window. Then I saw a small index card taped to the rear door. "Gilly, feed the boas" as one of them slid up a pole inside and scared the hell out of me with those beady eyes darker than the deepest well. That meant Bud might be gone for weeks or even months. On a hunch that Will said Bud was a Polack, I drove to the local PNA hall and struck fool's gold as it later turned out, because what Bud Shill related was more distressing than Les's version. He sat at the bar with an older woman whose yellow-slacked leotard covered the barstool like melting candlewax.

"Hey, nice to meet you. So what do you want? No, you can stay, babe. This won't take long."

I asked him the same questions I posed to Les a few days earlier in Glendale. "I'm an old friend of Will Melville and I'm writing this book based on his notes while on the Tern."

"Yeah, that kid of Captain Melville's. Sure. I'm familiar with it. Him. What's up?"

I started reading some excerpts from the draft about Alice Detwiler and the children's clinic. He took a long swig of his brewski and held up a torn gloved hand.

"Where did you get that from? Him?"

"Yes, from his notes."

"That's pure bullshit. Sorry hon. Are we talking about Melville's nephew here?"

"Yes."

"Well, you got the wrong Bud, bud, because I don't remember nothing about no island or rest home or whatever. What's your name again?"

I said to myself is this going to take an overhead slide show?

"You from the press by any chance?" He slid off his barstool for a second, brushed off his farts, then climbed back up.

"Please, Mr. Shill. I'm trying to get some facts straight. That's all. I'm doing this for his mother. She asked me to do it."

Bud raised his bushy eyebrows and said well, okay. If it's for her. But I want to let you know now up front I don't deal in facts." He brushed some peanut shells off the bar.

"What?"

"I deal in cash. Money talks, you know."

I agreed and wondered if I had enough money left to fly home or take the bus. I took a chance that a fifty would oil him up enough to tell the truth about Will and the Tern.

"Thanks. Can I buy you one?"

"Sure."

"No. That's not it. The Shapiros got too sick and we sent them sent back to the hospital in Charleston. They still there?"

I said I didn't know for sure.

Then Bud machine-gunned questions at me so fast, the tables were turned. "How do you know Will and his mom and where did you get all this erroneous trash about him on the yacht?" I said I read Will's diary and then broke his run by asking if he knew Will had been still missing-in-action.

"I heard. Not good. Should'a been here by now. Not good at all. Probably better off dead."

"Why do you say that, Bud? There's always hope."

He rearranged the five empty beer mugs in front of him into a straight column and wagged his head in apparent disgust. I could see that he had some difficulty pawing the empties with his right hand and mumbling about his childhood in Poland and how he came to America.

I asked him about the others.

"Les. That guy he's a real loner. I met him on the boat, but that's all. Captain Melville and me go a long way back. He calls me once in a while. Guess he's out there somewhere wheelin' and dealin'.

"How about Paola?"

The bleach blond next to him said, you mean Melville's daughter. Ouch! Bud! Stop it, honey!

Bud grabbed her by the hips and gently pushed her toward the front door. "Wait for me, babe. I'll be right there."

He finished his beer, liberated a final belch and said, "Look Mr. Scott. If you really want to know the truth, your friend Will was on the boat about a week and decided all of a sudden he wanted to get off. It happened just like that."

"But he wrote that"

"I'm telling you what I seen with my own eyes. I got no interest in lying about it, do I?"

At the front door, he wished me good luck on the book. "Nice knowing you, Mr. Scott, even if it doesn't sell."

He patted my on the back and I could sense he felt relieved kicking back into place the square manhole cover to his memories of the Tern. As I waved to him burping his Ducati in the parking lot, I wondered if this search for the truth was all for nothing. Even his jellyroll girlfriend knew about Melville's stepdaughter, but why wouldn't he tell me? How could Will write about this if he spent only a week on the Tern? Unless Melville somehow told him right from the get-go.

Bud swang his engine around about five feet from me. His torn gloves backed off the throttle. He looked straight ahead and shouted over the threatening innuendoes of idling exhaust, Hey! You know anything about two colored girls who broke into my place a few months ago. Huh?

"Heck no. You said break-in?"

"Yeah! That's what I said."

"Did they take anything?"

"Some personal stuff. You know, people shouldn't mess with a guy's stuff."

"You got that right, Bud. Well, take care. Hope you find them."

"You too, pal," and his back tire kicked up a hopper of pebbles into my slacks and shoes.

Bud, you son-of-a-gun. You ran out of the money and that meant I had to soak my hemorrhoids after a painful ten-hour bus ride to get home.

CHAPTER 34

When I got home the next day, I was so exhausted I almost broke down and cried when I got down on my knees and hugged little Josh and Becky. What a fool's errand I'd been on for over eighteen months. Neglected my kids, Roberta, my better judgment—what was left of it—for what? The truth? The facts? What the hell is that? Who really cares about the truth these days? There's so much moral equivalency out there, I can't even remember one single "true or false" exam question the whole time I was at Mundane. There's only change, like I mouthed back in college with a fist in the air, and I felt as hopeless as if that change were the few coins tinkling in my right pocket—the one that needed sewing. Watching the kids grow up; praying to Rachel that I'd be there soon for her; watching Roberta trying to hide the white strands around her temples; buying another junker. I was washed up and I knew it.

Flipping through the draft, I looked out the window from time to time at the light rain outside and wondered, is there any stretchable truth to the pathetic fallacy in literature that nature mimics our emotions, especially depression? My overboard intrusions into Will's story to refine and honestly elaborate the factual experience of my best friend had created a horrible mess. My hubris humiliated me worse than if I had stripped naked at Times Square. This went far beyond any contradictions Les and Bud brought up a few days earlier. The worst of it was I let down Will and Mrs. Melville, and eventhough she was gone and Will was as good as gone from this ball of candlewax, their presence beside me was more palpable than the tips of my fingers. Rabbi Schnitzler told me once that without the dead, there would be no living. I believe I laughed at him, especially when he added, "Even a tree in the dead of Winter has a beauty beyond its full bloom in Summer," but he was right. I wanted to weep for Will and his Mom, but I felt beyond my own redemption. My left shoe sole had a hole; my left sock was soaked and that wasn't the only part of me that was all wet.

I reached the pits when mired in the horrible nonsense that Will somehow betrayed my trust in him by abandoning me and ending his diary without so much as a word on the events that filled his tenuous days after the Tern. Like I said, I felt he literally deserted me when I later found out like a total stranger his "nowhereabouts" in that obscure *Free Press* column in September 1969 listing MIAs next to notices for lost pets and foreclosures, and the only reason I picked up the paper was to see if Ginger's Baby won the third at Garden State. I never felt so cheated in my life. I vividly recalled this on the glorious golden autumn afternoon they tossed me out for a second time at Brown and Shue, one day after they carried Ruthie's body out of the building. I stumbled into McGuffey's out of despair and by some miracle walked out sober with renewed longing for each hour of the day. To this day, I'm not sure how, because Terry McGuffey's wasn't a movie set. It was as if I took a leafy exit off the parkway I never intended to take but always wondered about. I looked into the mottled mirror running behind the bar, behind the blue and green and red and amber and crackled and clear and round and square vessels of bottled-up anger, lethe and forgetfulness. You might say in jest I had a pilsner epiphany. I was ashamed to blame Will for my situation, and then, in my mind, I did take that exit of leafy elms off the parkway and, as I pulled off onto a shoulder and stopped the car beneath the dapple of light and shade, I gripped the steering wheel and somehow mustered the courage to whisper, forgive me, Will. The guy next to me asked if I was all right, and I said yeah. Yeah. it's okay.

Roberta came in several times with hot tea while I rambled through the draft. She knelt beside my chair and reached up to run her fingers through my hair or lay her warm hand on top of mine on the arm rest.

"What are you thinking?" she said.

"Can't you tell to look at me? Honey, it's hopeless," I mumbled through the palms of my hands.

"Scott, something beautiful is going to happen."

"What?"

"Didn't you write that Captain Melville said something beautiful is going to happen?" She rose, kissed my forehead, then removed my hands from my face and kissed me again.

"Thanks."

"I read the whole thing while you were away."

"Great. So?"

"It's not a romance or one of those returns you used to bring home."

"So. What, then?"

"It's—it's different. Like you."

"Yeah. That's the problem. It's a piece of intrusive junk with my initials plastered all over it."

"No, honey. No. Listen." She closed the binder and put it on the coffee table. "No, Scott. You're the solution. That's why I married you."

"Oh honey. Please. Let's not go there again."

She casually rolled her left hand in a small orbit around her ring finger and said, "I really sensed the movement or turmoil between you and your friend in the way that you propelled the story along between the narrative and your footnotes. Sort of like an engine in and of itself. Does that make any sense, hon?"

"I didn't know any other way out. I lost my way. I should have listened to you."

With her fingertips guiding my chin, Roberta lifted my lips to hers. After we kissed, I looked straight ahead at the wind and rain brushing the boxwood against the windowpane.

"The truth is, you did it the best way you knew how." She sat on the arm of the chair and pressed my head gently against her warm and generous bosom. "You can write all the words you want, hon, but it's not going to resurrect him. You know, that's been tried before."

"So what should I do with this thing?"

"Add a few closing—what is it called, epitaph or epilogue—remarks about Will and let it go, Scott."

"But."

"Honey, let it go. It's done. You can't bring him back. Please, let it rest."

In despair, I deeply inhaled the sweet incense of her body and the soothing balm of her compassion, and I was uplifted. Then I felt Rachel's locket around my neck and knew it was time to move on.

And I did. It felt like a surgeon had miraculously exorcised a malignant rumor from my conscience and I could breathe on my own again. I promised myself never again to get so involved in a story or use blatant chicanery to deceive and frustrate a readership eager for a plain old good story. And I started enjoying the sheer child's play of ghosting teen romances across the river in Jersey. I even outlined a series of bird stories for children.

After I put to bed my fifth teen romance (*Prudence and the Tutor*)—I also banged these out every few weeks for Cherry Blossom Books— Roberta and I took the kids to the museum of art on a beautiful Sunday afternoon. Beautiful in the sense the sky was blue, a soft breeze rustled the new leaves now and then and everyone seemed to be at peace, smiling and walking nowhere in particular. I was one of them, and I couldn't have been more relaxed and comfortable than if I walked around in my ragged flannel bathrobe and flip-flops. We had a great time. This was one of Rachel's favorite places (Children's Puppet Playhouse). I noticed a woman with flowing golden curls who reminded me of the description of Paola in Will's notes; I never tried to locate her after Les and Bud; doesn't matter now. Becky asked if I could write a book for her; just for her and no one else. I told her you bet, sweetheart. (Aaron needs corrective shoes) (Roberta wants to go out for our sixth) (to live = vivere = leben = vivre) If I had gone ahead and spent the money right away to publish Will's story instead of the down payment on the used Pontiac, which we desperately needed, I already thought of a parting line: *So, if you're lucky enough to find this book in a Salvation Army store or yard sale down the street, I hope the true intent of this story exonerates my intrusions on your privacy and resonates enough in your imagination to assuage your disbelief, justify your patience and illuminate the path as you turn out the light.*

"Daddy," said Becky, "Who's that?

I said, Dr. Gachet.

"No, Daddy. Not the painting. Over there!"

CHAPTER 35[102]

[102] Since Scott didn't get around to writing the last chapter, I thought it only fitting to conclude Scott's book myself. He died last week (April 30, 1974) following an auto accident. The doctors said he succumbed to a massive heart attack halfway across the bridge and veered into oncoming traffic. He was on his way to my place to go over the draft of his book, based on my trite notes when I was on the yacht (the Tern) a few years ago. I was quite surprised and delighted he wrote it. I thanked him for taking care of Mom while I was gone and he said he was sorry. I understood. I haven't changed a word of his text; however, I'd like to briefly describe our reunion at the art museum. As you can see, I made it as abrupt as possible in a final chapter, because no amount of words could tell you how emotional it was for both of us. We both broke down like cry babies. A security guard came through and politely asked us to move before someone complained. What for? We didn't break any law. I should have been quicker on my feet—that is, wheels—and told him someone was two galleries away brandishing a boxcutter in front of the Van Gogh. I hadn't seen Scott for so long, I thought for a moment he was a character out of some paperback I read while at Walter Reed. It was about five years (by Scott's watch) and seemed like fifty years by my military experience. We lost touch and were total strangers for a time, and during my imprisonment in Vietnam, and right up until my recent return, I often thought of him and the good times we shared growing up on James Street and at Mundane University. It sustained me during some pretty rough times, along with my concern for Mom's health and well-being. After we regained some composure, I introduced my wife, Paola, and our son, Christopher. She frowned when Scott said he had already met her, but then we all laughed when he explained how he knew her from my notes on the Tern. Then I remembered and said My God, Scott; I still didn't believe it and he said he wrote the book for Mom. She wanted something to remember me by. I was embarrassed thinking of how he must have struggled to get anything out of

Roberta came over from the other side of the room with Aaron and Joshua in the stroller and asked if anything was wrong. "You look like you've seen a ghost."

"No. I'm looking at Dr. Gachet. Listen, why don't you and the kids go to the cafeteria. I'll be along in a few minutes."

"Sure? I don't think he's seeing patients anymore," she said with a smile.

"Let me ask him."

Scott's teasing reassured her he was okay, at least for half an hour.

When Roberta and the kids left, Scott turned around and began a tentative walk into the next gallery. Perhaps the next chapter, he thought. The woman with the long golden hair. He hesitated at the door. "Don't be a complete fool," he said in a low murmur. There must be a million like her.

She stepped back from a large canvas and sat down on a mahogany bench next to a young lad of about six, placed an arm around him and hugged him. A small group passed before them, stopped and then moved on like a small herd. They exited left and the room emptied for a few

---

those youthful ramblings I jotted down on the Tern. He wanted to push me to the cafeteria, but I said, no sweat, Scott; it's all-electric and right there he seemed a bit taken aback at my condition. Obviously we had changed, survived different experiences by choice and imposition and I think it bothered him a lot that, as I said, we moved on from the James Street of our carefree youth and the libertine frivolity at Mundane. Roberta and the children were charming. Aaron looked like his Dad. She and Paola hit it off pretty well, and that's saying something for my wife; she's been very protective of me; patient and understanding. I was right all along on the ship about her and I'm blessed she's in my life. Funny how Scott asked me what I meant in my notes when I began with, "When the lights came on, I knew I was in the dark." We both laughed a real good one about it for a few seconds. Scott said he couldn't believe it wasn't lifted from an old detective paperback. I told him nope and we could talk about it later when he dug out the manuscript and brought it over to the apartment; but for now, I said when Paola helps me into bed and turns out the light for us and young Christopher leans over the bedside on his tiptoes and gives us each a kiss goodnight, I lay in the dark and I can see everything quite clearly now. Scott gazed down at his hands resting on the table fiddling with a paper napkin for a few seconds, then looked up at me and said yeah, I think I get it now. Sounds like a pretty good ending, Scott. He did a real fine job. He was my best friend. GBY, Scott. William H. Melville (June 6, 1974).

seconds before a man in a wheelchair hesitated at stage right. A close beard; somewhat rumpled clothes like he had just stepped out of a canvas and grabbed someone's wheelchair to rest after a long journey. He adjusted his eyeglasses, brushed back his black hair and smiled at the woman and boy and moved over to them. Scott stepped closer while they chatted. Then he moved a few feet in front of them and they stopped talking to look up at the stranger.

"Will? Will?"

"Scott? Scott! I can't believe it. Scott!"

"Will!"

Scott bent down and hugged Will. He couldn't help himself and began to cry on the shoulder of Will's jacket. Then Will turned his head up into Scott's shoulder and wept. It had been quite a while.

CPSIA information can be obtained at www.ICGtesting.com
Printed in the USA
LVOW10s2049020715

444799LV00001B/7/P